T0354802

UGLIER

A Novel

BONNIE PALIS

AuthorHouse™
1663 Liberty Drive
Bloomington, IN 47403
www.authorhouse.com
Phone: 1 (800) 839-8640

Cover photo: Erin Mulvehill
Cover art: Greenbaum Marketing

Published by AuthorHouse 06/12/2015

ISBN: 978-1-5049-1582-3 (sc)
ISBN: 978-1-5049-1583-0 (e)

Library of Congress Control Number: 2015908861

Print information available on the last page.

My grateful thanks to family and friends who have lived through the ups and downs of ordinary life and loss.

To Mom, Dad and Jerry for the support through the years

ONE

This was the third year, so the prickly feeling at the back of her neck should already be familiar or gone. It wasn't. Once the year started, numbness would set in and her inner nose would become accustomed to the stench. Stink of the onion included adolescents, teens, teachers, the walls, the posturing, the habits, the lack of parenting; it all just stank. The onion might be a metaphor joke between two English teachers, but it was an accurate one.

Peel back a layer of that onion, do it now or it will never happen. Every year I have to peel back that first layer, the paper layer, the deceiving layer, then start into the soft, vulnerable flesh and the thinner, stickier layers that look as though they're gone, but annoyingly are not. I hate the onion, but I don't have a choice if I want my summers off. **She drove to the onion. The brick onion. It looked innocuous enough, but she knew better. She walked into her biggest nightmare each and every weekday for two semesters a year.**

Because of the recent incident, Tony now insisted she drive her ostentatious BMW since pinning McGinty to the side of his house and destroying his putting green about a hundred days ago. No longer was she allowed to drive Dad's old Bronco around town or to school.

That was the same day Tony accused her of being the female equivalent of a misogynist. She looked it up: "The equivalent is *misandrist* (a person who hates persons of the male sex), a rare word but seemingly much sought-after. The corresponding noun for the attitude is *misandry*."

"This is not funny, Bernie. I'm so rattled right now I can't even think of a word to describe your attitude, let alone understand your behavior. You're damn lucky he didn't press charges and have you arrested for intent to do bodily harm." She just looked at him through the numbness; the anger and rage were now dispelled. Tony was livid, as well he should be. But the issue that started it all was gone and her deed done as planned.

The whole complex was a lot like an onion she and Celeste had decided the previous year. Odd, she never noticed the similarity 14 years ago when she was a student here. The place could almost be smelled outside; just like an onion with the skin still on. An onion that is starting to get mushy inside, but you can't yet tell until you pick it up and cut it open. Opening that door today was going to be like handling that stinking piece of potential rot. Humanity cloistered in one place had a smell to it, school was no different.

Parking spaces were open and she found one close to the front doors, killed the engine, pulled up the parking brake and put the car into second gear; a life-long habit from driving a stick and an added safety precaution; could never be too safe. "'OCD,'" the doctor had said. *Who cared*?

Bernie knew that if she didn't immediately get out of the car and open the back door, grab the portfolio case and rush toward the building, that she would deter the dreaded trip into the first layer and prolong the agony. She wasn't about to drive away when this needed to be done today. ***I like kids, not school. Funny, I didn't like kids when I was a kid and associated school with pain and cruel kids. Now I associate the building with torture.***

She felt stupid wearing heels, a summer dress and pantyhose. The dress was not even as heavy as most of her t-shirts and she felt half naked as she walked toward the metal encased glass doors. She lived most of the summer in breeches, t-shirts and boots.

The school secretary, or administrative assistant as she was now called, looked up from her desk at sign in, "Hi Bernie, you're a few days early. How was your summer? Did you gun down McGinty again?" Chris Bard was in her early 40's and had gotten over the administrative decorum with teachers; a nice person who was outspoken without realizing potential embarrassments.

Bernie's face got hot and she sighed "No, I'm forbidden to drive the truck, Tony's orders." This was the talk of the town and it wasn't about to go away. In a village of 3,500 people, it was easy to keep the topic pot boiling.

"Ah, just as well. But you did what all the other females around here wanted to do. You really took a chance and we were taking donations for your bail."

"Very Funny," she looked toward the ceiling and sighed again, "Tony doesn't think it's so funny, but my

mother-in-law seemed to think it was the best thing she'd heard all year. The jury is still out with my folks."

Bernie signed the in-book. "Same room as last year I hope?"

"Same room."

"See you in a little while. I want to get my stuff in and the walls decorated so I'm not doing it last minute."

"Knock yourself out. The only other teacher here is, Mrs. Kresge."

Audrey Kresge was the home economics teacher. She always showed up several days early and started her shopping lists, ran some laundry and organized her leaflets and teaching lab; always a lot to do for her. She seemed to get the students the guidance counselor gave up on too easily. Good girls who no one seemed to notice or believe had aspirations; and the occasional boy whose mother was fed up with laundry and food issues. She had an excellent curricula and Bernie was personally grateful to her because she had her as a teacher years ago. When others were taking business class, she was in Home Economics learning to give dinner parties, cook, do laundry well, sew and decorate. To this day, here favorite color scheme for a room was monochromatic with accents.

All grades were in two buildings. Because of the size of the village, the confines of the buildings, and to allow students to mature, the seventh and eighth grades were housed in the high school. This was felt to teach students

to interact with one another and learn to blend better for cohesiveness.

Bernie went to her room on the first floor, slung the big portfolio on the desk, dropped her purse on the chair and looked around the room. *Ah, crap, I forgot to ask Chris how her summer was, gotta remember. . .*

Painted concrete block walls, an open beige canvas, to be plastered with examples, but not nailed or screwed into. Such a scene two years ago during her first full-time year when she pounded nails into the concrete blocks. She used "boogers" now. The hot glue gun wasn't much of a success, either, since it took her hours to scrape the glue off the walls. The new slightly sticky product found in attached magazine ads worked much better. *If Tony knew how I nickel and dimed things he'd have a fit. I don't even get receipts.*

The portfolio case was full of enlarged documents. The most interesting was the last will and testament with the names and property locations changed. It came from Tony's office and was just fascinating enough to possibly grab a kid's attention. The idea behind the posters was to get the kids to read the print and realize that English was important and served a better purpose than texting with abbreviations.

I should have brought a radio or a CD player or my iPod to get used to the upcoming continuous din. If it's quiet I can concentrate; next week I'll be flustered and dazed from the noise after a summer on the farm and riding and gardening with just nature sounds. I've got to start blasting the radio and the CD's in the car to prepare myself; I know better, it's the same the beginning of every

school year. God, I hate this place. **The distractions of the school year were many and thoughts on important subjects did not come readily or easily with the sound of students and school activities.**

Two hours later she was breezing down the hall ready to bolt through the doors when she remembered to stop and ask Chris about her summer. ***Gotta remember to be more polite and less terse.*** **Years ago office co-workers accused her of being so driven that she never asked them about their previous evenings, weekends or vacations when they returned. She just started right in on the day's business. Someone accused her of being "self absorbed."**

With the classroom done, she only had to submit her lesson plans for the semester and she was ready to endure another bout of hilarious but unruly teenagers and faculty drama and the meeting of the new principal in two days. She wanted to get the hell out of there before she ran into the new one. The old one looked like a portly hawk and was very critical of everything. If he had still been there she would not have a job after the end of semester debacle with McGinty. He and McGinty were also friends, as far as she could tell. Chauvinistic friends.

TWO

After going home and changing she headed for the barn. Noir was in the pasture with Dad's goats and wouldn't be much of a problem to catch for a trail ride. She had all afternoon before she had to be home to start dinner for Tony. August was such a lovely, quiet month to trail ride. Today felt as though it would be a little muggy, but tolerable. The Cicadas were humming in waves of sound again.

The horse was a bone of contention and a slight source of irritation to her father, but in the past year he had become more tolerant of Noir and Bernie had caught him talking to her in her stall a few times. Dad never thought anyone heard him talking to the animals as though they were people and was always caught off guard when discovered. She seldom milked with Dad because her day was the occasional Thursday evening when he took Mom out for the night. He was grateful to have the help since her two older brothers refused to do anything but hay season with him.

Noir saw her coming and decided that this was a good day to be caught. She wasn't always in the mood to leave the pasture and the company of other herd-bound animals.

A long time ago Bernie had forgone the brushing routine for a water hose and a scraper to get the dust and grit off the horse. The winter months were bad enough without having to end up dirtier than the horse with mud particles sticking to a sweaty face, neck and arms in the summer months. She haltered Noir and hosed her down outside the barn next to the hydrant and the tying post her father had built on a little concrete pad. Noir thoroughly enjoyed the cool water and sighed a few times.

Five years of companionship melded an understanding and an enjoyment of one another. Noir was a Thoroughbred Arabian cross with the Arab dished face. Rather large from her Thoroughbred side and hot tempered. Bernie always said she understood her because she was both a mare and had a temperament like hers. Most people refused to ride a mare and had their prejudices, but then, there were others who faithfully swore by their mares because they'd give their last ounce of energy and go the distance to get something done. Rather like most women.

Saddling and bridling were rote and she led Noir to the stump she used as a mounting block. She swung her right leg over, caught her irons and they walked off and down the lane toward the back fields. Over the years they had forged their own paths and trails and were quite comfortable just walking and trotting along together. The wildlife they encountered was predictable and didn't spook Noir. Today was just a short jaunt in a big circle to clear the mind and nostrils of the onion's stink. "I really need this ride, Noir. I'm glad you're so agreeable today because I couldn't really take much

resistance from anyone." They met no animals and no other riders were allowed on their paths at the insistence of her father, who proclaimed that he hated horses and didn't want anyone tearing up his fields. Because of horse boredom, Bernie had to mix up the rides and change the paths continually. Today was their little rhythm in the large circle. Some days, for excitement for both of them she rode up and down the country roads with the cars, trucks and farm equipment to change their perspective.

Her bridle paths where her own and the only times they encountered other riders was at the rare show. The trails were made by repeated rides and a chain saw bungied to the back of her father's four wheeler. Paths wove in and out of a large circular and wider path through the 40 acres of nontillable woods on the farm. Many afternoons were spent sawing and hauling logs to the side and standing on the four wheeler reaching and cutting branches to avoid being bashed in the head while riding.

She didn't have a truck or trailer and was at the mercy of other horse people when she wanted to a show or go to a planned trail ride. They were alone as a couple. Noir refreshed from her "bath" and Bernie refreshed from finishing her morning burden of school.

Dad was Dad, Carl, short for Carlton. Tall, thin, gray hair in a military style cut, pipe smoker, Scotch drinker. Quiet unless he had something to say and then he said it. He was an excellent teacher and had been a well-liked professor around the dairy barns in Madison, Wisconsin. Why he retired was a mystery to Mom, the boys and Bernie. They all missed Madison because of

what little Cold Lake gave back as a community and the lack of amenities available.

Her brothers, Josh and Matt lived in other cities. Matt was an automotive engineer and lucky to have a job in decrepit Detroit. Josh's interests were more computer oriented and after successive jobs, he started his own little computer shop for repairs and building servers for people. He was the egghead of the family, only because no one knew what he was talking about half the time.

Josh repaired and kept Mom and Dad's computer in great shape and always was on call to them if something went amiss. You saw him come home more often than Matt because he lived in Lansing. He'd be bent over the desk where the computer sat or under it, cussing about something.

Josh was the closest in age to Bernie being five years older. Matt was eight years older and had a hotter temper than Josh. He didn't have a lot of patience, and milking with Dad was not in his realm of reality. Josh could be recruited for a barn emergency if he was home.

Hay season was the only time Dad insisted that they help him with any farm work. There wasn't a lot of hay to do, only 20 acres and it didn't take them long for first or second cuttings. Dad's hay fields were a mix of alfalfa and grass. He would complain from time to time that both forages needed to be grown in separate fields and harvested at different times, but he didn't have much of a choice because of the lack of tillable acreage. The goats loved it and they statistically produced more than the average goat because of Dad's innovative feeding programs. The entire family thought this was a research

project on Dad's part and he would eventually write a paper on it. His latest addition to feed was microbials. His feed was carefully calculated for each goat and every ounce of milk was weighed before it was strained into the small bulk tank.

Years earlier Dad had found a group that made cheese and this is where the majority of the milk went. Mom and Dad drank goat milk and the kids naturally developed a taste for it. They kept cow's milk for guests and Mom was prone to freezing it because the family's preference was now from a goat.

Goat milk has an earthier flavor and is an acquired taste. When Dad first started milking goats the family balked at the taste after having had cow's milk their entire lives. Milk and cheese are main products of Wisconsin and their preferences changed a great deal after the move.

THREE

The kids' thing started in her apartment in Chicago, far away from Cold Lake and the Cold Lake School System. She thought she had escaped the tortuous place when she moved to Chicago after accepting a job with a large PR firm right out of college.

The offices were high up in a glass tower and she felt important walking into the building each day carrying a briefcase and wearing a suit. No one passing her knew she was just a lowly copy writer and publicist. When she went through those massive wooden doors and they closed behind her, her day in anonymity began.

Her high rise apartment building seemed to be teaming with youngsters ranging in age from seven to 17. Being single she did a lot of reading and her balcony was her exotic retreat. She managed to string a hammock between posts and installed a little Smokey Joe grill and a couple of plastic chairs and table. It was crowded and then crowded again with indoor trees and plants each summer. She loved that apartment with its quiet, other than slamming doors heard through the walls from other apartment front doors. It was on the fifth floor giving her a decent view of Lake Michigan and other apartment buildings.

Children were always in the laundry room because there was really no place to play outside in the Chicago winters. There were vending machines for soap and softener, candy, soft drinks and snacks; it became a congregating place. The laundry room took up a third of her floor and served two other floors. Parents and adults, alike, sat in chairs reading or tending to obstreperous toddlers. Bernie liked to sit through her entire loads and read. This was partially to keep her laundry from being dumped out and small pieces lost and a chance to talk to the teenagers who hung out. Some of them did laundry for their families, some of them just visited and some where just looking for a place to delinquent. Sunday was generally laundry day for her.

Although somewhat content to be single because of the freedom, Sunday was the worst day of the week. Sunday was family day and it seemed to her that everyone had a plan or a place to be on Sundays. There was the occasional date on Saturday and the once in a while Sunday brunch or trip with people from work, but Sundays were just plain lonely. If she didn't have to do laundry, she would sit and read and drink wine and ration out precious Godiva chocolates between chapters.

It started slowly with the kids. They became used to her being there with iPod buds glued in her ears and a book on her lap, laundry baskets at her feet. She was a Sunday fixture and late in the evening, after most families had returned home, the adolescents became bored and went to the laundry room. There was a game room on one of the lower floors, but she seemed to be more fascinating. She wasn't much older than them, being just out of college and having her own place was very interesting in their opinion. They were always talking about the day they moved out, got their own apartments, cars and were legally allowed to be adults. What they didn't know about were bills, bills, bills and the constant juggling. All they saw was freedom from their parent's rules and restrictions.

Parents were eventually introduced and kids were allowed to visit her apartment some evenings. She helped with homework, she served Sunny Delight, cookies and twenty-something wisdom. Eventually she bought a few board games and her apartment became another hangout on Sundays. Her fascination with books sometimes allowed her to discuss them and other times a kid would be sprawled across a sofa and she would be ensconced in a chair, reading and enjoying the silence between them. Occasionally she would invite a friend over to enjoy a home cooked meal. One of those friends was an attorney who would work on his briefs or read reports while she danced around the kitchen. Both were lonely and this was like pretend Sunday or Saturday marriage. They didn't sleep together, just enjoyed Scotch and the Scrabble board and the Saturday trips to the farmer's market before she started dinner. Timmy was good people and a fairly recent divorcee. He was just happy for the company.

Timmy didn't mind the kids since had had none of his own. The kids became used to just hanging out after school when Bernie returned from work. They seldom ate with her because they were expected to have supper or dinner with their families. It was afterward when the TV shows parents watched were boring that they'd congregate in her apartment. Everyone was kicked out

at nine o'clock because Bernie had to be up early and needed some alone time.

Scrabble wasn't high on their list of "cool" games, so they weeded themselves out of her life unless they loved to read or play Monopoly. Bernie wasn't keen on the game, but it excited the kids to beat her by buying up hotels and sending her to jail. She loved their ideas and felt they were original. It never occurred to her that these might be repeated from friends at school. Reruns of Miami Vice were favorites and one boy said that "Don Johnson was like the Jesus Christ of Jerusalem Vice." This was the sort of thing that kept her in touch with their thinking and the mindset of the youngsters.

There weren't a lot of people from work she socialized with other than the occasional Friday night drink or happy hour. People seemed to have their own lives, boyfriends, girlfriends, marriages and circles of people. Bernie was not unhappy to go home to a good book, although the absence of a man in her life would demolish any good Sunday moods when Timmy wasn't around. The romance just wasn't there for them; they were friends who needed companionship.

FOUR

Gail also worked in her office as a copywriter and was a single parent. She had an eleven year old daughter who was horse crazy. How a city child could become horse crazy was beyond Gail's comprehension, but she scrimped for the money for weekly riding lessons for Ashley. The riding lessons were nearly all the way to Wisconsin from downtown Chicago. Gail and Bernie ate lunch together on occasion and eventually began to share life conversations.

Chicago winters are almost as famous as Buffalo winters and Gail once asked Bernie to ride with her and Ashley to the barn so Ashley could take her regular lesson during a particularly bad snow storm. Gail was afraid to drive alone and Bernie had indicated that she was familiar with driving in the Michigan snow from her days at home on the farm in a place called Cold Lake.

Their first foray together to the barn was after both went home and changed into jeans and parkas and Gail picked her up in front of her building. Ashley, in the back seat of Gail's car, spewed a stream of horse related monologue during the entire 45 minute drive. Bernie didn't know what she was talking about, but Gail, being the good parent kept her talking. It was "mother time" according to Gail, who wasn't particularly interested in

this activity. "It keeps her busy and focused and away from the thought of boys because there aren't any at this barn." Bernie told her frankly that she knew nothing of horses, even though she had grown up on a farm. They weren't wanted creatures because they didn't make milk and years ago her father had been a professor in the dairy program at the University of Wisconsin at Madison; dairy country for sure.

Bernie was immediately taken by the smell of the barn when they arrived. It might be a blizzard, but the barn was warm, the arena was snow free and indoor and well lighted. Teens and tweens were everywhere. Girls of all ages and sizes in brightly colored riding outfits brushed, saddled, rode and loved on their mounts. The entire aura of the barn brought back serious and intense memories and feelings from her 4H years. Years spent in the utter euphoria of animals, people who loved animals and the smells of the barn, hay in particular, with the memories of the songs on the radio at the time. The whole place made her curious, jealous, brought back raw teen feelings of wanting to be loved and surrounded by want. She loved competing with her animals, she loved 4H judging trips, she loved the clubs she belonged to, and the people associated with them. This barn had a nostalgic magic on her.

Gail didn't refuse when Bernie wanted to accompany her and Ashley to the barn the next Thursday for Ashley's lesson. They watched the blossoming young girls in their candor with their horses and talked about work. Ashley started to talk to Bernie about her lessons and what she was trying to learn.

What struck Bernie as odd was that this was a type of riding she'd never seen in the 4H Club. It was all English and she had never been exposed to English riding. Previously all saddles she had seen had horns on them and lots of leather and people wore hats. These riders wore helmets and posed and posted in tiny saddles made with a minimal amount of leather. It all looked completely impossible to balance in that small space and jump over wooden rails.

It became possible to spend more time in that barn when she told Gail she wanted to take a lesson on the same days as Ashley, and if Gail couldn't get Ashley to her lesson, Bernie would. Gail wasn't too sure about the new set of circumstances and voiced her concern about Bernie breaking a limb and not being able to get Ashley home. Bernie said she'd start some exercise and tell the instructor when she wasn't comfortable, making it safer for her. Her main concern was to get Ashley to and from her lesson and then get a chance to experience this. Gail continued to drive through the spring until she was certain that Bernie wasn't hell bent on killing herself. Gail watched Bernie in her first three private lessons and then through group lessons until she felt comfortable enough to allow, the now 12 year old, Ashley to be alone with Bernie.

Just like a skier who endeavors to become better, Bernie bought her own equipment; a Collegiate all purpose saddle and hauled it with Ashley's saddle in her Jeep to and from lessons. The two of them became close and Ashley started to confide in Bernie when her mother wasn't available or just needed a Thursday night off. Another emerging teenager with the same problems as the kids at her apartment complex. They didn't know

how close they were as they shared a lesson with two others each week. Gail was the one who put the brakes on after about six months.

"Ashley got her period."

"I know."

"How do you know?"

"She told me."

"Do you know she told you before she told me?"

"No. Is that bad?"

"I'm her mother. I bought all the stuff, explained it all after the videos they had to watch at school and was looking forward to this development, no pun intended."

"Am I supposed to be sorry? I didn't know that. I don't know much about kids."

"Hell yes, you're supposed to be sorry for not telling me right away. She had two periods before I found out."

"How could you not know?"

"When I explained things to her I taught her to wrap everything in toilet paper. She empties her own waste basket because it's part of her chores. I don't exactly go digging in the trash."

"I'm sorry, I just thought you knew."

"What did you tell her?"

"Nothing, other than what to do for cramps with a heating pad and Midol."

"Well, I'm not happy about her confiding in a stranger before me."

FIVE

The conversation happened over one of their brown bag lunches in the company lunchroom. Both of them bagged it to save money; Bernie to continue her riding lessons and Gail to afford Ashley's. A distance happened that day and Gail insisted on driving Ashley to her lessons alone. Bernie changed her lessons to Wednesday nights and had to catch up to a more advanced class of younger children. There were no other adult riders and Bernie was surrounded by eight and nine year olds who had been riding for years. Their bodies were more supple and bent differently, they were more physically advanced due to years of riding and Bernie was struggling to keep up with them. The instructor said, "Adults are the most difficult to teach because they analyze everything and kids just do it."

"Wonderful, I'm in kindergarten and working harder."

"You're young, in great shape and you'll catch up. Just stop trying to think about it. You have a good position and soon enough you'll be doing what they're doing; you look good up there."

"Easy for you to say, you've been riding your entire life and I can't even get a handle on this animal's personality. Would it be a good idea to get my own horse, too?"

"Yes. Just like your own saddle, it helps to have the same horse under you each time. If you're really interested I'd recommend a Quarter Horse because they're level in the mind and more forgiving. We have two open stalls for boarding here and I can help you look. Right now, it's good for you to be mounted on as many different animals as possible to develop a good seat."

Little did the instructor and barn owner know what she had put in motion. Bernie subscribed to horse magazines and started studying breeds, hooves, grooming, feeding and personalities. This was not unfamiliar territory after cattle, sheep and goat studies in 4H. It was easy and pleasurable. Novels were suddenly replaced by riding books and magazines. Horse artwork started appearing in her apartment. Timmy was at first puzzled and then accompanied her on a Wednesday and got a gist.

"Interesting."

They were heading back to her apartment in the Jeep. "What do you mean when you say, 'Interesting?'"

"Well, I saw a whole new you tonight. You were lit up, you were concentrating, you were athletic and you were deliriously happy without conscious thought."

"Lit up?"

"Yup, the Sunday sadness has worn off and it seems you live for Wednesday. Our Scrabble games are suffering, but the Scotch bottle isn't. Do you think I would enjoy a lesson?"

"Right, corporate attorney in a class full of kids."

"No, I'm serious. It's an athletic endeavor and I don't do anything but sit in a chair all day. You look so concentrated and deliriously happy, that I want a piece of it."

Timmy started his first private lesson. The lessons led him to buying the same saddle because he had borrowed hers and found it comfortable. Wednesday nights were now covered with an activity that included meeting after work, changing from suits to breeches and boots and driving to the barn for lessons. Timmy wasn't the least embarrassed about having to wear breeches and found them comfortable. The little girls never noticed.

Horses became paramount without the pun. Scrabble games continued, the Scotch bottle was replaced regularly and they started going out for some weeknight dinners together.

Bernie would occasionally meet Timmy downtown for lunch now and stopped brown bagging it as often. She seldom saw Gail other than meetings. The rift was not going to seam together. Bernie still had no idea why this would drive two friends apart.

SIX

One of the places Bernie did not frequent was home. Holidays were mandatory because of the family being together, but she did not spend any time in Cold Lake, Michigan unless she had to. She felt she left the place at 18 and was not wanted then and had no desire to be chummy with people who were ugly and cruel to her when she attended school there. She would refuse to go to the grocery store for her mother because she did not want to run into anyone she had previously known and her brothers were always recruited for those trips.

Dad bought the farm there when she was in eighth grade and moved the family from Madison to Cold Lake. He retired his teaching position and wanted to raise and milk dairy goats. The move introduced her to 4H and she was hooked by all the activity, acceptance and friends who had similar interests; unlike the people at school. Life at school was miserable and even the teachers were nasty, with the exception of an English teacher and the Home Economics teacher who were kind. The teachers seemed to feed off the cruelty of the kids and were just as snide as the students.

Her first week was memorable when Bernie, struggling with the combination on the assigned locker, was accosted by another girl. She slammed Bernie's locker

door shut as soon as it opened, put her face near Bernie's and said, "I'm going to beat the shit out of you after school, new girl."

Bernie, not realizing the threat said, "My you're a pugnacious person."

"That's another thing," the girl snarled at her, "No one knows what you're talking about."

Cold Lake was primarily a farming community. The village had a population of 3,500 plus residents. The village center had a large gazebo in the middle of a park that the streets edged around. There was a Post Office, a pharmacy that sold gift items and pricier shampoos than the grocery store. Two lawyers, one car dealership, a real estate office, two bars, one pizza shop, one decent restaurant, two cafes, a liquor and hardware store, an auto parts, a Dollar General and two gas stations to complete the picture. Outside of town was a municipal garage that housed the snow plows and work trucks for the road maintenance. The primary employers were an abrasives plant and an auto related manufacturer.

Her parents valued high grades and her brothers were already either out of school or seamlessly blended in. She had to dumb it down to survive without having her hair pulled or cut, her books shoved to the floor or shredded. Her grades suffered steady C's all year. Dad and Mom were aghast. They didn't know what was happening on the bus or at school. If Bernie tried to explain it to them, they seemed oblivious to the threats. There was nothing she did to garner this type of interest, she just stayed in her own world and slumped down into it further each year. Her parents didn't care about anything but grades

and she was being browbeaten at home for studying. She purposely blew tests.

There were times ink was rubbed into her clothes that Mom had so carefully taken her shopping for. She dressed differently because Mom was used to good schools, good clothing and a decently high position as a professor's wife. Sloppy jeans and T-shirts were not condoned by her mother because she had gone to private schools during her youth and felt that a well dressed person had a better chance at success; at least Bernie didn't have to wear a uniform. At one point she begged to go to a private school, but the closest one was 40 miles away and Catholic. Getting in was nearly impossible because they were full and neither parent wanted her going to a Catholic school, since they were Presbyterian.

Her parents didn't have a clue that they had moved to a town where everyone knew everyone's business and had been together since birth. Outsiders were suspect and either cool or very uncool. Mom especially didn't know of the gangster-like activity of the kids and the town because she seldom left the farm. She and Dad were building the milking parlor and Mom was fixing up the old farm house to make it more "livable."

Their trips were often not to town, but outlaying cities like Jackson, Ann Arbor or Lansing to the big depot stores for supplies. Dad did business at the local mill and the farm implement dealer, but he was the typical professor, lost in his world, and didn't notice people's suspicions of him and his education. They knew that he had been a professor, but not of what. They did, however, respect that he knew the dairy industry, goats

and farming, yet it was a puzzle to them how he had this knowledge. Dad didn't talk about himself and he didn't much socialize with the locals.

With three children, in college, high school and junior high, they were oblivious to anything other than basic care like meals, lunch money, Matt's college needs, the farm and holidays. Bernie was awash in a sea of dangerous creatures intent on killing, maiming or eating her. Her parent's lack of socialization didn't help her matriculate into the mainstream of the village and its occupants. People actually stared at her for long periods of time at school making her very self conscious. It didn't help that while everyone else was developing breasts, talking about cramps, going gaga over boys, that she was rail thin, breastless and self-doubting.

Her father was six one and her mother was five eight, so tallness was going to be an issue to deal with for clothing and assumed basketball skills. Bernie didn't like team sports because she felt no connection to anyone, wasn't going to be picked anyway once it was evident that she had no athletic skills useful for a team and wasn't popular or a team player.

Gym class was an exercise in wicked games, taunts, flat out affronts and toss your lunch fear. They were expected to take showers, unless they were menstruating. You could tell the short, squat toad who served as the gym teacher "M," meaning you had your period. Since Bernie was underdeveloped, she didn't know when she was supposed to get her period or how many days there were in between. It was just easy to say, "M," and get out of having to shower after class. The toad dragged

her one day by the back of her collar into her office and said, "You can't have a period every class just to get out of a shower. You will shower and you will like it. So, I'm calling your parents and finding out what your cycle is and tracking it." Bernie wasn't thrilled to be physically assaulted by a teacher let alone have to deal with a call home. She hadn't even started her periods yet. The call was never made.

The teacher neither knew nor cared that girls would stand on the benches in the adjoining shower stalls and throw wet gobs of toilet paper at her. She would cower in her nakedness until they left. She was always late for her class after gym. The teachers were as bullying as the kids. One didn't exactly go to the principal's office and complain about a teacher. The office staff and administration didn't care about anything but behavior in the halls, the school budget and truancy. "Hey mosquito bite," didn't alert the teachers in the hall that people were making fun of her lack of physical development. The boys, too, knew what this meant. "Hey ugly, got any big words for us today?" One teacher actually referred to her as "Mosquito," when asking a question. The class fell over. He must have thought it had something to do with her long legs, and was pleased with the class's reaction.

Stepping off the bus at home was the biggest relief of the day and Friday's were the guarantee that one day was going to be good, Saturday. Sundays started out well and then her stomach started knotting up after dinner. She knew she'd have to go back to the vile place with the monsters and their terrorization.

She once had to phone home about staying late because Dad expected her to milk with him that evening. She went into the one and only phone booth, deposited her quarter and as the home phone was ringing; she read the wall graffiti, "Bernie is ugly." By the time her Mom answered the phone Bernie was in tears. The crying jag was chalked up to female hormones by her parents. Hormones she didn't yet have.

Talking to her parents had no effect on them. She tried to explain how her clothes were ink stained, how her backpack was destroyed, why her grades were suffering and they put the screws in tighter to study harder and get better grades. It was a hopeless situation because they did not socialize with the residents of the village and had no connection with the students she attended with. This was going to be Bernie's battle alone. Her brother Josh got wind of the fun at Bernie's expense, but didn't do anything to stop it. He was popular and this was his kid sister, what she did at school was her business. He already had a car and was dating. This was his senior year and he, too, had been relocated, so he was going to enjoy it and bolt away for college in the fall. Occasionally she could beg a ride home with him if he wasn't due at his job at the supermarket after school. He was one of the lucky ones to have gotten a part-time job in a small town. He was known to be reliable, polite and friendly. His interests weren't focused on his little sister's problems at school. Neither did he know of the constant badgering because of his age and distance between the high school and the junior high students.

Her junior year she became bolder and less affected by the teasing and taunting. The big event was supposed

to be the junior prom and she was seriously looking forward to being asked and going. There were no boys she had dated, but two of them were kind enough to her and she figured one of them would ask. It never crossed her mind that they were looking at younger girls and didn't consider her as a date. No one asked and her mother was insistent upon shopping for a dress.

"Mom, I don't have a date and no one has asked me. Why do I need a dress?"

"Someone will ask you at the last minute and you need to be prepared."

"I'm begging you to listen to me, I'm not popular and I will not be asked to the prom."

"Are you saying you don't want to go to what is considered a right of passage for high school? That's ridiculous."

Bernie resisted each and every trip. Her mom was relentless and told her that if no one asked her, she should ask someone herself. "Ask the most popular boy in school, he probably doesn't have a date". Bernie, of course, thought her mother had seriously lost her mind. She never did go to the junior prom because she started having headaches weeks before the set date. "We need to get your eyes checked. I'll make an appointment and see if you need glasses and that isn't what's causing the headaches. Maybe it'll help with your grades, too," her mother said.

The day of the eye appointment Bernie was doubled over at the nurse's office unable to function because of the severity of the headache. Instead of picking Bernie

up and going to the optometrist, her mother took her straight to the doctor's office.

The village doctor saw everyone and the one thing he saw a lot of was drug usage in teens. His first words before asking her about the pain were, "What drugs are you doing?"

He finally believed her mother and referred her to a neurologist. The headaches continued to the point that she could not climb the stairs to her bedroom. Her parents installed her on the couch in the living room. They were suddenly concerned before the neurology appointment. She lost her appetite and was only able to keep broth down because vomiting had become another symptom. The pain in her head was a continuous throb; she started losing weight and finally fell to 85 pounds. The neurologist found nothing wrong with her in his tests.

The only phone call from school was the principal asking why she was truant. No friends called. There were people who tolerated her to eat lunch with them, but they never called, either. However, three 4H leaders called. Bernie wasted away on the couch.

Her mother continued to make dinner for the three of them, although Bernie didn't eat anything other than a few crackers and broth. During dinner preparation her mother would listen to the radio in the kitchen and Bernie finally heard the words to "Take It Easy" by the Eagles for the first time. The phrase, "Don't let the sound of your own wheels drive you crazy" had a sudden effect on her. The phrase kept repeating itself in her head and her dreams. It was then that she decided

there was nothing wrong with her, but that she was making herself sick. Her appetite came back, school work was picked up and completed and her parents stopped worrying about her enough to send her back. Nearly two months of participation was lost, though.

SEVEN

Returning to school, she was a different person. The person she had become was a result of summers of showing animals and 4H projects, her confidence bolstered by what she knew and how much she had won over the years of shows and fairs and open competitions and public speaking projects. Suddenly Bernie was the Bernie she was all summer long. A laughing, happy, bright teenager with straight A's. Her accomplishments were her own and she now knew this. "Just let me get through and I'll be gone and out of this place," she promised herself.

Colleges suddenly were interested, and Mom took her to visitations. She wanted to be far away and her parents wanted her close to home in Lansing. Go to Michigan State they urged her. Unfortunately for her parents, Bernie's personality took on a confrontational side as well. "A state college isn't good enough for me, she yelled at them." She had applied to Northwestern, Syracuse and Columbia because of their excellent communications departments. Arguments were loud and verbally violent among the three of them. Her brothers were no help when they were home because they were in their own worlds and really didn't care where the high maintenance baby of the family wanted to go.

The guidance counselor at school suggested she go to cosmetology school because of her previous grades. He was no help and dismissed her like he dismissed most of the C students around her. She started fighting at school for higher classes and wrote essays to prove she was deserving of advancement. The teachers, upon reading the essays, fought the guidance counselor for her to enter their classes. The counselor wasn't too convinced and Bernie said, "I'm either in or I'm dropping out and you can lose your per diem per head." He refused and the next day she went to the school office and registered the drop out paperwork. She sat home for three days and read until the phone rang. It was the principal asking why she had dropped out when her grades had picked up. She explained the situation and the recommendations from the teachers and suddenly she was back at school in advanced placement classes. Battle won. All those years of being picked on for her vocabulary were not lost and she aced through the new classes with the exception of math.

Whether people wanted to be around her or not, was no longer a concern. But the strangest thing happened. Suddenly she was mildly popular with the brainiacs. She was invited at lunch to sit with her new classmates. These were some of the very same people who had participated in the toilet paper runs, the ink incidents and the taunts. They were slight misfits themselves and needed someone to pick on to fit in. She didn't forgive entirely, but forgave enough to eat lunch with them. Her comments were no longer kept to herself, but verbalized. She made some people laugh and others become uneasy.

That summer was the absolute best for 4H and showing. She won almost all of her classes at fairs, was a champion public speaker and had close relationships with other 4Her's from neighboring towns. She was selected by the county 4H to participate in State Fair and had some nice wins. She was popular with these kids and was asked out on dates. She had gained back her weight and developed enough that she was more confident about her appearance. She realized that she wasn't ugly as she was told over and over again at school. She started dating various boys from other towns and realized what fun she had been missing. Bernie even attended her first high school football game, albeit she rooted for the opposing team with her friends from that town.

Senior year was a breeze and only one taunt made her take a swing at someone. He sat behind her in Social Studies and was a whiz with the straw and a spit ball. The wet goobers slid down the back of her collar with regularity. On her desk she had a new book from her book club. She considered the shiny new cover, the perfectly formed corner, the fantasy world beyond the front cover. Bernie took great care of her books, like the treasures they were and she wasn't about to ruin a single page on someone's face. However, she was strong from working with Dad each and every day in the barn and caring for her own projects and animals. She clocked the guy with the book and broke his nose. For the first time she was called to the principal's office. "I don't get it, you've always been a quiet and a model student. Why did you hit Mark?"

"You haven't noticed these past five years, but I'm the most picked on student here. For the first time I chose

to stand up for myself. Am I suspended?" she asked without emotion.

"No, this is your first offense and Mark has been known to get into a lot of brawls. This was his first, however, with a girl," the principal said with a small smile playing at his lips. He probably got a charge out of a girl breaking Mark's nose when it deserved to be broken several years ago by another boy.

Mark with the bandaged nose requested to be moved to a desk on the other side of the class. People started looking at her again, only this time it was with a sort of grudging admiration. Her parents had, of course, been notified and grilled her about the fist fight. "Girls do not slug it out with men."

"Who are you calling a man? He's a boy who's been picking on me since eighth grade and you've both chose to ignore it all these years. What about boys don't hit girls? Suddenly you're interested because I fought back? Ha, ha. You never stuck up for me, my brothers never stuck up for me and all you're worried about is your reputation since you started going out to dinner in town. I've been begging and pleading with you to understand what's been happening to me since we moved here. I hate it here and I cannot wait to leave this place. Don't get me wrong, I love the farm and I appreciate all you've done for me with 4H and the various clubs, but you've ignored me long enough. So I broke the guy's nose. Big deal. What did he do to my spirit and self confidence through the years with the others? Did you see my prom pictures?" There were no answers to her questions.

College became Northwestern when the scholarship notification arrived by mail. They couldn't say a word to her; she was delirious.

Boys could be met, dated and disposed of at college. She learned that everyone was starting fresh, didn't know anyone else and knew nothing of her. It was a relatively easy four years. She learned that she was attractive and dated many young men. Other than her roommate of four years, she really didn't trust many other women and didn't have a close group of friends. The school newspaper was a different story all together. Those were people she loved, confided in, could be irreverent with and they enjoyed each other's wit and company. Graduation Day was meaningful this time and she did not dispose of her cap and gown on a cafeteria floor. She bagged it up and returned it as asked.

The counselor she had for four years was great at getting her to the placement office, writing letters of recommendation and pushing her unusual high school extracurricular activities. The placement office found her a job immediately and her parents found furniture for the apartment she rented in Chicago. Since the job started in the middle of milking season, Dad prevailed upon the boys to take vacation days and care for the farm while they moved Bernie to Chicago during a weekend. Bernie didn't feel that her brothers suffered much, besides, they were probably high the whole time. She knew them.

EIGHT

Burger Belt was one of the country's largest franchises and when her firm, Rand and Rand, landed the PR contract it included publicity and all press releases. They were Chicago based and so was their law firm, which included franchise attorneys, personal injury attorneys and a host of other specialties.

After two years of a very successful partnership, with everyone busting their butts to make the client happy and more prosperous, a party was planned at the offices of Rand and Rand. Most of the management team from Burger Belt were familiar faces at the company, but several ancillary organizations they worked with were not. Their law firm and several local vendors were also invited to the party in their honor. The party planners were buzzing for a month and over 500 people were expected to attend. An orchestra, open bars, appetizer stations and a sit down dinner were planned.

For expansion, a company had moved out of their building and the owners allowed Rand and Rand to rent the space for the huge party. A portable dance floor and a dais for the band had been brought in. Everyone at Rand and Rand snuck down a floor to take a peak at the decorations and planning. A portable kitchen was set up with a well known chef. The employees were

excited and had a difficult time concentrating through the activity for the formal affair. The Rand's had been extra friendly with their employees and were making the rounds to various departments in an effort to get to know people on a more personal basis. *Probably because they don't know us and want us to appear to be one big cohesive family for the party.*

"Are we expected to have dates for this event?" Bernie asked a co-worker.

"Yes, the memo isn't out yet, but we are expected to have an escort of sorts. I'm married, so I have a built in one and she's really excited. Women love to dress up. You say 'black tie' to a woman and you don't see her for weeks because she's shopping."

Bernie's wardrobe had grown considerably over the years, but it was suits, blouses, good shoes and riding clothes. She had Ovation, Tuff Rider, FITS; the latest riding and paddock boots, shirts, gloves, breeches and vests in an array of colors. A few good dresses and gowns were in her collection of clothing, but nothing for a night like this. A twinkling light night. An unfamiliar panic set in and Bernie started worrying about clothing. She assumed that Timmy would accompany her because she wasn't dating anyone at the time.

"Timmy, do you have a tux?"

"What a weird question," he said on the phone. "Why do I need a tux? I need a horse more than a tux."

She outlined the festive occasion and Timmy genuinely seemed excited. "Hell yes, I'd love to go. I'll rent a tux.

Always wanted to work for that law firm Berger Belt uses; it'll give me a leg up to meet some people."

"There's just one problem, I don't have a dress."

"So go shopping."

"Uh, I don't exactly have anyone to go shopping with. And, I don't know where to go. It's not like I'm buying a suit."

"Chicago has tons of upscale dress stores."

Bernie sighed, "Look, I'm asking you to go with me."

"Oh, I see. I'm the one you trust to approve apparel for this event?"

"You're a man; you would be honest about what looks good on me."

"Hey, Bernie, I got news for you, this ain't exactly up my alley."

"You mean you never went shopping with your wife?"

"No, that's probably why she divorced me."

Bernie's laugh could be heard down the hallways of Rand and Rand for minutes, "So you'll go?"

"Let me ask you a very pertinent question, how many days are we talking here?"

Their nights, other than Wednesday, became a flurry of visits to formal stores. "Burger chains have bizarre public relations problems and I've worked my ass off

for these people. I don't want to look like a freaking bridesmaid."

"What's wrong with looking like a bridesmaid?"

"Tim, you're hopeless."

The dress was found in a small shop off Michigan Avenue. The shop catered to special occasions. It was dark turquoise, sheered in layers and made Bernie look like a shimmering mermaid. Because of the sheering, it layered itself around each curve and was strapless. There was a small train and that was altered off the dress when the shoes were presented so that one could dance in it. "Do I look ridiculous? I like it, but it may be over the top for this. So many people are going to be wearing black."

Timmy stood back apprised and said, "No, it stands out a little, but that's what you want since you've become a senior copywriter and, if I may say, it makes your eyes look turquoise, too."

"I need a wrap for this because of the weather."

"Oh, good Lord, does that mean more shopping? I can't take any more, Bernie."

The sales clerk overheard and produced a soft black cashmere cape. "This can be worn with other outfits and doesn't detract from the beauty of this dress for your occasion."

"Sold. Please tell me you take plastic."

NINE

Timmy and Bernie were seated at a round table with other partygoers. Gail was seated with an unknown man at another table. The party planners had done a good job and purposely planted people from different companies together. Bernie and Tim joined the group at the bar, got drinks, tasted Hors d' Oeuvres and danced a little before the dinner meals arrived. They introduced themselves to their table mates and everyone seemed to be interested in each other's jobs and got along well. Wine appeared before each course and Bernie felt herself getting a little tipsy. Dinner calmed the alcoholic overload and she and Timmy danced when the band started another set.

"Hey, this is fun. I just wished we were sitting with some of Frank and Touey's people, so I could network."

"I can introduce you to who I know and after that you're on your own."

She steered dancing Timmy toward a table of people she recognized and stopped to introduce him. At the adjoining table was a tall man, Latin looking, almost like Julio Iglesias. They glanced at one another and he winked at her. Bernie felt her face flush in embarrassment.

Timmy didn't see and was engrossed in conversation and introductions.

They were invited to sit with the new acquaintances and Timmy talked shop. Bernie sneaked a peek at the adjoining table and was disappointed to see that the man who had winked was not in his chair. She scanned the dance floor and found him with a lithe blonde in his arms. The set ended and they returned to their table. Bernie purposely did not look again. Timmy offered to refresh their drinks and left. The chatter in the room was deafening and Bernie had a difficult time trying to converse with the wife of one of the attorney's for Frank and Touey. It just so happened that her daughter rode at the same stable on Tuesday nights. She was 16, an advanced jumper and rode many of the same school horses. They talked until the band started again and Timmy returned with their drinks. They moved back to their original table, eventually left their drinks and went to the dance floor.

Mr. Julio danced by with the blonde in the red dress. He caught her eye and winked again. Bernie did her best to steer Timmy off the dance floor. "Hey, what gives, I thought you were having a good time?"

"I am, I'm just getting tired and these shoes should have been broken in before tonight."

"OK, I'll get us a couple of fresh drinks, Dewar's and soda again?"

"Yes, that would be nice." Timmy left.

A second later the tall man with the dark mass of hair lightly touched Bernie on the shoulder. "May I have this dance?"

It was a slow one and Bernie was a little embarrassed to be held so closely by a stranger. "My name's Tony and I work for Frank and Touey. What's yours?"

"I'm called Bernie."

"Well Bernie," he held her a little closer, who do you work for?"

Bernie tried to put a little more room between them and said, "I work for Rand and Rand the party givers."

"It's a nice party. What do you do for them?"

"I'm a copy writer and publicist." What do you do for Frank and Touey?"

"I'm an attorney and handle smaller cases and some criminal work."

Before she could think to distance herself from what she felt was a dangerous cad she said, "Oh my escort tonight is an attorney. He does mostly corporate cases."

"Oh, so that's not your boyfriend?"

"Ah, no, we're just very good friends and spend a lot of time together and take riding lessons together."

"You ride, huh?"

"Well, I'm learning and trying to ride," she laughed.

He put his face closer to hers and said nearly in her ear, "I'm assuming you mean horses."

"Yes." She was beginning to be more nervous by this very good dancer who was holding her closely. "Is that your wife you were dancing with earlier?"

"No, that's a friend. I'm not otherwise engaged."

"That sounds like a line to me."

"It is a line, are you interested in a date?"

She smiled at the candor. "I only know your first name and don't know another thing about you, other than you are a very good dancer. Why would I want to go on a date with you?"

"I can tell you my life story in a minute or two and you can decide."

"Thanks, but I have as escort for the evening and he is back at our table with drinks. It was a lovely dance and thank you for asking me. I should return now."

"Your wish, my lady." He winked at her again. They walked off the dance floor as a faster number was starting. He steered her to her table, indicating that he knew where they were sitting because he had obviously been watching them.

Timmy graciously stood as they returned and Bernie introduced him to Tony. Tony works for Frank and Touey, Tim."

"Really? I was just introduced to some of your colleagues. Brent and Fran, I believe. Nice organization you work for."

"Thanks, it's a job. My interests lay in other areas outside of the granite high rises, though."

"My interest is in your firm. Any openings that you know of?"

"Well, you might try applying for starters. You never said who you work for."

Tony pulled up a chair and started questioning Timmy about his work and they spoke for several minutes. Bernie was content to just listen for a while and then she excused herself to make her way to Gail's table. It was killing her to know who Gail's escort was for the evening.

It turned out Gail had no one to ask but her brother, who was an accountant. Gail, as far as Bernie could tell, was not unhappy to talk to someone tonight. Bernie asked about Ashley's riding progress and got an earful about the instructor being a surrogate mother figure. Bernie wanted out of this conversation after the estranged relationship and excused herself to return to her table where Tony and Timmy were still talking.

"Tim, my feet are feeling better, a dance?"

"Sure, excuse me, Tony, the dance floor waits." He swung her into a high energy number and she was grateful to be away from Tony. "What did you say to him to let him know I was taking riding lessons with you?"

"He asked you about that?"

"Yes. He seems very interested in you."

"Well, I'm not too keen on him. I perceive he's a womanizer, just look at him."

"He seems nice enough to me. I found out there are some openings at Frank and Touey and I'm going to drop off a few resumes. They have a great reputation and are large enough to satisfy my aspirations. There are several departments I could work for."

"Good, just make sure Wednesdays are still open nights."

When they returned to their apartment complex Bernie said good night and shut the door softly. Timmy was acting a little strangely in the cab on the way back and attempted to hold her hand. She let him hold it for a little while and then decided that a Kleenex was needed from her evening bag. They did not spend Sunday together because they were both a little hung over.

Monday came a little too quickly after Saturday night's events and Bernie felt a little burned out and slow. Her fellow workers seemed to be in the same state of mind and not much was accomplished other than talk of the weekend party.

Wednesday rolled around and she and Timmy packed the Jeep and headed off to the barn for their lessons. Timmy told her how he had taken Monday off and arrived at Frank and Touey's doorstep to set an appointment in person with the human resources department at the

firm. He was in luck and they accepted his resume and gave him a brief interview on the spot. "Guess who I ran into?"

"I don't know, she said as she made the turn down the barn lane.

"Your friend, Tony."

"Oh, how did you run into him in such a large place?"

"He was in the human resources department at the time. I think his being there helped me get through the door so quickly. He shook my hand like he'd known me all his life."

No more mention was made of Tony that evening.

TEN

Two weeks later she answered the phone in her office to hear Tony's voice asking her to lunch. "I can't go today I have lunch plans, maybe another day."

"Well, how about tomorrow? I have a loose schedule right now and I'd like to get to know you better."

"Interesting you should find me without knowing my last name, and then call my direct line."

"Oh, I have ways of getting information."

"Apparently! I am a little busy right now, could we have this conversation another day?"

"Sure, how about at lunch tomorrow, I'll swing by and pick you up at your office."

"In the lobby?"

"No, I said, your office."

"You don't know where my office is, Mr. Tony."

"It's Romanelli and I do know where it is."

Intrigued and not having dated for a while Bernie accepted the lunch date and continued her work,

forgetting about him. The next day she woke in a sort of thither about what to wear to work for a date with a virtual stranger.

Women being women, she chose a taupe suit and a blue blouse to accent her eyes. She took extra care with her makeup and ended up being ten minutes late to work.

At 12:30 he arrived at her open door. He was holding a green tissue wrapped white rose, which he presented to her with outlandish flourish. She felt her cheeks burn brightly and the blush didn't go unnoticed by Tony. "I hope you like roses."

"Actually, I don't. They're the only flower, other than the weed goldenrod, that I don't care for."

"Well, let's solve that." He reached to her desk where she had laid the rose, picked it up and chucked it into the trash can. What flowers are your favorites?"

"Lilies, she stammered."

"Then the next time I see you I shall bring lilies."

"You're awfully forward, don't you think?"

"No, I don't think I'm forward. I just know what I like and go after it."

"You like roses, then?"

"I'm not particular about flowers. Shall we leave; I have a table reserved for us."

Bernie sighed inwardly and braced herself for what she knew was going to be a tenuous lunch.

"September is not exactly a good month for a picnic, so I made reservations at Chef Paul's Bistro. Have you been there?"

Bernie braced herself yet again because this was over the top for a first lunch. They walked side by side to the elevators and made their way to the lobby and out to the street where he hailed a cab. The restaurant was crowded, but their table was ready by the windows. He seated her and waved to the sommelier.

"I don't usually drink at lunch because of work. Since when does a restaurant have a sommelier for lunch service?"

He sighed aloud and said, "Listen, I think I'm going too fast for you, but I must warn you that this is not going to be a hurried lunch and you look like you could use a nice drink with lunch today. Am I making you nervous?"

"Yes, as a matter of fact, you are. I'm not used to be squired around and I barely know you; for heaven's sake, I just learned your last name two days ago."

The wine steward headed in their direction and Tony asked, "White or red?"

Bernie knew that if she ordered red her teeth would be purple at the end of lunch. The sommelier approached the table and Tony said, "George, we'll have a bottle of a nice white burgundy."

"How did you know I wasn't going to drink red?"

"Women only drink red at night because it stains their teeth," he said as cockily as he acted.

Lunch was a gourmet delight and gratefully accepted by Bernie who was happy not to have a microwave meal at her desk or in the company lunch area. Salmon in puff pastry, steamed asparagus, Caesar salad made at the table and the wonderful dry white wine.

"So tell me, are you a Chicago native?" He leaned across the table.

"No, I grew up in a very small town you've never heard of in Michigan. I'm originally from Wisconsin, but my parents now live in Michigan."

"What town?"

"I'm telling you, you've never heard of it. Where do your parents live?"

"In an equally small town you've never heard of. A traffic jam is four cars behind a tractor." They were passing the banter back and forth and having fun with it.

"You've never heard of Cold Lake then, have you?"

Bernie grew cold and the blood ran out of her face. "Is this some sort of joke?" She practically attacked him with her words. "I think this is cruel and unusual punishment."

Tony, cocked his head to one side, lost all expression in his face and asked, "Why would I be playing a joke on you? I just met you as well."

She folded her napkin and put it on the table. Nearly rising from her chair she said, "Listen, I don't think you're funny and I'm not going to be the blunt of another cruel joke from anyone from Cold Lake. How could you know I grew up there?"

His actions were catlike and he put his very warm hand on hers, instantly calming her. He urged her to stay seated and said, "No, I'm serious, I'm from Cold Lake, Michigan. I was born and grew up there. Did you grow up there as well?"

"This is a joke, right. There's a hidden camera somewhere and I'm supposed to throw this glass of wine at you, right?"

"No, I assure you, you're not to throw a glass of wine at me, there are no hidden cameras and I didn't know you might be from Cold Lake, Michigan.

Bernie started to visibly tremble. The shakes were bad enough, but what to think or do next was harder. She didn't have anything to say to this handsome man in this elegant restaurant. She wanted to run out any door and hide somewhere.

"Bernie, listen to me, please look at me. I don't know where you're from, I've never met anyone from Cold Lake, Michigan in Chicago and I am not lying to you. This is not some joke, I'm really from Cold Lake and my family lives there today. I am of Italian decent, my father is an attorney in Cold Lake, Romanelli, do you recognize the name?"

She sat with her hands folded in her lap, her head bowed, "Yes, I do, now, recognize the name of an attorney there. How could you possibly be from Cold Lake and we never have met before?"

"I don't know, it's a small town and everyone knows everyone else. When did you graduate?"

He calmed her and ordered a desert and Lemoncello for both of them. "I have a suspicion that you should not return to your office because the mention of Cold Lake has visibly upset you. I truly did not mean to rattle you, I wanted to get to know you and ask you out on a real date. Something stupidly fun and casual like bowling."

The absurdity of this and the previous conversation set Bernie to chuckling. Her chuckle was deep as was her laughter. "I'm sorry, but I have never met anyone from Cold Lake that I liked and I certainly would not associate with them if I knew they were from there."

"It sounds like you were in agony there. I can tell you small towns are cruel and it sounds as though you have had your share. I graduated before you arrived, so it makes sense we did not meet one another prior to this. I hope you'll forgive me for not lying to you about where I was from."

"You'd lie?"

"No, I wouldn't lie."

It was indeed a tenuous date and Bernie thanked him and returned to her office about four o'clock. No one

said a word about the strange man or her absence from the office. She took work home with her to catch up.

The next day she and Timmy went to their riding lesson. "Tim, what do you think Tony Romanelli was doing in the human resources department when you went over to Frank and Touey?"

"He was talking up the secretary when I arrived. I don't really know."

"Did you hear anything conversationally?"

"No, I got there just as he was saying 'Thanks for the info.' Why?"

"I had lunch with him yesterday and it was nearly a disaster. Did you know he's from the same small town I'm from in Michigan?"

"No, how would I know that? I was just grateful to run into someone I had met before. I really want to work there. What was such a disaster?"

"Well, you know part of my life story and how horrible I always felt there and how crappy people were. I thought he had set me up as a gag or something."

"Me thinks you like him. He's a looker, for sure and he had his eyes on you during the party. *The entire time.*"

"Really, I didn't notice."

"Yeah, well you're really good at missing male and female details sometimes. I wonder what else you miss as a copywriter."

"What the hell is that supposed to mean?"

"Nothing, I'm just teasing."

Bernie's lesson was on a new horse just brought in as a school horse. She was a black mare and high strung. "I think you can handle her as an adult. I'll warn you, she's got an opinion about things, but we've been riding her for a month and she's settled into her job. She's a five-year-old half Arabian, half Thoroughbred cross called an Anglo Arabian. We call her Noir because of her color. You don't ask her, you tell her, got it?"

"I think. Does this mean that she won't tattle on me if I give the wrong cue?"

"Right, she's a little green when it comes to lessons, but you can handle it. I just trust that you won't cheat and you'll be paying more attention to her than our regular school horses."

Noir proved to be all that and a box of Twinkie's. She would try anything once until she was corrected. Since Bernie had elected not to learn to jump, they were concentrating on a discipline called Dressage. One tap of the Dressage whip and Noir settled back down. She didn't need to be whipped or cracked, just tapped and her attitude went back to obedience. "Nice job, the teacher said. I didn't tell you we brought her in here for sale and I'm having everyone ride her so she's better equipped to handle a new owner. She came from a breeding farm where the owners are getting a little too old to ride anything other than trail horses. She's supposed to be good on trail. We haven't taken her out yet until I get a better handle on her."

"Bernie, breathless and spent from having to control the poundage between her legs said, "She's a handful. She knows her cues, but she tests every one of them before she obeys."

"Yes. I know you to be firm, so I put you up on her tonight. I've only had the advanced students on her until today. You look really, really good on her and she's tall enough to accommodate your long legs. You should consider buying her. I originally told you that a Quarter Horse would be something for you to look at, but she's a lovely mare and I think you can control her."

"That's a nice compliment, thanks. I'm sure you want a fortune for her."

"No, she's only one of two mares here. I don't trust mares too much and everything in the barn is a gelding other than the 19 year old pony and her."

Bernie asked the price and sucked in her breath when she heard it. The stable owner told her she would take installment payments and keep the mare ridden as a school horse until she was paid for. "But I only ride once a week, how could I ride her enough to keep her legged up?"

"We could work out a schooling lease agreement with you. We have other students who can control her; half board and she schools every day but Sundays."

"I'll think about it, but I don't know if I'm ready for my own horse yet."

The thought of the black mare with the two hind stockings and the small star on her forehead was exciting though. Black horses weren't seen much and if they were, they were privately owned because it was such a desirable color. Most of the horses Bernie rode were bay or chestnuts, mostly chestnuts, and all geldings and experienced and lazy school horses.

"Timmy, did you see the horse she put me on tonight? She's for sale."

"She looked like a problem to me. You were constantly saying something to her and she looked like she wasn't listening."

"She's comfortable, but hot."

"She's a woman!"

"Yeah, that part I get. I'm not sure if I have the skill to keep her legged up." She outlined the basics of the sale and Timmy said he was jealous that she had found a horse already. "Hey, I didn't buy her. I don't have that kind of money in savings to prepare for boarding a horse and buying it, too."

Timmy insisted on walking her to her door again and Bernie sensed something other than friendship on his mind. "Look, you want a game of Scrabble Saturday? I was planning on making a roast and you know that I can't eat the entire thing myself. Besides, there'll be plenty left for lunches we can split."

"Sure, sounds great. What about some fall vegetables before the farmer's market closes for the year?"

"Great, let's meet and go shopping and then I can work on my stuff, you can read briefs and I can get you to help me shop for a digital camera that you can learn to use. I'm really thinking about this horse and I want some pictures on her. She's really beautiful."

"Whoa, Lady, you just met the horse tonight and you're already planning on buying her, which you told me you weren't going to do. And, in what order did you want to go shopping? I suggest the camera first and we can fiddle around with it at the farmer's market."

"Sounds good to me, see ya." Again she softly shut the door on Timmy.

ELEVEN

Tony Romanelli wasn't on her mind much other than the extreme discomfort and embarrassment of their lunch. She certainly didn't want to be around him again and fell back into her pattern with Timmy. They went out to the stable on Saturday and both rented a horse to ride through the fall leaves and the trails adjacent to the stable. It was the first time they'd been allowed outside the barn and it was exciting to trail ride.

"I just thought of something you didn't think about yet," said Timmy. "You will have more expense than just board and paying for this mare you are in love with."

"Like what?"

"You haven't noticed that all the people here who own their own horses have their own equipment? You are using a school bridle, school curries and brushes and stuff. What about veterinary care, don't I remember you telling me about vaccinations and hoof care on a regular basis?"

"Oh, man, like a dog, yeah."

"Lots more expense than a dog, Bernie."

"I'll need a second job!"

"I heard there was an opening at that dress shop where you bought your fabulous gown," he teased.

"No, Timmy, I'm serious, I'd need a second job. What kind of job could I do without it interfering with my regular job?"

"Well, you're so interested in all those teenagers who hang out, why not tutor in something. How good are you in math, because that's what most people need tutoring in?"

"I'm lousy at math. I wonder how many need English tutors. That's a great idea. I could put tutoring money toward my horse endeavors."

And it began. She posted a flyer in the laundry room and immediately got a call from a parent who had already allowed her son to come to her apartment. He was failing English and wasn't the best of readers. She needed to get him through his current reading list and stay interested in it, as well as understand the words and nuances of the writer. He started doing better and word of mouth got her the next student. She enjoyed these sessions with the kids and was on her way to buying a horse and equipment.

Wednesdays were firm "no tutoring" days and she and Timmy continued to take their lessons. Timmy was finding it more comfortable than his first lessons and he was advancing. The instructor was pleased because she didn't have to stop as often to correct both Bernie and Timmy while attempting to keep the children interested in their lesson. Timmy now started talking in earnest about buying a horse. "She said she had two stalls open

for boarders. If you get a horse, I'm definitely going to be looking for one."

The only problem was that there was only one horse for sale at the barn and Bernie had first dibs on it. She was requesting and riding Noir at all lessons and Timmy hadn't ridden her. Timmy was going to have to take trips with the instructor to meet horses at various facilities and farms. These were going to have to be Sunday trips, leaving Bernie alone with kids and starting dinner for him when he returned from visiting sales horses. "This is a kick because we're both behind in our work and you just flash through the door expecting dinner. We might as well be married for the way things are working out," Bernie told him.

"I'm gun shy about marriage."

"Geez, I was only kidding. I just meant that you need to be pulling your weight around here because I cook and you eat and then leave for paperwork while I'm tutoring. It's amazing to me how much life has changed in a few months."

TWELVE

Thanksgiving was coming up and Bernie planned to drive home for the holiday. Her mother already had a big meal planned and everyone was decently excited. It would be good to see her brothers and her brothers' new girlfriends, who had accepted invitations to the farm.

She left on Tuesday and was home before lunch. Mom was in the kitchen with Dad. She had him peeling carrots and they were engaged in a conversation when Bernie came through the back door. "We didn't even hear you drive in, what'd you do get a stealth kit for your Jeep?" Dad asked.

"I have goodies to be brought in, how about a little help?

"Oh, I hope you didn't go and buy a lot of things because Dad and I have been shopping for a week and a half for all the things we need for this dinner," her mother moaned.

"No, just some things you can't get here and some things for Friday breakfast, like real bagels and lox."

"Well, that sounds lovely, I wasn't looking forward to eating turkey for breakfast on Friday morning," Dad said.

The boys arrived late Thursday morning and introduced their girlfriends, Bryce and Amber. Both girls were nice and fit in with the conversations and family teasing. Bernie approved of them for her brothers. Matt acted a little more attentive about his girl than Josh did and Bernie suspected it was serious, as in a getting married serious. She waited all day for the ring to present itself, but it never did.

About four o'clock when all the kids were outdoors having a wood chopping contest a dark blue BMW pulled in the driveway. "Who's that?" Matt wanted to know.

"I don't know, I don't recognize the car," said Josh.

"Neither do I," Bernie commented. Then she blanched as Tony Romanelli stepped out holding a cone of wrapped flowers. "I'm going to die right here and now," she told her brothers. "This guy is stalking me."

Both young men approached the tall man in jeans and a cream colored pullover sweater. "Can we help you?"

"I'm looking for Bernie."

"She may or may not be here," Matt said confrontationally.

"I can see her right there in the bib overalls."

"Does she know you?" Josh asked.

"Sort of. I knew she'd be home for the holiday and I wanted to pay a visit."

Bernie had recovered sufficiently to walk over to Tony and introduced him to her brothers and their girlfriends.

"What are you doing here," she whispered to him. "It's been a month since I have seen or heard from you."

"Well, hi to you, too," he presented the lilies to her. "Do you know how difficult it is to find lilies this time of year? I would have been here earlier, but I had family obligations, too."

"No one invited you, Mr. Romanelli." Her brothers had since walked off and were conferring together with the girls near the back door.

Matt yelled from the doorstep, "Hey, invite him in, it's time for sandwiches and leftovers and a football game."

Bernie felt trapped and Tony winked at her. "I do wish you'd stop that. It's insulting."

"What?"

"The winking thing."

"It's an affliction of affection."

"You have no affection toward me and I have no affection toward you," she bristled.

"Hey, I was invited in by the rest of the family."

"Asking you to leave my family home isn't going to deter you, is it?"

"No, Bernie, it's not. I wanted to see you again, but our first date was a small disaster. I too had to be home for the holiday and all I could think of was trying to see you again in different surroundings."

"Cold Lake?"

"Yes, Cold Lake. It's my home and yours, too. The least you can do is introduce me to your folks and let me join in for a while. It would be less embarrassing for me."

"I have a suspicion you don't embarrass easily and I find this to be very rude. This is my private space and my family time. You just show up as though you own the place. You could have called and warned me."

"What? You'd have run away."

"You're probably right." Her sigh was audible. "You might as well come in now."

Tony's easy, relaxed manner was accepted by her brothers who asked about his predictions for the game. Mom and Dad exchanged glances several times. Bernie's movements lost their grace and became jerky. They congregated in the living room, fed the fireplace, pulled out the backgammon and Scrabble boards and the TV was tuned to the big game.

"I really want to watch the game, but I heard you're a wicked Scrabble player," Tony winked at her again.

"Who told you that?"

"Tim, when I saw him yesterday at Frank and Touey, he was just hired into one of the corporate departments. He didn't tell you?"

"I haven't spoken to him since Monday and I have no idea why you are talking to him about me. I'll kill him."

"As I said before, I wanted to see you, so I asked him where you were going to be. If you were staying in Chicago I would have shown up at your door tomorrow."

"I wouldn't be home tomorrow. I'd still be here with my family and helping Dad in the barn." They were having this conversation in the kitchen while she opened a bottle of wine and got Dad ice and a glass for Scotch.

"Here, let me help you with that cork."

"I'm capable of opening a bottle of wine, thank you."

He stood close behind her, put his arms around her and pulled the cork.

"OK, it would please me if you kept your hands off me and kept your distance. My family has been gracious enough to invite you in and you make me uncomfortable."

"I need to repair our relationship."

"We have no relationship," she practically screamed at him causing everyone to turn around and look toward the kitchen.

"You need help in there?" Matt asked.

"Oh great, let's just draw attention to ourselves. I'd really like to speak with you in person, but we are trapped in here."

"We could go outdoors, but it'll be cold. I could help you get more wood for the fireplace. Did I tell you how cute you look in overalls and pigtails? Tell me you wore those through Thanksgiving dinner."

"Mr. Romanelli, you are becoming impossible to deal with. You show up here unannounced, uninvited, bearing flowers and expect an invitation to my private life. You nearly had me in tears at a lunch and now you want to spend time with my family? Who do you think you are?"

"Just another former resident of Cold Lake who needs to make amends for a lunch gone badly."

Bernie fidgeted with the glasses and bottles and ice. "Hey," called Dad from the living room, "Where are those drinks?"

Bernie swallowed hard, "Coming."

She turned to Tony, who was leaning on the counter watching her, "Look, I feel like you're stalking me and I'd appreciate it if you could put on good manners and we could get through this situation as decently as possible."

"I have excellent manners, am a *decent* person and know how to deal with families."

"What do you mean 'deal' with?"

"Come on, let's get a Scrabble game going and watch the game and enjoy the afternoon."

"I really wish you'd just leave."

"How would you explain me to your family, then?"

"There is no explanation other than we danced at a company party and you took me to lunch; we have nothing in common. Said and done."

She could tell by the set of his face that he wasn't about to leave so they made their way to the living room with a tray of glasses and bottles. She served everyone, but Dad a glass of wine. Dad got up and poured his own Scotch, lit his pipe and returned to his favorite chair. She chose a glass of red and so did Tony.

"I knew you liked red," he said as they turned the Scrabble pieces down.

"How did you know that?"

"I saw you slightly hesitate at lunch and that's why I ordered a bottle of white burgundy."

"If you're such a good observer of people, why haven't you observed how out of place you are and how uncomfortable I am?"

Bernie attempted to play Scrabble with Tony, while they sat cross legged on the floor and he kept one eye on the game. There were some cheers and high fives that included Tony, who apparently was rooting for the same team. Mom got up, and started putting food on platters and laying out a spread in the dining room. Bernie and the two girls went to assist. Condiments and pickles were put out that were not served with the big dinner and several desserts were placed on the table.

"So, Bernie, you didn't tell me or your father you had a beau."

"I DON'T have a beau. This guy invited me to lunch once and it was an absolute travesty. His family lives in

Cold Lake and he just showed up here. He didn't even know where I lived, for God's sake."

"He said he's an attorney. I assume because we're listed in the phone book is how he found you."

"Mom, I don't like or trust him, help me get him out of here."

"Nonsense, he's handsome, polite, obviously smitten with you and he's having a lovely time. It would be rude to dismiss him before we snack."

"You're not getting this. I don't know him at all and I want him to leave."

"If you don't know him, why did he bring your favorite flowers, Missy?"

"A good guess?" She was feeling trapped by her own family. But, she should know from past experience that they were mostly unconscious about her life.

"Halftime, halftime, Josh yelled, let's eat."

"What is this dish?" Tony asked of her mother.

"Creamed onions, Bernie makes it. She had a boyfriend whose family made it for Thanksgiving and Christmas and we incorporated it to our tradition."

Tony nodded his head at her in appraisal. They returned to their spots in the living room with laden plates. "So, you cook."

"Of course I cook."

"No, I mean you're not a microwave baby, you really know how to cook. That's one of my requirements."

"Requirements? For what?"

He just grinned at her while he bit into a huge turkey sandwich on Pumpernickel.

Tony excused himself after the game and invited Bernie to walk him to his car.

"That wasn't so bad, now, was it?"

Exasperated and showing it she asked, "What do you want of me?"

"Well from what I've already seen of you and how you handle yourself, I want to get to know you better. How about a date tomorrow night?"

"No, thank you. I think you're dangerous and I'm not reconciling with the residents of Cold Lake."

"Who said anything about Cold Lake? I was thinking more like Jackson."

"Look, thanks for the flowers and thanks for behaving around my family, but I don't think so. I think you're *pushy*."

"Great, I'll pick you up at six thirty and we can go to a movie and get some pizza. See you then." He just drove off with Bernie watching the taillights.

She walked back into the house and sat in the dining room with her fingers folded together and her head on

top of them. “Wonderful, my life is out of control again and all because of Cold Lake.”

Dad walked in, grabbed a pickle and said, “Nice young man.”

“Nice young man my ass, he’s a pain in it.”

“He really likes you, Bernie. Why didn’t you tell us you had a boyfriend?” he took a bite of the pickle.

“I don’t have a boyfriend, that’s what I’ve been trying to tell Mom. I met him at a company function and we had lunch together. It was a complete bust. He’s stalking me.”

“Young lady, you should see the way he watches your every move.”

“I’m telling you, Dad, he’s weird. No one openly stalks someone, shows up at their doorstep, and invites himself into your home without knowing you. It’s frightening already.”

“We’ve all been watching you this evening and you don’t look as frightened as you profess to be. You watch him as much as he watches you. You stared at him the entire time he was watching the game instead of your letters. Frankly, I think you’re fascinated. You’ve never had a boyfriend spend so much attention on you before. That’s all I’m going to say. If you want, I’ll help Mom clean this up and you can go to bed. You’ll need a good night’s sleep to think about this and for your date tomorrow.”

“You were listening? How could you be so devious?” she felt the blush rise.

“We’re all as fascinated as you are. Quite the relationship you’ve started there. He isn’t related to Guy Romanelli, is he? Guy did your Mom’s and my will. He’s a good attorney and they seem to be a nice family. You never met him before in Cold Lake? Hmm, I think there are younger kids than him in the family, too. You didn’t go to school with them?”

“Dad, I can’t believe you would eavesdrop on a private conversation; outdoors, no less. You’re incorrigible. And, no, I did not go to school with any Romanelli’s”

“It was an accident. It was hot in the living room because of the fire and we had opened a window earlier. Both your voices carried.” He raised his eyebrows and said; “Of course we were all quiet so we could hear,” and then he chuckled and walked out of the room.

Now Bernie was hopping mad at everyone. She just left the dining room and went upstairs to her old bedroom and shut the door. She paced for a while. The phone rang and was answered by someone downstairs. A moment later her mother yelled up that it was for her. She picked up the extension and looked at the caller ID, “Romanelli, Gitano.” She hit the button and made sure that she heard the phone click off downstairs before she said, “Now what?”

“Well, isn’t your voice melodious and sweet.”

“Look, Pal, I don’t know what type of freak you are, but this has to stop. I’m not going anywhere with you and if I have to, I’ll ask for a restraining order.”

“Cool, now we get to talk law.”

“There is something wrong with you in the head. My family heard our entire conversation outside.”

“So, Bernie is embarrassed and hurt.”

She couldn’t believe his nerve and started to laugh, “Is there some mental defect you have that you are ignoring?”

“Now, that’s a sound I wanted to hear.”

“What?”

“Laughter.”

The whole situation was so absurd that she couldn’t stop laughing. When she did he said, “I know you came home to the farm and weren’t exactly planning on going out, so that’s why I asked you to a movie and pizza. I’d rather we go someplace nicer, but you probably don’t have any clothes for that.”

“Tony,”

Before she could finish her sentence he said, “You know this is the first time I’ve heard you say my name to me. I like it. There is some distance that the phone affords you, so now we can talk. Oh, and I know your family heard the conversation because there was a window open downstairs in the living room when we were outside.”

“You, you knew?”

“Yes, or I would have continued arguing with you, it’s fun.”

"You're deranged."

"Been told that a time or two, but never by a woman. Mostly in court. Before you continue protesting, I just want to say a few things. I like your family, I like you, I want to take you out and see if we can reverse the last time out. I'm thinking we go see a comedy, stop and get a pizza and spend some time together. That's why I suggested Jackson, not Cold Lake."

"Do I honestly have a choice?"

"No, I will not let you off the hook."

"OK, but just this once so you get a chance to redeem yourself. I have good jeans with me and a sweater that will have to do. Nothing fancy, hear me?"

"Got it. And, Bernie, I'm looking forward to tomorrow night. Tomorrow during the day I promised to help my father catch up in the office, so I'll be coming straight from there. I'll be starving, too. Please be kind to me and just be ready. Goodnight now." He hung up.

Bernie stood with the phone in her hand. She needed a drink and walked back downstairs. She went to the kitchen, opened another bottle of wine and poured herself a glass and went to the living room where everyone was still watching TV. The dining room had been cleaned and the games were put up. No one said a word to her as she planted herself on the couch and tried not to look self conscious drinking her wine. "What had Timmy told him, when?" She was just too angry at Timmy to call his cell and too damned tired already.

The next morning she assisted Dad in the barn as he started winterizing things, saw the herd, talked to him about his breeding plan from the previous season and asked a million questions. The boys had slept in one room and the girlfriends had slept in another. She was the only one with a private room and she had really needed it now.

About eleven the family gathered for brunch and Matt announced that he and Bryce were getting married the next summer. Wine was brought out and toasting began and the ring was shown around. Wood splitting was the culmination of the day as a gift for Mom and Dad.

Typically, the girls cornered Bernie to ask about the handsome Tony. Bernie dreaded the high school maneuver. "Look, I really don't know this guy and we only had lunch once. All I can tell you is he feels terrible about what a horrible experience it was and wants to make it up to me. I'd appreciate not talking about my life. If you want to know about my job or my horse riding lessons, then fine, but we are not discussing this man. This is going to be a one time thing and then I'm going back to my life in Chicago." They were miffed to be put off. "Fine, thought Bernie, except one of them is going to be a sister-in-law and I'm going to have to suffer for this rudeness."

The "date" was fun and they returned to the farm slightly giddy from the laughs at the movies and the conversations they had over pizza. Neither of them drank other than soft drinks, so there was no worry about driving impaired or her being off guard. She found that she really didn't need to be on guard, either. She smiled as she prepared for bed.

THIRTEEN

Driving back to Chicago she called Timmy on his cell and gave him an earful. He was still at his parent's on Sunday. "What'd I do wrong? He asked me a couple of questions about the horse back riding and I told him about it. He likes you, what do you want me to say?" It was a hopeless attempt, so she talked about Noir and finally hung up.

Bernie continued the tutoring, but less dinner making for Timmy. Timmy started dating a girl and was spending time with her. "Fine," thought Bernie, "I was getting tired of the pseudo marriage thing, anyway." They still rode to lessons together on Wednesday's and Timmy even invited Nancy, his new girlfriend to observe their lessons a few times. She seemed uninterested in the horses and Timmy seemed to be disappointed by her lack of enthusiasm.

Noir had been owned and boarded by Bernie for almost a month. She accepted the trainer's offer to lease the horse back to the riding school because the fuel it cost to drive there several nights a week was ruining the budget she set. She just couldn't stay away from the mare which proved to be a wonderful companion. It wasn't much help that to ride after lessons were over was much later

in the evening and she was returning to the apartment more toward eleven PM.

Timmy was very happy with his new job and talked about it all the way to the barn on Wednesday. That's where he had met Nancy, who worked for another department. Timmy was not a very forward person and Nancy was very shy, they made a good couple with the exception of her lack of interest in horses.

Tony called regularly and they talked late into the nights. They had a double date with Timmy and Nancy and it went well. It was the first time since Thanksgiving that they had seen one another and a double date seemed safe. Talking on the phone was another story, entirely. They talked of dreams and aspirations. She found that Tony's father planned to retire soon and Tony wanted to take over his practice in Cold Lake. He knew most of the clients from his years of working with his father; he started in junior high just doing filing and paperwork for him. Law school wasn't too difficult because he had been exposed to talk and work about the law his entire life. He'd taken the Bar for two states and was allowed to practice in Michigan as well.

Bernie confided in Tony that since starting to tutor she had considered going back to school to learn to teach. She didn't need a lot of courses and most of them were taught at night. He urged her to continue this line of thinking and she finally filled out the paperwork and started night classes. This lessened the time she spent with Noir and tutoring. She only had two students now and the budget was straining to bursting point.

One week when she attempted to pay her board at the barn she learned that it had been paid in advance by "an admirer." Three months in advance! She questioned the stable owner, but the woman refused to tell her who had paid the board bill. This happened in February, after the Christmas holidays. She had been home during Christmas and Tony was there, this time by invitation. He surprised her with a new Pessoa bridle and a horse blanket as gifts. She had given him a leather bound notebook with his name engraved in gold leaf on the bottom corner of the cover.

This was the first time that her family learned of Noir's existence and new ownership. Dad was visibly not pleased and voiced his opinion of horses and how nonproductive and outmoded they were. Bernie barely heard him.

They had done the bowling thing outside Chicago and found that they were both hopelessly deficient. "Must be some sort of skill to this other than rolling the ball straight," Tony mused.

That was their first date alone and Bernie was a little nervous because she didn't yet trust Tony's intentions. He was a very good looking man and turned other woman's heads. Men even looked at him. Being at the bowling alley had relaxed her a little, but people were still staring at them.

"I see that men watch you, he had commented."

"Men watch me? What do you mean?"

"You're beautiful with that black hair and those sparkly eyes; how could they keep their eyes off you?"

"You're being ridiculous. I think it's time we leave. I've had one too many beers and need to use the ladies room." She excused herself and walked to the bathrooms. In the mirror she surveyed her outfit, a turtle neck, jeans and a riding vest. She really never looked closely at herself before because she always felt conspicuously plain because that's what she had heard through five years of Cold Lake comments.

An older woman walked out of one of the stalls and while washing her hands said, "You make a striking couple."

"Pardon me?"

"Your husband and you are a very good looking couple."

"We're not married. What makes you think we're married?"

"Oh, I just assumed you were newlyweds. Sorry."

Bernie was flustered when she returned to Tony. "Let's go, I'm bowled out."

"Want to hit a deli before we end the evening?"

"The way you eat and expect me to eat, I'm surprised I can sit on my horse without bowing her legs. We have to stop this food excursion thing you've started."

"Actually, I was thinking about asking you to a nice dinner next weekend. Something dressy and intimate."

“I don’t like the term *intimate*.”

“Bernie, there’s something wrong with you. I’ve never even attempted to kiss you. You have a thing about being close to people. You keep them at a distance and it smells like fear. Are you still afraid of me?”

“Honestly? I don’t know.”

“I’ll warn you right now, we’ve spent some wonderful talking time, some light and casual dates and I’m wanting to plant one on you.”

“How rude.”

“Yes, you always consider me rude, but I’ve yet to figure out why.”

“Public displays of affection are just that, public displays. Displays for whom, I don’t know, but they are embarrassing.”

“What about private displays of affection?”

“Are you asking me or telling me?”

“I’m asking you,” he had her elbow and was walking her toward the exit. He seemed determined to pursue this when he put his arm around her waist. He flagged down a cab and they got in. “You’ve never invited me to your apartment; I always meet you in the lobby. Don’t you think it would be nice to make a pot of coffee and sit and talk the way we do on the phone?” He gave the cab driver an address and she recognized it as her own and became very jittery.

Her first reaction was to fiddle in her purse for something, anything. Breath mints appeared and before she could think, she offered him one with nervous hands. Tony threw back his head and roared with laughter. "I swear I'm in high school on a first date with someone."

Bernie put her hand over her mouth in embarrassment and shock. "I was just looking for something and found them."

"I see that I still make you uncomfortable. I've never spent so much time with a woman and not kissed her a few times."

"You're a cad and I knew it the first time I saw you. I even told Timmy you were a ladies man."

"What is it about me that makes you so uneasy? I have never done anything inappropriate, never even attempted to kiss you. You squirm away from me when I put my arm around you. What? Just tell me what."

They had already reached her apartment building and she was grappling with the thought of him coming upstairs. "Um."

"Um, that's all you can say?"

"Well."

"Oh great, we're back to one word sentences again. What am I doing wrong in trying to court you?"

"You can come up for a few minutes if you'd like. I think the apartment is fairly clean, although there may be

some papers on the table and some books. . ." her voice trailed off. "*Be bold*," she told herself.

He was laughing at her as he helped her from the cab. "You're cracking me up; I can hear you thinking."

They rode the elevator to her apartment and she fumbled with the key. "Bernie, listen, this is making you a wreck. I'm sorry I invited myself into your private space again. If you don't want to have me in, then, fine, I'll just go to my apartment. It was just that we were having such a good time and you were so relaxed and trusting of me that I thought it about time to learn more about your world."

"No, come in, I'll make coffee."

When the door opened and the lights were turned on, Tony whistled, "This place is spotless; you're also a good housekeeper."

"What do you mean by 'also'?"

"I know you cook, now I know you clean. You should see my place, I have to wind my way around to find the bathroom. Now tell me what you were so nervous about downstairs."

"Nothing."

"Oh, it's something alright because you are either very confident or very uneasy with me. You and I already have a history through conversations. I've never had a relationship with a woman like this before. If you can't tell, I like you and admire you a great deal. Hell, I like

you more than I can say right now. What's the problem? You act like you're afraid of me all the time."

"I am afraid of you," she blurted. "I have no experience with men at all. Dating isn't high on my list of things I'm confident about, let alone the other aspects of a male female relationship. There, I've said it."

He stood still in the foyer and took a long, hard look at her. "What you're saying is that you are afraid of physical contact between the sexes?"

"If you have to put it that way, yes."

"Now some of this makes sense to me. No wonder you think I'm a cad."

"Would you like coffee now?"

"I'll tell you what, if you have tea, I'd rather have a cup of that."

She put the kettle on and they sat down across the small kitchen table from one another. He took her hands and said, "Bernie, I'm sorry. No wonder you always act afraid of me. I promise not to make you uncomfortable again. If things happen between us, then they happen. I can see how you thought I was forward. I've never met a woman like you before and I don't think I'll meet another."

She had a difficult time directly meeting his thickly lashed brown eyes. "Thank you, really, thank you for understanding."

"Well, I have a secret, too. One you may find amusing. I'm not unexposed to horses. I used to ride in college on the intercollegiate team. After, when I had the tiniest amount of time in law school, I started playing polo. I've been out to your stable and taken some lessons, and I've ridden Noir by request."

"You rode my horse? How did you even find out where my horse was? Did Timmy tell you?"

"No, I paid attention to who you were talking to the night of the party where we met and got myself invited to dinner at Brent's home. I asked his daughter what she was doing for extracurricular activity and it dawned on me what you might have been having a conversation about that night. I described you and I asked if they knew you, and the wife remembered you talking about the riding lessons. The gown you were wearing was stunning and it was bold because it wasn't the black that everyone else was dressed in. You really stood out that night so it was easy for her to remember you.

"When I found where she was taking lessons I drove there on a Saturday and set up a lesson or two. I've been taking lessons on Saturday afternoons to get my seat back. Just before you bought Noir I had my eye on her because she's fabulous and hot tempered; just the type of horse I like. Polo ponies are wired for sound, you know."

"You rode my horse?"

"The horse is half leased as a school horse and any rider capable of riding her is allowed to."

"You rode my horse!"

"Yes, I'm stalking your horse, too."

"You are stalking me, I knew it," she laughed. Then the tears started streaming and she began to cry. "Why do you always make me cry?"

"Oh God, I'm sorry. I thought this was a way to be closer to you. I've taken something precious from you and I didn't know it would have this effect on you. I do so truly apologize," he held her hands firmly in his, not allowing her to pull away. He stood and walked around the table behind her chair, bent over and put his arms around her, holding her tightly. "I'm so very, very sorry." He buried his face in her hair and turned her around and he kissed her softly on the mouth. The tea kettle whistled and he started laughing at the timing. She joined in the laughter and they set about the kitchen to make tea.

"How did you like Noir? I haven't spoken to anyone who's ridden her."

Instead of answering her, he was perusing the kitchen. Good God, this is the second most outfitted kitchen I've ever seen in my life. Is there any piece of kitchen equipment you don't own?" he asked as he opened cupboards.

"Just make yourself at home, Mr. Romanelli, it's what you do."

"No, I'm serious, only my mother's kitchen is this complete. I'm the take out king. It looks like you're the

cooking queen. Invite me to dinner. Tim did say you're a damn good cook. That much I wheedled out of him."

He spun around and swiftly faced and simultaneously grabbed her by the waist and picked her up and swung her. "Golly, lady, I like you more and more," he kissed her in earnest this time and it lasted more than a second. Face to face, eye to eye with him, she knew.

She didn't want to know, but she wanted to know more than all the longings in the world. She wanted to know more, too.

"Let's have our tea in the living room. I have some cookies here for the kids who hang out." She settled on the couch and he sat cross legged in front of her.

"This apartment is decorated nicely. It's contemporary with a warm feeling. I like your horse posters, too, very artsy. Where did you find them?"

"Downtown, in various galleries. I particularly like the Ratafia because I love watercolors. There's the Petrie, also. It's called Restrictions. The man thinks he and the horse are tied to the ground and he's restricted. He's calling to the other rider, but doesn't realize he can help himself through his dilemma and the only restrictions are in his mind."

"That's how I feel about you. I wouldn't pursue anyone like I've pursued you if they'd given me as much trouble and hassle as you have. I feel the restrictions are in my mind. Or maybe they're in your mind."

"Tony, it's a little early to be talking like this. I promise I won't put up as many barriers as I have and we can let the relationship you're asking for develop naturally. I need time, too. You move a little fast for me, figuratively and literally. I'm a slow learner and I need to learn very slowly."

"I promise to go as slowly as you need; the slower the better," he flashed that smile at her. She felt her chin start to quiver and an odd sensation spark through her body.

"I have the distinct feeling you're not talking about our relationship."

"Right, I'm not. You drive me absolutely crazy and I'm close to losing my mind. With that said, I take my departure. I'll call you tomorrow." He unwound himself, stretched up and walked to his leather jacket draped on the chair.

Bernie, would you like to go out to the stable tomorrow and we rent a horse and go for a ride? I'd really like to see you on Noir. I have a nice camera and we can get some photos for your office."

"I'll let you know tomorrow Mr. Romanelli." He blew her a kiss as the door closed behind him. She watched from the peephole as he walked down the hall.

FOURTEEN

Bernie was not about to quit her job and attempt to substitute teach while maintaining her apartment and waiting for jobs. She continued with Rand and Rand and completed her classes and certifications for Illinois. She spoke to Timmy about finding a house away from the city and having a mortgage instead of rent. It seemed a more prudent thing to her to start acquiring some equity. Timmy actually liked the idea and said he had thought the same thing many times himself. His parents lived outside of Chicago and it seemed to him as though a mortgage would be cheaper than paying the high rents downtown.

They decided to start looking at various areas outside of the city and contacted a few realty companies. "How'd you like me as a neighbor in a horse related community? Timmy asked.

"You're already my neighbor here in the building; I can't seem to think of being any closer than using the same laundry room!

"The only problem will be the commute."

Bernie told Tony of this latest development and he was against the idea. "Do you realize how much you'll need to have for down payment and closing costs? The

gas to drive to work and pay for parking will nearly bankrupt you."

"I was thinking that things already nickel and dime me to death, so where's the difference?"

Tony was more than discouraging and it dampened Bernie's enthusiasm for a few months. It didn't really matter because she had to be home several times to help prepare for Matt's wedding to Bryce. They planned a July wedding outdoors. "I think they should have waited for a cooler month because the heat and humidity will wilt all the guests, Bernie said to the three others on a double date one evening. My parents are putting in new carpet, even though the wedding will be held in the Lansing area. I think it's a waste of money, but Mom says they'll be seeing relatives they haven't seen in a while and she wants the place spruced up. Besides, a few of the groomsmen are staying there. I can't wait to see what type of people my brother hangs with."

Nancy asked if Bernie was standing up for the wedding. "No, I wasn't asked because I've only met the bride once and did everything in my power to keep from being asked. I hate bridesmaid's dresses and I hate the showers and all the stuff associated with weddings. I sent a check to my mother to pick out something for the shower and send it in my name. I'm just not into all the high school girl stuff."

"But your brother is older than you, right; and it's the first wedding in the family?" asked Nancy.

"Yes, he's older than me by eight years and has his own, established life, but the girl he's marrying still wants all the traditional rigmarole. It just doesn't interest me."

Nancy was starting to get on Bernie's last nerve with the frou frou stuff and she said, "Look, will you two excuse us, but Tony and I are going riding tomorrow and I want to get a good night's sleep." Her abruptness surprised Tony.

"What was that all about? Tony asked as he drove her back.

"Nothing, don't worry about it. It's part of having stupid shit happen from high school where someone would shove a ring under your nose and act as if getting married was the height of freedom. Nancy gets on my raw edge from time to time, anyway. She's just so, so, I don't know, girlish, I guess."

"What's wrong with girlish? I think she and Timmy make a good couple," he said.

"I don't. He seems to have grown tired of her, but has no other outlet for dating. I think he feels trapped. You know she's not overly excited about horses, too; and this is bothering him because it's an activity he can't share with her because she's just not interested. I think she went to college for her M. R. S. degree."

"M. R. S. degree? What's that?

"Mrs. Lots of colleges have female students intent on only being there to find someone to marry. Haven't you ever heard that before?"

Tony chuckled and shifted gears.

FIFTEEN

Matt's wedding happened as planned and Bernie invited Tony to escort her. They drove up together from Cold Lake to Lansing and Josh and Amber accompanied them in the back seat. All in all, the weather held and the wedding was lovely. The party afterward was slightly reminiscent of Tony and Bernie's first meeting. They danced, they drank, she introduced him as her "friend" to her relatives and he never once protested or acted hurt even though they were much more than friends at this junction.

To offset the apricot sheath dress she chose, she had been using a tanning bed some evenings and weekends because her job involved longer hours than years before. There was no sunning time on the balcony and she and Timmy had spent a great deal of time getting to know certain communities outside the city. It was a last resort "makeup" situation for her.

The dancing began and the band was quite good. Tony and Bernie danced, Dad danced with the bride, Tony danced with a few bridesmaids. One of the groomsmen, Aaron, asked Bernie several times. They talked on the dance floor and Bernie learned he was a graphic artist for an advertising agency in Lansing and related to Bryce as a first cousin. Bernie and Tony did their best

as a couple to keep things lively among the guests and Tony asked Bernie's grandmother to dance. While this was happening, Aaron, again, asked Bernie, to dance.

He got very close to her and bent his head down to her shoulders. The next moment was a little bit of a blur to Bernie. Aaron tried to kiss her. Either he was very drunk or he didn't know she had a "date" for the evening. Grandma got dragged across the dance floor as Tony tapped Aaron on the shoulder and politely asked to switch dance partners. Bernie was mortified for grandma, but grateful to Tony for the "out."

"What was that about?" Tony asked Bernie as he piloted her away.

"I don't really know, one minute we were dancing and the next minute he was trying to paw me."

"Did you encourage him?"

"What? How could I encourage him?"

"Well, you've danced with him several times tonight."

"That's because he asked me and I'm supposed to be family and aid in keeping this a pleasant experience for everyone."

"Well, I'm sure it was *pleasant* enough for him. Do me a favor and don't dance with him again."

"Why would that be a favor to you?"

"Because you're mine to dance with. As a matter of fact, don't dance with anyone else this evening."

"How dare you tell me who to dance with."

"Look, that guy's drunk and he obviously thinks you're available."

She frowned at him and said, "I am available. I'm not married and I'll dance with whomever I please."

He pulled her very close and put his lips on her neck as they continued to dance. An electric-like shock shot through her. "And when this dance is over, we're going for a walk. No discussions, no arguments, we're walking."

She hadn't yet recovered from the neck caress when the dance ended. He steered her off the floor. They walked around the grounds a bit and then he took her in his arms and gave her a difficult to break away from urgent kiss. "That's from me to you. Don't ever let another man kiss you again."

Breathless, she barely whispered, "What about my Dad?"

"Stop teasing me, I'm in no mood for this after that oaf."

"I'd kiss you back again, but you're being unreasonable and possessive."

"Yes, I'm possessive. I've never been possessive of a woman before, but I am now."

"It sounds like a trap to me."

"Would it be so difficult to be trapped by me?"

"What are you getting at?"

"Bernie, I see you and I want to be with you every waking moment. I want to make a life with you. I'm not going to spoil your brother's wedding here and now, but I need you to know that I've fallen in love and hope you feel the same way I do. It should have been us up there in front today."

"You want to marry someone you don't know?"

"Oh, I know a lot more about you than you think. You just don't know me very well. You're afraid to get to know me."

"I do know that you want to live in Cold Lake, and that has no appeal for me. That's the last place on earth I want to live, let alone make a permanent home there."

"Why do you think I've been discouraging you from buying a house in Illinois? This is something I've been thinking about for a year. You need a place to land. . ."

She cut him short, "I have a landing place and it's in Chicago. It's close enough to get home should I be needed and far enough away to make me comfortable. Cold Lake makes me uncomfortable."

"I want to be your copilot through life. I want you in mine, and after all this time, I would hope you'd want to be a part of mine. I'm not flashing off to Cold Lake for a little while.

"The next thing I want and need is for you is to meet my family. Sundays are family dinners at my folk's and I want you to come tomorrow for dinner."

"I can't, we have relatives who will want to hang out with my family before they leave. I would, however, consider living with you on a trail basis. There, I've stuck my foot into my mouth up to my knee already. You think I haven't thought about this, too, I have. I just wasn't going to ask you to marry me because I knew you want to live and work in Cold Lake."

My love, let's go dance and be merry for the family. Tomorrow we'll find a way and time for you to finally meet my family. I'm introducing you as my *girlfriend* and you'd better get used to it. It wasn't lost on her that he referred to her relatives as "the family."

SIXTEEN

Relatives and groomsmen left early and at five o'clock on the button Tony was at the door. He was wearing khakis and a Polo shirt. Bernie wore a peasant type blouse, a skirt and flat canvas shoes.

She was not prepared for Tony's family. Large family. Extended family. Hoards of people. It was as though the entire staff of some company had come for dinner. And children, children were everywhere. The Romanelli house was large, the yard was large, there was a swimming pool and a tennis court and a pool house and what looked like a little stable, it was really an implement shed for gardening tools. The privacy they had on several acres of land was tremendous.

Tony's mother was a slender woman with short, graying black hair and a regal bearing. She was gracious and in control at the same time. Guy Romanelli acted as though he knew Bernie her entire life and started their conversation with what wonderful people her parents were.

"Well you met the zookeeper and the ringmaster, what do you think? Tony asked.

"Your mother is the zookeeper. She keeps it all under control and your father is you, making things lively.

He's the ringmaster with a sense of humor and loves being surrounded by his extended family. Everyone is family to him, huh?

"Your brother is nice and so is his wife. But, I'm confused because you have three sisters and they seem to be around my age. Why haven't I met them before?"

"My parents insisted after my attendance at the Cold Lake schools that the rest of the family attend private school. Dad bought Mom a van and she was the bus driver. They never went to Cold Lake, that's why you never met them. They went to Catholic school in Jackson.

"My father used to come home with the stories of the hoodlums and they didn't want the younger children exposed to that type of environment. Dad spent plenty of hours in court for a lot of the people you went to school with. I know them all through their families and their court appearances. I've been working in Dad's office a long time. Mom and Dad didn't want any conflict of interest with the children of the town being associated with Dad's practice. My family has spent as much time in Jackson as here, maybe more."

Dinner at Tony's home was a hilarious mix of foods. Pasta and antipasto were mainstays, but grilled sausages, potato salad, Jell-O salad, three bean salad, cole slaw, hot dogs and hamburgers were also on the menu. "I am a little overwhelmed about what to eat here. I love the sausages and pasta, but July is a good month for a good ole hamburger."

"You can get a hamburger anywhere. Try the pastas because my mother is a wizard in the kitchen.

"Oh, and Bernie, watch out for the water balloons and squirt guns. The kids have no respect for clothing. I hope you like wet swimsuits because these children will plant themselves on your lap in a heartbeat. I should have told you to bring a second set of clothes. By the way, these kids are not all my family; some are children of my cousins. I'll introduce you when you get a little more comfortable. I realize that a family this large is a little overwhelming because your family is so dignified and sedate."

"My family is not sedate."

"Trust me, by comparison, this place is a circus. It will happen at some point, but my mother will pick up one of those water shooters and plaster my father. The place comes unglued after that. I can also guarantee you that someone has firecrackers hidden somewhere and there will be a lot of noise. Just wait till it gets dark."

"Hmm, do we honestly have to stay that long?" she laughed.

"No, we can leave anytime you're uncomfortable. I just wanted you to meet my family the way they really are, not in some quiet dinner where all conversation is polite and controlled. I'm not saying that's how your family is; it's just that this family is completely wound up all the time. What they don't get away with at work or school will play itself out here at the Ponderosa.

"With a family this large, there is a lot of drama. Italians are dramatic people anyway. We just know how to have a good time. They are already watching you for any sense

of play and then they'll jump ya. Just watch yourself, I'm warning you."

As predicted the pasta was supreme. Bernie felt comfortable eating in front of the family because they, too, were enjoying the food as much as she. There were all sorts of special desserts that Bernie had only seen in Chicago and she suspected that Tony brought them home with him for this occasion: Cannoli, Biscotti and Tiramisu. And the espresso flowed.

It was Mrs. Romanelli who commandeered her to the kitchen. "Look what I'm hiding," she said. She opened a cabinet door and pulled out a bazooka-sized water canon. She showed Bernie how to fill it and said, "Go get him in the back when he's not expecting it. You'll make the family roll because he tries so hard to be dignified, but can't resist a battle."

"I'm not comfortable dousing Tony with water. We just started dating."

"That's not exactly what I've heard or know. I know he's been courting you a while. It's time someone blasted him. If you don't do it, you'll be in the middle of the battle once the fun begins out there. I know. I've been his mother for 33 years; and if anyone will start something, he'll be the first."

"I was told you would be the first."

"Pssst. I know he and his father will start it. Someone needs to start before he does. Go ahead, surprise everyone. I promise it will be worth it. If not, I'll make it up to you somehow. I want to see him get pasted by

the person he suspects the least. Let me make sure he has his back turned before you come out the back door. I'll start some sort of diversion and get him to face the other way. Don't miss, whatever you do," she threw her head back and laughed so hard that a lock of gray hair fell over her forehead.

"What do you mean I brought the wrong flavor Cannoli's?" Tony was fairly loud with his mother. She was facing the back door and had positioned him with his back to Bernie's hiding place in the kitchen.

"It's now or never," she thought, as she charged out the door with a battle cry.

Tony was completely soaked before he could shut his gaping mouth and grab a super soaker to blast back. The battle had begun and the family went berserk. People were everywhere in the fake war, shirts, pants and skirts were soaked to the skin and hung provocatively on bodies.

Bernie and Tony exited the car just as Dad was finishing up in the barn. He took one look at them and shrugged. They were drying out, but visibly damp from the soaker party. They were a little disheveled as well because the kissing had begun in earnest after several glasses of Chianti. It was no longer a secret, they were a couple with stars in their eyes. Mom never said a word when Bernie walked through the house to her room.

SEVENTEEN

All day Monday her hands shook at work. She realized the night before and driving back that she had just committed herself to marrying Tony Romanelli. She wasn't quite sure how that had happened after her carefulness with her life. She always thought she'd meet some very nice guy and fall in love. Never in a million years did it occur to her that she'd meet someone from Cold Lake and nearly commit herself to a life there. The weekend was romantic, fun and hilarious, but was that a reason to marry someone? Many, many thoughts went through her mind as she tried to sort out the feelings and eventuality of the situation she found herself in. Who else could she date before making such a commitment? *Tony would have a hissy fit if he thought I wanted to date others. Oh my God, what happened to me?*

It wasn't helpful that she was up half the night in sleeplessness. She really didn't remember much of Monday or Tuesday in the office. It was on the way to the barn with Timmy that she realized what had happened and the finalization of it all.

"Tim, I think I'm getting married and I don't know how it happened."

"Are you pregnant?"

"No, why would you ask me that?"

"Well someone who suddenly decides that they're getting married and doesn't know how it happened, sounds likes a pregnancy to me," he said in a soft voice. My God, your hands are shaking. Are you OK?"

"No, I'm very nervous and on edge. I don't think I can ride tonight. I don't want to cheat the instructor out of a lesson, but I'm too shaky to ride and control my horse. Will you ride her for me and I can just watch?"

Tony called late after she returned from watching another person trying to control her mare. Timmy did his valiant best, but he was no match for Ms. Opinion. He said afterward that he was specifically looking for a gelding and that Noir had helped him make that decision.

"How'd your lesson go?"

"I didn't take it."

"Why not?"

"Tony, I'm a nervous wreck. I just committed myself to something that scares the hell out of me."

"After this past weekend, I still scare you. Hmm. I really thought we were on the same page here."

"I think we're on the same page, but it's a life decision that has me bamboozled. I'm terrified."

"I'm not. This isn't something I'm taking lightly just so you know. I have thought about it for a long time and it's

what I want, but I can't change your thinking for you. I thought we wanted the same thing."

"A water fight isn't a reason to get married."

"That's all it was to you, a water fight? Not family entertainment where you were the instigator? It takes balls to be the instigator in something like that with my family."

"Your mother put me up to it."

He laughed softly. "She already knows how I feel about you and probably thought it was a way for you to be comfortable around the rowdies. God love her."

"We have a lot to discuss. I'm not saying 'No,' I'm just telling you I'm frightened and uncertain about my life right now. It feels out of control and dizzying."

"OK, so what do you propose, no pun intended, we do?"

"Friday night. Let me make you dinner on Friday night. No one will bother us, we can stay here and talk this thing out until we're blue in the face."

"Alright. Let's utilize your balcony and your grill. I'd invite you to my place, but I'm afraid you'd be out of your element and less apt to speak frankly with me. I suggest that I bring over a couple of thick steaks and you do the rest. I'm bringing wine, too, Bernie. If this gets out of control, I want to be able to drown myself."

"You're being dramatic. It doesn't become you. You're too confident about your life and what you want in it, don't be dramatic."

"What do you expect at this point? I feel like I'm suddenly living a trauma drama."

"Let me just catch up on what I couldn't concentrate on in the office this past week and we'll start early Friday. How's that sound? I can get myself together and you can be here as early as you like. No one stays after five at my office on Fridays, anyway. Of course if there is a public relations emergency, I will have to stay."

"I'm bringing a change of clothes and my duffel because I think we need to go out to the stable and ride on Saturday. Let's make a long weekend of this and see if we can't work this out to the satisfaction of both of us."

"You're inviting yourself overnight?"

"Yes, I'm inviting myself overnight and bringing the wine. Questions?"

Bernie let out a long, slow breath, "No questions. I just want to sneak past Timmy, OK? I didn't tell you what happened tonight and he's a little uncertain of himself right now. I really don't want to get caught up with having to go out with him and Nancy, either."

"What happened?"

"This is telling you a lot more than I want to discuss right now, but I've got a major case of the heebies. I've had the shakes for three days because I just realized what I committed to with you. I'm nervous, I'm scared and I couldn't ride my horse. I asked Tim to do it and he didn't have a good lesson. Noir is a lot of horse to have to school. I don't think he was expecting it because we've

become close riding partners and it looked easy to Tim. She was an absolute brat tonight and he had to deal with it. I think he's embarrassed. I also told him what I was thinking of doing and he got really quiet."

"He's in love with you."

"Who, Timmy?"

"Yes, he's totally bowled over by you. It's very obvious. You just don't see it."

"That's what he was talking about."

"He told you?"

"No, he didn't tell me he loved me, it was a conversation about a year ago about me not seeing signs between men and women."

"Oh brother, has he got you pegged."

"What's that supposed to mean?"

"He knows you well and you just don't see it. You are completely oblivious to your effect on men."

"What effect?"

"Let's discuss this Friday, OK. I have some work to do tonight and I know you need to think about a few things before Friday. If you don't want me to stay, I won't. But, we really should go out Saturday and ride. We can ride together like the first time. Do you remember the first time?"

"OK, I'm hanging up now."

EIGHTEEN

It was a wedding. Not the kind of wedding Bernie's mother had planned for her only daughter, but a nice dignified, quiet wedding. It was held in Chicago and only immediate family was invited with the exception of Bernie's college roommate and her husband; she was matron of honor. The dress was simple and sheer. It was a fall wedding and the leaves were just beginning to change in early September. The honeymoon was a week in Bermuda and Tony signed her up to swim with the dolphins at the hotel. They rented motorbikes and toured the island when they weren't napping or sunning.

The motorbike rental was short-lived because Bernie blasted the fuel handle on hers and it reared up in the air dumping her on the rain soaked road. The bike lay sideways and Bernie sat on the ground stunned and looking at it.

"Are you OK, Mario?"

She looked up at him as he gingerly tried to pick her up. "I think so."

"You look dazed."

"I am. It didn't get up and run away."

He tried so hard not to smile but the tears of laughter poured down his face. "It's not a horse."

They moved Bernie's things to Tony's much larger apartment. She had only been there three times before and it was always clean. He finally confessed that if he knew she were coming over that he had called a maid service and had the superintendant let them in.

Tony was a messy person who dropped things or piled them everywhere. "What's this?" she pantomimed shooting a ball at a hoop.

"Basketball, two points."

"Yes, exactly, two points, so how come your underwear never hits the basket? Isn't that worth two points?"

"We've been married four months and you're becoming my mother. You're nagging me."

"I'm just saying."

Rand and Rand was still home base, but Bernie started putting a few feelers out for teaching. She was looking for a full time position and some experience. Nothing of value came through and she continued her regular job. "I'm not exactly equipped for teaching on the South side, although there are permanent positions there," she told Tony one night over dinner.

"I wouldn't be too worried about it, something will come along. You definitely need the experience as a student teacher, but we need the income to save for a house. Which reminds me, would you like to go to Michigan this coming weekend?"

"We could. If you don't mind, I'd like to cover in the barn for Dad so he could take Mom out for a night."

"I'm not sure what that entails, but it's fine with me. Just promise you'll have enough time with my parents for dinner one night. Nothing big, just a sit down so my folks can get to know you better. They haven't seen you in months and it's also time for you to start developing a relationship with my sisters. My brother and his wife won't be able to make it."

"How do you know?"

"They've been staying close to home because Sherry is close to delivering."

"I've got an idea, how about Dad and I start early and you get my parents an invite to your folks. Then we can all have dinner together. Or is that too forward with your parents?"

"Nothing is too forward with my parents."

"I know, but my parents are your dad's clients."

"Oh hell, he doesn't care. As long as he doesn't have to represent them as defendants in court, they're all family. We are all family now."

"Oh Lord, don't let there be a water fight."

"Not in my mother's dining room! I assure you it will be a quiet but lively evening without all the hoopla. I can't even tell you if two of my sisters will be there because they are both seriously dating. Saturdays at the Romanelli's is always a showoff evening for my mother

if we have company. Should we call our folks and plan it now so that no one is surprised?"

Tony, always a fast mover, had ulterior motives he wasn't disclosing for the coming weekend. He had noticed an impact on the village that Bernie wasn't yet aware of. Although they hadn't been home since the wedding, Bernie found that many of Tony's weekends prior to marriage were spent in Cold Lake.

Some farm land had been sold off on the edge of town about a mile and a half from the village center for a modern housing development. It was small with only three streets and about 25 homes. There was no home owner's association for the contemporary houses with landscaping and mature trees on large lots that each backed up to the golf course. Another road was etched into the land for the next phase. A lot of people from Jackson had moved into the homes and commuted, they were the ones who felt Jackson was getting too wild and wanted their kids to go to a smaller school system where they assumed the education was better and children would be in small classes with more attention. Ann Arbor wasn't that far and people were commuting from there as well. The small town had changed since she left.

They arrived Friday night and stayed at Tony's parent's home because it was larger and had more bathrooms and space. Three of the five were married and moved out, so they had a bedroom and bathroom to themselves. Early Saturday Bernie drove to the farm leaving Tony with his parents. She helped Dad in the barn and set up for the evening milking. It was close to the time that the milking of goats would stop for the winter and they

were engaged in farm chores all day in anticipation of winterizing. Bernie left Dad to clean equipment and returned to Tony. She showered and dressed for dinner and then went downstairs to help Mrs. Romanelli with the last minute preparations. Her parents arrived about six for cocktails. Dinner was well prepared and the conversation was lively. Bernie's mother had brought dessert and they had coffee in the patio enclosure with the fire pit going after the meal was cleaned up.

Tony hadn't said what he had done with his day and Bernie assumed he was working on office things. She found out the next morning that he had been to a new housing development and looked through the models and scoped out plots.

He took her there on Sunday morning instead of attending church with his parents. "What do you think?"

Bernie felt pressured now. Cold Lake was looming in front of her and she knew she had no escape from it. "What do you want me to think, Tony?"

"I want to know if this is a place you could settle into when we move here."

"That's awfully conniving and fast of you. I didn't think we had to deal with this so soon."

"I'm not being *conniving*, I'm asking you to start to think toward the future. We've discussed this and you said you could do it. I am going to take over my father's practice at some point and we need a place to live. You need to get this through the thought and acceptance processes. I'm looking for a place for us to settle down

with the least amount of pain for you, and where you really don't know anyone. The houses can be built with any plans as long as they are contemporary. I know that is a love of yours and I want to please you, but you have to give me some wiggle room here, Bernie."

"Gulp."

"I anticipated this reaction from you, so I want to return tonight to Chicago and give you thinking time. There is one corner lot that I like and want you to look at it. It's currently the lot with the most amount of privacy, which I know you like.

"Before you say a word, I want you to know that you are two miles from my parents and two miles from your parents. I like the development, it's all professional people, you don't know any of them because most of them are from Jackson and commute; and we need to set the wheels in motion soon. Dad wants to retire in two years and he'd like me to be there one year with him to ease the transition.

"Just do me a favor today, and take a look at the lot. OK?"

She swallowed and turned to look at her husband. "OK, Tony, I'll do it for you. Have you discussed this with your parents or mine?"

"No. Our lives are our lives. I wouldn't go making or discussing decisions without first talking to you. That I promise you."

The lot was just as he described and there was a grouping of mature Maple and Oak trees in the back near the golf

course. The front was open and ready for a home to be built. The dream of being a homeowner and the fantasy of building a home overcame her better judgment. Two months later they closed on the lot and had picked building plans for a layout they liked.

They chose a two story, high ceilinged home with a see through fireplace that served the living room and the kitchen. Lots of high windows, Hunter Douglas Silhouettes to let light in, but nosy eyes out. Hardwood floors, tile and carpet. Marble countertops, stainless kitchen, open foyer, three full bathrooms, four bedrooms, open staircase, nook in the kitchen overlooking a deck and backyard, two car garage with a mud room (came in very handy for Bernie when she returned from the barn), laundry room in the basement, which they finished in a casual style with a bar. Only thing missing was a pool. Part of the basement was turned into a gym with exercise equipment. The laundry room was a dream with a folding table, bars for hanging clothes and storage space and a chute from above. The family room included a pool table with a cover. Under the pool table they had installed an electrical plug and Bernie could plug in crafting equipment or her sewing machine or an iron, a big screen TV was able to be viewed over the back of the couch so she could iron and watch TV without messing up the top floors of the house.

The deck overlooked the backyard which was ringed with newly planted pine trees for privacy from the golf course. On the opposite side was a low row of hedges at the long edge of a fairway. Over the years only two golf balls had been found in their backyard.

NINETEEN

Celeste was short and round like a human planet, with an ass for days. Her name fit her; as in celestial, all encompassing. A true personality, not a false smile and a nod like other teachers. Celeste was prone to making outrageous faces or winking large if they passed in the halls. If you told her something her favorite whisper was, "No shit?" She and Bernie had private, shared jokes, descriptions of incidents, students, teachers, situations and the bantering back and forth with English, build your vocabulary puns.

She was a girl of sorts, with a frazzled brown halo of hair; hair that couldn't be tamed with any amount of anti-frizz product. Vulnerable like an apple doll, with slightly pink cheeks, short nose and giant brown eyes; Celeste looked like she would be the best nurse in the most extreme situation, caring, thoughtful, and overflowing with kindness. Not the type of person to put into a stressful scene or confrontation because she would take it personally and fret over it. Students sensed her kindness and vulnerability and were kind in return. She was lucky because students could be harsh on teachers. Celeste was always reluctant to comment on what she saw or what was on her mind. She was just a cheerful disposition waiting for another cheerful disposition to gel with.

Bernie had done her student teaching in Celeste's classroom two years earlier. It was just fortuitous that there was an opening as their house was built and Tony was starting to take over the practice.

The friendship developed as they milked together. It really started as an accident. Bernie had just arrived at the farm and was reading Dad's instructions for a feed change for one of the goats and remembered that she had lent Celeste an advanced workbook and needed it for the next day. She called from her cell phone to Celeste's home. Celeste asked where she was and Bernie told her she was working at her Dad's farm. Celeste offered to bring the book out. Bernie insisted she let her pick it up after she was done and Celeste indicated that she was bored and wanted to drive somewhere, anyway. So, Bernie gave her directions and met her at the barn driveway intending to grab the book and put it in the Dad's Bronco and have Celeste leave. Celeste got out of her aged green Explorer and walked Bernie to the truck while she put the book in the backseat.

"I really appreciate this, Celeste. I totally forgot to get the book this afternoon and I need it," Bernie said, hoping Celeste would go away. Instead of getting in her little truck and leaving, Celeste said, "I know you have a horse, is that what you're going to do, ride?"

"No, um, I help my dad on Thursdays with the milking." Bernie felt embarrassed because she didn't want to be perceived by the other teachers as a farmer with Tony's new position in town.

"No shit?"

"No shit."

"Can I watch?"

As comfortable at school as she was with Celeste, this was one of those times she'd prefer to disappear. It wasn't like she was in riding clothes and mounted on Noir and felt she looked magnificent because of the beauty of the mare. She was wearing bib overalls, jack boots and had her hair in a bandana to keep it off her face. She just didn't want to be perceived as a hick to anyone she worked with. The feeling of carrying a briefcase and wearing a suit was never going to wear off.

"Look, Bernie, you seem embarrassed for some reason. I'll go."

Bernie sucked in her lower lip, looked up and then down at her short friend, made an instant decision and said, "Hell, if you have nothing better to do and don't mind getting dirty, you can help me and I can get paperwork done earlier tonight."

"No shit?"

Bernie bugged her eyes out at Celeste, stuck her head out like a turtle and said, "No shit," and laughed. She put her arm around Celeste and said, "Welcome to my hidden kingdom. No shit."

When the entered the milking "parlor" Bernie said, "These are my subjects and this is the time I serve them for their serfdom."

Celeste took to the goats because of their trusting, sweet nature. She met the kids, she pet the nannies and

understood the reason for the pristine requirements for milking. She listened well and followed up so she didn't make beginner mistakes. Her questions were relevant and timely and Bernie was delighted at having to explain each procedure. She was more thrilled to have someone to talk to. Evenings in the barn were solitary and she learned that she missed working with someone. The job wasn't difficult, just singular.

The regular Thursday milking begat a much deeper understanding of one another and they worked in tandem, with purpose and lots of bantering. The goats, if they were listening, got an earful.

Talk did not center on school, but did touch on it several times a night when the girls milked together. Celeste became enamored of goats and had a few favorites. Goats don't bite, but will nibble lightly in a manner of affection. To Celeste this was the height of animal kindness. Each nanny had a name and Celeste was quick to learn them and call them by name. Dad had spent fifty cents on each one to have their names engraved on plastic tags that hung from their collars. The idea came to him when they were in a Petsmart and he saw the machine that made the tags. Celeste took the naming to a whole new plain and entire conversations were had with each and every nanny. Thursdays became entertainment nights for more than Mom and Dad because Bernie would sometimes just stop what she was doing to hear Celeste's sing song voice talking to the individual members of the herd as she worked.

It was one of the happiest days of the week for them. They had each other's company and the company of

some really lovely, giving animals. Noir got special attention, too on Thursdays because of Celeste's help. With Celeste making the job faster and easier, Noir got a better grooming and a little more attention to her feed. Noir was brought into her stall for each milking so that she could consume her own dinner or breakfast without getting pushy with the goats. Her rations were very different than lactational goat feed; and this insured she got fed properly without hurting a goat. Being in the same herd, the mare became the alpha animal and was prone to sending them on their way at times. Noir, did, however know that it was feeding time and walked right into her stall twice a day without following the herd to the milking parlor. When the goats were released for the morning or evening, so was Noir. Noir was so comfortable in her little herd that she often laid down with the goats as they chewed cud. Noir would just stretch out and goats would surround her.

Celeste had a fear of the big horse and would just watch and talk over the stall wall while Bernie groomed or fed her. In the winter she wore a blanket so there wasn't as much grooming needed if Bernie wanted to ride. Tony never did get a horse and Noir was quite happy to have a herd of goats for companions.

TWENTY

Originally, the pump house was a dilapidated building about the size of a 12 by 12 foot stall. Dad has lengthened it by four feet, replaced the overlapping cedar shingles with new ones, insulated it and re-caulked the three four- paned windows; the door was replaced with an insulated steel half window door and a burlap curtain. The well pump was in its own area and heavily insulted against freeze, the rest of the building was open. Over the years when someone would throw out a reclining chair, Dad would pick them up and put them in the pump house. He decorated the barn wood walls with rail road spikes, glass insulators, shelves, old horse shoes and pieces of farm equipment like a disc or an old pitchfork handle. It was decorating by Smith and Wesson, rustic and comfortable for him to just crawl into and cogitate. And, yes, it had a farm calendar on the wall with a pencil hanging next to it.

There were old coffee cups and a bottle of Jack Daniels, a bottle of Scotch and cheap peppermint schnapps on the shelf above the three recliners. This was Dad's retreat and the bald hanging light bulb was replaced by an old ceiling fixture that Mom didn't want in the house any longer. It didn't hold a bright bulb, but a low wattage one. This created atmosphere of near darkness. The fire from the wood burning stove added a dim glow.

This was truly a little cabin, stained blue on the outside with contrasting white paint on the window frames. He had installed a miniature picket fence around it where Mom planted bulbs and annuals in the enclosure. It was magically cute, like a child's playhouse from the outside.

It was several weeks of Thursdays before Bernie introduced Celeste to the pump house. No work needed to be done with the pump and the building was not in plain site from the milking parlor or general barns, so Celeste didn't know it existed.

"Hey, want to have a drink with me before we leave tonight?"

"A drink?"

"Yeah, a drink. We have a special place to just chill out and I thought I'd invite you."

"I'm not clean enough to go in the house, Bernie."

"I'm not talking about the house. We have some hooch stored in the pump house."

"The pump house?"

"It's where the well pump is located for water for the herd and barns. This well is separate from the house well because it has more sulfur in it and we don't drink it. We have to keep the pump somewhere and it has to be insulated so it doesn't freeze in the winter. It's out back."

"Another building? No shit?"

Bernie laughed, "No shit," she said through her smile.

Celeste followed Bernie through the barns and out back. "It's usually dark by the time we finish so you probably never noticed it before. Besides, I'm the one who takes the herd back to the pasture."

"Ohhhh, how cute," Celeste crooned when she saw the building in the dim light. The marigolds were already fading, but it was pretty obvious that this building has special significance by the outward appearance.

"Trust me, it's a whole different animal inside."

Celeste's eyes were wide, "It looks like it fell out of a fairy tale."

Bernie opened the door and beckoned Celeste inside. "Ohhh, it's a man's place," Celeste breathed out.

Dad has put an old Mr. Coffee in there and a dorm room refrigerator for his goat milk and some cheese and his vaccines. There was an old mouse proof metal bread box with crackers and beef jerky. A discarded end table completed the furnishings. "Feel comfortable sitting down, Bernie told Celeste, These are junked chairs and Dad spends a lot of time in here reading between milkings and chores so he doesn't make Mom crazy in the house and mess it up."

Bernie had long since contributed to the alcohol and added a box of her wine and a few mismatched wine glasses from broken sets from home. The boxed wine lasted a long time, but her favorite was a belt of Scotch after milking and to grade papers before going home. If her students only knew that some of their papers were read in this environment, they'd change their opinion

of her. This was Bernie's retreat on Thursdays during the spring, summer and early fall. She and her father never sat in there together because he was gone when she milked. He never said anything to her about the box of wine or the other bottle of Scotch.

She always visited the pump house after milkings and grabbed all the cups and glasses and took them to the milk house to wash them. They were carried back in an old milk crate and returned turned upside down on paper barn towels on the shelf. This was just her way of thanking Dad for letting her use his private space. The knives in the refrigerator and the cheese wrappings were cleaned and disposed of, too. Bernie cleaned up after Dad and Tony all the time and it just became habit; although, Dad was a little more detail oriented in the cleaning department than Tony would ever be.

Celeste spied the bottle of Jack Daniels on the shelf and said, "Hey, I'll have a hit of Jack, if that's OK."

"Sure, that's what it there for. I replace it every so often so he doesn't complain."

"This is truly your Dad's place, huh?"

"Sure is. I keep it cleaned on Thursdays during milking season and he doesn't complain."

"When do I get to meet him?"

"I guess we'll have to wait for a night in for them. He makes a really concentrated effort to take Mom off the farm at least once a week. They don't go out as much in the winter because I think they spend a lot of time

in front of the fireplace playing Backgammon. Goats don't milk through the winter months because they are bred back and just don't produce as much and need the nutrients to make kids," Bernie grabbed a coffee cup and poured a good shot of Jack for Celeste. "I'm glad you like the liquor selection!"

"Hey, this is great. I see your Dad has an ashtray for his pipe, too."

"Yeah, well I smoke in here because Tony doesn't know I smoke and it makes the liquor taste better. I started smoking again after I started milking again. It's one of my little secrets. The cigarettes are in the refrigerator if you want one. I shower and brush when I get home so Tony doesn't know.

"No, I don't smoke, never have."

"Did you ever try dope in college?"

"Yeah, it wasn't my thing. I got sick and threw up."

"Oh."

"Do you have some stashed someplace?" Celeste asked with a little surprise in her voice.

"No, but I've thought about it. My friend Timmy used to get his hands on it sometimes and we'd enjoy a toke on my balcony in Chicago."

"I can't imagine where you'd get it now that you're a teacher!"

"Good point."

"Do you miss your friend, Timmy?"

"Yeah, I miss our Scrabble games and lessons together. I really don't have any way to get to a riding lesson here and I haven't had any contact with Timmy, save once, since getting married. That and the Christmas cards." Bernie poured a little Scotch into a coffee cup and drank it in one swallow, and poured another.

"You know," said Celeste, "if we spend any time in here, we could set up a Scrabble board. I haven't played in years and my husband isn't about to play with me. He's gone so much that we just do household things and go out for dinner when he's home. Construction workers aren't exactly Scrabble players. If he plays anything, it's Poker with the boys in our neighborhood on the rare Saturday in someone's basement.

"Does that bother you that Mike's gone so often? Tony's been working a lot of late nights and weekends lately and it's starting to get on my nerves."

"No, I've been used to being alone for so long that it doesn't bother me. I have papers to grade and a lot of hobby things I do. I sew pillow case dresses for one of the local churches for missionary work in Nicaragua, so that keeps me busy. Hey, how about another shot of that Jack?"

Hence began the Thursday night drinks before leaving the farm. Celeste found an old Scrabble game and they put the box on the shelf. Many hours were spent in the pump house, making them both late getting home.

TWENTY ONE

There were deeper, darker fears among Bernie's regular days. Still not confident about her appearance and acceptance from people, she wasn't the most pleasant person in a retail setting. Tony had often remarked that she was curt with salespeople and seemed to go out of her way to be insulting to them. She always found an excuse to justify her behavior such as, "Well, I wasn't dealing with the high end of the evolutionary scale there," or "When I asked where something was I got a blank stare."

Tony, as driven as he was, was the kindest most smiling person to everyone. No one was beneath him and he made everyone around him feel grand and good about themselves. Bernie, on the other hand, made people feel small and insignificant, as though they had ruined her day. They were going to ruin hers, so why not start it? Her voice could be edgy and cutting.

It took a long time for Bernie to warm up and trust people. The people she worked with were just as mistrusting of her because of her sharp words and unkind glances. She was prone to staring a person down or making a disgruntled face if they made some remark she didn't like. Those blue eyes could turn stone cold gray when she was upset or irritable.

Agitation and irritation were constant emotions which she portrayed when disappointed or worried. Sometimes people were disposable in her opinion and that didn't make her many close friends. To others she appeared aloof and cold. What no one knew was how vulnerable and insecure she was on the inside. She would lash before anyone else could verbally hurt her.

TWENTY TWO

Cappy was their lawn person. After two years in the new home the landscaping had taken on a mind of its own and Bernie struggled to keep the place mowed, pruned and trimmed. Tony called a local lawn service and they did a decent job for a while, but Bernie wasn't entirely thrilled with their work.

At a parent teacher conference a woman by the name of Dot had started talking about her "partner," saying she owned a lawn service. She gave Bernie a card and Bernie called the woman. Cappy showed up in a rolled up T-shirt, jeans, boots and a cap on her head. She had long hair, but it was tied in a knot at the back of a ball cap. They hit it off immediately and Cappy surveyed the problems and told Bernie she could do a much better job for a much better price. They struck a deal and Bernie terminated the old lawn service. Cappy cut at diagonals and made the new lawn look like a baseball diamond with her zero turn mower. Her trimming was straight and she even clipped and pruned the topiary around the house with precision. Bernie was immensely pleased with the job, as was Tony. This gave Bernie even more time to herself during the summer months.

Cappy purposely did their lawn on Fridays at the end of the day because she knew that Bernie would be home

and would offer her a cold beer after work. This was fine with Bernie who always wanted a nice cold one at the end of the week and loved Cappy's company. It didn't hurt that through the weekend their lawn looked well manicured. She recommended Cappy to her in-laws and Cappy got their business.

Part of Cappy's problems with getting jobs was that she was female and quite obviously gay. She had to prove herself by doing a better job than her competition; and she did. Cappy and Bernie would sit on the deck in the backyard and talk about all topics on Friday afternoons until it was time to start dinner. She learned that Dot was the cook in their "family" and Cappy was the cleanup crew. It seemed like any normal marriage and friendship to Bernie. Cappy and Bernie became close.

Dot's daughter was only 14, but in an advanced placement class Bernie taught. She did not allow the flat chested Courtney to be picked on by the older students and was quite protective of her. She'd been there and wasn't about to allow it to happen to anyone else. If she heard anything in the hallways or through the student grapevine, she nipped it quickly and sharply with a threat. She never said a word about her mother's and Cappy's relationship and neither did Courtney. As far as Courtney was concerned, this was a perfectly normal relationship of two women living together and Court had two mothers. The other students didn't have a clue.

Because she was one of Courtney's teachers, it really wasn't proper to foster a friendship with Dot and Cappy at her home, but she did accept invitations on some weeknights to join them for food Tony wouldn't consider.

She'd leave Tony a plate in the fridge with microwave instructions, set the table and pick up some flowers and a bottle of wine and head over to Cappy and Dot's. Liver, onions, bacon, mashed potatoes and spinach was the big meal that no one else, except the four of them seemed to enjoy. Tony wouldn't touch liver with a twain pole. They'd eat dinner and Dot and Bernie would sit at the kitchen table while Courtney went to read and Cappy cleaned the dishes and kitchen. Dot and Bernie got into political conversations where they eventually agreed to disagree, but hashed out the details anyway.

It was always hilarious fun with Cappy keeping an eye on them over the kitchen counter while she washed dishes.

It's not clear how the conversation began, but Dot was telling Bernie about a friend she had years ago who was sometimes a jerk. She was either super nice or a real dork. She was supposed to take her medication because she was manic depressive and would refuse to take it.

"What happened to her?"

Dot leaned back in her chair and said, "She died."

"How?"

"Being an asshole."

"This sounds like one of your jokes, I know I'm being set up for something here."

"No, seriously, she died. She was in a manic phase and tore off on a motorcycle and got herself killed in a wreck."

"Why?"

"Because she figured she didn't need her medication and they couldn't do anything to force her to take it because she was an adult. I think it was some sort of road rage incident."

Bernie didn't say anything for a long time. Then she looked toward Cappy in the kitchen and asked, "Am I an asshole?"

Cappy paused in her dishwashing and put her head down for a second and then said, "I'm not saying anything."

"No, seriously, Cappy, if you're my friend, you need to be honest with me and tell me if I act like an asshole."

"Yeah, well I don't want to lose my job at your place."

"You won't. You'd be my friend by telling me what you really see. I can't see myself clearly and I'd appreciate the honesty."

"Well, sometimes you can be an asshole."

"Hmm. You know, Tony sometimes tells me I act strangely with people, but I never considered myself an asshole."

Dottie scraped her chair closer and put her elbows on the table, leaning forward. "Caps tells me sometimes she hears you on the phone or sees you with someone who comes to your house and how you treat them. It sounds like an asshole to me. She says you get all excited and sometimes yell and treat people badly."

"Cappy, do I treat you badly?"

"No."

"Who do I treat badly?"

"Oh, man, I don't want to get into this now."

"You'd be doing me a huge favor by telling me what you observe that I don't see; or I'm just not aware of. You two are my friends, and God knows, I have few of them."

Cappy put down the dishtowel and came to the table and pulled out a chair. Cappy was naturally a soft spoken person, in contrast to the assertive Dot, and her voice sometimes couldn't be heard. She was quiet in her speech now.

"You don't know that you are confrontational before something starts. Sometimes, if you'd just listen to people you'd be logical and figure out what needs to be said. You are a great conversationalist and you know how to talk to people, but you don't use those skills around everyone. You've never said or done anything to me or Dot to make us dislike you; and Courtney adores you as a teacher. She's never said a bad word about you. But, I hear things sometimes and wonder why you don't use the brain that God gave you."

Bernie was quiet.

Dot said, "I hear the stories because me and Cap talk about our jobs each night. You're the most colorful because of the things you do and some of the things you say to people."

"Like who?"

"Like that guy who delivers your frozen food," Cappy said. "He missed a week or missed a delivery or something and you went up one side of him and down the other. He didn't deserve that."

"He missed a delivery and didn't bring things I needed."

"See, that's what Dot's talking about, you didn't put in an order, but he missed you on his route and you just assumed he knew you needed something. I think his truck broke down that week. He was so upset," Cap said, "he looked like he was gonna cry."

"Yeah, and he didn't come back for months, either until I placed an Internet order. Then he had to."

"This is what we're talking about, Bernie," Dot leaned forward again, "You don't know what kind of effect you have on people. He's not stupid, but you treated him like he was a moron. You made him feel small. I wouldn't come back, either."

Bernie picked up her wineglass and swallowed the contents. "What else?"

"We saw the same kind of behavior in Susan before she died. She was like the imperious leader or something. Queen Diva. She'd be all quiet one time and raging the next. I started wondering if you had other traits like her so I asked Cappy to keep an eye on you. Cappy likes you too much to lose your friendship. Me too.

"Susan was a good person, but she had a disease or something. Her brain didn't work the same way other

people's did and she was either lots of fun or difficult. There was no in-between.

"She was in her late 20's and when she was on her medication she was fine and even tempered. But when she was off, you could tell immediately and she was this free spirit raging or flying off to some new dangerous adventure. She would just do stupid things. She made a lot of enemies along the way because she couldn't control her mouth, either, "Dot said.

"She drank a lot, too," Cappy said not meeting Bernie's eyes. I think it was like a medication to her or something."

Dot interjected, "Yeah, well we all drink a lot, except you, Cap." Cappy didn't look at either of them.

"Well, Susan wasn't intoxicated when she died. She treated that bike like she could fly on it. Like it was some sort of magical machine to use uninhibited," Cappy seemed to be talking to Dot. It was obvious they missed their friend, but they seemed to be having their own conversation without including Bernie at this point.

"She did weird things like disappear for weeks at a time and then show up and expect that you knew where she was. Or she'd tell some outrageous story of what she was doing while she was away. Sometimes it was obvious to all of us that she didn't use common sense. I'm surprised she didn't get a disease from all the men she was with. Remember the time she showed up in a truck with two guys and wanted to borrow some money for booze? Man, I wanted to smack some sense into her. They were both hanging on her and she could barely stand up she was so drunk. They were drunk, too." Dot reminisced.

“Who put her on medication? Bernie asked.

“She had to go to a special doctor or something, I really don’t know. I just know she could be a real weirdo and you could tell when she wasn’t on her medication. It was two different people,” Dot said to the ceiling.

“Am I like Susan? Do I act like her? Do I remind you of her? Bernie asked.

“YES,” they said in unison.

“OK, I’ll consider this and see what I can do. I didn’t know I was a problem child. Reminds me of that Joni Mitchell song, ‘Problem Child.’”

They looked at her with blank expressions.

“I guess you had to have heard it. It’s kind of funny. It’s really old and wasn’t wildly popular so you won’t be hearing it on the radio any time soon. I just happen to have the CD of her greatest hits. You guys don’t even know who she is, do you?”

“No.”

TWENTY THREE

School started Wednesday. Bernie had to submit her lesson plans for other teachers and the administration to review before school started. Many years ago the administration cut through conflict by having teachers review each other's lesson plans so the lower classes could prepare students for the next step in their education. It stopped a lot of "Oh, I didn't know you'd be covering that."

Monday there was a general meeting. It had been decided that each teacher would meet the new principle before the group meeting. Bernie dreaded this date. She did not want to be reminded of the afternoon at McGinty's and she certainly didn't want to be judged by someone she'd never met. Gunning down another teacher in a truck was bad enough, and embarrassing, but she had sought help at the urging of Tony and her friends afterward. The conversation with Cappy and Dot had pushed it to fruition. This, too, was embarrassing and she hoped no one knew.

She hadn't seen McGinty or his wife all summer and wasn't looking forward to the meeting of educators with him in attendance. In her opinion, McGinty wasn't about to change other than letting Chelsea play golf with the boy's team.

McGinty was going to be in the same conference room with her and the other teachers; Bernie was very nervous. Brea, Tasha, Todd, and Charlene were the ones she worried about the most because they were the gossip group. The divide and conquer group. The group most like the students she had attended school with as a kid. The group most likely to give her shit and catch her off guard with nothing to say. She tried to keep them out of her mind and concentrate on appearing nice and stable for her upcoming meeting with the new principle. She knew nothing about him other than his name, Gene Morgan. Celeste had already met him because he called her home and scheduled an appointment with her. She said he was in his mid 40's, good looking and very nice, "seemed like an understanding guy."

****

There was something about female gym teachers that made them either walk like men or slightly waddle. Brea was built like a dock piling. She had the utilitarian short haircut that could be showered on and fall into place without a comb or brush. They built gym teachers this way for a reason. Why?

This place is a study in hilarious stereotypical personality types. They don't mesh, they don't meld as a group, they were born to be teachers of certain subjects and look like it, **Bernie thought as she looked around the conference room. Todd refusing to sit and leaning on the door jamb, Celeste with a pile of dog-eared papers before her, Brea slumped in a chair, Tasha with a short skirt and one crossed leg swinging, Charlene with the points of her polished fingers making a steeple, Chris Bard looking**

efficient about to take notes and McGinty glaring at everyone. You couldn't have casted anything better if you tried. It didn't occur to Bernie to ascertain where she fit into this gaggle.

"Why did Brea's parents give her such a beautiful name and such an ugly continence?" She looked like the female version of a sumo wrestler. "How the hell could she teach PE when it looked like she could barely move in a straight line with any grace? How did she teach PE, anyway? Didn't gym teachers have to be athletic?" Brea was the farthest thing from resembling an athlete. She was fat, too. Or was that all muscle? Bernie doubted it was muscle because she'd never seen Brea do anything other than hoist the whistle from around her neck or carry a basketball. The students carried the equipment to and from the fields. Who set up the volleyball net? Another mystery.

Celeste had long talked about taking a gym class in her off period. What Brea might do to her was a scary thought; there was no respect there. Brea reminded Bernie of the gym teacher she had when in high school. What happened to her? She was married, she knew that, but to whom and how was not known. The woman had looked the part of a dyke and acted like a mean one, too. Brea, too was married, but no one had ever met her husband. They didn't attend the football games that Bernie knew about. She'd ask Tony if he ever noticed her. Tasha was in charge of the cheering squad, but she had to have some contact with Brea at some time, but Bernie had never seen them conferring or even together.

Brea might or might not be a nice person, but Bernie's own remembrance of gym classes reflected on Brea and she could see her physically grabbing a student who wasn't team oriented and dragging her. Brea didn't have a chance of humanity in Bernie's world. Brea didn't exactly interact with the other teachers, either, so it was difficult to gauge her as a person. She stayed in the gym and didn't even have lunch room duties for some reason. You never saw her in the teacher's lounge and Bernie wondered if she ate lunch in her office. What about a cup of coffee?

"Hey, Celeste, do you ever see Brea other than meetings? Like, do you ever see her outside the gym? I've never seen her eat lunch, grab a cup of coffee, or do anything unrelated to the gym. I see the classes out on the athletic fields in good weather, but I've never seen her alone, or even walking to the office."

"Never thought about it," Celeste had looked sideways while attaching a milker. "I was never keen on gym as a kid, so I really don't think about it. I know I need exercise, but the torture in gym class didn't do me much good. I wasn't picked for teams and I wasn't good at gymnastics, so I was a non-entity. I really should talk to Brea about joining them when they do aerobics, if they do."

Bernie remembered her gym teacher standing over her when she fell off the vaulting horse and knocked the air out of her lungs. The teacher just stood there and watched her, never attempting to comfort or help her. Bitch. The one thing Bernie was good at was gymnastics. That day she had vaulted right over the horse and fell.

Celeste brought her out of her reverie, "Why do you ask?"

"I was just thinking about school and the lack of communication between the staff. I never was big on gym class myself because I was picked on so often. I just couldn't hit a softball or volleyball and it brought back some memories. I actually had my gym teacher grab me and haul me into her office once."

"I was just ignored."

"You were lucky then. I was tall enough to play basketball, but had no skills. They weren't going to be taught or developed, either."

"Phys Ed wasn't my strong point," Celeste giggled at herself. "Soccer was the worst."

"Oh yeah, soccer is brutal. Everyone wants to kick the shit out of your shins and knock you on your ass.

"Hey, is that group done? I can let them down the chute and bring in the next group."

"Yes, the mommies are done and fed and they're ready to go."

The opened the chutes, sent the goats down the chute and stood by waiting for the next group of amicable animals to come in. "I think I love goats," Celeste said as she watched them walk to stations and refilled their grain boxes as she weighed rations.

"Well, Dad would tell you that they are wily little suckers that can get out of any opening in a heartbeat. It wasn't easy for him to build goat proof fences out there. Keeps Noir in, too. Not that Noir exactly wants to leave the herd."

TWENTY FOUR

The junior high science teacher was a royal pain in the ass. Her name was Tasha, short for Natasha. She came across as perceiving herself as exotic with an ego beyond all boundaries. She'd never been voted as teacher of the year by the student body, but she thought she was the best at everything and she let everyone know it. She was the coolest, the prettiest, smartest, the most creative and innovative. She was convinced that all men were falling and fawning over her if they started a conversation. She was known to make inappropriate remarks in mixed company, justly proving her beliefs about herself. She thought she was flirting and instead she was making those around her uncomfortable.

Tasha was not pretty, just mildly attractive. Some assets, no boobs to speak of, but tall, thin, long legged and very long dark hair that she swished around like a horse's tail. Slightly bucktoothed, she had big teeth with lots of gum showing. It was pretty obvious she did not wear braces as a child. Rumor had it that she'd been divorced three times. She was originally from Lansing, so no one knew her very well and most of the faculty avoided her because she would stand for hours and brag about her teaching abilities and techniques. She lived in Jackson and drove in. Her most irritating feature was the loud, raucous, braying laugh that made you cringe and your

head hurt at the same time. Children, family? No one knew.

Her computer was better than yours, her injuries were worse than yours, or anybody else's for that matter. Standing with one hand on her hip and her leg stretched out like a fashion model, she obviously flirted with Todd. Her room and his office were directly across the hall from one another. The gym doors opened on that end and the opposite hallway so that the gym could be divided into two sections for girls and boys PE.

They were the two teachers who were always seen talking. Todd couldn't resist talking any more than Tasha could. Neither of these two ever seemed nervous about anything, although Tasha was known to be bitter about some personal issues. Maybe they discussed them in the hallway, who knew.

Whereas Charlene was a pimple on the ass of progress, Tasha was a pimple; a simple annoyance to avoid or pop; preferably in the face. You couldn't miss her grating voice anywhere in a crowd or the school. Bernie had seen enough students cringe at her laugh to know that it wasn't just her individual opinion about how bothersome she was. Celeste said every time Tasha laughed it hurt between her shoulder blades and gave her a brief headache.

She had no credibility and a total lack of charisma, yet her ego refused to let her know it. What her students thought of her was unknown. Because of her "big" personality, students may have been intimidated and seldom was anything overheard by the other teachers.

Every teacher had a nickname based on their personality or their given names.

Girls had a tendency to call McGinty "McFlinty," but boys worshipped him as coach. Celeste was "Mama Cass," Bernie was "Burn it," (More so since the McGinty incident), Charlene was "Paste Face." Kids have the ability to know the personalities behind the faces and personas. They always know when a smile is false and pasted on and when a teacher has a serious desire to reach each and every one of them. Tasha was known as "Mule," probably due to her voice.

The petite woman with the short, stylish, frosted hair was Charlene the math teacher. She was a flashy dresser with all the accessories. Her nails were perfectly manicured, lipstick was always on and lined. If you didn't know she was on a teacher's salary, you'd swear the suits and shells were Dior or Chanel. She was always perfectly accented with the right jewelry or scarf, bangles, bracelets and rings. There was no mistake that she was a consummate shopper. Bernie could envision her driving from sale to sale, mall to mall in her little convertible.

What kind of ego lies behind that perpetual smile and syrupy voice? You could imagine her teaching grade school and saying, "OK, boys and girls, today. . ." How the teens and tweens tolerated it was beyond Celeste and Bernie's comprehension.

The conference room was full and everyone had a seat other than Todd. Todd was wall leaning with one arm outstretched to hold his posture of crossed legs.

Mr. "sex appeal." Yup, that was Todd. He was the boy's PE teacher. Bernie referred to him as the "Cowboy." Thin, tall, tanned and the postures to go with the type; always leaning on something like he was observing the turning of the earth, the corners of his wide mouth slightly smiling as though the world was a joke. When Bernie grew up she wanted to be Todd and know everything about everything because Todd had an opinion on all subjects, known and unknown. Where he obtained his information was suspect, but he had all the answers.

Their confrontations were legend among the faculty and students. Bernie could not contain her thoughts around him and often took him on. He thought English was a joke and that air was only to fill volleyballs. The female students couldn't take their eyes off him and the adolescent boys wanted very much to be him because they saw him as some sort of idol. The older boys had already adopted his mannerisms and these were not appreciated by the female teachers, who already felt threatened by the attitude. There was speculation about him being gay because he never talked about or was seen with any women other than Tasha. Bernie suspected that most of them felt the same way about him as she did and eschewed his company. "Jackass."

"Oh, I see the tanning bed is getting a good workout because your eyes are white again," Bernie sneered at him one morning at class change while they stood in the hall.

"I don't use a tanning bed; I work out and wear sunglasses."

"Oh, you work out in the snow," she thought she was being a smartass.

"I cross country every morning."

Curiosity got her attention and she asked, "What time go you get up to do this if you have to be here near seven?"

"Five."

Bernie hadn't considered that all a man has to do is shower and shave; and this one wore sweats to work. She felt foolish as he grinned at her as though he was looking down at someone short. They nearly stood eye-to-eye because of her height. She, too, woke at five and spent the time getting coffee and any breakfast Tony wanted and then getting dressed for school.

He made fun of Celeste much too often in front of the other faculty members and it grated on Bernie. He also took every opportunity to rub Bernie the wrong way, "Gaining a little weight there, Bernie. Are you pregnant?"

Her mouth flopped open, "No, it's due to a medication I'm taking."

He was unimpressed and unsympathetic. Bernie made a mental note to call the doctor and discuss the meds. She had read the contraindication sheets the pharmacy had provided and knew that one of the side effects of most antidepressants was weight gain. The doctor had said the same thing. She wasn't eating more or higher calorie food than before the prescriptions. She didn't feel a

little wine or Scotch was going to affect her weight, even though the directions were "absolutely no alcoholic beverages."

Morgan entered and politely addressed and thanked everyone for being present. He was a handsome man with a pseudo military haircut, blondish, clean shaven and bright blue eyes. He was in great physical shape from the looks of it. He started the meeting business fashion and conducted it with aplomb. There wasn't the usual bedlam of teachers arguing with one another, raised voices, and the usual teenaged physicality of throwing themselves at each other with barbs and arguments. Morgan had successfully, and apparently, met with each of them and laid ground rules for a businesslike meeting atmosphere. Kudos to him.

Bernie's own meeting with him was brief and not once was McGinty mentioned. She found that Morgan had an insurance background and had run a rather large agency in the past and decided he wanted to go back to teaching in the social sciences and move into administration with the business skills he acquired. It was a successful mix and she was comfortable with him because of his business background. He wasn't your typical teacher who had moved into administration without business skills. She liked him and felt she could reach out and confide in him when necessary.

TWENTY FIVE

Bernie drove to Ann Arbor for her appointment with a doctor about a week after her conversation with Dot and Cappy. He was a psychiatrist. Her first meeting with him was a full medical examination where she asked him if he believed in God. He paused and said, "I imagine you're asking me that because of my profession and because I deal with minds. I'm a full medical doctor, too. And, yes, because of what I know and have seen in this profession, I believe in God." Bernie was comforted by the fact that someone who deals in mental illness could still believe in God.

"You're medical exam checked out and you're in excellent physical health. What I'd like to do, based on your own diagnosis about being bipolar, is put you on an antidepressant and see how that goes. Because of your descriptions of your behavior, I'd also like to put you on a prescription that acts as an anti-anxiety drug. I suspect that anxiety sets off the behaviors you've described to me and I think it will help. Now you need to understand that all these drugs do different things and have side effects. One of the most common side effects is weight gain and initial dizziness. I suggest you start these on Friday night after work and take time to get used to any side effects. Many of these drugs cause dry mouth and you may be feeling thirsty. Some of these

effects will go away as you become accustomed to them, and some may cause you to be concerned. I recommend that you don't do any driving or operating machinery for a week.

Although you checked out physically, I do believe that the *illness* you described in high school was your first clinical depression. How you recovered from that without medical help is beyond my comprehension. I think you are a mentally strong person."

"I have to milk goats on Thursdays and that involves being able to think straight, follow instructions and use equipment. I also ride a horse on a regular basis."

"Well, I'm asking you to get someone else to do the job and not ride the horse until you get used to possible side effects. You call my office if any of this gets out of hand and we'll adjust the dosages. Right now you'll be on lowered dosages and we'll use that as a baseline. It would be good to keep a record or diary of any side effects and when they happen."

Going to a psychiatrist has its own stigma and Bernie didn't want anyone but Tony to know she had made and gone to the first two appointments. She filled the prescriptions in Ann Arbor because she didn't need the local pharmacy knowing about them. A small town was like a large sponge. You could squeeze just so much dirty water out of it and it still held dirty water.

The discussions with Tony were not pleasant because of the McGinty thing and her behavior around people she didn't know well. "I'm glad you're seeking help," he said one night at dinner.

"I'm not. I don't see anything wrong with my behavior. I did a lot of research before I went and I don't have any of the symptoms other than occasional fits of anger."

"I think you disguise mania as anger. What's this 'OCD tendency' thing mean?"

"I'm not sure. I guess that many bipolar people have OCD tendencies and shop a lot to make themselves feel better. I read that they buy the same things over and over and accumulate a lot of things that they don't need or are unnecessary in their lives. They also check and double check things like locking doors, turning off the stove; things like that."

"Sounds right to me when you consider the way you hoard food."

"I do not hoard food; we just have a well stocked pantry. You never know what you're going to need and it keeps from making frequent trips to the grocery store."

"Just because you don't like being seen in the local stores and don't want to go."

TWENTY SIX

The high school boys were in awe of Chelsea's prowess on the golf course and her reputation in open tournaments. McGinty still held a grudge against the girl; at least that's how it appeared to Bernie. McGinty's female students often complained that they were all but ignored in his classes and how he would make a study hall out of class and have all the boys gather around his desk and talk sports. His desk and chair were even placed on a wide dais that the shop students had constructed. Very little teaching happened unless the students did their assigned readings.

He coached the golf team and only boys were allowed. Allowed, being the key word. He played regularly at the private course and was never seen playing with women. Someone once told Bernie that the word golf stood for "gentlemen only ladies forbidden." The acronym fit McGinty's outward opinion of women and made Bernie remember Tony's accusation about her being the opposite of a misogynist. She didn't dislike all men, just those who treated women as an inferior gender. Wonder what he thought of gays?

Bernie had no idea that Brea golfed and wanted very much to have a girl's golf team. There was nothing in the budget and Brea brought in her own clubs and taught

the girls to tee off. She would impose on the system occasionally for a bus to take the girls to the golf course so they could go together as a group and practice hitting balls and walk the course to understand her passion for the sport. There wasn't equipment, but two girls did have their own clubs and they would have to share with the others. Chelsea was 15, had grown up in a golfing family and was really quite good. She had a beautiful swing and had been taught to keep her eye on the ball, so she was good at placing it.

Being in charge of the boy's golf team, McGinty meant to keep it his way. This was a chance for him to golf under the budget of the school system, although, he did have a putting green in his backyard. How he kept it prime and short was not generally known to the teachers. He actually paid to have the kid who cut the private course bring out the special mower to maintain his backyard green. The boy's golf team spent a good number of their evenings and summers on the course or at McGinty's house.

McGinty and Brea were in a silent war about not allowing Chelsea to play with the boy's team. She knew how good the girl was and Brea felt guilty about having her share her clubs with the other girls in gym classes. Brea was constantly searching eBay for golf clubs that were cheap and still useful within her teacher's salary.

The year before Bernie got wind of this through Tasha. Tasha was a talker, and apparently so was Brea. Brea didn't seem like the type to converse with someone like Tasha, but Tasha's relationship with Todd in the hallway had developed into a three way conversation with Brea.

Brea would often open the door between the boy's and girl's gym and speak with Todd. Todd, because he yakked constantly, told Tasha. Tasha was not happy that girls couldn't play golf. It wasn't entirely like that; it was more that none of the girls, save two, had any interest in the activity. Chelsea, because she was very good, and the other one because it was what her family did for outings. Tasha felt that Chelsea should be allowed to play with the boys. McGinty, being a jackass, was against Chelsea worming her way into his male clique.

McGinty was married to a soft spoken, gray haired mouse of a woman. She did what McGinty needed done and her life revolved around his as a silent satellite. Mrs. McGinty served soft drinks and Gatorade with cookies and assorted homemade pastry to the boys all summer long. She would only be visible when she brought refreshments to the picnic table and then she'd retreat back to the house. This was well known because of McGinty's offhand remarks and the boy's talk. McGinty supplied hamburgers and hotdogs all summer and sweet talked the parents into letting the boys hang out there. Mrs. McGinty was the food slave and the boys noticed it. They hadn't been brought up by their parents and sisters to ignore and behave that way toward women, but McGinty was coach, so they let it be. They all knew about Chelsea because she played the same course they did during the spring, summer and fall. Her great scores were legendary and even mentioned in a local paper.

It seemed to Bernie that McGinty felt women should be seen and not heard. How he became a teacher dealing with both male and female students was another one of

Bernie's puzzles. Only having been in the system for two years, she didn't know the ins and outs of the student body, their opinions or thoughts on him.

She wasn't aware of Chelsea's situation until Tasha mentioned it in the teacher's bathroom. Tasha was hot under the collar about the situation and fed Bernie's new found rage about McGinty. She put her hands on her hips and practically spat at Tasha concerning the situation that Tasha had just outlined. "What do you mean there is no girl's team and he won't let her play with the boy's? It's a team and as far as I know there are no gender restrictions for a team. It isn't exactly a contact sport, Tasha!"

"McGinty has known about Chelsea's outstanding game for several years and has purposely discouraged the girls from any participation; that includes speaking up in his classes."

"What? You're freaking kidding me, right?"

"No Ma'am, that's why I'm so pissed right now. I don't teach business classes and history, so I have no contact with him other than faculty meetings. I'd bust his head in if I could. Someone needs to take this to the administration."

"If you've known about this so long, why haven't you said something?"

The conversation made Bernie seethe all day. She was in charge of a detention group that day and several students missed the later grade school busses home. One boy in particular had no way to get home to help

with farm chores. Brandon was a good kid who lived on a dairy farm and was a 4Her. Bernie had offered from time to time to volunteer her father's farm to the local 4H clubs involved in dairy management and knew that Brandon needed to be home for chores. She offered to drive him. As she passed the golf course's main entrance the hair on the back of her neck stood up. She got angrier and angrier. Brandon didn't say much other than a profuse thanks to her when he got out of the Bronco. The second trip past the course entrance made her change directions.

Bernie knew where McGinty lived and drove into his driveway. There were four boys there on the putting green with McGinty supervising from the side. She dropped the transmission into second gear, pushed the clutch down and roared the engine. When the truck shot forward out of second gear she headed straight for McGinty. He ran to the other side of his house and she ran over the putting green, spun mud and grass and the truck lurched toward him, nearly pinning him to the side. She opened the window and yelled, "What's the matter McFlinty? You scared that a girl is gonna hurt you? She shifted into neutral and gunned the engine. McGinty was almost crushed into the side of the house and he looked frightened. One of the boys called the police from his cell phone and a few minutes later a police cruiser pulled up with Tony right behind it running and puffing into McGinty's backyard. He had run all the way from his office after hearing the police scanner in the office.

Tony's face was florid from running and anger. He pulled her out of the Bronco, ran to McGinty and dislodged him

from the wedge between the truck's grill and the side of the house. Bernie was still yelling at McGinty about not letting girls play with the golf team and Tony had to physically restrain her before she pasted McGinty. He held her arms behind her and tried to reason with her. She was out of physical and mental control and he was just as surprised as the boys and McGinty. Mrs. McGinty never came outside during the commotion.

Tony spent a good half hour talking to McGinty and soothing him. They sent the police cruiser away after McGinty agreed that no real harm was done other than the destruction of his putting green. McGinty kept staring at Bernie as though she had lost her marbles and was going to physically attack him. He had apparently never been assaulted before, let alone by a woman. He looked really frightened and Tony was a soothing patch on the event.

Tony called her father. Her mother drove Dad, and Dad drove the Blazer home. Tony dragged her down the street to his office and closed the door. He sat for a long time just staring at her as though it was the first time he had met her. Not a lot was said in his office and Bernie dreaded the trip and conversation at home. The only thing Tony said over and over was, "Bernie, what happened out there?" She had no answer for him other than explaining the girls and the golf thing. Tony seemed unconvinced that such measures were necessary and that this could have been taken up with the school administration in a civilized manner. Bernie wasn't feeling too civilized at the moment and the adrenaline started to drain little by little until she slumped into the chair in front of his desk; spent and exhausted.

It wasn't an hour from the time of mental explosion to the time the town was already talking. The staff at Tony's office had already heard many of the details and Candy the paralegal high fived Bernie on the way out the door when they left. Tony glared at Candy. On the way to the car Tony could feel people staring out shop windows and said under his breath to her, "What is this some sort of sick female conspiracy? I don't get it."

"Those women were probably McGinty's students at one point. You wouldn't get it. You don't live with it every day and do not know what's happening at school. He refuses to let a talented girl play on the golf team. He's gone out of his way to shun her when she can best any of his boys."

"So what? Isn't there a girl's team?"

"No, that's the problem. He's a complete idiot and ignores even the girls in his classes. I don't think they get an education other than how to keep their mouths shut in his class. He refuses to consider a girl on the team."

"There are other ways to handle a problem like that, and your choice was not viable or prudent. This was a rash act on your part."

"He looked scared and that's what he needed, a good fight."

"Then why didn't you challenge him to a pistol duel? That's about the equivalent of what you just did. Someone could have been killed and you arrested."

"I wasn't arrested and there was no damage to anyone."

“We’ll be responsible for fixing the yard and that damn putting green, Bernie. I don’t know what this is going to cost, but it seems to me that it’s going to cost more than money. You need to see someone about this rage of yours.”

“You’re just worried about your reputation.”

“I’m also worried about yours. You could lose your job over something as stupid and senseless as this. Good God, woman, what were you thinking? Never mind, you weren’t thinking. I’m shook right now and I don’t know what types of repercussions are going to result from this. I think we should not talk until we get home, people are staring at us and our voices are loud. I don’t want to create any more scenes.”

****

McGinty glared at her during the entire meeting and then started to stare down Brea. Bernie felt a strange kinship to Brea and Tasha during the meeting, but kept her eyes focused on Morgan. She never expected Morgan to mention anything and was surprised when he announced that the girls and boys would be participating in some mixed gym classes this semester. Bernie’s head sprang up, she met Brea’s eyes. Brea kept a stone face and Tasha smiled. Tasha said she could use some boys on the cheering squad if any were interested. Bernie had set in motion something, but what? Maybe she had peeled an onion layer.

The meeting ended and teachers either went to their rooms or out the door to their vehicles.

Bernie got a case of the shakes and headed home to change and then in search of Noir. She ran into her father in the barn and they just exchanged glances. It had been several months since the McGinty incident and they said nothing. Dad and Mom were used to her teenaged blowups and had not said a word to her about the use of the Bronco or Tony's edict about driving her car now, as though they approved of his supervision of her.

She saddled up Noir and headed to the woods. The ride didn't calm her much and Noir sensed her tension and was extra jiggy on the ride. It was a good hour and a half before she relaxed enough to calm the horse.

****

During the year there were times when the bathroom was a necessary trip and the teacher's restroom was occupied or full. Bernie would just use the girl's bathroom. She'd duck into a stall, get her business done and leave. It was impossible not to hear the girl's conversations as they smoked their cigarettes in the adjoining stalls. She wasn't one to say anything to the girls because she, herself, snuck a smoke once in a while at the farm. She had tried smoking in high school because it gained a little acceptance from the other girls; and she wasn't about to bust anyone. Where they got their underage smokes was none of her business and she didn't care.

One such trip allowed her to overhear a conversation between two girls. She thought she recognized the voice of one, but wasn't entirely sure. "Jake is getting a new Camaro from his grandfather."

"Really? Cool. How?"

"He's telling everyone that his grandfather sexually abused him when he was little. He figures the old man is too senile to deny it and he's going to tell everyone and have it settled by getting the old man to buy him a car to shut him up. He figures that the old man can't deny it because there's no proof. I'll be drivin in style with my man, let me tell you."

Bernie froze. What if none of this was true and the kid were blackmailing an elderly man? Who were these girls? She had to pay attention and listen; and then listen in class to recognize the voices. This wasn't something to be taken lightly. Child abuse was bad enough, but to blackmail someone for a non-existent act was the height of evil. She exited the stall and didn't even bother washing her hands. This was terrible and something had to be done and stopped before someone was indelibly damaged for no reason. Jake? Jake who?

The name Jake probably stood for Jacob. Which students did she know named Jacob? It was Thursday and she and Celeste milked tonight. She'd ask Celeste if she knew of any Jacobs who had girlfriends. The girls were famous for starting arguments and physical fights over perceived infractions concerning their boyfriends. Celeste knew more because she was more tuned in to the kids and paid more attention to the gossipy details between them. It was entertainment for her.

Bernie had a tendency to ignore the adolescent banter and was sometimes considered one of them because of her use of the bathroom and ignoring the cigarette issue. The door to the girl's bathroom had been removed years

ago to be able to see into it by passing faculty members. This was an effort to stop underage smoking and did little other than expose the tampon machine and clusters of girls in there. Sure, every girl with her menses wanted to be seen putting money in the machine by passersby. Few students complained about the smoke, but many complained about the bathroom door being taken off. Inexplicably, the door to the boy's bathrooms were left on, even though as much smoking went on in there. It was probably because the urinals were on the wall facing the door. It wasn't fair and it didn't stop the nicotine abuse. The female teachers should have been so discreet. It was obvious when entering the teacher's bathroom that someone had just finished a cigarette and flushed it. Bernie suspected Tasha as being the worst offender because Tasha often smelled like lingering smoke. The teacher's bathroom was on the second floor allowing Tasha easy access because her room was on the first floor near a staircase. Bernie would never have seen her walking past her room because they were on opposite sides of the building.

What students did in her lab when she was absent was another mystery; knowing how much trouble they can get into by just joshing around. Bernie thought she'd instruct her students to read a chapter and visit Tasha one day. *What excuse to use to talk to Tasha, though? Hmm, it'd better be a good one. Was there some famous scientist in their readings that she could connect somehow?* She'd be thinking about this. She just wanted to catch Tasha with a butt to her mouth. With luck the door would be unlocked.

Bernie wondered how many male teachers smoked and if it was as obvious in the male teacher's bathroom. Both had locks on the doors, even though they had two stalls. Being an adult and hiding a habit like that seemed foolish to Bernie, but Bernie was a closet smoker herself.

TWENTY SEVEN

Milking was done at 4:00 and finished in about two hours. Forty goats that gave a little more than a couple of quarts a day by mechanical means were not time consuming. The last half hour was the most strenuous because of the cleaning and putting away of equipment.

"Hey Celeste, I've got a new word for you."

"Yeah, what?" asked Celeste dipping teats and stripping them before attaching a milker.

"Trice."

"Twice?"

"No, T.R.I.C.E."

"What's it mean?"

"Insignificant."

"I think I know someone named Trice!"

"Well then, they're insignificant!"

"OK, how about 'dolt?'"

"Todd"

"Close enough."

When they finished washing up and putting everyone outdoors, they headed to the pump house for a game of Scrabble and a drink. "Any papers to grade tonight? Bernie asked.

"Nope. You?"

"No, or I wouldn't have suggested a game. I have an interesting piece of school gossip for you and wonder if you could help me fit the pieces together."

"Sure, I love my educational gossip. What's up?"

Bernie told her about the overheard conversation in the bathroom and stressed the seriousness of the potential situation. "Know anyone named Jake?"

"Yeah, two kids. Both just got their driver's licenses, too. But I can't tell you who is dating and who is not. I'll keep my ear to the ground and see if I hear anything about a new car, or see anyone acting close to a girl. Would you recognize the girl's voice if you heard it again?"

"Dunno. I thought I did when I heard this, but can't make up my mind now. I can tell you whoever it is smokes, though. I have one senior named Jacob, but I don't suspect him. He's very studious, very extracurricular and already has early acceptance to college. Who do you know?"

Celeste put her finger to her chin for a second,"Jacob Nash. Trouble maker, too. A junior this year, not serious about school, hangs out with a group of juniors and sophomores. Seems to be the ring leader, too. Doesn't

seem to be in any clubs or after school activities and just puts in his time. Doesn't apply himself to his work, just skates. Not real talkative, either, in class; slumps in a chair and exists."

"What makes him a trouble maker?"

"Fights."

"When? I never hear about this stuff. I don't know the kid, either."

"After school stuff. Townie, parents are supposedly alcoholics. Has a sister in tenth. Her name's Tamara and she's a pretty good student. They don't dress well and seem neglected. Who knows what goes on behind closed doors at home."

"Does he seem like the type to cook something like this up?" Bernie asked as she poured herself another glass of wine and put her letters on the board.

"Couldn't tell you. His writing is sketchy at best and he seems like the type they promoted to get him out of their hair. I just don't know enough about him because he doesn't participate a lot. From what I can tell, he does the minimal amount of reading or uses Cliff's Notes. He appears to know what he's writing about, but sometimes it's too technical for his demeanor.

"His sister is in one of my other classes and she is a good student. Seems like she could be better groomed, doesn't say much, either, but her work is very good."

"Keep your eye on him, OK?"

Bernie shuffled some letters around and told Celeste about smelling smoke on Tasha and that she'd been in the teacher's bathroom a few times and smelled smoke there as well. "Your room is right down the hall from Tasha's. Do you see her walking down the hall a lot during class hours?"

"Yeah. She leaves the kids to their experiments and walks past my door a lot."

"I just knew it was her. I wonder how much she smokes. I'd just love to catch her in the bathroom with a cigarette in her big mouth. I wonder if she'd be embarrassed or not."

"Why do you want to catch her? It's her business."

"We're supposed to be a smoke free environment. It's bad enough that the north corner upstairs reeks of cigarette smoke from the girl's lavatory, but Tasha should have better control."

"You're getting into someone's business that's not yours. Let it be."

"I'm just saying."

"Yeah, well, my friend, let her be."

"You sound like you're defending her."

"What she does is her business, not mine. As long as her kids don't blow up my side of the building, I don't care."

"I'm just being nosey. Besides, she irritates me."

"She irritates a lot of people. If you ignore her, she won't irritate you. I bet you irritate the hell out of McGinty!"

"You didn't need to bring that up."

"Why, it's hilarious. Out of control, but hilarious. A lot of people were afraid you'd be fired, but it was after school and on your own time. You didn't get arrested because your husband is a local attorney and well liked. I'm surprised at McGinty for not taking you on, though."

"Honestly? I think he was too afraid that day and he knew that the day was coming when someone was going to call him on his ways and methods. He's skating on thin ice, too."

"You could tell he wanted to cold cock you in that meeting last week. Then he turned his attention to Brea. What's the story behind that?"

Bernie filled her in on the eBay buying of golf clubs and what Tasha had told her. She also confessed to having a bad day thinking about it throughout school and outlined the sequence of events leading up to the moment of "impact." They hadn't talked about it earlier and Bernie had a few glasses of wine that loosened her tongue. Celeste was the type to accept her friendships when they came and not ask a lot of questions. Bernie was now talking a lot and the Scrabble game stopped. "It's really the first time I ever spoke to Tasha other than passing in the halls or at lunch time. She was pretty burned up about the entire situation. I didn't know that she and Brea had ever exchanged a word. I even wonder if they did, and it wasn't Todd who outlined it all for

Tasha. Those two spend a lot of time in the hallway talking."

Bernie envisioned Tasha standing with one hand on her hip and her leg outstretched. Like Todd, Tasha had an endless supply of stories and was always right about everything. Bernie thought the kids should refer to Tasha as the "rooster" because she crowed about every little thing.

"You know I didn't plan it that day, it just happened. I drove past the golf course entrance twice and I kept getting angrier. I knew where that son of a bitch lived because I'd passed his house so many times and have seen the boys out there. I just wanted to smash him in the face. It kills me that a good student and a talented athlete is forbidden from exercising her talents on an intercollegiate team. The other schools don't seem to have that problem, why us?

"I don't know what hit me that day. I just lost control and turned into someone else. I was so angry I was shaking, but I was in control of the Bronco and maximized my inner terrorist."

"After all the things you've told me about high school, I'm surprised you let loose. McGinty's been at this school a long time and he could have annihilated your career."

"I know. Want to know what's strange? I don't feel any remorse other than we had to pay for the repair of his lawn and putting green." Bernie could feel the vitriol rising again.

"Listen, Kitten, I've got to get home. Mike's coming in tonight from a big bridge job and I want to make him a nice dinner and sit curled up in his lap. I'm leaving. OK?"

"OK. Sorry to have unloaded on you. I just kinda felt like talking for a change. I can't talk to Tony any longer because he watches me out of the corner of his eye. He seems to be coming home later and later and saying less and less. We don't talk about school and we don't talk about his clients any longer since the McGinty thing. I'm just feeling lonely. You have a good night. I'll clean up here."

Celeste left and Bernie put another log in the wood burner. She poured herself another glass of wine and put the Scrabble board back. She sat in the near darkness just thinking. Nothing specific, just thinking. She sat long enough to pour another glass. "I need to eat something or I won't be able to drive home," she thought. "Screw him. He thinks he's perfect, let him get his own dinner for a change. It's leftover night anyway. Dad's got cheese and beef jerky here, I'll just eat that."

She felt sober enough to drive the two miles home after about an hour. The house was dark and Tony's BMW wasn't in the drive. "Damn good thing we don't have a dog that needs to be taken out," she thought. She let herself in through the garage, stripped off her clothes and dropped them down the chute and went up to shower. Before the shower, she found her box of wine and poured another glass. When Tony arrived he found her passed out in the bed with the reading lamp on.

TWENTY EIGHT

Friday morning did not start off good. First she had a wicked headache; second, Tony was not happy with finding her passed out. "You didn't answer your cell phone all night, what happened? He asked. "Did you go out drinking with the girls or something? I found you unconscious in the bed. Did you even bother to eat dinner last night? I called and left you several messages about bringing a pizza home for us. What the hell happened?" He was clearly agitated. "You were drinking and you know you're not supposed to be drinking with those medications. Where's your head?"

"I can have a glass of wine once in a while. I'm an adult and don't need you to make my decisions for me."

"You've been on those medications for several months now and you can handle about two glasses of wine, but you'd had a lot more to drink from the looks of it last night. I'll go make you some protein for breakfast and you'd better eat it if you want to make it to school on time and be halfway productive."

"Who do you think you are? My parent? Even my parents treat me more like an adult than you do lately."

"Bernie, when you start acting like an adult again, we'll treat you like one. Either you're out of control again or you've been hanging out with teenagers too long. Maybe this whole teaching thing was a mistake. Now I'm going down to make you eggs and sausage and some toast. I suggest you drink as much liquid as you can possibly hold and see if you can't get rid of what looks like a bad hangover. You ought to see the circles under your eyes."

A few minutes later he climbed the stairs with a huge glass of orange juice for her and put it on the bathroom counter. "See if you can't get some of this down. I'd give you a Bloody Mary, but you don't need to go to school drunk."

Groaning, she got out of bed and dutifully drank down the juice. She looked in the mirror and damned him because there were dark circles under her eyes. She wasn't known to wear a lot of makeup, but there was some concealer in a drawer somewhere. She showered, felt a little better and made her way downstairs to the kitchen. She was ravenous and consumed everything he put in front of her.

"You didn't eat last night did you?"

"Yeah, I had some cheese and beef jerky at the farm."

"Look, I'm going to be late, but I'll make you a protein shake to take with you. I suggest you drink it about two hours from now to see if you can stay sober enough to teach. I love you, but I don't understand you lately." He left for work. She wondered if he had bothered to eat dinner last night. She looked in the fridge and there was missing chili. She didn't feel so guilty.

Todd was either the only one to notice or the only one to comment on her appearance. "Looks like you had a bang up night there, Bernie."

"Mind your basketballs, Todd." This exchange happened outside her room before the changing of the tide (students moving from class to class).

Celeste cornered her at lunch, "You look like hell."

"Oh, not you, too, thanks very much. Todd said something already."

"What'd you do, stay and drink last night?"

"No. Well, yeah, and I didn't eat, either."

"You want me to buy you lunch?"

"No, I can handle it. Tony made me breakfast and a protein shake."

"Bernie, how much did you drink last night and what time did you get home?"

"I drank another glass or two of wine and waited to drive home."

"That's not responsible. Even if you drank, you shouldn't have driven home, but stayed at your parents'."

"Aw, Celeste, I got home OK. I just forgot to eat."

"No one forgets to eat! Did you drink more wine at home?"

“Hey, let’s not discuss this now. I’ll get a good lunch and make a good dinner. Tony’s upset with me, too. I don’t need another one on my case.”

Food was discussed often because they both loved to cook and the topic came up at least twice a week. Standing in the hall for the tide change, Celeste asked, “What’s for dinner tonight Bernie?”

“Beef Stroganoff.”

Todd, walking down the hall heard this and said, “Fancy Hamburger Helper.”

Both Bernie and Celeste turned in his direction and said to his retreating back, “Dolt.”

TWENTY NINE

Winter came and Bernie and Celeste were missing their Thursday evenings together. Cooking conversations and recipe exchanges were the more common topics. They decided to do the cookie swap thing, but bake at Bernie's house because she had more counter space and two ovens. After Celeste unloaded bags of ingredients and trays from her little truck they sat and decided on which recipes they would do and divvied up the kitchen. Celeste made Bernie laugh when she put on an apron. "I don't even own an apron. I just wear an old T-shirt. You're killing me, Betty Crocker."

"Hey, remember the conversation about a 'Jake?'"

"Yeah, did you find out who it was?"

"It's who I figured it was in the beginning. It's the Nash kid."

"How'd you find out?"

"Heard him bragging in the hallway about getting a new Camaro for Christmas. He was telling everyone he picked out his color and the interior and the engine and all that."

"When was this?"

"Today during tide change."

"Where were you?"

"I was headed up to the bathroom and he was on the landing with a group of other boys and a girl hanging on his arm. I'm not sure who the girl is, but she looks to be in middle school. I'm guessing an eighth grader. But, I don't have her in any of my classes this semester."

"Hmm, what's an eighth grader doing in the upstairs lavatory? I heard that conversation a few months ago. Those classes are mostly on the first floor with the exception of me, Brea and Charlene. Weird. Did you hear anything else?"

"No. I just mentioned it because you were so upset and it upset me, too. I finally confirmed it and wanted to let you know. Something needs to be done about this before it gets out of hand and someone is accused of something that didn't happen."

"Yeah, I know, but what?"

"Maybe you could talk to Tony."

"That's one possibility; if he'll listen. Lately he hasn't had much to say and a lot more people end up in court during holiday season than any other time of year. It has something to do with money, depression, arguments and holiday tension he says. He's really busy between Thanksgiving and New Years."

"This is the sort of thing that disturbs me about parental involvement. The Nash kid is a junior and someone is letting a potential 14-year-old daughter date a high

school kid. He's eighteen, by the way, he got held back in primary school. He got his driver's license almost two years ago. I just thought it was new because of the other kids talking about driving," Celeste mused.

"Sounds like you've been doing some digging."

"Yeah, well I was pretty upset the night you told me about this. It just makes me mad that I can't stop or prevent it from happening. I know I told you I heard his parents are alchies and I confirmed it the other day, when I went to the liquor store for some brandy for one of the cookie recipes. His parents were in there and they were falling all over the place trying to buy whiskey. He was sitting in their car because you have to be 21 years or older to enter the store. There's no doubt in my mind that they are bums. Makes you wonder about the girl's parents, too. I wish I knew who she was. I bet Tasha would know because she has all the younger kids for science. How to approach her without her opening her giant mouth is going to be a problem."

"Yeah, but she had to have this Jake Nash as a student at some point, too. You could ask her if he was a good student under the guise of his having potential and you wanting to know if he had any trigger points that lit his buttons in science class," Bernie felt good about this suggestion.

"That might just work. I'll do it. I'll tell her he's an underperformer and I think he's smarter than that. She's so nosy that she'd know who the girl is."

"Oh shit, we've been talking and I forgot to set the timer on these press cookies. Do you have any idea how long they've been in there?"

THIRTY

Celeste was successfully convincing with Tasha and it turned out the girl was Addison Turner, a 14-year-old overdeveloped underachiever in eighth grade. Her parents weren't overly supervising and never made it in for parent teacher conferences, so Tasha didn't know a lot about her, other than she was failing her science class.

Bernie got a bead on the Nash kid by someone yelling in the hall, "Hey, Jake, wait up." She turned and recognized the boy immediately. Flannel shirt, baggy jeans, dirty sneakers and dirtier hair in desperate need of cutting. Now she knew her target.

It hadn't snowed yet and Noir was getting ridden regularly after school. Tony was extremely busy in the office with a lot of small cases and court appearances in the county seat. Bernie would have loved to have shopped for and bought Tony a horse of his own, but he would never have time to ride it. The practice had mushroomed and his father was a regular part-timer in the office. They had all the work they could handle and the holidays made it exceedingly difficult on both families. His father was putting in as many hours as Tony and the Christmas spirit just didn't seem to be as

bright. Thanksgiving was split between the two families and seemed rushed and out of sync.

Between the Thanksgiving holiday and the Christmas break Bernie saw a group of boys standing around Jake Nash during tide change. She approached them and walked right into the middle of the group. "You, Nash, I heard about your scheme to get a new car by lying about sexual abuse as a child."

Nash's eyes got wide and he looked at the unfamiliar teacher in shock.

"Don't look so stunned, it's all over the school that you're lying to frame an old man who did nothing."

"Mind your own business, bitch."

Bernie lost it. She grabbed his grimy shirt and spun his ass around to face her. She was a lot stronger than she looked and her suit belied it. "What did you just call me?"

The kid's Adam's apple bobbed. "I didn't say nothin."

The group of boys scattered off to various classes and the hallway emptied, Bernie didn't let go of the shirt, which was now firmly attached to the arm she was holding in a vice-like grip. "I heard about your little plan and I also know you're 18 and boinking an under aged girl. They call that statutory rape in legal circles."

He tried to pull away from her and she grabbed his other arm and pulled both behind him. Standing at his back she put her mouth to his ear and said, "I am more than willing to go to court on both accounts and your

ass will end up in the slammer for blackmail and rape. Fun, huh?"

She released him with a shove, but not before another teacher, Todd, came up the stairs and saw them. "Bernie, what's going on? Did he assault you?"

"No, we were just having a very interesting discussion and I was straightening his shirt for him," she pivoted on her heel and walked down the hall.

It wasn't fifteen minutes before she was summoned to the office. Sitting in a chair was Jake Nash with a smug look on his face. "We'll see now, bitch," he said under his breath as she made her way to Morgan's office.

Bernie's adrenaline was up and she felt like screaming. Gene Morgan gestured to a chair. "What just happened in the upstairs hallway?"

"I stopped a case of blackmail."

"OK, that makes no sense to me. Expound. But, first tell me if you laid hands on that student sitting in the outer office."

"I grabbed his shirt."

"That's not what he tells me."

"Did he tell you I'm a bitch, too?"

"Listen, Bernie, I have to sort out stories here and I usually side with my teachers. You are in no way to lay hands on a student; he tells me you physically assaulted him in the hallway with witnesses."

"What witnesses?"

Gene sighed, "Look, let's not play games here. Did you lay hands on him?"

"Wanna hear a story?"

"Yeah, sure, I want to hear a story. Is it as good as the McGinty one I heard last summer?"

"Oh, that's low."

"Well, I know about it, but you have an exemplary record, so I chose to ignore it. This story had better be damned good."

He pressed the intercom button on his phone, "Chris, tell Jake to go to class and I'll see him tomorrow after his first class. Find out what class he's supposed to be in for second period and let the teacher know.

He turned back to Bernie, "So spit."

Bernie felt like a child and was surprised her feet actually touched the floor from the chair she was sitting in. "I'm not sure where to start, it's a two-fold story."

"Who's in your class right now?"

"No one, I'm sitting here."

Morgan pushed the intercom button again, "Chris, have Amy go proctor Bernie's class. Tell her to have them read the next chapter in whatever they're working in." He turned back to her.

"OK, I needed to use the restroom a few months ago and the teacher's was locked so I used the student lav. I overheard a conversation" She outlined the conversation and the puzzle about who the perpetrator was. She did not mention Celeste or Tasha and purposely did not mention Todd seeing the tail end of her pushing the Nash kid.

"I also know this kid is 18 and dating a 14-year-old girl. That's statutory in my book."

"We can't do much about attraction between the high school and younger kids. Yes, some of them are adult age, but it's going to happen and we have to rely on parental good judgment to prevent it. I'm like you, I don't want to see that happening, but there isn't much we, as educators, can do about it. The other story is a little more disturbing, though."

"Yes, we can. We can expose their little scams and games and let them know we are aware of them."

"Not to the point where we touch them in any way. This is a big problem. It used to be you paddled the hell out of the kid, called his folks and the problem ended until a new one got thought up. This is a different situation. He's accusing you of physically abusing him."

Bernie swallowed. "Does he have any proof? If he doesn't, then it's his word against mine."

"That would be fine, but you already have a reputation for a physical attack on a fellow teacher. It's not documented, but it's well known.

"Bernie, his parents aren't exactly pillars of the community. I know them through various channels and they are problem parents. They really don't care about their kids and they have a girl who is a model student. How, I don't know, but this situation is one I have to deal with and I don't know where or how to start. Did you pin his arms behind him and push him down?"

"No, I did not push him down." She toyed with the idea of telling the truth, but she knew she had crossed the line; an action that was drilled into them over and over. She thought back about the gym teacher in high school who had grabbed her by the collar and dragged her into her office. What had happened in that situation? No one had complained, so it went unreported.

"Did you physically lay hands on this student?"

"I grabbed his shirt."

"At no time did you physically touch him?"

"Do I look like I'm going to wrestle a monster like that?"

"That's not what I'm asking you. Did you physically manhandle him in any way?"

Bernie was trapped between the truth and the situation; she hung her head and said, "Yes, I grabbed his arm through the shirt."

"Christ. What am I supposed to do here? The kid is in perpetual trouble through fights inside and outside of school. I know he needs to be disciplined, I know the story you told me is true, but I don't know what to do. Usually we suspend a teacher for a certain amount of

time. That involves calling in a sub. Right now we have a librarian proctoring your class. Thank God, it's the last class of the day. I suggest you go home and think. I'm going home to think. I have to deal with this boy tomorrow and I don't want to lie to him, but at the same time I know the truth. I'm also wondering if I can trust you any longer. It's pretty obvious to me that he's a player. I'm surprised that he hasn't dropped out yet. His grades are deplorable, he has no adult supervision and he's about to commit a crime that is bigger than the school can handle. I'm in a huge quandary.

"You report for classes tomorrow like this never happened and I'll let you know what the decision is. I have your home number and we may have to discuss more of this tonight. Go back and dismiss your class. Be aware that this has already gotten all over the school because that kid is trouble on the hoof. He will exaggerate this to proportions we cannot even imagine. He's also one of McGinty's followers, just so you know."

"Oh great. Does he play on any teams that McGinty coaches?"

"Not that I'm aware of, but I do know about the McGinty situation here at school. That doesn't make it easier on you, I know, but I'm aware of tenure and the male clique up there. I don't agree with it, but I can't do a damn thing about it right now. For the record, when I heard the McGinty story I couldn't wait to meet you; and you're the only teacher I didn't meet over the summer because I didn't want to have any preconceived ideas. You present yourself as a classy lady, but I'm afraid you're going to mess someone's face up if you don't get

this under control. And, it can't happen here at school. Yes, I thought the whole thing was funny, but it's not funny when *I* have to deal with it.

"You are well aware that these are children. They do not make adult decisions. Your decisions right now do not appear adult-like. I can't say I wouldn't have wanted to do the same thing, but I have to restrain myself. I usually have to deal with the kids, not the teacher's behavior. Audrey has classes full of pregnant girls and she freaks just worrying about their futures. This is an entirely different situation and I have no idea which way to go. Would you consider counseling? I know that sounds harsh, but it sounds like you take on situations beyond your control in a vigilante way."

Bernie listened in thoughtful silence then said,"I don't know what to tell you. I manhandled the boy because of what he was doing to an old man. My husband is a lawyer and I know what happens to people once they are accused of sexual abuse to children. I didn't want that to happen to an innocent person and the kid get rewarded with what he most desires. I don't know this student from Adam, but I overheard his *girlfriend*'s comments. I didn't know at the time that she was only 13 and has just recently turned 14. This seems to me to be a cockeyed situation. I don't know what I'd do in your position. I'm angry right now because when I went to school, you did not tattle on teachers for your benefit. This kid needs to be quashed.

"I'll release my class and go home. I don't have any detentions today and I need to think about this. I am very sorry to have put you in this situation, Gene. I'm

sorry, myself, for being in this situation. Some things just set me off and that was one of them. It's been on my mind for a long time, too. I just didn't know who the person was and when I found out, I lost it. Again, I'm sorry."

****

"Tony, I need your help. I got myself into a situation today and I don't know what to do about it. It may be legal," She had called him at his office at the end of the day.

"Oh, sweet Jesus, what? You sound stressed."

"Could you come home early and have a glass of wine with me and I can tell you about this? I'm a little freaked right now and I really need your help and legal counsel."

"Bernie, are you OK?"

"Yeah, I guess so."

"I'll be right there. Do I need to stop at the store for anything for dinner? Can I take you out and get you out of there? You don't even know how your voice sounds right now."

"No, this should be discussed in private. I thawed a couple of pork chops and we have frozen vegetables and I will make a salad. I just need you home right now because I'm scared."

"I'll be right there."

They ate in the living room, sitting on the floor near the fire. Tony listened to every word; ranting and all. He was the old Tony. The Tony she dated, not the side glancing husband she had come to know.

"Bernie, this is out of my hands. There is nothing I can do for you; it's up to the administration at school and you better pray they are forgiving. True, the kid is trouble and it's only a short time before the girl gets knocked up if she's not on birth control, but that's another set of circumstances. What made you grab him in the first place?"

"After he called me a bitch, he was about to walk away. Classes had already changed and there was no one in the hallway because his friends beat feet out of there when I confronted him. He's 18, Tony, and he thinks he can get away with this. I've heard what happens to sexual offenders and I don't want the only decent person in his life to be labeled so he can drive a new car. Let him go out and get a job like my brothers did and earn a car."

"Yeah, I'm listening, but still this is not going to help you. You can have all the opinions you want, but you're not to touch a student. It's bad enough with the town talking about the McGinty thing from last year. I know that most of the people who have mentioned it to me agree with you completely, but what you did was wrong. This is wrong, too. I have no idea what to do for you and I can't give you any legal advice because, again, this is up to the administration. I just pray that Morgan lets this slide and you are not on probation or fired."

“I honestly thought I was doing the right thing. Todd saw me push the kid. He was coming up the stairs as it happened.”

“So there was a witness to part of this?”

“Yes, and I’m not Todd’s favorite person. We get into it over a lot of petty shit.”

“At this point, the story is going to be believed by all the kids and administration because of past events. You just bought yourself a label. Whether you wanted to do good or not, is not the point here. You have a label on your forehead.”

“Great, and I have the kids reading “The Scarlet Letter” right now.

“Look, let’s sleep on this and see what Morgan does tomorrow. He told you to show up to teach, so you show up and teach and we’ll pray that things level out. Bernie, I’m really concerned about you and think you need to see the doctor again; maybe get some counseling from a third party. You can’t go around falling on your sword every time some infraction happens. Do you want me to go with you?”

“God, no. I don’t need your input. It’s hard enough to face this bipolar stigma myself and be honest about it, without you adding your two cents.”

Tony sighed heavily. He started cleaning up the dishes and taking them to the kitchen. “Let’s just pray about this tonight and hope it gets better.”

School was strangely quiet as well as strangely noisy the next day. Students could be seen in little groups in the hallways during tide change. It was pretty obvious what was being discussed and why. Her students were very respectful, had their work done but the class discussions were not the usual rowdy and lively ones. Second period came and went, and she heard nothing from the office.

During the lunch period, she walked to the office to see if she could meet with Morgan. He was stationed outside the lunchroom and not in his office. She walked in that direction then turned around and headed back to her room. She didn't want to face him. At some point in the day, she knew she had to, but chickened out.

At fourth period Todd knocked on her door. She set the class to reading the last of their chapter and met Todd in the hallway. He wasn't wearing his usual laconic face and Bernie was on alert. "What's up?"

"Listen, I'm going to bat for you because I believe in what happened yesterday. I've been a coward and have known about this little scam for a few months. It's not that the kid is good or talented in any way and deserves a car or anything else he can get. I'm not your biggest fan, but you did what a lot of us wanted to do yesterday. I just want you to know I'm on your side.

Bernie was flabbergasted and didn't know what to say to him or even how to act. "Has the faculty been contacted about this and I don't know about it?"

"Yes, there is a meeting after classes today regarding your situation."

"Todd, is the McGinty thing going to come up, too?"

"Fred and I are coaches and we have to get along. I'm not all into his male clubiness, either, but I do have to get along with him. I really and truly believe that Chelsea was getting the short end of the stick with the golf team, but I have to get along with everyone. I'm not exactly who you perceive me to be. I thought the story about you and the truck was funny, but I couldn't tell him that. And I certainly wasn't about to tell your smart ass my feelings on that issue, either. He smiled at her.

"This afternoon is going to be rough because you're not going to be there and battle lines will be drawn. I know most of the faculty likes you, but you don't chum around with anyone but Celeste. I honestly don't know how many real friends among the faculty you have. I just wish you the best this afternoon and wanted to let you know that I'm going to stick up for you. It's not entirely you, either. Nash has caused a lot of problems in my classes and in the locker room. If I could, I'd get his stupid ass suspended so I could have some peace in my own classes. I even tried to be sensitive and teach the boys about meditation at one point. That was a total bust because the Nash kid thought it was an opportunity for a soliloquy from him.

"You looked surprised that I'd know that word."

Bernie laughed. "Well, Todd, you aren't exactly promoting the honor society on your end of the building; what'd you expect?"

"Yeah, well, like I said, you don't know a lot about me. Good luck this afternoon." He walked away and

Bernie stood in the hall looking in at her students for a few minutes. When she opened the door, every student looked up and stared at her. "Look, gang, I'm going down to the office for a second to make a phone call. I'll be right back. Think about what you'd like to discuss about the mindset of the people she has to deal with."

Bernie grabbed her purse from the desk drawer and headed upstairs to the teacher's bathroom. It was locked. She knocked. The lock clicked and Tasha opened the door. "Sorry."

"Tasha, we all know you smoke, you don't have to lock the door because I don't think you'll get busted."

"I know, but this is a smoke free zone and I just have to have my nicotine. I tried the patches and they don't work." Tasha's face changed, as though she realized who she was talking to and what was about to happen that afternoon.

Bernie immediately noticed it and made a mental note that this was not a friend. "Ah, Tasha, my kids are unusually sedate today and I just needed to make a private phone call. If you want, I'll head down to the phone booth. Just don't let Audrey catch you in here because she's the only one who will complain. I used to smoke as a kid here in this school and she once put her arm around me and asked me if I had been in the lavatory smoking. I lied and told her I had been in the lavatory and didn't smoke. I wanted her to think it was second hand smoke, but I know now she knew the truth because second hand smoke isn't as strong as a smoker's smell."

Tasha, usually the talkative one, just stared at her without interruption. "You used to smoke?"

"What, I look like an angel to you? I still sneak a smoke now and again. My husband doesn't even know."

Tasha was still staring at her when Bernie left the bathroom. She never made it to the phone booth and returned to her room. The discussion was its usual lively one and students debated character after character. *I really believe they read this stuff,* she thought to herself. About 2 o'clock her hands started shaking. At 2:15 she grabbed her purse and coat and left the building.

She didn't go to the farm and called and asked Dad to feed Noir for her. She said she needed some time to do a few things at home. Whenever she needed to think she would cook. She dragged out the mixer and soufflé dish and started the process for a cheese soufflé and added ingredients to the bread maker for a crusty loaf of French style bread.

Tony returned early again and they ate in silence in the kitchen. The fireplace didn't seem to warm the kitchen much and Bernie wasn't talkative. She put more wood on the fire and turned toward Tony. "I am very nervous right now and don't know what to say to you. They were having a meeting that I wasn't invited to after school. I don't know the outcome. I really want to call Celeste and find out what happened, but I'm a coward. I just don't have the nerve to find out right now.

Tony wasn't overly talkative, either. "I guess you didn't go to the farm today because you made a soufflé for dinner. It was good, thanks."

The phone rang and Tony answered it. "Yeah, she's right here, Celeste." He handed the phone to Bernie and went downstairs to the TV.

"Hello?"

"Are you OK? You sound tentative."

"No, I'm not OK. I'm nervous and edgy and in need of company and medical supervision. How's that for an answer?"

"Bernie, it was a terrible meeting. Everyone was yelling and arguing and Morgan had no idea how to control them. It's the first time I've seen him lose control of a meeting. He just sat down and let them go at each other."

"Do I have more enemies than I think?"

"You have more supporters than you think! Strange ones, too. Even Tasha stood up for you. Todd blew my mind when he said he agreed with your actions and wished he had done it himself to prevent you from having to take the fall. He just blew me away. Todd!

"Morgan found out that some kid had called the Police Department and told them everything. I guess it was bothering the kids, too. They dragged Nash into their offices and that's where he is right now. So are his grandfather and parents!"

"You're kidding me?"

"No, I'm dead serious. The whole thing came out; and so did the story about the girl. I think you'll be OK, but you're going to have to watch your back. I also suspect

it was one of your own students who called the law. Your students love you.

“What’s going to happen at school or at the Police Department, I can’t tell you. I wish I could. They can’t suspend the kid from school for blackmail, but they can prevent him from doing this to his grandfather. I have no idea what his parents are saying at this point.

“Bernie, are you there?”

“I’m here, I just don’t know what to say. What do I do next?”

“Nothing. It’s got to be embarrassing in light of the McGinty thing. McGinty was really loud, too. He said he should have pressed charges against you, but your husband prevented it. He said you were mentally and physically dangerous. That’s when Todd started in. McGinty and Todd aren’t speaking any longer, from the sound of it. You divided the entire faculty. Kresge even spoke up and told McGinty he was an ‘ass’ for the way he treated females. I’ve never heard her say a word before and I don’t think I will again. She was furious with him; so was Tasha. Tasha and Todd, go figure. What did you do to Tasha that made her defend you?”

Bernie told her about wanting to make a call and lied and said she wanted to call Tony. She was really going to call the doctor’s office. She relayed the conversation in the bathroom with Tasha. “I don’t want to speak too much because Tony can hear me downstairs if the TV isn’t really loud. We can talk about this later?”

"You have no idea how many people took sides against McGinty and how many defended you. It's like you're some sort of folk hero. I wouldn't want to be you tomorrow at school. What we thought was a faculty divided, is now a real division. Even the shop teacher told Morgan that he wanted to slap the shit out of Nash a few times. He was just surprised that anyone even attempted to."

"I have a confession. Todd saw me push the Nash kid, Celeste. I had his arms pinned behind him and then I shoved him forward when I let go. Todd was walking up the stairs. I'm just lucky that the halls were empty and kids were in class. I feel like an asshole right now and don't want to go back to school tomorrow."

"You have to."

"Yeah, I know. I better go tell Tony about this. What was the outcome, am I still teaching?" She asked as she doodled on the pad by the phone.

"Morgan didn't make any conclusive statements either way. He just told everyone to go home and enjoy their evenings. I think he got an earful just sitting there and letting them bash each other. I don't think he was surprised that you were the catalyst for all this, either. I'm betting you'll be called in for discussion, though, before anything is fully resolved. If I hear anything about Nash, I'll let you know. I don't know where I'd hear it, but I'll let you know. Get a good night's sleep; you're going to need it."

Bernie walked downstairs and relayed the information to Tony. He stayed quiet and looked thoughtful. "Honey,

I'm going to bed. I think I caused enough problems for a lifetime and I need to try to sleep. I'm expected at school tomorrow and I'm not looking forward to it.

"Did you tell your father anything about this?"

"No," he said softly, "I imagine it will be all over town tomorrow and he'll hear about it at lunch at the café." He turned off the TV and walked upstairs with her.

"I'm going to bed, too. I'm exhausted by all this. Bernie, we have to talk about this behavior. I know you didn't do anything really bad, but you know you can't touch a kid. Now you've divided a group of people who need to stand together over certain issues and be cohesive. What bothers me the most is you're off the hook again and are taking no responsibility for this. Sure, you're embarrassed, but don't suffer any consequences again. In my opinion, this is not good. You really need to seek counseling. Have you called your doctor?"

"Why do I need a doctor to have an opinion? I'm allowed to have opinions about certain issues. It's like you want me to be meek and quiet and not take any action against things I feel strongly about." She put her hands on her hips.

"You can feel as strongly as you wish about any subject you want, but you can't take anger out in physical action. You could have maimed or killed a man this past summer and you thought it was funny. It didn't help that half the female population of this town, including my mother thought it was hilarious. They just enabled you to continue. "Your behavior is not like that of an adult."

"Now you sound like Morgan."

"He's right, damn it."

"I'm going to bed."

"You do that, I'm sleeping in the other room. I'm not sure I want to be near you right now. I don't like sleeping with strangers. Good night."

THIRTY ONE

Thursday Bernie showed up at the farm even though she didn't have to milk. Dad was feeding hay in the sheds. He didn't look at her as she started breaking open bales and assisting.

"Daddy,"

He interrupted her with, "Look, I'm thinking right now and don't need any help. Thanks for coming."

"Dad, I really need to speak to you."

"Someone needs to speak to *you*, that's for sure. Today I heard about the latest incident at school and I'm not happy. What the hell has happened to you?"

"Nothing happened to me. I haven't told you or Mom, but I'm under a doctor's supervision."

"Yes, I already know about that. Your husband and I had lunch together here today with your mother."

Bernie froze. "What'd he tell you?"

"He filled in the details of the incident with the teacher at the end of last semester and told us about bipolar disorder. He called it Manic Depression and said it's usually hereditary. Apparently, he's been doing some

research. I understand you've been doing a little research yourself. He also said it starts to manifest itself heavily around age 30. He also told us about the student you accosted. He told us a lot of things. I'm thinking right now and your mother is in a panic about mental illness. We know Matt has a temper, but he's never done anything close to being arrested. Your mother is in denial and I'm trying not to be.

"My best advice to you right now is to go home. I have nothing to say because I don't know what to say."

"Dad,"

"Go home, Bernie. I don't think your mother is in any mood to talk, either. Just go home. I need to be alone. Oh, and I started to look up a few things and the alcohol in the pump house will be removed. I understand that's a form of self medication."

"What are you talking about?"

"Go home," his voice was firm and loud.

"What about Noir?"

"You didn't come dressed to ride and the weather is crappy. I'll take care of Noir. Her, I can predict. Now go home."

The meeting with Morgan included another woman. The counselor the school system used for troubled kids. Morgan introduced Cathy Jones and excused himself. Cathy was an attractive woman in the mid 30's with chemically streaked shoulder length hair.

"I usually don't have to speak to teachers, they refer kids to me. I'm a little uncomfortable here, but this school has indicated that you might need to speak to someone and they don't want to terminate your employment. Gene filled me in on the student and the accusation. He also described in his words what you told him after the incident with the student. I'm not sure where to begin with you or what you are thinking right now. Is there anything you'd like to tell me?"

Bernie wasn't expecting this and red flags went up. *Be careful what you say and how you say it.* She cautioned herself. *Go back to Chicago, you're a PR professional and you can handle this.*

"Well, Cathy, I'm not sure where to begin. First, I'm sure you're aware that Jake Nash is not my student, but I overheard a conversation concerning him wanting to blackmail a relative in return for a new car. Are you aware of these circumstances?" She threw the questions back at her.

"I'd really like to hear the story from your standpoint. I am not scheduled to speak to the student because the system doesn't consider it a school matter. Please tell me your story."

Bernie briefly outlined the overheard conversation in the girl's bathroom, the identification of the student and the shortened version of the incident in the hall. She purposely did not touch on the rage she was feeling when she approached Nash and his groupies.

"What were you feeling when you approached him?"

"Angry. I knew it was going to happen, it was months of knowing about it and it was confirmed that he was still going forward. I knew an innocent person was going to be labeled for life and I wasn't about to let that happen. He needed to be called out on his scam and motivations."

"You say you were angry; how angry?"

"Angry enough to confront him. How would you feel?"

Cathy was probably used to hearing students bitch about parents and restrictions and wasn't prepared for a question back. "I don't know how I'd feel. I'm not the one in the position you were in. Did you feel rage?"

"Define rage."

The woman was clearly getting upset and not expecting questions back. "I understand you physically assaulted the student."

"I grabbed his shirt."

"And you admitted to holding his person and threatening him with jail, from my understanding."

"Who told you that?"

"Is it true?"

"Yes, it's true. I told him that what he was doing was going to land him in jail. I also mentioned the under aged girlfriend and statutory rape."

"How did you feel while this was happening?"

"I felt angry, as I said before."

The questions were the same, the answers were the same and the interview came to no conclusion. Bernie told Cathy that if she felt she should talk to someone, she would be more than willing to speak to someone in the private sector, but was not comfortable with speaking with the same counselor the students were allowed to speak with. They parted amicably enough, but wary of one another. Bernie never mentioned the doctor or the drugs she was taking.

The doctor's office scheduled an appointment for Thursday after school. He greeted her like an old friend. "Skip the niceties, I'm mentally and physically out of control and sliding down emotionally."

She gave it to him full force, sparing no words or emotions. "The antidepressants aren't working and I'm enraged half the time by the stupidest things. Right now my husband and I aren't sleeping together, people are avoiding me and I'm depressed. It's affecting my work and my relationships with people as close as my parents. Do something. They had the kids' counselor meet with me at school. This is getting out of hand and I have no control over it. Right now I'm feeling bouts of road rage, too. Just getting here today was a chore. I'm throwing this in your lap."

"Very typical."

"What the hell is so typical? I am not myself. Hell, I don't even know who I am any longer. People look at me funny, I get mad over the smallest, pettiest things, I don't feel like doing my regular work and I fell no joy at all. I'm slipping here and no one is there to pick me up

at the bottom of this hill. And, you're saying 'typical.' What the hell is that supposed to mean?"

"How do you feel right now?"

"Hollow."

"Apt description for depression."

"Am I depressed? I feel pissed."

"I told you once before that I thought you were a mentally strong person. I think you fight depression with anger. When you feel helpless and hopeless, you get angry. This is called rapid cycling. You, my friend, are a rapid cycler. This means you go from up to down quickly. You're not going to like this because of the complaints about the weight gain, but we need to adjust and increase your meds."

"Oh great, I can't wait to be gorked out of my mind again."

"This too, shall pass."

"Say you. My parents aren't even speaking to me right now because they were told that this is possibly hereditary. My mom is in complete denial, but I remember her stories as a kid. She used to describe various family members who either drank a lot or did very weird things. I don't think what I did was weird; those incidents were set off by something that I could do something about. Whether my actions were prudent or not is up for discussion. My husband was the only person who knew I was seeing you. He went to my parents. This is ridiculous already. I am fairly newly married and he's

sleeping in another room. I don't want to be drugged out of my mind to keep him happy and me in some sort of stasis."

"Bernie, running someone over with a truck is not *prudent* behavior. Talking to them is a little more normal."

"Yeah, well you didn't have to see the pain he was causing a 15-year-old girl and a group of scared boys, too intimidated to say anything. Furthermore, he is not a person you can talk to or reason with. He sees nothing wrong with what he does or how he behaves toward students."

"At this point, I can only increase or adjust the medications. They work, but they take time to work. Your brain needs to basically rewire itself. The alcohol is not helping; it's acting as a depressant and keeping the drugs from working. How much have you been drinking?"

"I don't drink much," she lied. "I have a glass or two of wine with dinner and occasionally an aperitif."

"You've never drunk so much that you passed out and couldn't remember how you got there?"

"No," she lied again.

"Alcohol on these medications is very dangerous and can spin you out of control. You don't sound like you are in complete control now, but you don't sound like you've been drinking, either. I'll be completely frank with you, but most bipolar sufferers lie about their

alcohol consumption. It's a quick and legal solution to just pass out from too much and forget their actions or reactions."

"So, no wine with dinner?"

"Right, no wine with dinner. Try some juice or water flavorings. Many of my patients find that these are good substitutes. If you want, drink them at room temperature and it feels like you have a glass of wine."

She just looked at him with nothing to say. No wine with dinner, no after dinner drinks, no parties, no holiday imbibing. Would people think she was pregnant? Did people expect her to be pregnant? Would Tony ever want children who could inherit this?

"Drinking on these medications will only exacerbate the effects of the meds. You'll also be more intoxicated."

"I've been drinking almost as long as I've been smoking. I drank a lot with my friends in college and can't even play a game of Scrabble without a drink."

"If you want to get better, there needs to be lifestyle change."

"Do you drink?"

"Yes, I have wine with dinner and the occasional drink with friends."

"So how would you feel if someone told you that you could not longer do that?"

"That's not the question here."

"Answer me."

"OK, it's social and I enjoy it, but I'm not taking the medications you're taking."

"That's not an answer that's a deflection."

"You're right, it's a deflection. I, however, am not taking the medications you are prescribed, and you can't medicate yourself with alcohol. If I were on those medications I wouldn't drink because I know the repercussions. It's that simple, Bernie."

Her drugs were increased and the side effects started again. The biggest was the weight gain. It was hard enough to zip and button her suit pants and skirts without increasing the dosages and gain more. Hating to shop wasn't helpful, either. She had gained 15 pounds when she began the medication and the thought of buying bigger sizes wasn't making her any happier. The gain had her more depressed than events happening around her. It never occurred to her that her alcohol consumption was adding calories. She did not stop her wine at dinner or while cooking.

Things settled down at school and with Tony. He was sleeping in their room again and they discussed her latest doctor's appointment. She did not mention the alcohol, but he did. He'd been doing Internet research on self medication and started in on her when he saw the wine glass on the kitchen counter while she cooked dinner.

"You're not supposed to be drinking."

"It's just one glass of wine."

"And, you'll have another with dinner."

"So how can two glasses of wine hurt me?"

"I know it's not one glass of wine because our garage has a pile of wine boxes against the wall. You didn't bother to hide them. Are you taking them to recycling or am I?"

"I don't have anything to hide because I've done nothing wrong. I disagree about a glass of wine now and again."

"Bernie, it's not a now and again thing, it's a continuous drink from the time you arrive home until the time you hit the sack. How can you even grade papers in that condition?"

THIRTY TWO

The hollowness was ubiquitous. It wasn't just inside; it was in everything outside, too. Lack of energy, but restlessness for something to happen, something to take her away from the lowness. People didn't live up to expectations, weren't interesting; their lives, too, were boring and nondramatic. People and life in general was just plain empty.

Chores, routines and tasks were just that, routine, rote, done by auto pilot. There was no sense of fulfillment, excitement or creativity. Even cooking had become mundane and unexciting.

Noir stood in the pasture or the stall. Hay, grain and water were "administered," but not given with any sense of care or vigor. Bernie even forgot to see if her salt block needed replacement. The horse became the charge of Dad.

It was the restlessness that was the most irritating. Having been used to being on the move a lot, Bernie found herself listless, and tired all the time. Conversations at work and home were lacking and short. Wine boxes piled up in the garage. Tony spent more time at the office and late nights, too. He didn't help the situation

with engaging conversations and Bernie felt abandoned as well.

Cappy came to start the winter cleanup of the property. She raked, pruned, trimmed, and edged for the last time.

"Hey, Cappy, want a beer?"

"Yeah, that sounds about right."

They sat on the deck and each hoisted a bottle to the other. "Cap, you ever get down and can't get back up?"

"You mean fall on the job?"

"No, more like feeling blue."

"Ah, I guess, but I've got a pretty busy life and business. Our daughter is 14 now and Dotty and I keep her busy all the time."

"Oh."

"Why, you feeling bad?"

I want to take a self defense course to beat the living, shit out of someone. "Here, take this and this and this. The lovely impact of flesh upon flesh. The spurt of blood, the swipe of sweat, the splurge of possible pieces of skin peeling off. Splatter."

Cappy just looked at her, finished her beer and left Bernie sitting on the deck.

THIRTY THREE

The winter and holiday season passed and spring kids were born. She started milking again on Thursday afternoons. Celeste was ecstatic to be back in the barn. Since Dad did most of the regular chores, their only job was to feed, milk and clean up on Thursdays. The pump house was the retreat and Celeste noted that the liquor bottles had been removed. Bernie had brought a box of wine from the trunk of her car and a bottle of Jack for Celeste. She just had to remember to put take them away when they left in the evening.

It snowed a lot that winter. Not driving the Bronco had caused her to have to fight unplowed roads to the farm. She felt this was not a good use of the car and she was ruining it by wearing her barn clothes. She hung her overalls on a hook in the milking parlor and put them on over her jeans when she got to the barn to keep the seats cleaner, but she wasn't about to put on a freezing pair of boots at the barn and little bits of hay and debris found its way into her car.

She and Celeste were close to finishing when they heard a car crunch on the gravel drive to the milk house. There was just enough melting snow on the ground to hear a car pull in.

"Oh crap, looks who's here." Celeste waved at her.

"What's this about?"

"I don't know, but I don't like it at all. For Christ's sake, she's come to a barn." Celeste was looking out the window. "What does she think she is going to do, help us? She's wearing freaking starched jeans, good boots and a sweater."

Bernie met Charlene at the entrance to the milk house because that's where the lights were on and it was obvious this was where the activity was. "Hi Char, what are you doing out here?"

"The whole faculty is talking about your love of farming and your horse. Can I see your horse?" Everyone wanted to see Bernie's horse as though it was some unicorn, rare and special, like they'd never seen a horse before. Bernie had no problem "showing" her horse to anyone who wanted to see because Noir was big and black and showy.

"Sure, I'll introduce you."

"Oh, I'd love that."

Bernie walked Charlene through the various barns until they came to Noir's stall. Noir was completely uninterested in visitors because it was feeding time and she was yanking out mouthfuls of hay, her butt to the stall door.

"Oh, she's so big. I didn't know horses were so large."

“*Duh, dipshit,*” Bernie thought, “*You thought they were as large as goats and sheep*?” Bernie inwardly sighed because she didn’t get to say aloud what she was thinking.

“Well, she’s not that large, she’s sixteen hands, but she has bearing and it makes her look larger.”

“What’s bearing?”

“She’s full of herself and she knows she’s adored.”

“She’s taller than me, that’s for sure.”

“*Anything is taller than you, except Celeste.*” Bernie considered saying.

“What’s a hand?”

“A hand is approximately four inches and it’s how people used to measure horses. It stuck in the modern world and is used to describe how tall they are at the withers.”

“What’s a withers?”

“Her withers are the point of her shoulder blade. They measure them from the shoulder to the ground, or the ground to the shoulder.”

“So, if my calculations are correct, four inches times sixteen is 64 inches tall, but she looks taller.” Leave it to the math teacher to instantly calculate the math.

“She looks taller because she still has a head she holds up on her neck.”

Charlene turned her head from gazing at the horse to Bernie and said, “I can see that.” Her voice indicated

that she knew she was being condescended to. Bernie was growing bored with Charlene and wanted to get back to the chores.

"Char, I need to get back to milking because it's a favor I do for my father on Thursdays. Do you mind?"

"Oh, I'm sorry, I didn't realize there was a schedule to this. I can help if you want me to.

"Why is she wearing that thing?"

"It's a horse blanket. It both keeps her warm and clean so I can ride her with a minimum amount of grooming beforehand."

In the pump house pouring their drinks Celeste said, "I thought it was hilarious you setting her to washing up. Bet she never comes back after all the splashing water and milk residue. I even bet she ruined her outfit with Chlorine. Can you imagine her out here with us regularly?" Celeste was laughing and obviously excited.

"I didn't know what else to do with her and she wasn't about to leave. We couldn't even have a conversation with her standing there.

"She is conniving and talks behind backs. I wonder what she says about me when I'm not around. I don't trust her at all. I was even afraid to mention any of the kids because she's the type to use information against them.

"I bet she was surprised to see you out here milking. That will be the talk tomorrow. Plus Noir lifted her tail and farted in her direction."

"Don't care, I love this job. If I could, I'd have a goat as a pet."

"Celeste, do you have any pets?"

"We have a fat old cat that doesn't do much; he doesn't even play any longer. Mike lets him sit in his lap when he's home, so I guess you could say he likes him. We talked for years about getting a dog, but I really don't know much about dogs because we neither of us had pets as children."

"Why don't you and Mike have kids, if you don't mind me asking?"

"We tried for years and found out that Mike's swimmers aren't very good. I'm so overweight that it would probably be a high risk pregnancy if I were to get pregnant. I really need to go on a diet. I'm not very good at diets."

"I've never been on a diet in my life because my lifestyle was so active. Now I have to."

"Yeah, I didn't want to say anything, but you've gained weight this year."

"Ah, Celeste, I haven't been telling you everything lately. I had a major life change last year. Some of the things that happened at school were the result of something I cannot control by myself. I have bipolar disorder and I'm on medication right now. Its biggest side effect of the meds is weight gain."

"Why didn't you tell me earlier? We talk about everything else."

"I was embarrassed and confused. I really don't want anyone to know about this. You'll keep my confidence? Even with Mike?"

"Sure. What is that exactly? I've heard of it before, but wouldn't know how to recognize it or what it does."

"You're my closest friend, so I'll just tell you straight. It's a mental illness. I'm mentally ill and need medication to keep me stable and from doing things like what happened at McGinty's. They say your brain neurons don't fire properly and they get crossed. It causes depression and it causes manic episodes. There are various levels of it. I got from high to low very quickly. Things that depress me also make me angry. The doctor I'm seeing says I fight my depressions with anger. He also calls it a chemical imbalance.

"A lot of times you see it in teenagers, but mostly the depression. Sometimes it doesn't really show up until your 30's and gets out of control. I was starting to get out of control. I didn't consider my behavior a fault or a problem. All I see is something that is happening and no one doing anything about it. Like the whole issue with Chelsea and the golf team. McGinty's personality and behavior toward women doesn't help either. He really should be teaching, if that's what he does, at an all boy's school. He's such an old fart with farty old ideas. I don't like the way he treats his wife either." Her speech was getting excited and rapid as she went off on this tangent.

Celeste just sat quietly and listened to Bernie's extended tirade about McGinty. She hardly moved and barely sipped her drink. She just stared at her friend in the semi-darkness of the little room. She'd seen and heard

Bernie's speeches like this before, but this one seemed especially passionate and loud. She seemed more agitated and irritable. Of late, Bernie had been less patient with people and animals. Celeste noticed that Noir wasn't getting her usual attention and that Bernie hadn't ridden in quite a while.

"Bernie, are you depressed right now?"

"I don't know."

"You are talking fast and you seem to be agitated."

"I'm writing a book on the seven habits of the highly irritable.

"Yes, I'm depressed. I've gained weight, my mouth is always dry, I feel out of touch most of the time and it's all due to the drugs they have me on. Plus my father has gotten on me about drinking in here. Tony is on my case about it too because I'm not supposed to drink with these prescriptions. I'm getting frustrated with everyone who wants to control my life, and, if I do have an opinion it's suddenly the illness talking. I'm no longer allowed to have opinions or get worked up about anything." Bernie rambled for another ten minutes and managed to down three cups of wine. Dad had removed the wine glasses and only left the old coffee cups.

THIRTY FOUR

A green mist over the landscape seemed to appear overnight as the months got warmer and April approached. By the end of March the serious snows had stopped and the girls were in full Thursday swing as the sky stayed lit longer. Bernie had adjusted to the upped dosages of the medication, but didn't feel as though she was fully functional; she still felt slowed down as though life were an exercise in swimming through pudding. At her last appointment she was told this feeling would also wear off. She considered changing doctors, but didn't want to go shopping for psychiatrists. It has been almost a year and she felt she wasn't any different from her starting point.

Noir, having been somewhat neglected and stalled most of the winter was full of excess energy. It took a few weeks of lunging before rides were possible without incidents and spooks. Since Bernie has always ridden in the prior winters, Noir was not used to being idle in the past and Bernie had to earn her right to ride the high strung mare again. Noir expressed herself by being slightly girthy and fidgeting during saddling. It was a good month before she settled down enough to be trusted to not bolt off when mounted. Noir was not a patient horse and Bernie's legs and seat were not up to par. There were rides that made her sore again.

They came out of the woods to a clearing with large, flat limestone outcroppings and Noir nickered. Bernie had never heard Noir make much noise other than at feeding time. She scanned the edge of the woods and saw another horse and rider. Two thoughts came simultaneously. She heard her father's voice in her head about not wanting riders on the property and she got angry that someone had invaded her space. She rode up to the other horse.

"Hi neighbor" a beautiful tenor voice said.

Bernie stopped for a short second and then met the other horse face to face. "This is private property and you're not supposed to be riding here."

"Oh. I thought this was part of the woods I ride." The man was blonde, blue eyed, wearing a hat and mounted on a chestnut wearing a western saddle. His plaid flannel shirt was open at the collar, showing a little bit of blonde chest hair. He was also wearing a pair of chinks like some cowboy.

"No, this is private property, as I said, and no riders are allowed here. My father doesn't want his land ridden on and his fields torn up by other riders. How in the world did you get in here, anyway?"

"There's a fence gap in the woods back a ways."

"Where? I made these paths and I know just about every inch of Dad's land."

"Look, lady, I'm sorry. I didn't know I wasn't supposed to be here and I'm not entirely sure where I am. I'll let my horse take me back."

"Back to where?"

"Where I board him at Brinker's."

"Who are the Brinkers?"

"They live down state road 17."

"I've never heard of them. Their property doesn't back up to this land. You've ridden quite a way then."

"I've been riding about two hours. It's just nice to get back in the saddle after this past winter. I'm sorry about the trespassing. My name is Jack Reems and this here is Red."

"Very original name."

"Yeah, well he's red," he didn't seem apologetic or embarrassed by her sharp words. "That's a beautiful horse you've got there."

Always delighted with her trophy horse, Bernie warmed a little. "Her name is Noir. Thanks. We didn't ride much this winter and she's getting used to being back outdoors. We've never encountered another rider out here before because the land is posted. There were no posted signs where you got in?"

"Really wasn't looking, to tell you the truth. I just followed a deer path this way and into these woods. The gap I came through must be the property line, but the posts are rotted out and have fallen down."

"I'll have to check that. You best be on your way before it gets dark." She turned Noir around and rode away.

"It was nice to meet you Noir," Jack Reems said to her back. Bernie didn't acknowledge or stop.

Neither did she mention to her father about the rider in the woods when she saw him in the barn after she put Noir away and fed her. Kidding season was close to over and full milk production was up. The chores had increased and her father was always busy. She could have offered to help clean up, but was still angry with him about the liquor conversation and she knew she'd be here on Thursday, so she just got in the car and left.

There was no awareness on her part of how rude she had been to the other rider. But, she did think about him and puzzled over how he had gotten through fence lines and who was boarding a horse for someone she'd never heard of before. He was a good looking man and the horse he was riding was not bad, either.

At home she immediately started dinner. Tony was coming in earlier in an effort to spend more time with her. Bernie felt it was more a supervision effort than wanting to be with her. She felt he was overly critical of all actions, thoughts and comments from her. After dinner he would go downstairs to the TV or read. She spent time on the computer or in bed with a book after dinner was cleaned up. They existed in the same house, but she felt caged and studied.

I don't have a life any longer other than school and goats," she thought. They talked through dinners, but he made no effort to not drink a glass of wine with his. Not fair. This whole bullshit thing is not fair. I made the effort to diagnose myself and the least he can do is honor my efforts. It's like he's throwing this in my face.

I didn't choose to have this problem. Maybe I don't have a problem and it's his perception. No one else mentions it, other than Dad because Tony went to him and Mom.

The anger she felt toward Tony started her on a slight upswing again. It was not something she could sense. There was only a vague feeling of anger and hurt, like he was making fun of her. It wasn't mentioned. Bringing up the subject would only bring up feelings of guilt about the Thursday night drinking and the bottle of Scotch hidden in her closet. It was nice to have a glass of Scotch while reading. He couldn't tell because he would take his second glass of wine downstairs with him so she hid her glass under the bed. *Like Tony would ever look under the bed. He certainly couldn't smell it on her if he had wine with and after dinner.*

I need to get out and meet some people again. I'm boring myself to death with Celeste and goats and other teachers. Thank God for papers to grade and books.

****

Typical of schools, there were always clubs, activities, science and book fairs and sports to keep the kids occupied. Bernie never volunteered for any of the after school activities because she had Noir. Tony never missed a home football or basketball game; she didn't attend with him. He was a booster and his practice had banners at the games. He also sponsored two softball leagues. His job introduced novel and new things to him daily and he met with a variety of people. Bernie's life, by comparison, was static.

She continued her visits with the doctor and refilled her prescriptions in Ann Arbor. Although she shuddered each morning about teaching the children of the very people she went to high school with, she continued to go. Her students were the only brightness on her horizon. They kept her laughing, kept her challenged and were worth the effort of getting out of bed.

Dietary changes happened in her house. She still cooked delightful meals for Tony, but ate smaller portions and took a salad to lunch with her. Her breakfast consisted of instant oatmeal. Mom had made oatmeal every morning of her schooling that she could remember and she developed an abhorrence of it. Putting a spoon into something gray didn't much excite her. She knew that it would sustain her eating urges, keep her full and was fibrous enough to not make her want to overeat at lunch. It wasn't easy to find a brand of oatmeal that she could stomach, but she finally found one at a health food store in Ann Arbor. Because of the included Flax, it smelled and tasted different. Her wine was cut down to one glass a day at dinner. Her official diet had begun. If the medications were not going away, she was still going to fit into her clothes. As much as she disliked jogging, she purchased a pair of running shoes and started out walking and then running when the weather allowed it. Tony joined her in the morning jaunts. They shared an activity in common again.

Celeste, too, became motivated and felt that she had become stronger and more toned by milking on Thursdays. She started on a similar diet, minus the running shoes. She wanted to know if Carl needed any help on other nights, but he insisted he didn't. She had

finally met him late one winter night around kidding time. He told her how grateful he was to her for her help and her friendship with Bernie. Celeste was in awe and developed a crush on him.

Tony relished the morning runs and Bernie hated them. It was just good discipline to do it and she needed to counteract the effects of the antidepressant on her waistline. She felt as though she'd like to paste that bumper sticker on the rump of her running sweats: "I'd rather be riding."

Noir was getting back into shape, becoming a more willing and obedient partner and actually wanting to explore her riding environment again. Bernie rode every day except Thursdays and on Sunday mornings if Tony was going to be in the office for a short period of time. It was on one of their rides that Bernie remembered the man in the woods and went looking for the spot she had met him at the edge of the property. Like most wooded areas, there were deer paths and trails laced across. Finding the one he had mentioned seemed an impossible task. The pair did more standing around and side passing than riding. She found it at about rider height in a tree. It was a pink piece of flagging tape tied to a branch. Visible under the plastic tape was a deer trail.

She and Noir edged their way into the narrow space and cautiously walked the weaving trail to the edge of the barbed wire fence that was the property border. Little paths led off and she wasn't entirely sure where to look for the gap he had mentioned. She was also concerned about getting stuck between trees and Noir's general

resistance to backing up. This was serious trail riding because the horse needed to perform maneuvers like a seasoned trail horse, not the walk trot pony she had become. *I need to follow the largest and most used path because that's where a horse would easily get through. Stay off the smaller narrower paths and I'll be able to get back.* It never occurred to her that she could get lost.

The widest path led to a barbed wire fence and a "gap." Gaps were old fashioned gates made with a moveable post and looped barbed wire that hooked on the loose post. One moved the post back to the supporting pole and dropped the moveable post into the bottom loop and took the top loop and hooked it around the post, closing the gap. The gap was still open and the posts were, indeed, rotted as the man had indicated. She managed to get Noir to turn around and they headed back to the barn to look for something to replace the post. She also wondered again about the man, whose name she could not recall. Again, she did not mention him to her father when she returned. She did, however, go looking in the post pile for two cedar posts that she could use to fix the gap, borrowed some old barbed wire and the fence tool and took the four wheeler. The four wheeler was too wide to get through the path and ride over fallen trees. She parked it and walked down the path to the gap. Noir had been placed in her stall with her dinner and there was just enough light for her to get back.

She again noticed another pink plastic ribbon near the gap on the other property marking the trail. Hoof prints indicated someone had been there recently and it was a well worn trail across the aging fence. He had marked that side of the fence to find the place again or to warn

him not to enter the path. Now her curiosity got the best of her and she walked through the hole in the fence and wandered down the trail a little way. The sun was beginning to wane and she decided that it was time to head back. The barbed wire had proved too thick to cut with the fencing tool, and she had brought no staples to attach it to the cedar posts she had carried back there. One more post was needed and some sort of wire that could be cut and worked with. She left the two posts, found the four wheeler and returned to the barns.

Carl was milking and she fell in step beside him. It was Tuesday and she really didn't want to immediately go home. She needed to find where Dad kept his larger and stronger tools. There was very little barbed wire on the farm because they had built goat proof fences. "Wiley little suckers," Dad had said when they were building pastures, "They can get over or under anything. They can even jump up and out." They had strung an electric wire on the top board to discourage the more ambitious ones. This was the wire she decided to use, but had no idea, since the building of the fences, where any left over might be kept. She'd need to do a little investigating in the barns.

Bernie decided that washing udders and putting bag balm on them after milking was the most useful job she could do that evening for her father. This was the most time consuming activity and it was appreciated because milking got done early and Dad had only to wash up the equipment and clean the milking parlor. Bernie left for home about 5:30. Dinner would be easy because she had chicken breasts and lemons and capers and she could make him a scaloppini and a salad and he'd be in heaven. Veal was too expensive and not available in the local grocery store. If she wanted veal she'd have to pick it up in one of the better stores in Ann Arbor and she wasn't due to return for a month.

Tony appeared through the garage door and said, "Smells like goat in the mud room."

"Oh, yeah, I was out on trail longer than usual and felt sorry for Dad, so I helped a little in the milking parlor. You really need to come out and see for yourself sometime. You drink the milk, but you don't know where it comes from and you haven't met the nannies or seen the kids. I think it's about time you wrestled yourself from your desk and got a different kind of education. Any day but Thursday would be good. Celeste and I like our gossip time on Thursdays."

"Well, I'm not exactly a farm animal person, but it seems to be a big part of your life and I'll do it for you. Will I smell like goat when I return?"

"No, we don't expect you to do anything, just observe the process. Besides, you don't have any clothes we could put you into that could be ruined by the disinfectants. If we get clingy visitors, we make them wash equipment!" She told him about Charlene's visit.

He laughed at her penalty job description. "Dinner looks great. I'm going to get the monkey suit off and be back. Why don't you dispose of the goat smell in there." Before putting the chicken in the pan she dutifully grabbed her old jeans, socks, sweatshirt and T-shirt and shoved them down the laundry chute.

After school the next day she returned to the farm and found what she needed to make a new gap for the fence and took off on the four wheeler. She hiked back into the area and made new loops, dug up the old posts and put in three new ones and strung wire. It was finished and she was wiping mud off her face when she saw the horse coming through the woods. She was just about to haul the shovel, sledgehammer, post hole digger and tools back, but stopped to watch. He didn't see her at first, but the bright pink jacket she was wearing gave her position away.

"Hi again Noir's mommy."

"Ah, yeah, I guess I never told you my name. It's Bernie. I can't remember yours, though."

"Jack."

"How was your ride today, Jack?"

"Lovely, as usual. I really like this trail I've discovered and have been riding it regularly."

"I see you marked the gap and the property line for me. I fixed the gap."

He smiled down at her from his position on the chestnut horse and said, "Well, I guess you were very serious about not being on the property."

Bernie pursed her lips slightly and said, "I can't say that I always like riding alone, but my father has some very severe prejudices about horses and his property. It took him nearly three years to get used to the idea that I owned a horse and two years for him to accept her on

the farm here with his goat herd. He doesn't want his hay fields ridden on and doesn't want manure in his hay. At least he lets me keep Noir here and I don't have to board off the property. He has been good at taking care of her when I'm not around for one reason or another.

"No offense intended, Red." She reached up and stroked the horse's forehead.

"He's a fine looking horse, what is he?"

"He's Appendix. Half Thoroughbred and half Quarter Horse. He was bred for barrel racing, but never got that far because I bought him as a two-year-old and trained him to just trail ride. I imagine he's got some speed on him, but it's never been tested. I'm a trainer and I just wanted a nice looking, level-headed horse for my own personal down time."

"Where do you train?" She squinted at him through the fading low sunlight."

"I'm the resident trainer at Thousand Pines in Jackson. It's a hunter barn. I'm the only western rider, but they don't know that because I work with the hunters. This is my little secret. I am allowed to have a horse over there, but I like having my own space and time. I get off at two o'clock each day and travel over here to take a ride when I can. Me and my family live on the premises."

"How do you get out of work at two?"

"I start at four."

"Oh," was all she could say. It made sense; basically an eight hour day.

"Do you teach as well?"

"Nope. I just train. Most of the students start coming in after school."

"Sounds like the barn where I started in Illinois."

"Are you originally from Illinois?"

"No, I worked in Chicago and got started with a group of adolescents."

"Do you work on your father's farm?"

"Yes and no." She was wary of giving the good looking blonde too much information about herself.

"Sorry. I was being nosey. When you took off your gloves I noticed that your hands aren't exactly farm worker's hands."

She blushed. "I'm a teacher now. I teach here in Cold Lake and help my dad on the farm when needed. I milk on Thursdays, so I don't ride on Thursdays or Sundays unless I get a chance or it's not milking season for him.

"I've got to go because I have to feed Noir and get back to the main farm before dark. Nice to see you again, Jack and, you too, Red," she turned and walked off carrying her tools with her through the woods.

Celeste invited her over for dinner Wednesday and she accepted. She had made lasagna not realizing that the best Italian meals were eaten at the Romanelli's. The meal was good, though and Bernie enjoyed sitting at the kitchen table with Celeste and talking. There was

one bottle of red wine and after it was finished Bernie wanted more.

"I never heard any more about the Nash kid, but I know he doesn't have a Camaro or a Mustang or any hot car right now. I never did find out what happened at the Police station. Never heard a word," Celeste said.

"I haven't heard any more either. It would have been so easy for the school board to terminate me. It's hard being a teacher because you can't correct anyone's kid or make changes other than setting an example for them.

"Have you seen the girl around at all?"

"Nope. I haven't seen her in quite a while. They may well have transferred her into another system. I can't worry about that because I have my own kids to work with. Funny, though, we haven't heard anything since and you still have a job. I think that did go to the school board, though, and they decided you were not detrimental to the kids' welfare. You were lucky. I was really surprised that Todd stood up for you. I can't wait for the next meeting to see what happens and the subjects that are discussed," she said.

"Tony's still angry. He watches me like a hawk. I feel like he'd hide the knives if he could. He doesn't trust me any longer and I do not trust him because he went to my parents with the story of the incident. I just wish we could get it back on a level playing field at home. I miss his sense of fun. He usually goes downstairs now after dinner and I'm left reading a book or grading papers.

"Hey, I just started a journal with my classes. I'm trying to get them to relate to the fictional characters they read about. It's interesting because they do relate to them in a modern sense. They find some of the ideas old fashioned and that's where we have our best discussions about a writer's voice depending on the era."

"I'd like to do something like that, but we are still in the grammar and punctuation phase of things. We do read a few books, but mostly it's short stories for them. I have a few good readers and I can't wait to hear about what you think of them when they hit your classes."

Bernie helped Celeste clean up and went home. Tony was already there and chowing down on microwaved left over's. "How was dinner?"

"Sure not like your mom's. Celeste made lasagna. But, it was good and I didn't have to cook. She made it with goat cheese! How was your day?"

"Fair to midland, as they say. I was wondering if I could go out with you two tomorrow and watch the milking process. I know you don't want me to go on Thursdays, but it seems like it's going to be the only day I will have a chance with the current schedule. We'll take two cars so you can 'gossip and I can leave early."

"Sounds good to me. With the two of us there, we can explain things that my Dad wouldn't because he expects everyone to know them already. Celeste is a great teacher and very patient. We can meet here at three and change and drive over. I'll let Celeste know tonight so there are no surprises and we can hide the men, she joked."

Tony was actually fascinated by the whole process and helped clean up the equipment like a pro. He felt comfortable in the barn and stayed with the two of them to the end. He even went with Bernie to feed Noir, but Bernie purposely did not show him or invite him to the pump house after milking. It was a secret she and Celeste needed to maintain.

Watching Noir munching on her hay Tony said, "I really miss riding and I should start to set aside some personal time for thinking about getting my own horse and riding again. You seem to be very calm and centered after your trail rides."

"Tony, you are not going to take the time after the initial fantasy wears off to get out here every day and feed and exercise a horse."

"You can feed it when you feed Noir."

"No, that's not how this works. I come out each day with few exceptions and take care of my animal. I'm not going to take on another one because you have a whim right now. Nor is my father going to be happy about another horse here. He built this stall and the wash pad for me, he's not going to respect someone who shows up occasionally like a rich kid expecting the horse to be groomed and tacked up all ready for riding. I won't respect you, either, if that happens. I already know your schedule and it just ain't gonna happen when the novelty wears off. You're no different than a kid with a crush on a teacher. It will wear off.

"For me this is a habit, a responsibility and an obsession. To you, it's just a fleeting thought. I know that you will

go out and buy the very best of everything and none of it will ever get used, just like those golf clubs in the garage. At least, with those, if someone wants to hit some balls, you've got the equipment and can take a quick lesson without having a year long stone around your neck. And, you are not putting that stone around mine. You are welcome to ride Noir at any time when she's in shape and won't dump your ass. It took me a long time to get her back into shape after my low period and she's ready to be ridden by someone else. As a matter of fact, I've been thinking about taking a few lessons with her, but have to find a way to get to lessons in Jackson. I've become a walk trot queen and need help again with the canter and not losing my irons because I'm using my knees to balance again.

"Of course, unless you're willing to buy me a truck and a trailer. . ."

"I don't think you need a truck and a trailer right now with one horse and all this property to ride on."

"Well, I'm thinking about calling around and seeing if I can borrow one or get someone to take me to lessons. Dad's truck would work, but I don't like bumper pull trailers and think gooseneck ones are safer in the long run. I am going to start putting away the money for one and ask Dad if I can pay to put a gooseneck hitch in his truck. Then I won't have to depend on anyone. I know we have a steep mortgage and a lot of expenses, but I figure I can put a little away at a time and eventually there will be enough to make it a reality."

"Hey, what are you guys doing? Celeste walked into the barn.

They turned around in surprise because the conversation had gone on so long and been so tight between them about dreams and aspirations again that they forgot they were supposed to be cleaning the milk house. "Oh, we got to talking about Noir and forgot where we were. I'm so sorry, Celeste, it's not your job to be stuck doing all the work as a volunteer.

"Oh, hey, I get paid in goat cheese."

"Cute," Tony said.

"No, she really does get paid in goat cheese. Dad started leaving it for her on Thursdays before he and Mom take off. You haven't lived until you've eaten her goat cheese lasagna!"

"Seriously?" Tony raised his eyebrows.

"Seriously," Celeste beamed.

"By the way she hoards the stuff, you'd think King Midas himself had left her a golden egg or something."

The three of them strolled back to the main milking barn and finished cleaning. Tony profusely thanked them for allowing him to participate and they each drove out at the same time. Bernie didn't miss the trip to the pump house because of her conversation with Tony about the future and her plans.

She had put a new plan into motion and didn't know where it came from. It wasn't something she was consciously thinking about, it just came to her out by the stall as they were talking. She didn't think twice about her new plan, just knew it was going to be a reality some

day. She had set another goal and it was nice to have them again. "But, why? Where had it all come from?"

Not being one to over analyze things, she just forgot about the new plan and went home and made dinner.

Friday afternoon Bernie called directory assistance and asked for a number for Thousand Pines Stables. Nothing was listed. She drove to the farm and saddled Noir and went back to the spot where she had met Jack. The afternoon was beautiful and they played around for a while and she decided to venture into the path off the property. She climbed down, held her reins and unhooked the gap. She found a rock and remounted and ventured onto the deer path. It was a different environment and Noir's ears were twitching back and forth listening to sounds and her rider's commands. They never ran into the man, but they had an exciting ride into unknown territory. She returned to the farm and put Noir up for the night and drove home.

On Saturday Tony announced he wasn't going to the office and they were going to spend the day together in Ann Arbor. He had gotten tickets for a play and they headed out early fully dressed for an evening on the town. Tony wanted to go suit shopping; and his tastes were not such that he bought off the rack. They stopped in several shops and he purchased two custom made suits. They then went dress shopping and refilled her prescriptions.

Like two giddy kids they got through dinner at a Thai restaurant and made their way to the playhouse. It was a small theater and the play was Ibsen's Peer Gynt. They found their way to their seats as the house lights

came down. The play opened and Bernie recognized the actor playing the main character: Todd. Her shock was evident and she whispered to Tony that he was one of the gym teachers at her school. Now she knew what Todd had meant when he told her she didn't know much about him. He was quite good and energetic in his part. Afterward Bernie told Tony she wanted to go backstage and tell Todd what a great play it was and say hello. Tony was game, but told her he didn't want to stick around.

Backstage the usual theater pandemonium was afoot and they had a tough time finding Todd. Todd was equally surprised to see Bernie and finally meet Tony. Tony and he got to talking and invited Todd out to have dessert with them. Todd suggested a diner close to the theater and they walked there.

As they seated themselves, Bernie eyed Todd and said, "I had no idea you were involved with the theater."

"Been doing summer stock my entire life as a student and a teacher and I've been lucky to get several leading parts. What did you think about the play tonight?"

"I know the story and really appreciated your interpretation. How much was yours and how much was the director's?"

"We get to interject our own interpretations and the director moves things along so the audience keeps up and doesn't get bored."

"Well, I liked your input, then. I'm just surprised to see you doing this and being a gym teacher."

"Well, as I told you, you don't know much about me. I don't have to think too much to be a gym teacher and a coach, so I can concentrate on learning lines and injecting myself into a part. I really wanted to go into acting as a full-time career, but my parents went berserk, so I got through college and this is what I do on weekends and some nights. That's why I only coach football."

"Any larger offers?"

"What do you mean?"

"TV, movies, etc?"

"Oh, I've done a few commercials for some national companies and a few summer tours. I also direct some from time to time. I'd rather act, though. As far as Hollywood goes, that's not going to happen. I'll be a little thespian throughout my life. Hey, the cheesecake here is fantastic, you should try the Midori or pumpkin. Maybe we should all order a different flavor of cheesecake and split it."

"Marvelous idea," Tony said.

They parted back at the theater and Bernie told Tony how shocked she was to see Todd. She outlined some of the posturing and dancing at school to illustrate her point.

"I didn't know it was so political there."

"Oh, you have no idea. I found out rather recently that Todd stood up for me over the Nash kid problem."

"You didn't think he would?"

"No, he seems as though he is making fun of me and Celeste all the time, so it was a surprise to both of us."

"That situation was a mess, and you needed all the people on your side you could get. I don't want to dredge up old stories and problems, but that's the second time you could have been fired. Your salary is as important to us as mine and I don't know what we would have done if you were let go. I imagine you could have started driving each day to a PR job in Ann Arbor, but the likelihood of that happening is slim. You had a great job in Chicago and I don't know why you didn't have people problems there."

"Tony, that's not fair. I didn't have to deal with immature people and children all the time. You were given an assignment and trusted to get it done in the best way possible. This is an entirely new animal and, they are animals. The teachers are just as bad as the kids most times. You're not dealing with it on a day to day basis, so you have no right to make judgments.

"I really enjoyed the day and want to drop the subject right now and remember a great day, Tony."

"Fair enough."

"I hate that phrase."

"I know, but it's the only one I have right now."

Silence was maintained on the drive home.

Bernie never had a chance to tell Celeste of her discovery Sunday because it was family day at the Romanelli's and she knew that Mike was home for the weekend and he and Celeste were probably doing something together.

Monday she arrived at school early and bee-lined it to Celeste's room to tell her the news. As they were standing in the hallway Todd walked by and nodded to both of them, "Ladies, good morning."

"Oh my Gawd. It's for real," Celeste's jaw dropped at the change in Todd's attitude. Neither of them saw him as the cocky coach any longer, but the well educated, athletic man he was. Views changed considerably.

"Now that we have a professional actor in our midst, what do you think of involving him in the junior senior play this year?" Bernie asked Celeste.

"I think I'll just turn it all over to him because he commands attention and I am ignored as the organizer and director, Celeste said.

"Celeste, it's a lot of nights and weekends, he may not be able to do it. You need to sit down and talk to him first. What did they choose for performance this year?"

"Nothing yet. They are still deciding. Musicals have been a bust because no one wants to sing on stage. Those who do are always the same kids and so many are left out. We need a play with a large cast to involve as many kids as possible who want to be part of it all. What if we publicized Todd's ancillary activities?"

"I really think you need to talk to him first. I'll help. This year I promised to get more involved after school. I have been selfish about my horse. Tony is involved, so I should be too.

"I remember when I went to high school and there was a music teacher involved in all this. I was chosen to be a dancer, which was hilarious because I have two left feet. The music teacher made fun of me, but didn't change my spot to something else. I wasn't about to get up in front of people and dance with two others in a kick routine if he kept at it. I just stopped showing up for rehearsals and they eventually let me go. I was so embarrassed to be in front of people. Funny thing was, though, that I had no problem giving a speech in 4H. I just wasn't about to dance in front of a crowd. Mortifying."

"The kids have a meeting after school tomorrow and I'll try to corner Todd before then. Do you know his schedule at the theater?"

"No, I didn't ask him. I think it's a short run performance. It's really good, you should go see it."

Celeste did manage to converse with Todd for a few minutes and ask him to assist her. He seemed pleased to be asked and Celeste managed to get an after school commitment out of him when he wasn't acting in Ann Arbor. Overall, she was grateful to have the help and someone who would get the kids' attention this year. Now, just to get a play finalized. It wasn't that the juniors were pitted against the seniors, it was more of a disagreement between those who liked the spotlight and those who were literarily inclined. "This is not going to be an easy decision because we need to get an audience

to pay for tickets other than the parents of the actors," Celeste moaned to Bernie.

"Maybe they can pick something interesting to all and we can make it exciting and fun to watch. What kind of input do you need?"

"I'd like you to be there during the next meeting and see if you can't give them some ideas. I think something funny would get a wider audience. Let's face it; the only ones who attend are parents. Maybe we could reach the wider community. With what, I don't know. If the kids are given a chance to put a spin on it, they will be more involved."

Bernie attended the meeting and was surprised to see so many of her own students. In an attempt to involve many students, they chose "The Music Man." It was a musical, but it had a large cast and they could utilize the school marching band. These were the kids who never seemed to get attention off the football field and they were delighted to be included. Being typical kids, they couldn't wait to mess up the music in the beginning of the play and hyjinks were planned. These conversations were overheard by the teachers in attendance and a sense of excitement overcame the group. Todd showed up at the last minute and approved their selection. He promised to help direct and coach the actors. Celeste introduced him as a professional actor and the kids were fascinated that their gym teacher and coach knew anything about theater. Todd's standing seemed to grow that day.

THIRTY FIVE

Monday Bernie returned to the farm and went in search of Jack. She rounded the corner to the open area and Noir nickered. She knew that a horse was nearby. Jack appeared at the gap and Bernie asked him about his training at the hunter barn.

"Why do you ride western if you train English horses all day?"

"I retool Thoroughbreds off the track that they pick up cheaply or for free and make them safe mounts for advanced beginner riders. A lot of ex-racehorses have no job after their racing days are over and it takes some pride and skill to give them a new job. It sure beats the meat market for them. I wear breeches, ride in my saddles and equipment, but trail riding is a different set of circumstances for me. It gives me an opportunity to just relax. Red, here, just wants to walk and trot a little and be out in the woods. He enjoys getting off the Brinkman's place and he's an only horse, so my attention to him is appreciated. Red has only child syndrome!"

Noir was resting a leg as Bernie sat and listened to Jack's story. "You know, I tried to call Thousand Pines and they have no listing. I was attempting to get information about lessons since it's the only place I've

heard of nearby. No one rides English out here and I am in need of a few lessons. My only big problem is that I don't own a truck or trailer, so I can't take Noir. I'd like lessons on my own horse. It seems pointless to take lessons on someone else's horse when this is the horse I'd like to show again.

"I did a few dressage shows back in Illinois and enjoyed them so much. They just load up the student's horses in their trailers and all you had to do was show up at the show grounds early enough to get your horse ready. I learned to braid because I didn't want to pay someone else to do it. Noir was good about it, too. A lot of horses don't want their manes pulled or braided, she didn't care.

"I know you work for a hunter barn, but there has to be someone there interested in dressage, right?"

"As a matter of fact, there are. They are older women and there is an instructor allowed to come in just for them. They have a group lesson on Thursdays. I think there are four of them. Do you want me to find out for you?"

"Yes, but how do I get hold of you?"

"I'll give you my business card and you can call me. The facility isn't listed because it's privately owned. They do, however, have a website. I'll put it on my card, so you can look it up."

"Um, I still have a problem, I can't get my horse there."

"Maybe we can work something out. I own my own rig and I don't mind hauling your horse for you for gas money. Where am I, anyway?"

You're on the outskirts of Cold Lake. That's why I don't know where you board your horse because it can't be in Cold Lake. You've got to be in another town bordering here. You said you ride two hours so that puts you several miles from Cold Lake. You actually ride four hours a day after training all day? You must have an incredible seat and core strength."

Bernie did not expect the deep, low laugh. His face lit up and crinkled at the same time. "I never thought of it that way. I ride totally differently in one saddle than I do in another. Red's saddle is simply for sitting in. He only has to be trail savvy, not jump fences, etc. A lot of work I do is also ground work. Retraining a former race horse is a lot of calming. They only know how to do one thing, run in a straight line and go left. My training is to make them safe for the owners of the facility to sell them to their clients. I pick them out, pick them up, start them over again and ride the tar out of them to get them used to all kinds of things. It's not just a riding job. Ground manners are important as well."

While he was talking Bernie watched him fish in his shirt pocket for a card and a pen. He wrote on the back of the card and handed it to her. She didn't have pockets, so she put the card inside the upper part of her glove. She wasn't about to pull her shirt up to attempt to put it the tiny little pocket on the inside of her breeches. "Thank you. I'll let you know after I check out the website and investigate the facility. Nice to see you again."

"Yes, it was nice to see you and Noir again. I have to tell you I laughed when you told me 'Red' was an original name for my horse because your horse is named Noir; means dark."

Color shot through her face. She did remember the brief, snotty remark and felt contrite. "Sorry. I was just flustered about anyone on the property that day. I still haven't mentioned your presence to my father and don't think I will. He'll get all paranoid and start posting more signs. If you saw him talking to Noir, you wouldn't believe that he doesn't love her. He just says he hates horses. He tells me he can predict her more than me!

"Well, I've got to go and get her fed and then head home. Have a safe ride back. Nice to see you again."

The Thousand Pines website was simple and mostly photos of students and postings about shows. There was no mention made of Jack or his training. Bernie wondered how long he had been there and exactly what type of work he did for them. From his description and his business card, it sounded like a subcontract with the facility. The card simply had his name, phone number, address and "Independent trainer" on it. It was not a card for Thousand Pines. There wasn't even a logo on the plain white card.

She called the number listed on the website and inquired about lessons. The dressage faction was relatively new and small and they were currently working on a quadrille, so hopes of joining that particular group were dashed. There was hope because quadrille meant they were planning on showing together.

She made an appointment to view the facility after school and when she knew that Jack would not be there. It was important that she get a look at the place and learn their philosophy without having someone she had already met as a guide.

She plugged the address into the GPS system and drove over Tuesday. The facility was nicely kept up, but old. There were two indoor arenas and three outdoors. It was pretty obvious that they were a hunter and jumper barn because brightly colored and painted jumps were all over the outdoor arenas. Students were starting to descend on the place and Bernie was concerned that there would be no one to give her a tour. She asked a student picking out the hooves of a horse on crossties if Sue was around. She had made an appointment with someone named Sue. The rider barely looked up and said, "Yeah, she's over there and has a green vest on," and pointed in a vague direction, Bernie walked a little further into the barn and saw a very tall blonde woman wearing a green vest and light green breeches. No doubt the latest outfit from some heavily advertising manufacturer.

"Sue?"

"Yes?"

"Hi, I'm Bernie, I spoke to you on the phone about lessons here and we made an appointment for a tour today."

"Oh, yes. Nice to meet you," she extended her hand. "Could you give me five minutes to solve this scheduling conflict?"

"Sure."

Bernie listened to Sue talking to a gal who was obviously a trainer with a scheduling problem with another teacher in an outdoor ring. While she stood there she looked around and watched mothers dropping off girls, who immediately went to stalls and started bringing horses out to cross ties. Girls were everywhere within a 30 minute period, obviously after-school students in their teens and preadolescent phases. Tack was carried from various lockers and tack rooms between stalls. The dirt floors in the aisles were level and raked clean. Shovels and rakes were strategically placed at intervals for clean up. The entire barn was bustling and clean. It was a well oiled machine.

The facility was three times the size of the barn in Illinois and Bernie was fascinated by the activity. There were Paints, Thoroughbreds, Warmbloods, Quarter Horses and the occasional Arabian. One of the Paints looked like a Warmblood, but had draft horse features. "Must be a cross," thought Bernie.

Sue, upon closer inspection, was a very tanned, weathered looking older woman, probably in her late 40's. She stood slightly bow legged and Bernie assumed that her legs were formed around a horse's barrel. She was well over six foot, too. "Hey, Kaylee" she shouted, "clean up after your horse before you leave the cross ties."

"Yes, Ma'am," the little girl said. She raked horse poop into a shovel and put it in a wheelbarrow.

"Ma'am?" thought Bernie. She hadn't seen this much respect from preteens in a long time. There must be a code of conduct here, too.

"Well, welcome to Thousand Pines," Sue said as she extended her hand again. I usually don't do tours during lessons times because of the activity level, but you indicated you couldn't get here any sooner. You must work."

"Yes, I'm a teacher and the earliest I can get out is 2:15, then I have to drive over from Cold Lake."

She started walking and Bernie followed her. "We have about 20 to 25 students a night. Each night is a different group. There are a few individual lessons, but to accommodate this number of students we schedule group lessons early and private lessons later in the evening. This is our busy time of day."

Sue explained the rules and regulations for conduct and mentioned that prima donnas were expelled because they just did not have time to deal with behavioral issues from teenagers. "Their parents are informed of the proper conduct and expected to keep them in line. We are not a babysitting service, either. We have a viewing room upstairs so parents can watch lessons in both barns; they're connected by the viewing room with the office underneath. That way we can keep an eye on things and prevent accidents. Bathrooms are two to a barn and we expect them to be kept clean. If mud comes in, it should be swept out. Laundry is the owner's responsibility and we do not wash blankets or pads here. It should be hauled home and cleaned. We are on septic tanks and don't need the added expense or maintenance.

"We have two full-time instructors for hunt seat and we are just getting people interested in dressage. Right now we only have five people interested; that's what you wanted, right?"

"Well, I started with dressage because I was not confident about learning to jump. Right now I've schooled myself and my horse into a walk trot hole and need to get out of it. If I initiate a canter my mare bucks and I lose my irons. She likes to canter after she's done it a few times; it's just that I've lost my confidence out there. I've owned the mare several years and moved her from Illinois to Cold Lake. I essentially just trail ride now because I don't have a truck and trailer and haven't been able to find a lesson barn."

"Do you have a place to practice or will you be boarding with us?"

"No, I have my own trails and an area that can be made into an arena. I board at my parent's farm a few miles from my home."

"How'd you find us?"

Bernie stammered a little. "I met your horse trainer, Jack."

"Oh, he's a good guy. He picks off the track horses and auction horses for us that might fit the bill for sales here. Then he retrains them for our sales and school horses. He does a good job and he and his family live on the premises."

Bernie was grateful that Sue asked no more questions about how they met. She didn't want to give away Jack's secret. Although, right now the secret seemed stupid.

Sue stopped and opened a door to a stairway. "Come, I'll show you the viewing room and you can watch two different lessons in two barns. They ascended the stairs and Bernie found herself in a large open room with a fireplace and several sofas and mismatched chairs. Adults sat around or looked out the viewing windows.

"Why don't you watch some lessons tonight and let me know which group you'd like to join. Your canter sounds like it needs work, so the group on the left there, may fit the bill. They are beginning to canter and that's always a good point to start again. I have to go down to an outdoor arena and teach a lesson. I'll look for you in an hour." She walked away and was gone before Bernie could get her bearings.

The lesson Bernie watched seemed too advanced for her current ability. The kids were cantering over trot rails and judging distance. None of the horses seemed to give the riders any problems and none bucked. *Oh*, she thought, *What would Noir do in this situation? She'd disrupt the class the first time I put my leg on her. I may need a private lesson and some reschooling for her first.* Bernie ran her tongue around her molars while thinking. *Maybe Jack can get on her and canter her into the ground so she stops her dangerous behavior. I'll have to ask him about private training. But where? Hmm, I don't have an arena, but there is an area that could be better cleared with the bush hog that's flat enough to use.*

I'll have to ask him onto the property when Dad's not around and show him and get an opinion.

Sue returned and asked in a very businesslike fashion if Bernie liked what she saw. She was rather curt and Bernie could tell she was interrupting yet another lesson. They made plans to speak on the phone in a week. Bernie got in her car thinking as she drove home.

I wish I didn't have to drive this damn car for one. They see me coming and assume I'm rich or something. I've got to get back Bronco privileges. I can't be driving to lessons in this thing. Damn you, Tony. I need a truck like the rest of the world. It's bad enough that I drive this car to school. The rest of the teachers are barely getting by and drive older models. I have a brand new BMW and it's too flashy. **Tony, prior to the wedding had traded his sportster and her Jeep in on two four door matching cars. Because of the farm chores, and Noir's rides, hers was always dusty. Once a month he hired a kid to come out and wash and detail the cars. It was usually someone Bernie knew from school and Tony knew from juvenile court. He was all about giving kids a chance. The car had to go.** ***I'm sure Tony thinks they look like they fit the picture of the modern couple in the modern house in the modern world. Shit.***

She returned late and didn't make it to the farm. She called her father asking that he feed Noir because she was investigating riding lessons. "What do you need lessons for? I thought you knew how to ride."

"No, Dad, I need lessons because I'm having problems advancing in my riding and Noir and I are stuck in a hole. It's a little hard to explain because you're supposed

to advance, not be in stasis. Riding is supposed to be continuing education."

She decided to grade papers after dinner in front of Tony and the TV. There needed to be a plan and it had to be a faster solution than saving for a trailer and a truck. He'd have a cow if she asked for a truck after the McGinty incident. *A truck and a BMW? Ha. I'll just start to observe him a little closer and see what I can cook up. Maybe I should invite him to the barn when I start lessons. Oh, yeah, how am I going to start lessons without my horse? Crap.*

The TV proved to be a major distraction and she could not concentrate on literature essays. Tony didn't notice, he was laughing at the latest comedy show. She gathered her papers into two folders and went up to her desk in the bedroom. As soon as she sat down her concentration came back and she was able to finish grading and moving papers to the done folder.

The Scotch bottle came out and she poured herself a good dollop and downed it, hiding the glass under the bed. *Think, think, think, what can I do to get a truck and trailer?*

They were living well, eating well and dressing well. She had a good health insurance plan and Tony was on it, so prescriptions were minimal costs. What could be cut back on, without damaging their current lifestyle? *It's not like Chicago and saving for a horse, this is much larger and I have to find a second income that doesn't interfere with my job. I could teach summer school, but that was just busy work, it didn't pay really well. Tutoring*

was time consuming and you didn't really want to tutor your own students. Think.

She exhausted herself trying to wrestle an idea loose and fell asleep before Tony came to bed.

Jack Reems was waiting for her when she and Noir rode up. She outlined the conversation with Sue and told Jack about the idea of putting in an arena. Albeit, without fencing to begin with. She never knew when Dad was going to need more pasture and edge into her riding area. She invited him to step over the dividing line and ride over to the area she thought best for an arena.

They rode side by side a short distance and he immediately saw the flat area she was thinking about. "Looks as though that's your best spot. You won't have any spotters around, though. Are you sure you're safe out here alone and what you've told me about her?

He frowned, "What's your sudden interest in an arena after all those years of just riding trail?"

"I don't know. I really haven't completely thought it out. I did show a little bit in Illinois and think I want to again. I'm at a complete loss over a truck and trailer though, and if I can't get to Jackson, I can't even take lessons. Noir is a talented horse and I'm just wasting her riding around in circles."

"Red is talented, too, but content to be just trail ridden. I could teach him so many things and compete with him as well, but I don't. Are you sure you wouldn't be happy just riding in those circles? It's something you have to ask yourself."

"No, I've made up my mind about wanting to compete. Compete in what is the question though."

"Well, sounds as though you're going to have to work that all out before investing in a truck and trailer. I offered to pick up your horse, but the more I thought about it, the harder it seemed. I'd have to bring you back, too, after an hour's lesson. That'd be some mighty expensive lessons.

"How does your dad transport goats to market and places?"

"He has panels on his truck and just loads them in. He doesn't often pick up or drop off, people come here to pick up wethers and some of his older does when he decides to sell. He castrates the males and raises them enough to be sold for meat. Since they are dairy goats, many of them just go as pets because they don't yield a lot of muscle for meat. Although, he has been known to take a group to auction. It's just not his main business and he's unconcerned with that part of it. He has to feed them anyway and they have great pasture other than the winter. He usually sells the wethers in the fall so he doesn't have to feed them during the winter; that's when the pastures start deteriorating."

"I see," he looked thoughtful. "What about putting a hitch on his truck and buying a trailer?"

Bernie bit the inside of her lip a little. "Ah, I don't drive Dad's truck." That was all she was going to say and left the conversation hanging.

Jack persisted, "You can't drive a truck?"

She bristled, "Yes, I can drive a truck just fine. I'm just not inclined to do it right now. I can't ask my father to lend me his truck for horse shows. I need my own equipment."

"What does your husband think about all this?"

"How do you know I'm married?"

"Ah, duh, you're wearing a ring. I can see the outline of it through your gloves. I saw it when you reset the gap."

"Right. Yes, I'm married and my husband is an attorney here in town, He isn't keen on me driving around in a truck all the time. I haven't really discussed this with him, she confided.

"You're married, any kids?"

"Yup, married 13 years and two kids. Everybody is horsey. I have a boy and a girl, and the girl is an excellent jumper, she's going on 13 this year. My son, Aiden, is 11 and he is getting to the point where he can help warm horses up before a ride. He's small, though and I suspect he's about to go through a growth spurt. He mostly warms up the horses of the adult riders for evening lessons, when the older women come from work and are changing into riding clothes. They don't have as much time after work and they want to take their lessons or practice and go home to dinner with their families."

"What's your daughter's name?"

"Kaylee."

"She wouldn't have, by any chance, have taken a lesson yesterday, would she?"

"Yes, she takes a group lesson every Tuesday. Why?"

"I think I saw her at the stable. She referred to Sue as 'Ma'am.'"

Jack laughed, "She'd better. That stable is our bread and butter and she knows she's privileged there. They don't treat her like an employee's child, but like all the paying customers. I'm glad to hear that."

Bernie switched gears. "Would you consider getting on Noir and working on her canter. I can pay you to do some light training here."

"Not here. I have no safety net like an enclosed arena. If you had her over at Thousand Pines, it'd be a different story. She's well schooled and just sounds like she doesn't want to work too hard and only enjoys playing with you right now. Getting on her the first time she may not like my cues and may present me with some behavior problems. She's very used to you just riding at a walk and trot. I don't need to get hurt and lose my job."

"OK, that's an honest answer and one for which I'll have to find a solution.

"Hey, I'm going to have to get back to the barn and feed Noir and get home to start dinner. I really appreciate your input on this arena thing. Do you think you can find your way back to the trail head?"

"Yes, sure, if I can't, Red will. He will be wanting his dinner, too. Glad to be of assistance. Let me know what

you decide about the lessons and a way over there. Good to talk to you Bernie. Ready to go home, boy?" He turned toward the woods and they walked off.

Carl was milking when Bernie entered the barns. He was almost done so she started washing equipment. "Hey Dad, I've got a new goal in mind and I need your input on it and some permission."

Carl never looked up, "New goal?"

"Yeah, I want to find a space near the trails that doesn't interfere with any pasture you might want to expand, but build myself a small arena. I don't have any place to practice specific maneuvers without the prospect of Noir trying to evade me and get loose. What do you think about that?"

He still didn't look up, "Don't know. Do you have a place in mind?"

"Yes, it's a flat area where the rock outcropping is. You don't currently have any stock out there and I need a level surface to start back into competition practice again."

He stood up to full height and looked over at her. "Compete? Where?"

I found a place to take lessons in Jackson, but I need a place to practice here or my money will just be wasted on a lesson."

"Where in Jackson?"

"A large stable called Thousand Pines."

"Ah, Sue Riker."

"You know her?" Bernie was surprised and it was evident in her voice.

"Sure, I've sold her a few goats as companion animals over the years to keep Thoroughbred horses calm. I don't think she has any more, though. She used to come here ten years ago and buy a few wethers. One at a time. Something about racehorses and goats being companions. That's where the phrase, she told me, 'get your goat' comes from. On race days if someone wanted a horse to lose, they'd steal the horse's goat and the horse would become agitated and lose the race. Get your goat."

Bernie was not happy to know that Dad knew Sue and was familiar with the stable over there. "So she would come here or you'd deliver a goat?"

"No, she'd show up with a horse trailer and pick out a calm one and trailer it back to her place. I've never been over there, but from what I've heard, the place is nice; large too."

Bernie was a little relieved that her father didn't mention the trainer. She wasn't entirely sure why, but just glad that he didn't know about him. They probably didn't need goats with Jack over there.

"So, do you want to show me where this spot is?"

"Yes, but I need to get home to start dinner for Tony pretty soon and it's going to get dark. Are you taking Mom out Thursday?"

"No, we decided the weather was so nice, we'd grill and stay in. Do you want to go while Celeste starts milking?"

"No, that's not fair to her. She's your volunteer slave and I hate to leave her alone. I did it once with Tony and felt guilty about it. How about Friday afternoon before I ride we take the four wheeler out and I show you?"

"Sounds like a plan. Go home, I'm almost finished, and thanks for the help."

The spring weather was balmy and nice so she decided to stop at the grocery to pick up a few steaks for Tony's dinner. Her mind was preoccupied when she got to the small store and she wasn't expecting to have to stop to talk to anyone. She was still wearing her breeches and tall boots and wasn't thinking about running into anyone.

"Hi, looks like you just went for a ride." The man was her age and looked slightly familiar, but she wasn't sure. He didn't look like any of the parents she knew from conferences and she sure hoped it wasn't someone from high school. "What can we get for you today, Mrs. Romanelli?"

Bernie was so preoccupied with the thought of trucks and trailers and lessons that she was blindsided to be addressed. Her voice was sharp, "Pardon me?"

"Just wondering if there was something special you had in mind tonight. Most people are grilling out and I've had special orders all day." He was short, tubby and wore a butcher's apron.

"How do you know me?"

"You're Tony's wife. I've seen you in here before."

"Oh," she was brought out of her reverie and started listing names in her head of people she should know. "Um," she looked for a name tag and there was none. "Sure, I thought we'd grill out, too. Apparently, it's not an original thought today."

"No ma'am, everyone has spring fever. What'll it be?"

Not wanting to flaunt their good status, she decided not to order steak, but thick pork chops.

"There you are, Ma'am. Enjoy in good health. Do you need any potato salad to go with the picnic theme? We've also got some California sweet corn in."

Bernie was very cordial to the man she never met before, at least not in her memory, and said, "Oh, that's such a good idea. I'll do that. He'll just love to have a picnic on the deck."

Thank God there was no one in front of her in the checkout and she managed to get out of there in a hurry. *Geez, just get me outta here*, she thought as she zoomed away toward home. *God, I hate Cold Lake.*

At home she struggled with the grill cover and cleaned the bars with the wire brush. *This should be Tony's job, he's the one who likes to grill.* She became resentful again because she was always the one to cook dinner, the one to clean up, the one to think about what to cook, the one to do all the preparations. . .

Tony arrived home in a fine mood and was just delighted with the dinner choice. "Sounds like spring to me. Let's grill. Did you season the chops for me?"

"Sure did," she said, resenting him more. "It's prepared and all you have to do is cook them."

"Love this grill. Great investment for us."

***Yeah*, she thought, *You don't clean it, put it up for the winter, keep the propane tank filled or even hose off the cover from the pollen*. Her hair was in a pony tail and she started swishing it around like Tasha did with hers. She was fairly broiling herself when he came down in a pair of sweats.**

"I poured you a glass of wine and everything is ready to go when you are."

"Thanks, Babe." He bussed her cheek and walked to the back deck with the chops.

***Thanks, Babe*, she intoned to herself. She had purchased the store-made potato salad, made coleslaw and bought corn. The table outside was set and all that needed to be done was the chops. She poured herself a glass of wine and went outdoors with a plate for the cooked chops.**

"I've set a new goal," she said to his back.

Tony turned around from the grill and asked, "A school goal, a personal goal or a life's goal?"

"A personal goal. I want to show again and I need lessons. In order to take lessons on my own horse, I need a truck and a trailer. I could possibly use Dad's truck,

but I'd have to pay for a hitch and then I need a trailer. I can't get to lessons without one. I have no place to take a lesson with a traveling instructor because I don't have an arena. Friday Dad and I are going out to look at a flat spot in a clearing and see if I can't use it to build an arena to practice in. But I still need a truck and trailer."

"I'm not especially keen on your driving a truck again. Didn't we just have this conversation?"

"Tony, you are not understanding what I'm saying. I need a truck. I am embarrassed to drive the car to school because it's flashy and looks like I think I'm better than anyone else. It isn't even American made. I want a truck."

"We'll discuss it at a later date."

"How later? I need lessons now. I keep putting off learning and advancing. I can't just trail ride in circles for the rest of my life.

"Nor can you hold me a prisoner here all the time. If I can't go forward with my life and my ambitions, then what do I have? Nothing. I'm losing my mind, getting depressed, getting angry at you and everyone else who wants to control my life over something that isn't even proven. You prove to me that I'm bipolar. Just because one doctor says so, doesn't make it so."

"Hey, hey, you're the one who went in search of a doctor. I didn't tell you to go."

"Your certainly did, you told me to seek help. I'm not getting any from you, either. All I get from you is side

glances and the feeling that you are controlling my every move. I can't even have a glass of wine without you jumping my shit." Her voice was getting louder.

"Did you decide to grill out so the neighbors could hear an argument?"

"No, I just feel resentful toward you today. I go to work, too, work with my father and have an avocation that I like. You come home like the imperious leader and order me around."

Tony put his hands on his head and smoothed back his hair. "Have a glass of wine, Bernie, it'll calm you down."

"I am calm, I'm just tired of being controlled and treated like a child around here and at the farm. My father watches my every move too. You'd think I was carrying a machete around with me and everyone was on edge because I was going to slice off their heads. I just damn tired of it. This marriage is a sham, too. What happened to the fun and amorous Tony?"

"Oh, you're going for the throat today, aren't you?" He rolled his eyes, smoothed his hair again and turned toward the grill.

"Don't turn you back on me, Mister. We need to sit down and discuss this like we used to discuss things. I am a living shell in this house. I'm playing Susie Homemaker for you and you do nothing but walk in the door expecting dinner, your laundry done and everything else set in place for you. Who do you think you are?"

"Bernie, please, this is not the time or the place for this discussion. Let's just sit and have a nice dinner and we can discuss this some other time"

"What's wrong with discussing it right now over dinner? Unless you want me to sit here and eat like the zombie you want to be married to."

"Do you love me?" He turned and looked at her with earnest eyes.

"I love the Tony I married. Not the one I'm currently married to. What happened to that Tony? He disappeared under a pile of laundry somewhere."

"What does laundry have to do with your current problem?"

"See, it's *my* problem. You take no part in it. I'm not supposed to be drinking any alcohol, but you flaunt that glass of wine at me every night at dinner."

"You're all over the place with this conversation. You can't even stick to one subject. It started out about driving the truck and now you're on laundry and zombies."

"Maybe all those things are on my mind at once. We really need to sit down and hash out a lot of things. It's all building up inside me and I'm about ready to walk out the door at this point."

"You're thinking of leaving me?"

"Not exactly, just doing things I like again. I'm not saying I don't like to make dinner and sit with you each night,

but you're latest thing has been to remove yourself, leave your plate and go downstairs and watch TV."

"It hasn't occurred to you that I have a stressful job and that I'm swamped?"

"You sure don't walk in the door stressed each night."

"That's because I try to keep work at work. I can't be dragging that stuff home with me. I thought my Dad's practice was so easy because he only gave me the easy stuff to do when I helped him before. The little things that were annoyances to him, but I never got to the meat of it until I took over."

"Oh. This is news to me. You don't talk about your practice to me. You don't even come home with any good gossip."

"I don't gossip. It's a small town and people have or create problems. I don't think it's your business to have that burden on you or be that nosey."

The chops were done and they set the plate in the middle of the patio table she had cleaned and set earlier. He put a napkin on his lap and forked a chop onto his plate. "Are you depressed again?"

"Yes, damn it, I'm depressed again. You depress me. It's the same routine every night, night after night."

"We just went to Ann Arbor and a play, what do you want from me?"

"More. I want back the Tony I married and who was always up to something exciting."

“You make it sound like we’ve been married for a hundred years and I left you or something.”

“You did leave me, Tony.” She started to cry and when he reached for her hand, she pulled away.

“Aw, come on, let’s not do this now. I had a very bad day with the kid you assaulted.”

“I did not assault anyone. That’s another myth. I grabbed his arm. What happened to him?”

“Well, his grandfather is angry. He was the boy’s only salvation after I met the parents. They’re so drunk all the time, I’m surprised they even know they have kids. His grandfather practically raised both the boy and the girl. Did you know there was a girl?”

“Yes, Tamara. Morgan says she’s a model student and has high grades. No trouble to the teachers, either. You just changed the subject.”

“No, I really didn’t, I’m telling you about my day and the office.”

“But I want to talk about a truck and a trailer and my horse.”

“OK.”

“But I still want to hear about the Nash kid. He really upset me this year.”

“Bernie, I love you, but you have to concentrate on one subject at a time. This is one of the symptoms I looked up. You go from subject to subject and expect people

to catch the ring as the carousal goes round. I can only talk about one subject at a time. This is where I think you need to talk to your doctor. Do you have these wildly changing subjects with him, or do you carefully control yourself to conceal this? I know you can do that when you slow down and think. I'm not picking on you. I just want to finish one conversation before starting the next.

"How would you feel if I said, 'You look lovely tonight' and in the next breath said, 'we need to clean the cars?' You'd think I was absolutely off my rocker or really didn't mean what I said in the first breath. That's how you come across to people. Think about it for a moment before you say anything. You may not even be aware that you're doing this. It's like a serious case of ADD."

"I do not go from subject to subject. I just want to know so many things at once. Why are you telling me this now? You never mentioned it before."

Tony sucked in a deep breath before he answered her. "Are you even aware that you're speeding in a conversation? It's like someone wound you up tightly and you you're dancing too fast. No one can keep up with it. I, personally, don't remember you like this when we were dating. You've only gotten this way in the last two years. I so, do, truly love you, but I can't go much longer with the speeding conversations. How the hell can you concentrate long enough to even cook or teach? Those are things you do well, but I'm amazed every day how you can function in this mode. This is the manic phase that they talk about. It's as though you put on a sock, go brush your teeth, go back and put on the other sock, come back and comb your hair, leave to start

breakfast, stop halfway down the stairs and go back up and put your blouse on. . . "His speech trailed off.

"I do not do things like that."

"I'm not saying you do, but you talk like that. You skip from one subject to another in a heartbeat. How do you finish a thought?"

THIRTY SIX

On her lunch break she called the number on Jack Reem's card. Jack answered and it was evident that he was on a horse at the time. "Hi Bernie, what can I do for you?"

"I just wanted you to know that my father is going to accompany me out to the trails on Friday and I don't think it'd be a good idea for him to run into you near the property line. The less he thinks there are other horses around, the better."

"Oh, sure, I understand. I'll ride my old trails for a change. It'll be good for Red and me."

She thanked him and hung up.

She never mentioned her goals or Jack to Celeste when they milked. For some reason she just didn't feel as though she wanted to tell one more person about the new goals, and she certainly didn't want anyone to know about her new friend. There wasn't a lot of certainty about the direction of the acquaintance with Jack.

Summer was coming up fast and the population of the school reflected the lighter atmosphere and hope in the air. Kids were sillier, had shorter attention spans and seemed exhausted all the time. Teachers were having problems keeping their focus in class and on their work.

"Is it my imagination, or are the kids more tired lately," Celeste asked Bernie.

"I think it's the weather and the longer days. They seem to be distracted and I recall it happening each year at this time. Summer is approaching," she said in a fake ominous voice.

"Do you think your dad will let me do hay with you this summer?"

"OK, you've lost your mind or you need to ask the purchase price on this place. Hay is not fun to put up. It's also dependent on the weather. We will know when it's time to cut when the weather says it won't rain for two days, and then we have to be ready to bale at a moment's notice. Summer showers come up fast and with no warning. I can't tell you how many times hay's been rained on and ruined because of a freak summer shower. I'll ask Dad about it, but it's strenuous work and you need to be able to sling those bales up on the wagon, or lift them high enough to stack them. I'm sure Dad will let you walk behind the wagon and put bales on for someone else to stack. Be prepared to lose about five pounds in sweat, too, because hay is done in the hottest season."

"Well my diet is going well and I'm losing weight. I had to buy new pants for school because I can't fit into the old ones without having to hitch them up over and over. I'll be taking those in soon. How's your diet going?"

"I've been jogging with Tony, which I hate. Between eating smaller portions, I seem to be maintaining so far. The drugs are killing me, though. I really want to tear into some of Tony's Mom's pasta and I can't."

"Hey, this doe is kicking."

"Let me handle that one, Celeste. Dad just started her and he said to watch because she isn't too keen on being milked and he thinks the machine is scaring her. It's her first run at this job. I should have told you ahead of time that the newbies have to learn how to do this. They come in for their grain and follow the others, but you have to teach them how to milk."

They finished at their regular time and snuck out to the pump house for a drink.

Bernie took riding clothes out with her the next day and changed in the car. She saddled up Noir and told Carl which direction to drive the four wheeler. She eventually passed him and arrived at the spot she wanted. Her glances toward the opening in the woods were not noticed by her father and she was glad. She half expected to see Jack there.

"Looks like a nice level area and free of rocks. What you'll find under the dirt, though, is a different story."

"Yeah, it has to be raked up a bit to create a softer footing. I was thinking we surround it with temporary electric fence and put your wethers in there to eat it down. What do you think about that idea?"

"They'll eat it down, all right, and it won't take them long. I don't want them losing weight for fall market. Kids need a decent amount of fat on them for market; but you know that."

"My main concern is will you be using this area for pasture? I know it's back in the woods, but I didn't want to impose on anything."

"Nah, it's fine with me. You will have the job of putting up the fence and herding the wethers to this area, though. I don't want to get involved with it. Remember, as soon as the food disappears, they'll get loose and be out of there because electric fence strands won't hold them long. I figure about a week and you're finished. You'll also have to haul water out here for them. We have an old tank with a spigot on it that you can put in the wagon and pull behind the four wheeler that ought to do the job. I will air the tires up on the wagon and make sure it's working right. I really don't need another project, but that one's been on the list for ages. We stopped using that wagon a while ago. It's in the equipment shed; I'll leave it to you to pull out for me."

He left and Noir and Bernie just rode in and out of the network of trails for half an hour before returning to the barns.

Her cell phone rang as she was stuffing hay into Noir's rack. "Hey, it's Friday, you want to go to Jackson and see a movie and get a pizza like old times?" Tony asked.

"Sure. What brought this on?"

"You said I was ignoring you. Do you want to eat first or see a movie first?"

"Eat. That was a rhetorical question."

"Yeah, I know, but you sound like you need choices."

"Stop. What time do you want to leave?"

"How's 5:30 sound? That will give us 30 minutes to get there and then we can decide which movie we want to see. Do you have anything on your movie list right now?"

"Nope, don't even know what's out there. I've been busy with other things and haven't watched any of the trailers or papers to see what's current. We'll just have to take our chances and hope we find a good one. Thanks. I need off the farm for a while. See you at home."

Bernie hopped into the car, got back out and went to the milking parlor. "Dad, Tony's taking me for pizza and a movie in Jackson, so I've got to run, but I wanted to thank you for allowing me to put up an arena. You're the only one who seems to understand goals; and I thank you for that."

She arrived home, showered, put makeup on and was ready when Tony walked in the door. He changed into jeans and a sweater and opened the car door for her, "Let's roll, Lady."

Bernie wondered what changed and if he was going to miss any good TV programs tonight.

The owner of the pizzeria was all smiles to see them again and made the pizza himself. It felt like old times

and Bernie felt buoyant again. But, she was waiting for that other shoe to drop after Wednesday's dinner.

"I've been thinking about this lesson thing and the truck and trailer. What if you boarded your horse at that place for a month and took a few lessons a week to catch up?" Tony said, as he neatly folded a slice of pizza in half.

"That's a good idea, but not practical. I basically pay for my board by milking on Thursdays. It would be a waste of money to drive over there every day to ride her and I want to compete, so I need to extend the lessons. One month won't cut it. It would be nice to do that initially, but I really need to continue on. Besides, how am I supposed to get to a show without a trailer?

"I could talk Dad into letting me put a hitch on his pickup, but I still don't have a trailer. It needs to be discussed and I need to look for a trailer. Dad is letting me put in an arena at the back of the trails. He and I looked at it today and he's being gracious about it."

"Bernie, let's put the horse over there for a month and start that way. You'd love being in a barn full of people again, too. Is there a trainer over there we could use to get her back into show shape? I know you said you were having problems at the canter. If she stops bucking, you can concentrate in lessons and not disrupt everything. What do you say we start there?"

The night was light and uneventful. They stopped at the grocery store just before it closed in Cold Lake to pick up orange juice and eggs for breakfast. Tony went in with her and they picked up their favorite orange juice,

some Texas toast and eggs. When they got to check out the clerk said, "We have the store orange juice on sale right now, if you didn't know."

Bernie said, "This is the kind we like."

The clerk just rang up their purchase and they left.

"Bernie, you were so rude. Why didn't you just say something to the effect of 'this is good enough for tonight?'"

"I wasn't rude. I buy what I want, no one is going to tell me which orange juice I can buy."

"That wasn't the point, she was just being helpful by telling you the special."

"Oh, drop it."

Thousand Pines was called, a stall was confirmed, Noir was moved and Jack began retraining her. Bernie drove over every day except Thursdays to ride and took two lessons a week on her.

Jack seemed to be there every time Bernie took a lesson and she started to wonder about Red's trail rides. "I'm an independent contractor, and as long as I work with the horses here every day, I can take in other clients, but they must board here," Jack told her when she asked.

"Bet you're missing rides on Red."

"Yeah, I am, but I wanted to make sure you were happy with the canter and lead swaps. It seems as though she has forgotten a lot of cues because you weren't using

them or her to full capacity. She is a handful. I think she's even more keyed up because she is around horses again and not docile goats. She really gave me a run for the money the first three days she was here. It took a lot of work to get her to settle into a job again."

The conversation was hushed as they stood in the corner of the viewing room. It was past group lesson time and Sue was teaching an older woman on a Warmblood. They watched while they spoke. No one else was in the room and it seemed a little silly to be nearly whispering. They had nothing to hide other than having met before and acting as though it was the first time around Sue.

"I'm working on my off days putting up an arena near the rock outcropping by the entrance to your trail."

"Do you need help with that?"

"Right now I have it fenced off with a solar fence and goats eating it down to the ground, but pretty soon, I'm going to need help putting in posts for rails. I don't want you to be involved with this. You need to ride your horse and enjoy your time off."

"Look, Red ties to trees because I have to whiz once in a while and he can stand tied while I help you dig holes. What kind of posts are you using?"

"I went and bought treated posts and will be calling the sawmill when I'm ready and ordering boards to paint. I am not asking my father for any help because he has the entire farm and the herd to care for. I can't ask my husband because he isn't exactly a farm worker or have the passion I do about this project."

Charlene made another appearance on Thursday and this time Celeste was the one to put her in charge of washing equipment because she didn't think Charlene wanted to touch the animals. There was some talk of school and students this time, but nothing revealing about anyone in particular. Char had the foresight to wear usable clothes this time. Celeste took charge of inspecting Charlene's work to make sure it was up to cleanliness standards and Bernie did most of the milking. The offered her rubber gloves to work with, but since they had been worn by someone else, she seemed put off. Charlene left early and Bernie and Celeste had a drink in the pump house.

"Why do I feel this is going to come back to bite us in the ass with her out here?" Bernie asked.

"Why do you feel that way? I think she doesn't have anything to do other than shopping and this is someplace she could go."

"Have you noticed that she really doesn't want to be around the animals and won't touch them?"

"Yeah, but it takes an animal person to like this job. I don't perceive Char to be one."

"OK, then, why is she coming here? You have to ask yourself that question. I don't trust her and feel she wants something, but what? I don't want to be rude, but she was not invited in the first place and she isn't going to land here for entertainment. My suspicion is she'll reveal herself the next time she shows up."

"We'll see."

"Do you speak to her often at school? I never see her much other than shared lunch room duties or in the hallways since we're all on the same floor. I'm telling you, Celeste, there is something afoot here and I don't trust it."

Bernie drove to Thousand Pines almost every day after school and took lessons on Tuesdays and Wednesdays to better remember her lessons if they were consecutive. The lessons and group of adolescents reminded her of Chicago and the barn there. She also got a chance to watch the Dressage instructions and the quadrille practice they had switched to Wednesday.

Noir had settled into the barn's routine and didn't seem to miss the goats. She was a calm and willing partner. The canter had become easy for both of them again.

She learned from Sue that Noir had become a special project for Jack and he worked the horse longer than other horses. "She's a beautiful horse, Bernie and she has a lot of talent. You really should consider jumping her because I've seen Jack take her over a few and she picks those knees up to her muzzle."

"Well, I thought about jumping, but I don't have any spotters at home and jumping is dangerous to me. I really think I'm more interested in Dressage, but I'd be willing to let her go to a show or two if you have a student who wants to jump and show her. Of course, I'd have to be there and meet the student before I did something like that. Do you take your students to shows, or do most of them have their own trailers?"

"We have two trailers and two trucks here. We can transport eight horses to a show. Jack also has a trailer and will take payments, as well, for transport. Some of the adult students have their own trailers and they haul their own horses. Those are the trailers you see parked out back."

"When is there a show that I might fit into?"

"We've already gone to one show and the next one is in May. You might be able to do a hunter class with some of the other students. Should I get you an entry form? They're out already and most of the students have signed up. I'm fully booked, so you'll have to arrange your own transportation.

"Regarding a student who might like to jump your horse, I have an adult who would be perfect. Cat takes lessons on Tuesdays and I'll find the time to introduce you to her next week. I think it's a good fit, too because she doesn't own a horse and doesn't especially like showing our lazy school horses. She has good control of a horse and I think she and Noir would be a good fit. You could split the transportation costs to the show. Jack's been working her over jumps at night and it's pretty obvious she likes it. He's doing well with her. You, I have to say, have laid a great foundation for her."

"Thanks that would be good for Noir if she really likes jumping. I'd have to meet the rider before I let her on my horse. Tuesday, you say? Does she take lessons at the same time as me?"

"Yes, she is schooling in the outdoor rings with my daughter's class."

"Oh, I didn't know you had a daughter who taught."

"Yes, my daughter is a nurse and she teaches on Tuesdays; her day off. I should have introduced you two earlier, but I'm always so busy around here with lessons at this time of year. Plus, it's the time that Jack introduces new horses to the barn. This is the beginning of our busiest season, fast food, no housekeeping and laundry on the fly," she laughed.

Bernie was completely blindsided on Tuesday at the barn. The "adult" student was none other than Cathy the school counselor. Bernie's space had been invaded by the school again.

When Cathy appeared in the barn behind Sue, Bernie's head starting aching. *Oh, God, let this not be the person to ride my horse. I don't need her in my private space and I don't want her in my world.* Her head was pounding. *Beam me up, Scottie, beam me up NOW!*

"Bernie, meet Cathy Jones, the student I mentioned for jumping Noir."

Immediately Bernie extended her hand and said, "Cathy, so nice to see you again." It was evident that she wanted Cathy to keep her mouth shut about the school incident.

"Oh, I didn't realize that you two knew each other," Sue seemed mildly surprised.

"Yes, we know one another from school, Cathy is the kid's counselor and we interact from time-to-time," was Bernie's warning sentence to Cathy.

Cathy understood at once and reached for the extended hand. "Good to see you, Bernie, good to see you. I understand you have a beautiful horse just starting to jump and I'm excited to meet her."

"She's right here in cross ties. Noir, meet Cathy she's going to ride you today and you will have to behave," Bernie gave Noir a treat from her vest pocket. "Would you like to give her a treat? It would give her a chance to smell you and not surprise her. This is a horse that doesn't like surprises, Cathy. I didn't know you rode."

"It's my guilty pleasure with two kids. It's the only thing other than haircuts that I spend any money on with my salary."

"*Haircuts, my ass*," thought Bernie, "*Your hair is frosted. You lie*."

"Well, I guess with two children it's hard to have the disposable income to ride all the time. Is that why you don't have a horse? Bernie was prying with steel blades.

Cathy's face turned the shade of pink that was perpetually on Celeste's cheeks. "I'm divorced and have custody of the kids. They are my first priority and this," she waved her hand, "is my little bit of paradise."

Sue had walked off and Bernie felt like hissing at Cathy, *Do not say a word about counseling me*. But, she didn't, she graciously, with gritted teeth, introduced Cathy to Noir and told her a little about her and what they were doing at this facility. She did not mention her father's farm, goats, and her plans for the arena or Jack. She

finished grooming Noir with familiar strokes and a businesslike attitude.

"I ride in an all purpose saddle, do you own your own saddle, or will you be riding in mine?"

"Ah, I have my own saddle and I am comfortable in it. I understand from Sue that Noir can be fractious at times and she needs a firm hand."

"Noir is here because I dug her into a walk trot hole and she needed help with the canter and lead changes. We're past that now, but I'm not a jumper. Sue recommended you because you could be firm with a horse. This horse is trigger happy and sensitive. I have very light hands and she doesn't need to be pushed or pulled on."

Instead of taking offense at this, Cathy seemed to be listening intently to Bernie's words.

Oh great*, thought Bernie, *I just said 'trigger happy' to the school psychologist. She probably thinks I'm trigger happy, too."

Cathy ran her hands over Noir's forehead and down her neck. "She's beautiful, what is she?"

"Anglo Arabian; half Thoroughbred, half Arabian."

"Will I be allowed to ride her today in my group lesson?"

"Yes, that's why I haven't tacked her up. I was waiting for the new student and to find out if you had your own saddle. I prefer that you use one of my pads so there is no cross contamination. I might be a little paranoid,

but Noir lives at home with me and is only here for reschooling."

"I keep my saddle here, let me get it."

Cathy walked off and Bernie looked at Noir with tears in her eyes. "Noir, I sure hope she does right by you and that Jack did a good job with you and Sue is trustworthy." She swiped her eyes carefully to not smudge her mascara and give tell tale signs of tears.

Cathy returned and was allowed to saddle up Noir. "I'll take her out before the lesson and do some flatwork to get a feel for her, if that's alright with you."

"Of course, that's why I'm early. If you don't mind, I'm rather possessive of my horse and want to watch. I'm not taking a lesson today so you can work with her. I'll go to my car and get a chair. Which ring are you going to be in?"

Jack's work with Noir was evident and she was a perfect partner for Cathy. Bernie's heart beat a little faster as she watched another rider on her horse. Cathy was not only confident, but Noir was a tattletale and she did nothing to misbehave in Cathy's competent hands.

Bernie expected Noir to misbehave at least once but the horse was unfazed by the group of other students and horses. Bernie sat in her lawn chair and watched the lesson. Noir was, indeed, a good jumper with excellent bascule and lead swaps. Cathy was giving with her hands and Bernie's opinion softened toward the woman and the use of her horse. When the lesson was over, Cathy was a little breathless.

"Oh, my, she has her own thinking processes, doesn't she?"

"Yes, she does. What do you think?"

"If you're willing, I'd like to enter the May schooling show in Ann Arbor. Are you planning to show as well?"

"Yeah, but we have to go over the schedule so we have enough time for a tack change." Bernie was surprised at how quickly she accepted this concept.

"I have the forms in my car, Do you have time to look at them now? The classes shouldn't be too close together, other than I'm going to enter the low green jumpers with her and I don't know what classes you'll want to enter. Can you get away on a Sunday? I have to get a babysitter for my kids because I don't want them distracting me with a new horse that day."

"Yes, I planned on entering the show. Can you split the transportation cost with me?"

"Of course. I budget for three shows a year and this one was on my schedule. They do the Dressage portion on Saturday and the hunters on Sunday. I'm interested in watching the Dressage portion, but that day I'll have to bring my kids."

"Where do you live, Cathy?"

"Right here in Jackson. I can get their father to watch them on that Sunday and half of Saturday if I tell him now. They don't get to see him often and I have to force the issue." Cathy was opening her world to Bernie and Bernie didn't have a clue what to say, knowing that she

was not good at parent things other than parent teacher conferences. She remembered Gail and her mind traced back to the menstrual conversation.

"Let me put Noir away and we can look at the schedule."

Cathy went to her car and brought the paperwork in because it was already dark and they could study it under the barn lights. Students were leaving and private lessons were arriving. "Let's go to the lounge upstairs."

Bernie felt a little shudder between her shoulder blades and hoped that Jack would not be there. Although, she needed to get to Jack quickly to reserve a space on his trailer since the other trailers were booked. She just didn't want to run into him tonight.

Driving home she had some ambivalent thoughts. *I just crossed a personal barrier and allowed someone to take control of my horse and part of my world again*. It didn't feel wrong, though and Bernie looked at it as a business decision.

Tony was home and cooking when she arrived. A salad was made and pasta was boiling in a pot. "What's this all about?"

"I thought I'd surprise you and get some dinner up. I knew you'd be late tonight. I cheated, it's my Mom's sauce. I know you're eschewing the carbs, but it sounded so good to me."

"Thanks, Honey, that was really thoughtful and pasta sounds so perfect right now."

"It was a rather weird evening for me. You're not going to believe who the jumper rider is. She's the stinkin counselor they had me meet with after the Nash thing. I really shouldn't refer to her that way, because she had great control and was easy with Noir. They made a good team out there and I honestly think she has a chance in the ring with her." Bernie described the evening and her thoughts to Tony as he moved around the kitchen. She refilled her wine glass without thinking. Tony didn't seem to notice.

They took their plates and salad bowls downstairs on a tray to the TV. Tony had his favorite program on and Bernie became interested in the story line. Thoughts of horses and shows were forgotten in the stuttering light reflecting on the walls.

THIRTY SEVEN

Noir's one month of boarding and training was over and Bernie and Tony had to make a decision about staying another month and her driving back and forth or bringing the horse back to the farm and have no rides with Cathy. Bernie didn't want to invite Cathy to the farm and the arena wasn't even started yet. The show had changed their plans and budgetary decisions had to be made. They opted for one more month of boarding and one lesson a week. Jack was called and a space was reserved for Noir on his trailer.

Bernie had another conundrum to deal with. Her breeches were all full seat and a hunter show doesn't allow full seat breeches. She couldn't fit into her old ones and knew she'd have to buy a pair of breeches with patches on the knees for the show. She had never purchased a Dressage coat, but hoped her old coat would fit the new fuller figure. She was no longer rail thin and her calves had bulked up due to running with Tony. The boots were going to be the biggest expense she realized after attempting to put on her old ones. She discussed this with Tony and they decided that the credit cards would be used for buying the correctly fitting clothes.

This was the first time Tony acknowledged that the medications were raising havoc with Bernie's weight

and the clothing budget. "I hope this is not something we have to do on a regular basis. I've tried to keep our expenses low because of the mortgage and taxes, but this show dream of yours might break the bank this month."

"What? You thought the irritability was just due to being bipolar? Ha. The weight gain is enough to depress anyone by itself."

"I really didn't notice the weight gain until you tried on the tall boots. I also didn't realize that shows require proper clothing. I only played polo a few times and we always wore the same thing. You have tons of breeches and paddock shoes, but it never occurred to me that you'd have to go out and buy boots again. I guess we're getting older, too." He smiled at her and gave her a hug. "Hey, there's more to hug now."

She pulled away from him in disgust.

She scheduled her trip to the tack store to coincide with her next doctor's visit. She was euphoric during the appointment and he immediately noticed it. "You're on a manic high right now. Do you feel it?"

"No, I just feel good about myself and my new goals. I'm going shopping today for new clothes for a horse show after I leave here."

"How do you feel about your chances at the show?"

"Well, I have the most fabulous horse and she's been in training, so I just know we'll win. Besides, I'm a very good rider and I like to show."

"Are you sure you're not having grandiose thoughts right now?"

"What's grandiose about confidence?"

"From where I'm sitting I can't tell the difference because you've never been this upbeat before. I'd caution you to watch for the symptoms of over confidence and manic highs."

"I'm not high, just feeling good about this upcoming show and what my horse can do. I do well in lessons and am much better than the other riders. My mare is fabulous. Would you like to see a photo of her?"

"Sure."

Bernie extracted the small photo album she carried in her purse and flipped it open to a page depicting a shot of her and Noir from several years earlier. "Here she is. Isn't she the greatest looking horse you've ever seen?" Her actions and speech were quick and choppy.

"Well, I don't know anything about horses, all I can tell you is that she's a pretty horse and you look happy to be on her."

"Oh, she's more than *pretty*, she's a stunner. Just look at her conformation, and her attitude and that beautiful head with those little fox ears. She far outperforms other horses in her class."

The doctor nodded.

She also told him about Cathy's upcoming ride at the show on Noir and who Cathy was.

"How do you feel about this woman riding your horse?"

"At first I just wanted to die when I found out who the rider is, but she does a lovely job with Noir, that's my horse's name, and I'm quite proud of them together. Noir loves to jump and so does Cathy. We really haven't spoken much about the conversation we had at school. I'm more concerned that they win at the show."

"Bernie, you are going into a competition that you say is a 'rated show' where competitors will be skilled and practiced and you're not the least concerned about losing. Why is that?"

"Because we just can't lose, that's why."

"Why can't you lose?"

"We're just better than the competition out there, I just know it."

"I see. I wish you luck and confidence through this endeavor. Our time is up and I need to know if you have any questions."

"No, not right now. This is the best I've felt in a long time. I am working on the weight thing and today I get to go shopping for the proper attire that will fit my new body. I can't think of anything I need to discuss with you for a while and if I do, I'll schedule an appointment. Right now I don't feel as though I need to see you each month."

"I rather think that's not a good idea since this is all so new to you, you are new to me and the medications have

been changed and upped. It would be wise to continue until I feel we are on a more even keel."

"I disagree with you. I've been feeling good for about a week now and don't want to come back unless there's a change."

"Hmm. I can almost guarantee there will be a change, I just can't tell you when it's going to happen. I think we should keep our regular appointment for now."

Bernie was already standing, purse in hand, and said, "I'll let you know when it happens," and went out the door without stopping to reschedule another appointment.

The tack shop smelled like heaven. The smell of leather being heavy and combined with the scent of various liniments, hoof preparations, supplements and a new clothes smell. She wandered around for a bit before going to the boot department. She explained to the clerk what she was looking for and insisted on her regular shoe size in a wider calf. It hadn't dawned on her that her feet might have gained inches with the rest of her body, and when the boots didn't fit, she became a little irritable. "This is my size, but I can't get my foot into the boot. Let's try a different model."

"Ma'am, the young clerk said, "I think you need to go up a boot size to get your foot in."

"No, they just need breaking in, that's all."

"Honestly, I fit boots all day long and I believe you need to go up at least one half size. Let's just try it in the boot you picked out and see what happens."

"I'm telling you, it's the model of the boot, not the size." Bernie's temper was flaring.

Another model boot in Bernie's size was brought out with the same result.

"Ok, let's try a half size larger in the first boot," Bernie acquiesced.

This time the boot went on easily and came off with not much effort. Bernie was disappointed and confused by this. But, she finally had a pair of tall boots that fit and all she had to do was start riding in them to begin the breaking in process. She would wear them to milk in on Thursday because the milk house was clean and there was enough water splashing about to wet the boots for a more custom fit. They could dry on her feet to mold to her and fall properly.

The jacket she had did not fit, either, but she had failed to mention it to Tony. She purchased a hunt coat, two pair of breeches, four pair of riding socks, new gloves and two new blouses with chokers. When she went to ring up the purchases she noticed the stock pins and stopped and asked for assistance at the glass case. She added two of those to her merchandise and then decided to look at belts. It was a rule that hunters wear a belt in the ring and many ties in equitation classes were broken by the rider having to prove they were wearing a belt. The one's that looked like reins were the prettiest and she added one of those to the pile.

Her pile grew again when she realized she didn't have any idea where her snood was hidden and that an extra pair of gloves would be a good idea if it was raining

that day. She checked out using her credit card and hauled her cache to the car; the smell of new leather intoxicating her on the drive home.

At home she carefully unwrapped all the show clothes and put them in the section of the closet reserved for riding clothes then went down to start dinner.

Tony walked in late and asked her about the doctor's appointment. She explained to him that she didn't feel the need to go back for a while because she was feeling pretty upbeat. He, like the doctor, frowned a little.

"Are you sure about this?"

"Of course, I'm sure. I feel pretty good and some of the weight is coming off. Trying on breeches today made me feel a little better because I got into a size smaller than I expected. The boots, however, were a little different and I had to get a half size larger to accommodate my feet. Is it possible to get fat feet?"

April birds were singing and the sun was setting in the clouds, so they decided to eat outdoors.

"So how much did you spend today?" Tony queried.

"I don't know. I just got what I needed for the shows. I chose white blouses and beige breeches so I can use them in hunter shows and the lower levels of Dressage."

"What do you mean 'blouses and breeches?'" he asked. "I thought you were getting one set of clothes for the upcoming show. That sounds plural to me."

"It is plural. I need two sets of everything except a hunt coat. If I get dirty, I can change at the show."

"Bernie, what else did you buy?" He had a suspicion that she had gone overboard on the spending.

"Just the things I need. I needed a new coat because I can't button mine across my chest. I'm bigger there right now."

"That wasn't in the original conversation."

"Oh, I thought you would know that I can't wear my old one and needed to get a new one."

"How much did you spend?"

"I don't know, I just gave them my credit card and I have the receipt upstairs."

Tony pulled his lips inward and looked thoughtful for a moment. "I think I'd like to see the receipt now, if you don't mind."

"What's the problem? We discussed this and you agreed that I needed to get the right clothes to fit for the show. You know damn well I can't fit into my old stuff."

"Bernie!"

"Oh, Ok, I'll go up and get the receipt." She left the deck and went upstairs to find her purse. When she looked at the receipt, it totaled about $1,900. She hadn't looked at the piece of paper she signed and had just stuffed the receipt into her purse at the store. At that moment, it wasn't apparent to her that this might be a problem

because she never bought anything for the house or herself. They had furnished with things they brought from their apartments and only added a few pieces over the years. Their furniture had been newly purchased when they were single and it all worked in the new house. Her couch and end tables were downstairs in the family room, Tony's leather set was in the living room and her framed posters where on the walls and going up the stairs. Nothing set off alarms to her.

The alarm went off with Tony. "What were you thinking? Look at how *much* you spent. You know we have property taxes due this month. That's almost $2,000 in clothes for one horse show. You're going to have to return these extras and return them and get a credit on our cards. I can't pay property taxes with this kind of spending going on. We agreed to keep your horse at the stable one more month and that's $600, plus lessons. You have to pay to have her transported and I don't even know what the entry fees are for this."

"Noir needs a current Coggins test pulled on her before the show, so get ready for a vet bill. Plus she needs a health certificate from the vet to show. She also needs new shoes."

"What?"

"That's right, you can't show unless you send your entry in with a current Coggins and a health certificate. The stable required one, too, but that has expired. Dad paid for it last time because the vet was out working with the goats and he just had it done for me. It expired while she's been in Jackson, and I need a current one for her. I can't ask Dad to pay for another one, and I don't know

if he needs the vet out there, so I'll have to pay for a farm call, too."

Tony exploded, "Damnit, Bernie, you just broke the bank here. How am I supposed to support your fantasies and keep us afloat? This is irresponsible and selfish."

"I wasn't being selfish, we discussed this a few weeks ago and you told me to use the credit cards."

"Just tell me why, according to this receipt, that you need two of everything else?" His color was quickly rising.

"I plan to do more than one show this spring."

"Have you noticed the two machines we have in the laundry room? They're called a washer and dryer."

Later, online, Tony noticed that she had not only maxed out the card, but gone over the limit. His wrath was not to be ignored. "You'll have to drive back to Ann Arbor and get credit for the extra stuff."

"That will cost more in gas, is that wise?"

"I don't care about your supposed wisdom, just do it; and very soon. We are paying a mortgage, a lawn service, utilities, food, work clothes, dry cleaning and cannot afford this show stuff. You can very well wash your clothes and iron them for shows. I need to keep my suits dry cleaned and you have school suits that need dry cleaning. This is intolerable and irresponsible."

"You just don't understand the showing thing. I can't very well show two days in a row and clean my clothes and expect them to dry before the next day."

"I thought you were only showing in the Sunday show and doing the hunter classes. Now, you're showing in the Saturday Dressage portion?"

She looked sheepish and said, "I considered it, that's all. My horse is going to be there in a stall and I thought, 'why not?'"

"You mean we are paying for two stall days?"

"Yes, they take the horses in the day before the show starts and they stay there. Cathy rides on Sunday, and I ride on Sunday. Then I thought I might enter Dressage Intro A and B for Saturday. I also planned on riding her Saturday to keep her in shape and ready for Sunday. Either way, I was going to ride her.

"No, you're not showing on Saturday. That means more entry fees and having to put you up in a hotel for two nights. One on Friday and one on Saturday. Can you split a room on Saturday with someone?"

"I don't know anyone from that barn other than Cathy and I don't want to spend a night with the school counselor. It's bad enough they recommended her to ride my horse."

"You agreed to it. Why did you agree to it if you didn't want her to ride?"

"What was I supposed to say? I kinda got roped into it and then found out that she rode Noir well. Noir likes to jump and I don't."

"When I don't want to do something, I say 'No.' This is total Bernie logic; meaning it's not very logical."

"It's a onetime thing."

"I thought you were going to show all spring and summer. What makes it a onetime thing? Are you going to take the horse from her after the show? What if she wins her classes? Are you going to say, 'Now that you won, I don't want you riding my horse again?'"

"Oh, Tony, I don't know. It's all confusing to me. I have to keep her out of my life and separate from school. I don't know what I'm really going to do. I just was bamboozled by this whole thing. How could I know who they had in mind for jumping my horse? This is a situation that I don't know how to change."

"Well, you'd better think about it and correct it. Also, don't forget to take those clothes back and get credit. Maybe if you laid off the wine a little more, you'd not be consuming empty calories and adding weight to your diet."

"That's not fair. You eat whatever you like and don't gain weight. You're not taking medications that make you fat. You have no empathy at all."

"I have plenty of empathy for you, but not for the situation you put us in. I thought you were only going to watch the Dressage portion of the show and stay one

night and ride the next day. What is this Cathy woman doing to get to the show?"

"She's bringing her kids to Saturday's show and having their father drive over and pick them up Saturday afternoon. That's all I know so far."

"I suggest you get to know her better, share a room and split the expenses and work together for Sunday's show. I don't want to take the show away from you because you've been practicing for it and have your heart set on it, but you have to give us a little leeway here. The clothes need to be returned and you need to get down to a size to fit into your whites if you want to show in Dressage, too. I'm not paying for sixty pair of breeches for one show season because you suddenly forgot how to use a washing machine!"

She was angry all the way back to Ann Arbor the next afternoon. Angry at not being able to drive to Jackson to ride her horse, angry at Tony, angry at not being able to afford the things she wanted at this time and angry at the world for unfairness. Although the spring day was beautiful, she saw nothing but road before her. The tack shop was gracious about the returns because she had just purchased them the day before. The gloves and stock pins were returned as well as the breeches and the extra blouse. She was in a foul mood and wasn't very patient during the return process. Her previously high mood was dampened. She drove home and resented that she was not able to ride her horse. *Yeah, Cathy gets to ride Noir today, but not me.*

Her anger was taken out on Tony by making sandwiches and salad for dinner. She was in no mood to cook and

felt he didn't deserve anything better. She had put a full day in teaching and had a small run-in with McGinty. Some boys looked as though they were about to start a food fight and she nipped it quickly. McGinty was on lunch duty with her and told her they were just letting off steam due to finals. She countered him by telling him that the girls always behaved during lunch and the boys got away with everything short of murder and it was his fault for not disciplining them. They squared off outside the cafeteria glaring at one another.

Celeste seemed to be in a fairly bad mood, as well. She avoided Bernie during classes and during lunch duty. Bernie tried several times to get her attention, but Celeste either didn't see her attempts or was ignoring her.

Thursday afternoon Celeste didn't show up at the barn. The thunderstorms started as she arrived and she wondered where Celeste was. She called her cell phone and her house several times. Because Celeste wasn't there, Bernie had to do all jobs herself and realized how much she missed Celeste and how much longer it took without help. She was fairly throwing things by the time she started washing equipment and cleaning up. She called Celeste two more times, but it went to voice mail and her answering machine. Bernie was not looking forward to driving home soaking wet and making dinner for Tony.

"You get in late?" Tony asked when he came through the garage door.

"Why?"

"Well, I see you assembling sandwiches again for dinner. But there's soup."

"I didn't make it, it was frozen." She said testily.

"You aren't in a good mood, I can see."

"Nope, something's up with Celeste and she didn't show tonight. I had to do the entire process myself and it took longer than usual. I went yesterday to return the clothes and didn't get to drive to Jackson to ride Noir. I'm not the happiest camper right now."

"Honey, thanks for returning the stuff. We'll be in a better position after the property taxes are paid and I get my fees collected. Right now we have a number of clients who haven't caught up and it's causing some problems in the office. I may have to lay off one person for a short period of time. Just when I was thinking about an intern, too."

"Oh, that's nice." She said without much enthusiasm.

"We've got Candy on collections. One thing you don't want to do is pay your lawyer! Candy is not happy about making calls, either. Seems everyone is in a bad mood lately."

"Look, I have papers to read and grade, I'm going to eat my sandwich upstairs at my desk. Sorry not to be good company, but I'm better off alone right now." She picked up her plate and bowl and left the kitchen leaving Tony standing there in confusion. He followed her upstairs to change his clothes and left when he saw her open her folders.

She took the bread off her sandwich and ate the contents, slurped up the soup and returned her dishes to the kitchen, disposing of the bread in the trash compactor. *Fine, I'll just cut out as many carbs as I can and get back into those breeches. I'll run farther each morning and start walking with Noir instead of riding her when this show is over. You'll see, Mister.* She fumed.

She attempted to call Celeste's home one more time before bed and, again, the answering machine picked up. "I wonder if she's not feeling well. I hope she didn't get some disease from school." She washed her face and got ready for bed, pulling out the current book. She didn't dare bring out the bottle of Scotch because she had no idea when Tony was going to appear for bed. As it happened, she could have because he had taken his own folder of work downstairs with him and read during commercials. She was already asleep from mental exhaustion by the time he walked into the bedroom.

Friday morning Celeste didn't appear at school and a substitute was brought in for her classes. *Wow, she must be sick. I wish she'd call me and let me know, though.*

She drove to Jackson after school and rode Noir in a class practicing for flat classes in the hunter ring. Noir did well and Bernie was pleased with her. Her sweeping gait was powerful and Bernie's continence changed considerably. Cathy came over to get the horse to practice their jumping and Bernie broached the subject of sharing a hotel room with her. "My husband doesn't want me to spend money on two days and thinks

I should seek out a roommate. I know we don't know one another well, but it will save us both some money."

"Well, Bernie, I was afraid to ask and budgeted for a single room. If you don't mind, I'll take you up on the offer. Should I make the room reservation or will you?

"I have the recommended hotels on the show bill I saved and I'll be happy to do it.

"You can just give me the cash when we check out Sunday morning. OK?"

"Sure, that works for me. And thanks, it will save me money and maybe I can enter another show this year. If we show at the same ones, we can keep splitting a room."

Bernie didn't know how to broach the subject of not showing together and for Cathy to find another horse to ride and show, so she didn't say anything. "OK, we've got two weeks until D day. Let's focus on getting her ready. If you're going to be there Saturday afternoon, I'll ride her and you can ride her, then we'll bathe her and I'll braid her mane for the next morning. The jumping portion is in the afternoon and I'm up in the morning. That ought to give her a little time to rest between classes."

"Oh, can I at least watch? I've never braided before and it would be good for me to see the process because I just learned how to pull a mane. This show has me cranked."

"Well, sure. I'm used to braiding for Dressage, so I'll have to look up the braid for hunters. I don't know if they need to be removed before jumping or not. I'll

check. Either way, I have to look it all up because of my ignorance about hunters. Thank God they're teaching us how to work a ring for the group classes. Noir's mostly been ridden alone and we've been partners for four years; just us. Having to be in with other horses was difficult for her in the beginning since she's been alone so long."

They were sitting in the lounge talking like old friends and Bernie found herself teaching. "Cathy, do you have all your clothes together for the show?"

"Yes, I got tall boots and a coat and show gloves. I should be ready."

"May I make a suggestion?"

"By all means."

"Put all your show clothes, and only your show clothes in one bag. Like a hanging one. Then check to see if you've remembered everything, including your underwear for that day. That's what I do and I don't touch it until the morning of the show. That way I know that everything is in one place and I haven't forgotten anything. Do you have a stock pin? Keep it in a box or a Ziploc bag with your gloves and hair net. That way you can find it and they don't fall out and get lost."

"Yes, I got a stock pin, too. That's a great idea. Then you're not running around nervous that morning looking for things."

"Yes, and everything is protected from dirt in the bag. I usually wear my show breeches and a long shirt or top

over my blouse. I wash my hands before putting on my chocker and stock pin, then wait until the last minute for my coat and gloves. And, whatever you do, don't forget your helmet. I usually stuff mine into the same bag."

"OK. This is good advice."

"When we're done washing and braiding her, I'll put a blanket on her and a slinky to keep her from rubbing her braids out and if she lies down during the night, she'll stay clean and keep shavings off her. It'll be just a matter of brushing down the coat with a soft brush and cleaning her tail.

"I have to check to see if shavings are provided by the show, or if we have to buy them there or bring them. I should talk to Sue because she knows. Do you know where she is?"

"No, I didn't see her tonight. Well, Bernie, I'd better be getting home to my kids. I have to pick them up from daycare and get them some supper."

"OK, I'll find out about the shavings and see you next week. I'm having the barn's farrier come and put new shoes on her. Nothing fancy because you're only doing the 18 inch and the two foot. She doesn't need caulks or anything now. See you later." Bernie went in search of Jack.

She found him near the trailers parked in back. "Hey, stranger."

"Hey, Bernie, how are you?"

"Getting ready for the big show. I'm sharing my horse with Cathy and we are doing our planning. I need to ask a few questions about the show that you might be able to answer."

"Shoot."

"Who provides the stall shavings for the show? The show or us?"

"You have to buy them there and then strip your stall before we leave because they will charge you a stall cleaning fee. Some shows make you leave a cleaning deposit check when you register. Each show is different."

"How are we supposed to do that?"

"Sue carries pitchforks and brooms and rakes with her and a wheelbarrow. You just get it done before we pull out. The grounds have to be left clean or she gets charged and then charges it to you. Don't make her mad. She keeps this place spotless and expects her students to repeat the same habits away from home."

"Will we have any problems getting Noir on the trailer?"

"I doubt it. When are you taking her home again? I miss our meetings in the woods."

Bernie blushed. "I'll have to have someone haul her home after the show."

"Look, I can load her last and stop by your father's place and unload her first if you follow us. You just need to let Sue know that she's headed home after the show."

"Yeah, I really wasn't thinking about that until you mentioned it. I'd better find her and let her know that I won't be boarding here after that Sunday."

"When are you going to be building your arena? The offer to help still stands."

"I've already spent the money and had all the posts and boards delivered. My father knows, but my husband doesn't. He's keeping me on a tight budget right now and he doesn't need to know that everything has been purchased."

"I thought you worked full-time."

"I do, but there are some big bills coming up and he's got us on a budget."

"What does he do for a living?"

Bernie felt uncomfortable telling Jack what Tony did. "He has a law practice in Cold Lake. It's a small practice for a small town."

"Oh, I see. I think I remember you telling me that." Jack seemed uncomfortable knowing this.

"Well, let me see if I can track Sue down. Do you have any idea where she might be right now?"

Jack looked at his watch and said, "She should be starting a private lesson in one of the indoors right now. You might be able to just catch her."

"Thanks. I'll see you later. What are you doing, by the way? I thought your work day was finished."

"I'm checking all trailer tires for wear and air so if we need anything; it's not a last minute purchase. Just one of my jobs."

Bernie caught up with Sue just as she was about to enter the West indoor arena. She explained what she had told Jack and his suggestion. Sue listened intently and asked, "So you won't be showing with us for June?"

"Yes, I'd very much like to show in June, but I've got to save money and Noir has her own stall and pastures at home. I'll just come back, I guess."

"We may not have any stalls available by then. I'll keep you at the top of the list for open stalls during show season, though."

"Thanks, Sue, I really appreciate that. I just have to budget like everyone else. Noir needs some pasture time, too and a rest." She purposely did not mention that she was building an arena at the farm because that may have moved her down a notch on the list. The less Sue knew, the better their chances for a stall before the next show.

On the way home Bernie started thinking about the building of the arena and how she could convince her father that she did it herself without involving Jack's name. She had already decided to take Jack up on his offer, but knew that two people doing the work meant it was going to go a lot faster than one woman. How could she hide the fact that she had help? *Why didn't she not want to tell her father or Tony about Jack's offer*? Why hide this fact? Hiding things, other than alcohol, was not in her nature; but she didn't give this much thought.

She was still angry at Tony and angry with her father. By the time she pulled into the garage she was seething again and had no idea what she had issues with.

Celeste still wasn't at school on Monday and wasn't answering her phone. She appeared Tuesday and acted as though nothing had happened. She didn't appear to have been sick and didn't go out of her way to talk to Bernie, nor did she explain her absence.

Bernie sought out Charlene and asked her.

"I have no idea, she's your friend, why don't you ask her?"

"I haven't seen her in several days and she seems really busy."

"Not my problem, Bernie." Charlene walked away.

Tight ass*, thought Bernie. *I wonder what the problem is with her. I didn't do anything to deserve that snub.

Thursday Celeste returned to the farm, but was a little distant. She did her usual excellent job with the animals and cleaning, but wasn't very talkative. Her lack of information grated on Bernie's nerves.

"Celeste, are you not feeling well?"

"Why?" Celeste asked with disinterest.

"I don't know. You missed several days of school last week and I couldn't get you on the phone. I just wondered if you were sick or something."

"Nope, just needed some personal time. The sub didn't do any damage and all is well."

Bernie heard the curt replies and the lack of enthusiasm in Celeste's voice and decided not to press it further. She went about her chores and let Celeste do what she did, but noticed that Celeste didn't much talk to the goats. Celeste left Bernie to clean up and drove away after her portion of the job was finished. Bernie felt the missing pieces, but could not define it. It was as though Celeste wasn't really there. She might as well have just done the job herself and let Celeste have a break. Maybe that was it, Celeste was tired and needed a break. How could she let her know, if she didn't pick up the phone? It was useless to call because Bernie had tried every night since Celeste hadn't shown up last Thursday. She bit her lower lip while washing equipment. Not much went through her head and thoughts were slow to come.

Tony's demeanor wasn't much different when he came home. He was distant and not very talkative. She asked him about this and his reply was short as he expressed exhaustion from his day. Bernie again felt alone for the second time that evening. She didn't bother to mention Celeste's lack of pep to Tony; he seemed as though he didn't care much and parked himself in front of the TV after dinner. She went upstairs to the Scotch bottle and her book. A light sadness descended on her; much like the Sunday sadness when she was single. No one to talk to, no one to play or work with. She was alone again.

She was restless and started packing her clothes for the show. After she packed them, she unpacked them and tried them on just to be sure. Looking at herself in the

mirror she liked the formal attire, right down to the gloves. Tony entered the bedroom and started laughing. His laughter lightened her mood and she said, "I just want to make sure these fit before I pack it all in one bag. How do I look?"

"You look great, Honey."

"It feels good. I'm looking forward to this show. Are you sure you can't come and watch?"

"I'm sorry, but I really promised I'd play golf with my father. It was decided well before you entered. It's the Chamber's golf scramble and Dad thinks we'll do well. So we'll both be in a competition on that day. Also, I'm one of the sponsors and it would not be good for me to not attend. Seeing you dressed, however, makes me want to watch you show. Maybe the next one.

"Are you planning to go to Jackson tomorrow to practice?"

"Yeah, why?"

"Could you be home in time to shower and change and we can go catch a movie? I thought it would be nice to get out of here for a night. We can grab some dinner too. How does sushi sound?"

"Oh, that's a wonderful idea. Are you sure you don't want to do something else after? I don't know of any movies, unless you've got one in mind."

"Um, not exactly. I haven't been keeping up with current movies. Maybe I can pick up a paper tomorrow and decide before you get home. It seems almost silly to be

in Jackson twice in one day, but we don't have much of a choice. Remember, we have dinner at my parent's on Sunday."

"Yup, looking forward to it.

"Tony, I need some extra cash for the show because I have to eat the night before and have some for breakfast and lunch. I can grab a breakfast sandwich at some fast food place with Cathy that morning, but I'll need to eat lunch at the show. Any budgetary constraints that I need to know about?"

"No, but when you show, you should already have thought of that and budgeted it in. Just saying."

The week at school flew by. Either she was distracted or things moved fast, she couldn't tell. Thursday came and Celeste showed up at the barn for milking. Celeste was abnormally quiet again and Bernie didn't press it. She had other things on her mind about the upcoming weekend, so she wasn't as concerned about Celeste's frame of mind as much as she should have been.

Dad appeared in the milk house halfway through milking and Celeste lit up, stunning Bernie with her normal talkative nature.

"I just wanted to know how you girls were doing here this evening. Mom and I decided not to go out because we are both tired. I thought I'd just check in. There are some new does and I wanted to see how they handled. Anything I should know about?"

Celeste spoke right up, "Not really. We've had a few kicks out of the new ones, but nothing we can't handle. We just go slowly with them. You do have one here," Celeste pointed to an older nanny, "that isn't producing as much as she did last year. Any thoughts?"

"Ah, Gracie, yes. She's getting old. She used to be one of my best producers and I'm afraid she's going to have to be sold soon. I'd probably do well to sell her while she's still lactating than wait. Glad you mentioned it, Celeste. Thank you."

Bernie was a little miffed because Celeste hadn't mentioned this to her and she hadn't noticed Gracie's lack of production herself. She didn't have anything new to report to her father and, if she did, she would leave a note for him. She was embarrassed for not noticing because it was her job to weigh the milk before it got strained into the tank. Obviously, Celeste paid more attention to the animals and their particular quirks than Bernie did. This job was starting to get old, but she needed a place to keep Noir, so she kept her mouth shut. *I'd better wake up soon. It's got to be the drugs*, she thought.

Carl left the milk parlor and Celeste became quiet again. "I'm losing weight, Celeste. The diet and running is working. I got into a size smaller breeches when I had to shop for my show clothes."

"Good for you, Bernie." Celeste's voice sounded obligatory.

"How's your diet coming along?"

"I'm sticking to it and it's working. Just hard to keep remembering that I'm on it is the only problem. Habits die hard." There was no spark in her voice again.

They finished up and Celeste drove out before Bernie could offer her a drink. *Strange. Wonder what I did? She seems to be taking something out on me, but I don't know what it is.* Bernie cleaned up and went to the pump house herself. She poured a glass of wine and sat in the near darkness alone, but no thoughts arrived. She sat and looked at the wall. A half hour later she was in her car and headed home to make dinner.

She woke early Saturday morning, dressed in schooling clothes and made English muffin egg sandwiches for her and Tony; she left Tony's for him. He was sleeping while she drove to Ann Arbor. Since she had loaded her show clothes the night before, all she needed to do was grab her overnight bag and she was off.

The drive seemed to fly by until she got lost. The car's GPS system sent her in the wrong direction and she couldn't find the fairgrounds. She got frustrated and worried that she'd miss the lower level classes she wanted to see and show in. Her horse had been hauled in and settled the night before by the Thousand Pines staff and all she had to do was show up. Eventually she stopped at a gas station and asked directions. She was only one road over from the show grounds, but the GPS didn't recognize the road because it only served the fairgrounds. She found her destination and hurriedly found a parking space and practically ran to the rings.

Classes had not yet begun and she looked around for anyone familiar. This was not her group from the barn

and she felt a little lost and out of place hauling her folding chair out of the trunk and looking for a place to set it up. Her distraction was such that it didn't occur to her to find her horse and check on it. She had a single-minded goal to watch the Intro classes to assess whether or not she'd have a chance showing without instruction. The only Dressage instruction at Thousand Pines was on Thursdays again. She took her regular lesson on Tuesday now and she didn't have a way to haul to any barns where there might be specialized teaching for this.

Someone had done a lovely job setting up the lettered markers and decorating with flowers. The judge's booth was freshly painted and also adorned with flowers. The judge, wearing a showy hat, sat in the booth with the scribe. Bernie could feel her pulse start to race. *Oh, I wish it were me today instead of tomorrow. I don't have any idea what I'm supposed to do tomorrow other than what we've been shown. I just don't feel comfortable.* Nor was she comfortable sitting alone watching the first rider enter after the bell ringing.

Watching the rides, she realized she didn't know the current tests or have a current test sheet to follow. She felt self-conscious and hoped to memorize the pattern of the test through successive rides. She saw and understood more than she realized, but her discomfort detracted from learning anything other than correct circles and good use of corners. One rider, a young girl, had a reader for her test. The reader appeared to be the instructor, who called out each maneuver before it was to be completed. When the girl's class was finished the caller dropped her copy of the test into the waste can.

Bernie got up and fished it out. She finally had a copy of Intro Test A and stapled to it was a copy of Test B. Bernie could follow the pattern now, but there was only one more rider for Test A.

"Hey, I was looking for you." Cathy appeared with her own folding chair and set it up next to Bernie's.

"Hi."

"What'd I miss?"

"All of Test A. But don't worry, I didn't understand any of it until the last ride because I didn't have a copy of the test. I do now. I dug it out of a garbage can. I've got Test B right here if you want to look at it. Do you understand any of this?"

"I've been reading about Dressage and have a basic idea. I want to follow this discipline, but Dressage horses are expensive. Hell, all horses are expensive. I'm really grateful to you for letting me ride Noir. How'd she settle in?"

"Ah," Bernie's face colored, "I don't know. I haven't checked on her because I was late getting here and didn't want to miss these two tests because I'd like to compete at this level to start Noir back into Dressage." Bernie swallowed, "Did you check on her?"

"Yes, that's why I was late. She's fine. She's eating hay and seems uninterested in her surroundings. You can relax. There's no need to be embarrassed. You want to compete and you paid to have your horse transported and cared for at this show. It's clear that I made you

uncomfortable. I didn't mean to. I just didn't know how focused you were on this. I apologize."

"No, I apologize. I was a bad mommy. I got caught."

"Well, you didn't even have to be here today because we don't show until tomorrow. Or, not do any work until this afternoon. I, too, am very interested in Dressage, or at least the part of it that is involved in three day eventing. That's my goal." Cathy sighed. "If I can ever afford a horse, that is. And, you shouldn't worry about being a bad 'mommy' because I left my kids at the concession stand to eat breakfast! I was looking for you first."

While scores were being tallied, riders were warming up in the practice ring. The second test hadn't begun yet and Cathy and Bernie chatted for a few minutes about riding goals.

"Hey, how long do you think you want to leave your kids loose? I don't know anything about them, but loose kids at a horse show can make you fast enemies. Do we need to go look for them?"

"Nope. They each have a folding chair and instructions to come over here when they're finished eating. They should be headed this way soon."

"Should we look for them?"

Cathy stood up, shielded her eyes with her hand and said, "They're headed this way now. I'll go help them so they don't get in the way or run anyone over or spook any horses with their chairs." She left and returned with

a boy of about ten and a girl who looked to be around12 years old. The boy carried a small cooler slung over his shoulder. "Noah and Marci, meet Mrs. Romanelli."

Both children extended their hands to shake. Bernie was a little surprised at their good manners and took both their small hands and lightly shook them. "So, do either of you ride?"

"I ride," said Marci.

"No, you don't ride. You've been on some pony rides. These kids practice and have their own horses."

"I saw a girl my age on a pony a while ago and I can do what she was doing."

Not wanting to engage the child in an argument, Cathy said, "I'll tell you what, you sit here with us and watch this next class. If you think you can get on a horse and do what these kids are doing, I'll get you one riding lesson where I learn. How's that sound?

"Also, there is to be no talking while riders are in this ring because it's prohibited to make any noise; which is considered rude. Do you both understand me?"

The children nodded. Noah set the cooler down, plopped down in the chair and leaned over and unzipped the nylon, extracted a can of soda and handed it to his sister.

"Hey, that's for lunch time. It's too early to be drinking soda. Put it back, Noah," Cathy admonished him.

A rider was coming up to the ring and riding around it. When the bell rang she seemed to leisurely make

her way to the gate. She entered at A at a posting trot and stopped squarely at X, smartly saluted the judge and proceeded. This went on for 12 more rides. Cathy's children grew restless.

"When do we get to see the horse you're riding?" asked Marci.

"When these classes are over and we go up to the barns," answered Cathy.

"This is boring," whined Noah.

"Well, you had a choice, spend the day at a horse show or spend an extra day with your father. You made your choice, so you'll have to live with it. We are very interested in this show because this is what we want to do."

"Can't we walk around?"

"No, not unescorted. I don't need one of you to get run over and I don't want you to spook a horse by not knowing how to behave around them. You could get someone hurt by moving too fast or running. Do you notice any children running around here? No one is running or playing because they all have horse experience and most of them are showing their horses here today."

"Even the girl on the pony?" asked Marci.

"Yes, even the girl on the pony. There will be several more ponies competing today. This is where people who know how to ride show, and horses get used to being around a busy place so they know how to show and not be spooky and dangerous."

Bernie listened to Cathy as she talked to her children. She was impressed with how well the kids listened to her and didn't argue. Cathy obviously had done a lot of disciplinary work with them. Watching Dressage, someone once told her, was as exciting as watching grass grow; at least at the lower levels where they basics were applied. Sitting for hours in a folding chair couldn't have been the most exciting thing they could imagine doing. She guessed correctly that their idea of a horse show and the realities were two different concepts. It was clear that Cathy had never taken them to her lessons.

Bernie said, "Let's wait a few more minutes, watch a few Training Level rides and then I'll introduce them to Noir if you haven't already done so."

"I wouldn't think of opening that stall door until you gave me permission. I just looked in at her on my way down here."

"Yeah, well, I'm still a little uncomfortable having someone share my horse, so thanks."

"I perceived that when you first allowed me to jump her. Don't worry about it, she's your possession and you should worry about her. Did I ever tell you how beautiful I find her?"

"No, thanks so much. But, I'm prejudiced because she's mine. That means a lot to me."

"Well, it's an honor to be able to ride her, let alone show her tomorrow. I hope we both do well. I'm very nervous and I imagine tomorrow I'll be a wreck."

"Oh, all you have to do is remember the first lesson you got through and you'll do fine. Of course, I can dispense all the show advice I want right now because I'm not showing today!"

The May sun was beginning to heat up and Bernie found that sunglasses weren't doing the trick. Cathy noticed Bernie starting to perspire and said, "I've got a straw hat in my car if you want to borrow it."

"No thanks, I forgot a hat, but I bet they sell them at the tack trailer. I'll go look in a few minutes after we see Noir. They picked up their folding chairs and headed to the barns.

Noir's and the Thousand Pines stalls were indoor and shaded. The older group of Thursday night Dressage riders were actively working with their horses in anticipation of their classes. Bernie made a mental note to introduce herself to them. Maybe the instructor would teach on a night other than Thursdays again.

Jack wearing breeches, boots and a farm logoed polo shirt was holding a horse for a student who was putting on her coat. "Hey, I wondered where you were."

"Hi Jack. Cathy and I've been watching some of the Intro tests." She introduced Noah and Marci and Jack suggested that they join a group of other kids under a trailer awning. Apparently, Thousand Pines, or someone, had foresight because there were games, coloring books, a muck bucket filled with ice and soft drinks and lots of folding chairs. Cathy was visibly grateful. The trailer with the awning was parked behind one of the barns,

but within eyesight of the Thousand Pines stalls so the children could be watched.

"Do you want Noir ridden while she's here?" He said. "I have extra time on my hands this afternoon as soon as the Quadrille group is done. They go in around lunch time as an exhibition."

"No, thanks. Cathy and I are going to ride her and then bathe and braid. I think it's better to deal with whatever she decides to do now than have to eat crow tomorrow. So, how'd she travel for you?"

"Great, no problems at all. She settled right in last night. I think it was a wise decision to move her to Thousand Pines before the show, because she seems unaffected by all the activity. She hasn't made any noise at all. Listen, my wife is watching the kids out back if you two want to return to watching the classes."

"Thanks," said Cathy. "They were getting bored."

"We have lots of parents here and no babysitters, so we do this as a service. All we ask is that you feed your own kids."

"I'll run by a store before we ride and bring some treats back for the kids in repayment for the babysitting. Just watch Noah, he wanders off when he gets bored. Their father will be arriving this afternoon to pick them up and after that I'll be free. If you need some relief just let me know." Cathy offered.

Jack looked surprised, "Oh, that'd be great, Cathy. Thanks. We don't often have volunteers here because they are so wrapped up in their classes."

Bernie and Cathy were ringside again in their chairs when Bernie said, "Oh, now I wish I had copies of the other tests. I know I could at least do a Training Level with Noir at the next show. I plan to enter Intro A, B and C." She didn't mention the budgetary restraints that Tony had imposed or offer to let Cathy ride in the next show. She thought she'd just deal with it as it happened. Bernie found Cathy to be a pleasant companion and she was grateful for the company.

Around noon Cathy looked at her watch and said, "I need to check on my children and see if their father has arrived yet. We agreed that he'd take them to lunch before going home. I want to make sure that he's on time and get them off. I'll be back." She left Bernie watching the riders.

About 30 minutes later she returned and asked Bernie if she wanted to go to the grocery store with her to pick up treats for the kids under the awning. "I looked at what they had and I decided that veggies and ranch dip might be healthier than the cookies they have up there. Kids seem to like that and we can just pick up a tray in the deli. I passed a grocery on the way here and it wasn't far. You game? Or do you want to stay and watch?"

"No, I'm watched out. I'll go with you. Do you want me to drive?"

"They're my kids and they got watched for free, so I'll drive."

When they returned it was time for their schooling rides. Both had come dressed to ride and all they had to do was find their helmets. Cathy had one helmet to be used for show and schooling. Bernie had a schooling helmet with her and her show helmet packed in her show bag.

They took Noir out of her stall and lunged her in a sandy paddock. Each took a turn lunging her and then Cathy gave Bernie a leg up. It seemed to Bernie that they had been friends for a long time. Indeed, a very strange feeling considering their first meeting circumstances and Bernie's possessiveness with Noir.

Cathy watched Bernie school her horse and then they switched places and Cathy rode Noir to the practice ring with the jumps. "I'm not going to over jump her today or tomorrow before her classes. I just want her to be comfortable on the grounds and then we can grab some lunch and get her bathed and beautified. How's that sound to you?"

"Sounds perfect. She can hang out in her stall for a few minutes while we eat."

Noir was quiet during her bath and stood in cross ties while Bernie braided and Cathy watched and handed her pieces of yarn. "How'd you learn to do that?" she asked.

"Lots of practice. I knew I'd have to do it at some point, so I taught her to stand and I practiced until my fingers bled. Honestly, they bled. Horse hair is coarse and it takes two to do this; a quiet horse and a steady hand. I like the braids tight so they don't come out. Hand me

that hairspray can, so I can set these braids before we put her hood on."

After they finished, they went to their respective cars and Cathy followed Bernie to the hotel. They registered and dragged their baggage to the room. "Which bed do you want? Bernie asked Cathy.

"Your horse, your choice."

"Ok, I want the one closest to the phone because I need to get up the earliest. How long do you think it will take you to get ready tomorrow?"

"It depends on how long you need. I am going to wear my hair in a net under my helmet, so I don't have to curl it or anything. You're the one who has to be ready first because your class starts at 8:30. You tell me."

"I was thinking a five o'clock wake up so I can use the bathroom and shower and get my makeup on before we grab breakfast. Noir only needs to have her hood and blanket removed and be lunged before I warm up. I figure if we leave here by six, we should be good. Can you get in the shower after me?"

"Works for me."

They decided to find a Chinese restaurant for dinner and took Bernie's car. At first Bernie was going to suggest that they take Cathy's minivan, but nixed the idea. "She'll just have to get used to the idea of what I drive. Everyone knows about the car, anyway. Let her make her own assumptions; there's nothing I can do to hide it. *Oh, a truck would be lovely*, she thought.

Bernie had two glasses of wine with dinner and Cathy had one. Bernie brought up the subject of how well behaved Cathy's children were at the show.

"They were threatened within an inch of their lives. I told them I'd never take them to a horse show again if they didn't listen to me. They are not always that well behaved. You deal with kids all day long, so you should know."

"No, I deal with older kids all day and they can be a disrespectful handful. I'm not exactly patient with younger children. Your girl is how old?"

"Marci just turned 12."

"Oh."

"Bernie, what does your husband do for a living? I see you wear a ring. I'm surprised that he isn't here with you today."

"Tony and his father are playing in a golf scramble sponsored by the Chamber in Cold Lake tomorrow. He's an attorney with his own practice in town. What does your ex do?"

"He's a math professor at the community college in Jackson. He is involved with a woman right now and doesn't always make time for the kids. They aren't as much fun as they were when they were little and into Disney, so he doesn't exactly spend as much time with them as he should. This just started and it's been hard on me and the kids. At least I don't have to deal with abuse and civil disobedience like I do in my job."

"Yeah, your job. It has to be difficult to counsel teens all day long."

"It's not all teens. They're not the most difficult because they love to talk. It's the younger children who get to you because they don't know how to express themselves as well."

Bernie's mind started to fidget because she hoped that the Nash event wouldn't be brought up. *How did this conversation start, anyway*? she mused.

Her segue was abrupt, "Well, let's us get to the hotel and start to get rested up for tomorrow.

The hotel bar was active and Bernie asked Cathy if she could buy her a glass of wine. There was a live band and they both enjoyed more than one glass of wine while tapping their feet to the music. *At least it's noisy enough in here that we don't have to talk much,* thought Bernie. *I sure don't want to talk school and I hope she doesn't bring it up again. I've shown before, but maybe she's just nervous enough to be distracted.*

At ten thirty Cathy nudged Bernie and pointed to her watch. "I guess we better head up or neither of us will get up tomorrow."

In the elevator Bernie's cell phone rang in her purse. "Hello, my love."

"Where have you been all night," Tony seemed agitated.

"What do you mean?"

"I've called three times tonight and it went to voice mail."

"Oh, we were in the bar and there was a live band. I didn't hear it."

"Oh, great, a bar. How much did you drink?"

"Oh, just a couple of glasses of wine," she tried to sound casual because of Cathy. We are on our way to the room now," she said hoping he'd get the idea that someone was with her and she didn't want to have this discussion.

"I sure hope you can get up in time tomorrow. You have to realize that this is an athletic competition and athletes shouldn't drink before competing."

"Oh, don't worry, Honey, we are fine," she tried to hint to him again.

"Why did the phone go to voice mail?"

"Because there was a band and I couldn't hear it."

She hated to play this card, but she did, "I will have to talk to you tomorrow morning because we need to get some sleep right now. We're in the elevator and the service is terrible," she disconnected.

Five o'clock came very early for two women drinking the night before. Bernie groggily answered the wakeup call and tried not to groan about the headache when she slipped out of bed. Cathy was wakened, but didn't move.

Bernie showered and then came back to the bed and set up her makeup mirror. She applied some shadow

and waterproof mascara because she knew she was going to sweat with nerves. Cathy made her way into the bathroom and emerged a few minutes later. "Do you need the bathroom any longer? I've showered already."

"No, I'm fine right now. I just wish we had coffee."

"I can make this little pot and we can split it until we get to the fairgrounds. How's that sound?"

At the show they both made it to the concession stand and both ordered two cups of coffee before arriving at Noir's stall. Bernie's show trunk, carefully loaded and unloaded by Jack held their second cups of coffee while they removed her blanket and hood. Noir had fared well during the night and looked a little fresh. Her ears were up and she was swishing her tail in annoyance.

"She looks a little hot to me. Probably because she is not used to a morning schedule and wants her time off. I think she needs to be lunged more than yesterday. She'll just have to gather her energy back between classes, Cathy."

"Yeah, she looks crabby."

Cathy acted as Bernie's groom. She even went back to the concession stand and got them more coffee. She had paid attention to how Bernie took her coffee and fixed it perfectly. Bernie was thrilled to have someone who didn't hassle her in the hotel and who had shared a partial girl's night and understood what show nerves were all about. They lunged Noir and the mare settled down.

The first classes were lead line and Bernie watched atop Noir while Cathy stood nearby. "Oh how cute. I wish my kids had a chance to experience this for themselves. One day their father will get with the program and spring for riding lessons for them. At least for Marci. I don't think Noah is interested in anything like this at all.

"It looks as though your class is ready to enter. I'm glad you showed me how to register and get our numbers. Good luck in there. I'd say 'break a leg,' but I don't think that's appropriate here!"

"Thanks, Cathy. I need a tranquilizer because I've never done this before other than at the barn. Let's hope she doesn't get peeved about anything in there and behaves and strides correctly. Bye. Pray," Bernie said and walked to the gate.

The class seemed to last forever, yet went by too fast to concentrate. Bernie placed third in a class of seventeen. She wasn't happy and it showed.

"I just got whipped by a tween on a pony," she gritted her teeth.

"I thought you did very well for your first hunter class, Bernie." It was Jack standing ringside. Congratulations. Sue is happy, look across the ring."

Bernie glanced across the ring to see Sue giving her a thumbs up. Cathy seemed ecstatic.

"You just need to relax," Jack cautioned her. "Your next class is equitation and you have to be perfect, Noir already knows what to do. If you give her a little bit

of leeway, she'll carry you though. You've got a good chance to win that class. I know your horse and what she can do. The same to you, Cathy, let her have her head a little and she'll perform. She's a natural ham."

"Oh, speaking of ham, Cathy, do you have a camera with you? I left mine in the tack trunk and I don't have any show pictures of Noir."

"I can get it or you can walk up with me. You don't go in for a few classes and it will give you a chance to relax on your horse. You looked good in there and I'm glad you placed."

"Thanks, I was hoping for first, though."

"Different kind of show for you. I'm proud for both of you."

Bernie stayed mounted and worked on breathing exercises while they walked to the barn. She didn't take Noir into the barn or very close because she didn't want the mare to get the idea that her work was over and that she could return to her stall and her hay. Cathy walked out with the camera and they walked around the fairgrounds.

"Let me find a nice background for a photo, Bernie."

Bernie's second class, the hardest for her, was a success and she took a first. Sue came to her side immediately. "Very nice ride, Bernie. You looked fabulous out there and I placed you first, too. Thank you."

"Thank you?" Bernie was confused.

"Yes, thank you for representing our barn. We need all the ribbons we can get to display from this show. It brings in more students and presents us as professionals."

"I don't get to keep my ribbon?"

"Yes, we hang them in the office for one month and then turn them over to the riders."

"Oh," Bernie was disappointed she didn't get to take it home with her to show Tony.

They took Noir back to her stall and let her rest and eat hay. Before noon, they got some lunch. "Don't eat anything too greasy because it will make you queasy before your classes, Cathy." Eat something bland. I saw they made turkey wraps and that's what I'd recommend. Make sure you pee before your classes, too."

Cathy was showing visible signs of the jitters. "Thanks. I really wanted breakfast, but now I'm not sure I can eat."

"You've got to eat because we skipped breakfast. You need something in your stomach."

They were standing in front of Noir's stall during this conversation and Jack approached with a plastic cup in his hand. "Ginger lemonade is what you need to settle your stomach, Cathy. Here." He handed her the cup. "Bernie's right, eat now and let your lunch settle a little before you take the mare out again.

Cathy was saddled and mounted after lunch. "How do you feel?" Bernie asked.

"Nervous."

"Then take her for a ride around the grounds and get your legs. I'll be right with you. Don't worry, you just do what you need to do and trust Jack when he says she knows her job. I paid to have Jack retrain her and he trained all the horses you rode previously. Just keep that in mind and you'll do well."

Bernie positioned herself near the best decorated jumps for photos of Cathy. Cathy was visibly relaxed by the time she was to enter the ring for the first time and Bernie felt good about the team.

Sue watched from ringside too. She edged close to Bernie, who was squatting at the side of the ring, camera in hand. "She looks good. What'd you guys do, slip her a tranquilizer?"

Bernie laughed. Nope, told her Jack trained the horse and all the horses she's ridden at your place. Stretched it a little and she relaxed."

Sue laughed.

Cathy placed first and third, respectively in her classes. She was delighted and jubilant. She immediately got off the horse as she exited the ring and loosened the girth as a reward. "Oh, I'm so happy. I never thought I'd even come close to placing at this show."

"I told you she was a good horse," Bernie beamed at her. Cathy threw her arms around Bernie's neck.

"Thank you so much for making a lifetime dream come true."

"Lifetime dream?"

"Yes, that's all I ever wanted to do since I started riding. I just want to take my ribbons and put them in my office. It would be inspirational to the kids I counsel who think they are abject failures in life as teenagers."

"Ah, I've got bad news for you. Since we showed under the wing of Thousand Pines, they keep the ribbons for one month in the office first. We don't even get to take them home and gaze at them."

"Oh, that sucks."

"Yeah, I know. Speaking of which, I better call Tony and find out how they did at the golf scramble today or he's going to be miffed at me."

Bernie slipped behind the barns and let Cathy put the horse away after hosing her off. "Hi Honey, how'd it go today?"

"Oh, we're speaking again?"

"I didn't know we weren't speaking. Last night I had someone listening to our conversation and I didn't want to get into it with you. You didn't sound very happy."

"I was overprotective. I apologize. You just know you're not supposed to be drinking on your meds."

"How'd you do," she changed the subject again.

"We came in tenth and Dad did not win the car."

"Oh, there was a car given away?"

"Yeah, if you played a hole in one, you won a new Caddy."

"Did anyone win the car?" she asked with surprise and doubt in her voice.

"Of course not. We're just a bunch of hacks out here having a good time. We're at the clubhouse now having a few cocktails."

"I see." Bernie started a slow burn. It was alright for Tony to have a few drinks, but not her.

"Well, I'm packing my stuff up and heading your way very soon. What time do you think you'll be home?"

"Bout five."

"Ok. What do you want to do for dinner? I am really tired and hot and don't feel like cooking."

"We had a big catered lunch at the club, so I'm not hungry right now. "Did you forget? We are supposed to have dinner with my parents."

"Yeah, I did forget. Can we cancel them? I'm just too tired and I have to be at the farm because they are dropping off Noir and my tack trunk. I hate to say this, but what about just a pizza? We could get two and ask my parents to make a salad. I'll call them and let them know the horse is coming in and ask about a salad and dinner together."

"Fine by me. I haven't seen your parents in a while and we can spend some time together."

Bernie didn't want to ask Cathy to join them, but she felt guilty now that the hoopla was over and Cathy had to

go home to an empty house. "Listen, Tony, we did well today and Cathy is alone, could we I invite her as well?"

"Is that the gal who did the jumping for you?"

"Yes, and her kids are with her ex right now. I hate to let her down from such a big day."

"I'll call your parents because they don't like to be bothered and they would not say 'No' to me as easily as they would to you."

"Thanks. Good point."

Bernie walked back into the barn and noticed that most of the horses were already loaded. Noir was crying out as the lone horse to the others. "Hey, lovely lady, you're about to go home and be with your goats again." Bernie whispered to the horse.

"What are you telling her?"

"Oh, Cathy, I didn't see you standing there. I was telling Noir that she was going home and she could be with her goats again."

"Goats?"

"Yes, goats. My father has a milking herd and Noir is going back to the farm. I can't afford to keep boarding her at Thousand Pines when she has her own stall and herd mates at my parent's farm."

"Goats." Cathy said to no one in particular. She seemed to be looking into space and a little lost by the concept of horses and goats together.

"Ah, we have to strip Noir's stall before we leave or we don't get the deposit back. I'll start and you chase down the person with the checks. By the time they load her and my trunk, we should be good to go."

"No, I will strip her stall and you find the deposit check. I'm just happy to have had a horse to show and won two ribbons. I want to thank you. I was nervous today and I feel spent right now, but I still want to remember to thank you. Are we going to be showing again?"

Bernie was dreading this conversation, but had found nothing unlikeable in Cathy, other than her knowing about the activity at school. Cathy didn't seem as though she was going to bring it up and Bernie had unconsciously decided that Cathy was a good person, with a tough situation; both at home and in her job. She told her about the pizza and asked if she'd like to come.

"Oh, are you sure?" She looked hopeful.

"I'm positive. You can see where Noir lives most of her life. I'm going to be building an arena there and I'll have my own place to practice for my Dressage. Look, Cathy, don't get too freaked out, but I milk goats on Thursdays for my father and Noir's board. I know this concept seems unusual to you right now, but I want you to see the other part of my life. Another teacher, Celeste, also milks with me. She is in love with the goats, but afraid of Noir. Probably because of her size. You are welcome tonight and you're more than welcome to help me build the arena if you are handy with nails and hammers."

Cathy was very spaced out and appeared not to be listening. She still seemed to be fixated on the word goats. "Noir lives with goats?"

Bernie couldn't help herself and roared with laughter. "Yes, goats. Come, and you'll understand. Besides, you're only going home to an empty house. We won't be late and you will not be too tired to drive back to Jackson. Come on, let's get started."

Jack walked back into the barn as Cathy was cleaning the stall around Noir. "Where did Bernie go?"

"She went to get the stall deposit check back. I'm cleaning up and then we can follow you. Noir is going to be housed with goats."

"Yes, she is going home."

"Did you know about the goats?"

"Sure. I picked her up to bring her to Thousand Pines. It's a lovely farm. Noir is spoiled and happy there."

"Ok. It just sounds so weird. You don't hear about goats every day and I just see Noir as living a fantasy life as a fancy horse. I've never seen her outside of Thousand Pines, either. Goats sound so ordinary to me."

Jack looked at Cathy as though he were looking for signs of dementia. "Cathy, have you had enough liquid to drink today? I'm wondering if you might be a little dehydrated from the show and the sun. We still have water in the coolers if you need one."

"Why do you think I'm dehydrated?"

Bernie walked back in about then and looked at Jack. "What's up?"

"Oh nothing, I am just concerned that Cathy just survived the show, but may need some more liquid and may be dehydrated."

"Gee, Cathy, I never thought to tell you to keep yourself well hydrated at a show. You can get very confused if you're dehydrated. I'll go get you a bottle of water."

"Why does everyone seem to think I'm confused?"

Jack worked hard at trying not to smile. "It happens and you don't even notice it. Your fixation on goats is the clue."

Bernie handed Cathy a water bottle and said, "Goats? Fixation?"

Cathy got a little agitated and said, "I'm not fixated on goats, it just never occurred to me that Noir lived with goats. All I see is this beautiful horse and I think of goats as dirty. I just don't see her living with them. I'm not dehydrated at all."

"Drink the water anyway, Cathy. You never know.

"Bernie's parent's farm is lovely and they have a milking herd of goats. You are driving back to Jackson, right?" Jack asked.

"No, I'm having dinner with Bernie's family at their farm."

"Oh, so you'll be following us, too. Ok, when you get there, you will see that Noir is a spoiled baby and lives in paradise."

Bernie listened to this and puzzled about how Jack could know anything about her parent's farm other than the back acreage. "I'll follow you until we get to the turn off, then I'll pass you and lead you in." She said to Jack.

"No need, I know how to get there."

"How do you know where Noir is going?"

"I picked her up a few months ago. Didn't Sue tell you? She sent me for the horse."

Bernie's obsession with keeping Jack a secret friend surfaced. She set her facial expression to show nothing and was on guard. "Okey dokey, then, we'll just follow you."

Bernie and Cathy carried the trunk to the truck and it was set in with the others around the gooseneck hitch. When the caravan pulled out, they were right behind them.

Tony was already at the farm when the truck pulled in and Bernie grew more nervous. *Why am I so nervous for Jack to meet Tony? It's apparent that Jack has already met my father and knows the farm, what's the deal here Bernie?* she asked herself as she parked in the driveway near the house and walked to the barns. Jack was already unloading Noir and Noir let out a loud, high pitched whinny.

"Boy, she sure knows she's home. She's calling for her herd," Jack laughed. "You're home, girl. Settle down. Bernie, do you want me to walk her to her stall or is she to be turned out?"

Again, Bernie wondered how much Jack knew about the farm if he knew where Noir's stall was. "I'll take her to the pasture, Jack. She hasn't had any turn out in a while and I think she'll be grateful to see everyone again. Milking is done and the herd is back outdoors. Thanks so much for all your help. Listen, my tack trunk, just leave it here and we'll move it back later tonight."

"Oh, you and I can carry it back to her stall area with no problem, then you can have dinner with your family and not have to worry about being too full and carrying it."

"How did you know we were having dinner together?"

"Cathy told me you invited her. I just couldn't tell earlier if it was the goat herd or if she was dehydrated. She sure acted weird. She's out in the driveway right now with a bunch of people."

Jack leaned over and gave Bernie a hug. "You did really well today and you should have been first in your first class, but it was obvious that you were nervous and Noir picked up on it. Either way, you did really well and I'm happy for you."

Bernie both relished the hug and was repelled by it. She looked around to see if anyone had seen them, and disengaged herself from his strong arms. "Thanks. Only you and Sue said anything. I haven't told my husband yet, because he didn't ask!"

"Well, I'll be seeing you. I've got to get this load back to Jackson and unload and clean trailers." He was walking away when the group from the driveway entered the barn. Tony was showing Cathy where Noir's stall was and Jack stopped and shook Carl's hand.

Tony stepped in front of Jack and extended his hand and introduced himself. "Thanks so much for doing this today and have us avoid another hauling fee to get her mare home. I'm Tony Romenelli, Bernie's husband. You are?"

"Jack Reems, trainer for the horses at Thousand Pines and all around hand."

"Well thanks, Jack. You'll have to join us some time for a beer. I haven't been out to the stable yet, but I will when the next round of shows happen. I want to see the facility and the other horses. Anyone play Polo out there?"

"No, Sue has a few mallets in the tack room, but they look like they've never been used."

"I used to play a little and would love to swing a mallet again. I don't suppose you ride English, though, do you?"

"I'm an English trainer, I'd better. I might take you up on the offer after I study the sport a little. We could just use one of the outdoor arenas and hit a ball around some. Nice to meet you. I have a trailer load of horses that need to get home and get rested." He left the barn and a few minutes later they heard the sound of the diesel starting.

"Cathy, have you introduced yourself to my parents and Tony?"

"Yes. I see now that Noir is a happy horse here. The farm is lovely and well cared for. I'm sorry that I thought that goats were dirty animals."

"You should come during milking to see the stringent standards that have to be adhered to. My father washes goats just like we wash Noir. He clips their udders and keeps their feet trimmed. This is a well maintained herd."

Bernie's parents and Tony had walked off and Bernie gave Cathy the tour of the property and showed her Noir's stall. She had years ago painted the interior white and stained the outside boards a caramel color. It was the only stall and it looked like a room for a princess horse.

Cathy brought up the subject that Bernie had unconsciously been avoiding. "That Jack guy is sweet on you."

"What do you mean?"

"Oh, I can just tell by body language and how he makes sure you're comfortable and watches you. He came to the ring while you were riding and watched your classes."

"He's a nice guy and probably wanted to see how Noir did. He retrained her while she was boarded there. I hadn't been cantering her and she was starting to buck when asked to canter. He fixed that in record time and got her used to group classes so she didn't kick out at

anyone or buck during my lessons. He was probably just concerned about her showing."

"I'm telling you, he's attracted to you."

"Oh poo. Let's head to the house and get some chow. I'm famished all of a sudden. Doesn't pizza sound just like the perfect fit tonight?"

They ate in the dining room and listened to stories about the show and the wins. Cathy was animated about Noir's first class and her blue ribbon. She wasn't disappointed in the class with the larger jumps, either. She kept up the conversation and everyone seemed genuinely interested in the show.

Tony was still in his golfing shorts and he looked sunburned. "You two really got some sun today. How was the weather over there? Ours was clear and the sun was hot on the course."

Cathy engaged Carl in a question and answer session about milking goats and the babies. She seemed fascinated and listened to every word. *What is it about my father's ability to teach by holding attention and engaging everyone in the subject?* Bernie thought while she listened to the conversation.

About an hour after the pizzas were gone, two bottles of wine where finished and the salad bowl was empty, everyone helped clean up and went their own way.

When Bernie got home she stripped off her breeches and blouse and walked them down to the laundry room so that they didn't end up under a pile of clothes dropped from the chute. She sprayed some spot remover on them.

Tony was sprawled out on the couch by the TV and said, "So, you had a good day. What do you think of this Cathy person now?"

"Honestly, I like her a great deal. We met under tenuous circumstances and I'm grateful for her not mentioning the subject during the weekend. Her kids are well behaved and she seems to have good control over them. Horse shows are boring for non-horsey people, and they were very good. I trust her, Tony. I didn't when I first met her, but I do now. I think she sees so many juveniles that she just takes it in stride. I'm thinking about building that arena at the farm and inviting her to practice out there. She will still take her lessons at Thousand Pines, but I'll have a place of my own to practice. I can't wait."

"Hmm, when do you plan to start this project?"

"Ah, soon." She didn't mention that the posts and board were already purchased and delivered. One more money conversation would ruin a perfectly good weekend. The money was taken from her savings from her salary in increments and he didn't need to know the details.

Sluggish from the mentally and physically exhausting Sunday, Bernie had a difficult time getting out of bed for work the next morning. Tony seemed a little slow as well. They met in the kitchen as they both grabbed for the coffee pot at the same time. "Morning, she mumbled."

"Yeah, I'm feeling like you sound. I forgot how much you walk on a golf course. I wonder how my father

feels this morning. I'll find out soon enough, because he's due in the office this morning to help me work on a complicated case. I hope he feels better than I do. He golfs a lot more than I do, so I think he's in better shape than me."

"Oh, I'm so not looking forward to today. I have to start a new book with the seniors before graduation and we will have to rush through it. Starting a new book with them at this junction is difficult. I'll have to make them understand that it's on the final. They have a serious case of senioritis right now and getting them to concentrate is work. We spent so much time discussing other books that we're going to have to speed through this one. Many of them have mentally checked out already. They're pushing their limits and don't seem like the same kids that started class in January. All they can think about is graduation and summer before college." She sighed heavily and cut a grapefruit in half.

"Sorry I don't feel like running this morning, Babe." Tony smiled at her with empathy.

"Wise guy."

"See you tonight. Last night was fun. Next time you show I'll make sure I accompany you so I can watch. Did you get any good pictures we can use for framing?"

"Oh, I completely forgot, and my camera is in my tack trunk. I'll drive out after school and pick it up. It would be nice of me to have one or two photos for Cathy printed so she can use them in her office or at home. She was a doll to work with and I really think I like her. She may be a new friend. Now, if I could just figure out what the

problem was with Celeste, I'd be much happier and relieved. She hasn't really talked to me in weeks. I'm concerned that I might have done something, but I don't know what."

"Oh women, they worry about relationships too much. She'll come around. It's probably nothing. See you tonight."

The onion had a sense of excitement about it lately. The school year was ending and everyone seemed to be amped. Even the teachers seemed to be more relaxed about disciplinary issues and were in better moods.

Charlene was on lunch duty with Bernie and didn't say anything to her or get close enough for a conversation. She almost acted as though she were avoiding her. Bernie didn't think much about it, Charlene wasn't at the top of her list of warm fuzzies. Celeste was absolutely avoiding Bernie and this set her on edge. "I'll find out Thursday what the problem is when we milk," thought Bernie.

Celeste never showed on Thursday and the weather was also a mood dampener. The rains started early morning and kept driving in all afternoon. By milking time, many of the areas near the barns were flooded or puddled. Bernie was alone again in the barn and set out with determination to not let it get to her. She called Celeste's cell phone a few times and it went straight to voice mail. She also tried the house phone and it rang busy. "The least she can do is call me to tell me she's not coming to milk. It's just a courtesy."

Noir had a few good days off but the weather, with May rains, wasn't conducive to riding. "Better that she settles

back in and get some rest from being ridden twice a day. I'll ride her tomorrow on the trails and see how well she likes being home. We are definitely cantering. All that training is going to use. I need to look at the arena area anyway and Noir needs to learn to ride around and across water. There ought to be plenty of it after this afternoon, she thought, while she milked.

On Friday Noir didn't want to be caught. She had associated Bernie with work and being free again in the pasture was exactly what she wanted to do. Bernie doggedly kept following her until she tired of evasion and was finally caught. She gave no more resistance and was tacked up and ridden into the woods. As predicted, she shied at the water puddles and refused to cross a few of them on the path. Bernie kept after her and she eventually leaped over one of them, nearly tossing Bernie from the saddle. "That's why I don't like to jump. I don't feel comfortable being airborne, Noir." Noir eventually settled down and they came to the clearing. Jack must have been waiting a long time because his horse was already tied to a tree and he was drinking out of a water bottle.

"Hey, stranger. Miss seeing you around the barn."

"Jack, why didn't you tell me you were the one who picked up Noir when we moved her?"

"Never crossed my mind. I pick up most of the horses for Sue. She's busy teaching and I have a more flexible schedule. I use her truck and trailer because mine is my own."

"So, you've met my dad before, then? Did you say anything about the arena to him on Sunday?"

"Subject never came up. Doesn't he know?"

"Of course he knows, he just doesn't know about you or that you've been riding on the property with me. Or, that you've offered to help me put it up."

"It's our secret then."

"Well, it might not be because I told Cathy that she could help if she knew her way around a hammer and nails."

"Well, you'll have to dig post holes before a hammer comes into play."

"Yeah, I keep forgetting to ask my father about the tractor and the post hole digger. This is his busiest time of year and I don't want to burden him with one of my projects."

"Would he let me help and use the tractor?"

"I don't think that's such a good idea. He would be wondering how we met, how the conversation came up in the first place and then he'd find out about Red and you on the property. I'd ask Tony to help, but he gets home too late to be of much use and his weekends are usually full of some activity. I need to think about this a little."

"Well, you'd better start because you'll want to get it up soon. The Thursday Dressage class is rescheduling to Tuesday because someone has a conflict. They did a

nice Quadrille at the show and are itching to start again. Individually, each of them did fairly well, too. Did you get to see them?"

"I watched a few of the drill teams, but I didn't know who was who, so I can't answer that."

"Speaking of students, Cathy was out for a lesson on Wednesday and she seems to be missing Noir. She had to ride a school horse and got impatient. She was a little pissy with Sue and they had words. I think she was spoiled by Noir. She said she'd be practicing out here with you. Did you invite her to practice in your arena? The arena that's not built yet?"

"Uh, I don't remember much of Sunday afternoon because of all the excitement. I may have, Jack."

"Well, do you want to ride off the property today? I can show you some of my trails."

"How muddy are they? Noir seems to have developed a diva complex and is being fussy about puddles and water."

"Oh, good, she needs to be back to being a horse, I'll help. Red is a great leader. Let's go."

The woods past the farm smelled of early honeysuckle and dampness. It was very different from Bernie's manmade trails and Noir had to carefully watch the placement of her feet over roots and fallen branches. They rode the largest path moving away from the farm. Bernie could hear woodpeckers and morning doves in the woods. "I love the sounds of the woods. I can't think

of a better place to enjoy them than from the back of a horse. Thanks Jack."

"Thank you. I've been wanting to show you these trails for a while, but you are always so busy. Do you have time to ride toward Red's barn?"

"I don't know. How far away is it?"

"Another half hour's ride."

"I don't think so. I need to head back and get home. I have obligations and a teaching module to review so I can enjoy my weekend."

Jack rode up next to her in a clearing area and stopped. "I really wanted to compliment you on the equitation class Sunday. You really surprised Sue and me. I think that Dressage training paid off for the two of you and Sue is suddenly interested in the discipline more than she has been. She mentioned it to me yesterday. I believe she'll be looking for another instructor to bring in. Your subtle use of aids was the clincher for the judge. Noir just did what she was supposed to while you worked on your position and won the class. That impressed Sue, who had initial reservations about you entering a hunter equitation class. He leaned over to Bernie and patted her gloved hand.

Bernie didn't pull away and realized that she was attracted to this man. The knowledge of keeping him a secret was revealed to her at that moment. She found him attractive and interested in her activities. She admired his way with the horses and his way with people. The strangest feeling went through her and she wanted to

kiss him. She overcame the urge and moved her horse around to head back.

Jack looked dangerous at that moment, as though he were thinking the same thing. She concentrated on backing Noir and turning her to the main path again. "How far do you have to ride to get to our farm?" She asked as a distraction that broke the mood.

He gathered his composure and replied, "A few miles. The barn isn't that far away from where we are right now. I used to follow the deer paths, but they've become wider since I've been riding out to your place. You can follow them right to Red's barn without a problem now. I carry a hand saw with me to cut branches and it's already pretty well marked."

"Look, I think I can find my way back alone. Thanks for the lovely ride. I want to get back before the sun starts to set. I'll see you soon."

"Remember, the offer to help with the arena still stands. Just call me and we can get it up in no time once the holes are dug. I'd offer to dig them by hand, but if your father has a post hole digger, it would go a lot faster."

Her discomfort faded, along with the urge to kiss him. "Thanks, Jack. I'll give you a call. I haven't set up any more lessons with Sue and I haven't talked to Cathy this week. I'll give her a call, too." She figured that three people would be safer than her and Jack working together since this attraction had surfaced.

They parted on the trail and Bernie had no problem following the hoof prints back to the clearing at the farm. She put Noir in her stall to eat and left for home.

She showered to remove the feelings left on her tingly skin and started dinner. The previous day's rain had left everything fresh and the air cooler, so they ate outdoors again. Tony went downstairs after dinner to watch TV and Bernie followed him with the saddle pads from the trunk of her car. She filled a tub with detergent and water and soaked them for their eventual trip to the washing machine, glancing every so often at Tony through the laundry room door. He was in TV land and he didn't seem to notice anything different about her, but she felt different and slightly sullied by the afternoon's activities and the realization that she was attracted to another man. Her clandestine meetings with the rider in the woods bothered her a little.

Saturday, while Tony decided to work half a day in the office, she drove to the farm and talked to her father about the tractor and the post hole digger. "Dad, we are on a tight budget and I never told Tony that I bought the posts and the boards already, so I'd appreciate if you didn't say anything. I bought them months ago when we were in a better position, and he wouldn't understand the need for an arena right now. He doesn't want me to board at Thousand Pines for a while because of money constrictions, but I need a place to practice. I did really well for my first hunter show and I'd like to keep this between us. The money is already spent and I need some help getting the holes dug for the arena posts. Do you think I can operate the tractor and post hole digger myself?"

"That's generally a two person job, Bernie. I think I'm going to have to set aside a little time and help you. I can run the tractor and you can set the auger in place. We really should go up there and take a look at how large an area you've mowed down and where the posts need to go. We need to mark them off with spikes and string for it to come out well. When do you want to do this?"

"I can't ask you to stop work in your busiest season. Hay is coming right up, too. Maybe one of the local kids could help me."

"You'd have to pay them and you just said money was tight this month."

"Right, duh. Um, I don't know how to answer the question because I don't know your schedule. I was offered some help, but the holes need to be dug first. What are you thinking?"

"All those posts and boards need to be moved up there first. When a hole is dug a post should be dropped in so if it rains the hole doesn't fill in all the way. Just like we did with the goat fencing. Each post is going to have to be tamped and then leveled. This is no minor undertaking, it's going to need a crew."

"I can use the small wagon behind the four wheeler and start moving the posts and boards up there next week. At least they will be out of your way and in position. Do you think the boys might help?"

"No, it's too close to hay season and it's like pulling teeth to get any work out of them as it is. Besides, marriage has removed one from the family."

"I have an offer from two people to help, but they both live in Jackson. It would be a serious burden to ask either of them to commit to something that will be just mine." She purposely didn't mention Jack's nearly daily presence in the clearing.

"Don't any of those kids you teach owe you favors?"

"Forget the seniors, all they can focus on is graduation and skipping right now. I might be able to get a group of junior boys together, but I can't pay them."

"What about a promise of food, like a barbeque?"

"I'm not that close to any of them. I might be able to get Cappy to help me. She's just starting back into the lawn cutting, though. She's a friend and she might just help one day."

"If we get those holes drilled, we might be able to get the posts in and the boards up in one day. Might as well make a party of it. Talk to Tony, he needs to get out and do some work instead of sitting behind a desk all day. He really needs to get involved with your passion, too. It would do him good. You two aren't as close as you used to be. Just saying."

Bernie was stung by the last comment. She knew that Tony wasn't interested in her activities and never volunteered to help her with them. He ate the Christmas cookies, listened to her horse and goat stories, but didn't involve himself in what was previously an obsession with her. His interests hadn't changed that much. He just wasn't as attentive as he used to be. Was she not

as attentive to him, she mused. "Are you using the four wheeler right now?"

"No, go ahead."

"Thanks, Tony won't be around until lunch so that gives me a good hour and a half to move some posts up there." She hooked the trailer to the four wheeler and started loading posts. They were heavier than she expected and found that she had to unload some of them to be able to tow the trailer. It was a start; the details she'd work out later.

On the way home, she stopped at the feed store to buy another pair of leather work gloves. Hers were dirty and needed to be washed, and they would take two days to dry and then oil again. By the time she got home, she was gritty and sweaty. She showered and put on a pair of shorts and a t-shirt. Tony had worn shorts to the office and he came through the door in search of a beer. "Hey, where've you been? I called twice, but there was no answer."

"I was at the farm moving posts up to the clearing for my new arena. It was laborious and I just got back and showered. What's up with you?"

"Nothing important. I thought I'd clean the garage and see if my parents were thinking about cooking out tonight. You seem distracted and we spent time with your parents Sunday, so I thought we could spend some time with my family this weekend. Wanna help?"

"Sure," she said, "the garage is getting to be a tight fit for cars. I can run the recycling in while you start. How's that sound?"

Tony loaded the plastic and glass and paper into her car and she made it to the recycling center a few minutes before it closed. When she returned the driveway was full. "It looks like we're having a yard sale out there," she said when she entered the garage.

"Just where'd all this crap come from? I thought it was your stuff and horse stuff, but most of it is just things we didn't put away after use. I'll feel better when this is done because you keep the house so clean and I seem to be responsible for the mess in here."

While they worked at organizing things back on shelves and into cabinets, she told him about the arena project and her father's suggestion. Jack's name didn't come up on purpose. Tony listened, but didn't say much.

Around five they finished the garage project and checked to see how much room they had with both cars in. They both showered again and headed off to Tony's parents. Grilled t-bones hit the spot and the fire pit was lit. Bernie had brought a flannel jacket and she needed it while they sat around the pit. Tony told his parents about the arena project and Mr. Romanelli made a suggestion.

"Tony, you sponsor a few softball leagues. Why don't you enlist their help for this project if it would only take one day to finish?"

"That'd cost me new uniforms, which I can't do right now."

"They owe you. You said a barbeque would be provided, so what's the harm in asking? You might get a few skilled guys out there and get the job done in half the time."

And that's how the arena got built. The little league painted the posts and boards and everyone got to meet everyone else. Bernie supplied all the food and Mom and Dad manned the transported grill from Bernie and Tony's place. Carl even allowed another person to operate his tractor; albeit another farmer.

"The only thing missing is a gate," said Bernie. I can use a rope for a while. This is great, I have an arena and we had a party. A football appeared and post tops served as goals and a game of football ended the afternoon.

School was due to let out and another horse show was about to take place. Hyjinks were at an all time crescendo and teachers were short on patience as finals neared.

Cathy was invited to drive over and practice on Noir with Bernie as spotter. They made their own jumps from concrete blocks and leftover posts. For fun one afternoon they painted them and stood back to admire. The colors were chosen from leftover paint from their homes and looked a little ridiculous, but they had jumps. Disposable plastic plates served as Dressage markers nailed to boards. The arena was finished with the exception of a permanent gate.

Celeste had been absent for many Thursdays and Bernie, unable to pin her down on the phone or in person, just let it be. It bothered her that their friendship was on edge somewhere. She had no clues about the rift; and Celeste certainly wasn't going to be forthcoming with

information. Dad never asked, probably because he didn't know. He and Mom had gone out each of the Thursdays that Celeste had been absent from the barn.

Jack appeared in the clearing one afternoon and surveyed the newly erected arena. "Wow that seemed to happen overnight."

My husband had a lot to do with it. He sponsors two softball leagues and they repaid him by building this and having a barbeque. I'm so happy. I just need better footing, but I'll get there as time goes by. What do you think?"

"I think it looks great and it's finished. Good for you. I see some jumps, too, has Cathy been out here yet to look?"

"Cathy was the one who suggested how to make them and we painted them together. Neat, huh?"

"Yeah. What's Noir think about all this?"

"She spooked the first time we came up on it. Now she's used to seeing it there and just ignores it. I haven't had her in there alone yet because we are waiting for the boards to dry; it's asphalt based paint and it takes several weeks to dry. I really don't want her to rub me on one of the boards and ruin a set of breeches."

"Ok, then let's go for a trail ride."

Before she could think twice, she had accepted. They entered the woods and went off on a different path than their previous ride. Jack didn't attempt to kiss her or even touch her and she felt comfortable thinking that

they both had considered the ramifications of such an act. They parted at the main trail and Bernie decided to introduce Noir to the ring. Noir swished her tail in annoyance and Bernie had to tap her with the whip. She probably thought that they were headed straight to the barn. "No you don't, Missy, you will behave. You have a job and I have a job. My job is feeding you and you're job is to work for feed. You've become a spoiled brat. Let's work a pattern for a few minutes and then I'll reward you by taking you home."

Noir was picked up again and taken back to Thousand Pines for a two week stay in anticipation of the next show. Cathy was more able to get to Thousand Pines than the farm and they worked in tandem again. Their routine of working with the same horse was set and it became a partnership. Their friendship was deepening and growing. Cathy confided in her a little more and Bernie relayed things from school. She never talked about Tony or Tony's job; and she certainly never mentioned Celeste. Celeste was a raw spot in Bernie's heart.

"Hey, Bernie, why don't we switch lessons? I'll do flatwork and you can learn to start jumping."

"Oh, I don't know about that. I've been launched over a few logs and puddles before and I don't feel comfortable."

"You don't start jumping immediately, you learn to go straight over ground poles and steer your horse from a two point position. You'll enjoy it. It's very satisfying."

They agreed on Bernie entering the beginning jumper lessons and Cathy took the group lesson from Bernie.

Bernie did, indeed, feel a sense of satisfaction and enjoyed herself. The new sense of accomplishment caused her mood to heighten and she started a rapid speech pattern. Of course, she didn't notice it, but Cathy did. "Do you have any idea how fast you're talking right now?"

"I'm talking fast? I didn't notice." Bernie knew what this meant, but she ignored it because she was feeling good. "I guess I'm just excited to be learning something new. I feel like I could enter one of the jumping classes at the upcoming show."

The instructor overhead this conversation and interrupted her, "No, you're not even ready for cross rails yet. You could get hurt from what you don't know. If by the fall shows I decide you're ready, we'll talk about it then. Right now Cathy will do the jump classes."

Bernie was disappointed, but listened because she didn't want to get hurt. She'd seen quite a few tumbles and people ending up tossed over a fence or two. The thought of breaking a bone didn't entice her to pursue that line of thinking very long. But she did have an idea for Cathy. "What do you think about entering a flat class at the next show? We don't have a lot of time to prepare for it, but you're more advanced than me and if you can afford it, I know where there's a horse!"

"Really? I didn't want to ask you to overburden Noir, but I've been thinking about a flat class. I plan to enter the same two classes as last time. What are you entering?"

"The same two, but let's look at the show bill and see if there is a flat class you can enter. I think Noir could

do five classes at one show. She's in excellent shape and didn't suffer any, from what I saw, at the last show."

They talked to Sue and she found a suitable class for Cathy. All arrangements were made for the Lansing show. They decided to drive separately again because of the distance between their homes and because Noir would again be dropped off at the farm. The reserved hotel was the same one that the entire show group was staying in. It was a Saturday show and everyone arrived Friday evening. Tony had to work, so he couldn't fulfill his promise of attending Bernie's next show.

Friday evening after bathing and braiding Noir they found themselves in the hotel bar again. Half the adult barn goers were there and they pushed several tables together to accommodate the group. Jack was there and not on night duty. Sue had taken his place and slept on the grounds in the living quarters of her trailer. There was also a live band and many people got up to dance. Their moods were high. Most of them, after the third show of the season were already into a routine with their horses and had finished early. Many of them considered this a mini vacation and had eaten earlier in the hotel restaurant.

"I want to eat in the hotel restaurant," Bernie said, "but I don't know your budget, Cathy."

"It's good, let's do that."

When they rejoined the group, Jack was dancing with someone from the barn. Everyone wore riding clothes and it was a sight to see everyone in breeches on the dance floor. Jack asked Bernie to dance the next dance

with him, but it was a slow one and there was a little unease between them. Bernie felt strange putting her arms around his neck and he purposely kept his hands high on her back. The group fired each member up a little and more alcohol was consumed than monitored. Bernie was feeling a little more comfortable as the dance progressed and she hugged him a little closer than earlier. The spark was there and it became evident to both of them on the dance floor. They were slow to part and decided to dance the next number together.

Upon returning to the table, Cathy said to Bernie, "He likes you. I told you before."

"Nah, I think we're just becoming friends. He retrained my horse for me and got to know me through her."

"He's retrained a lot of these people's horses and I haven't seen him dance twice with the same person other than you."

"You're reading too much into it, Cathy. He's married and I'm married, we are just friends; or becoming friends, I should say."

"Ok, whatever you say."

The Thousand Pines group took the show by storm the next day. Albeit, everyone was a little sluggish from the party the night before. Their turnout and winnings were excellent. There was an air of jubilance among them and a lot of cheering and congratulations were offered up. The group seemed to bond and were no longer strangers. The children of the group immediately sensed this shift and were just as wound up. People not having their

classes until later helped each other with small details. Boots were cleaned after a rider was mounted, jackets were handed up and people were ringside to cheer on their new friends. Many blue ribbons fluttered in the light breeze wafting through the barn aisle. Bernie won both her flat classes and Cathy took a fourth, she won both her jumping classes. Her jumping instructor had come along and was very pleased with Cathy's placings. Everyone was happy for Noir. Noir took more blue ribbons than any single horse and became the day's star.

Bernie lapsed into rapid speech again and, once again, Cathy caught her. "You don't even know you're doing it, do you?"

"I competed with people and horses who've been riding or together longer than us and I'm just happy, Cathy. This is a great day. And, it's Saturday, so I get to rest a little tomorrow before work. School's been tough lately with the seniors and the restlessness of the kids."

"Ok, those are two separate thoughts."

"Not really, I just feel relaxed and happy. I get to totally shut down the school from my head and pretty soon the semester will be over and we'll be free."

Jack, too, was in an elevated mood. "Hey anyone here dehydrated? We still have a cooler full of water and Gatorade. Don't want anyone going delirious on me before we have to leave and drive."

"Nope, good here," Cathy yelled back. "I really think he was right at the last show. I was so nervous I didn't think

to drink much water and started fixating on things in my head."

"I get irritable when I'm dehydrated. Makes you wonder how a horse feels, huh?" Bernie said.

Noir was, again, the last to load, but stayed quiet this time. Jack helped Cathy carry Bernie's tack trunk to the truck and they heaved it in. Bernie went into the dressing room of the trailer to retrieve her suit bag. It was dark in there and she had a difficult time telling which one was hers. The tack room door opened and closed and a pair of lips sought hers. He didn't ask permission or give her warning. She was not surprised. His kiss was tentative but penetrating. She dropped her suit bag and returned the affection. They heard Cathy calling for her and scrambled to find the lights and the suit bag. Bernie was worried that she was blushing and it would be evident to perceptive Cathy. Jack grabbed Cathy's bag and exited the trailer, Bernie followed a minute later and watched as he handed Cathy her bag.

"OK, guys, I'll follow you to the farm. Cathy, I'll give you a call this week. I have a lot of farm chores to help with and this is hay season, so I may not be at the barn for a lesson depending on the weather. Hay is very important to my father and he wants it done just right," Bernie said as she got into her car.

The long drive back gave her time to compose herself and think about what had just happened. There were no questions about why. She had known from the first meeting that he was an attractive man and she was definitely attracted. In a sense, he reminded her of someone from college. Very lean, athletic and

accomplished. And married. She reminded herself that she, too, was married and wondered what type of behavior this was considered. The thought of a manic high and not having good judgment skills did not cross her mind. She didn't know she was on an upswing. All she could think about was doing it again. And, Jack's moral status wasn't in question, either.

After the mare was unloaded at the farm, Bernie shook Jack's hand in front of her father and he shook Carl's hand. She couldn't make eye contact with either of them. Tony wasn't there this time, so she didn't have to deal with her feelings about the kiss until she got home. "It was just a kiss. Yeah, but it was a passionate one. Obviously he's been planning this for a while. Well, I almost kissed him myself in the woods," were the thoughts she had driving to the house. The house was quiet and Tony wasn't yet home. She felt grubby and showered in an effort to forget the incident in the trailer dressing room. It didn't work.

She made a hot German potato salad, a nice crisp lettuce salad and pulled brats out of the freezer. They would grill out tonight. Being in the night air might make the feeling of sin go away. She was wishing that Tony would not return until late, but guilt got the better of her and she called him at the office. "What's happening?"

"I'm to the wall here. I could use help filing since I laid off an employee and I find myself thinking of high school. Filing is not my favorite job and we seem to have an extraordinary amount of it right now. If I don't get all these files put away, we're not going to be finding

anything quickly. It's amazing how fast files pile up around here in.

"How'd you do today?"

"Two firsts and Cathy took two firsts as well as a fourth. She's happy and gave me a hug. We had a great show, overall. Everyone was in high spirits and there was a sense of teamwork we haven't had before.

"What time do you think you'll pull in?"

"I just can't answer that question right now. I feel overwhelmed with secretarial duties. If you get hungry, just go ahead and eat and leave me a plate. I don't think I'll be in any time soon, Hon."

She was secretly relieved that he may not appear until after she was asleep. She poured herself a glass of wine and sat on the back deck and analyzed the happenings of the day. One happening in particular. There wasn't exactly a feeling of guilt, but puzzlement about what to do next. Yes, she wanted to do it again, but crossing the line was crossing the line. Where did she go to draw the line? What was the line? She had no one to discuss it with and started to feel the creeping of guilt around the edges of her heart.

She loved Tony, albeit, she felt trapped at times and their activities were very far apart, but she was very attracted to Jack and his excitement about the horses and showing. What exactly, she mused, was she attracted to? His casual manner, his ability to keep a secret, his attraction to her starving need for attention, the man, himself? Nothing stood out in her mind as being a major point. She really didn't know much about him, had never met his wife or kids. He was a father, he was a husband. As far as she could tell, he didn't own anything other than a truck and trailer and he had said they lived on the Thousand Pines property. What was he, a contract worker? Like a migrant worker? What was the attraction? She had previously been attracted to very intelligent and polished men. She just couldn't see Jack at a decent restaurant, but he sure looked good in breeches. Was that it? A physical attraction?

The questions came without answers and she poured herself another glass of wine. Where was this headed, anyway?

She decided she needed to keep herself busy to think, so she made some brownies for Tony, did a load of laundry, spotted her show clothes, unloaded the saddle pads from her car trunk and soaked them, went through the house with the vacuum, and looked for other jobs to occupy her hands while her mind spun. Eventually, she quit, grilled the brats, ate outdoors and left a plate for Tony and went to bed.

Her dreams were terrifying and she woke with a start several times. Tony was still not home, or at least not in bed. What would it feel like when he climbed into bed after she had been necking with a virtual stranger? She didn't want to think about it and got up looking for the Scotch bottle. She opened her current book and fell asleep reading it.

Tony was snoring in soft snuffles when she woke the next morning. She looked over at his handsome relaxed face and shuddered. "Will he know?"

They were expected at the Romanelli's for a barbeque Sunday afternoon and Bernie just wasn't feeling it. "Will Tony do his usual and pretend to be attentive to her, or has that worn off as husband and wife?" Who would notice that she had been changed and strayed? Had she really strayed? It was just a kiss, for God's sake. It wasn't like they ended up in bed together. What would happen if they did? She shuddered again and Tony saw it.

"What's up, Babe?"

"Oh nothing, I was just thinking about the jumping classes and the thought of getting tossed just crossed my mind." She had learned, too easily how to lie to him. She was becoming a good liar with family, him and the doctor.

Several times that morning she replayed the kiss over again in her head. It happened fast and she had responded in kind. Why? *Oh, for God's sake, it was only a kiss; a passionate one, but just a kiss. Harmless and impulsive, forget it.*

The Romanelli's were out in force and the summer weather was perfect for the opening of the pool and the expected water fights. Bernie had learned to pack clothes for both her and Tony because the super soakers would be in use. It was fun to run around like a kid and have a water fight. Mrs. Romanelli had apparently shopped and found a soaker that held a full gallon of water and used it all on Tony's father. They laughed and played and swam and ate. The evening ended early because of the mosquitoes and people having to work the next morning. She was glad. At least she forgot about her conundrum for a short period of time and relaxed with the family.

June rains moved graduation inside and teachers were expected to attend. They were a disrespectful group. It was as though they just wanted their summer off, too, and weren't in the least proud of their former students. Bernie found this slightly irritating, especially the talking amongst the teachers during the ceremonies. These were the kids they were supposed to be nurturing and preparing for life and college. What was wrong with these people? Celeste sat next to Charlene and away from Bernie. McGinty sat scowling at the end of a row. Bernie was located between Todd and Tasha for some reason. There weren't assigned seats, it was just the way they took them upon entering. Ceremonies were finished with mortar hats being tossed. Bernie got in her car and left. The first day of summer vacation was about to start and she wanted to be home as soon as possible.

Since it was a middle of the week ceremony, Tony wasn't yet home and she drove out to the farm and saddled up Noir for an evening ride. She was going to stick to her paths and avoid the clearing near the arena. She didn't want to run into Jack and it was already late, so chances were slim. Noir had shown her happiness to be home by bucking after being put back in the pasture and Bernie certainly hoped it wasn't going to be a habit. They rode until nightfall and Noir got her dinner late. Dad was finished in the barn and had gone to the house. Bernie made a trip to the pump house and sat there for a while. She saw the Scrabble board and missed Celeste. Maybe she could engage her in conversation tomorrow when they milked.

It seemed as though it rained every Thursday now. The downpour was expected and Bernie made it to the barn early to check the herd and read instructions. Since the information on Gracie the nanny, she was extra vigilant about paying attention to the animals and their production. She checked former production records on each doe and tried to remember them for milking this afternoon. The rain was relentless and all animals came in soaked. The smell of wet goat permeated the air in the milk house and almost became overwhelming to her. Celeste never showed and Bernie started on milking and calling Celeste's home phone over and over. It rang busy each time. *I'm going over there after milking,* she thought. *I'm getting to the bottom of this. I've done nothing I can think of to be treated this way and something is up that I'm not aware of. Maybe she's depressed about something and can't talk about it. But, she didn't sit near me at graduation, either. She sat with Char.*

Because she had started early, she finished early. If it wasn't raining the skies would still be light, but the low clouds were blocking all light and it looked like night out there. She drove to Celeste's house.

The rain was coming in sheets and Bernie had a difficult time seeing where to put her feet as she attempted to reach Celeste's front door using the walkway. Obviously the front walk wasn't used a great deal and the weeds were starting to edge into the paver stones and cracks. A light was on in the front room and Bernie could see the flickering of a TV. She banged on the front door and after a minute or two the porch light went on. Celeste opened the door.

"Are you OK? I've been trying to call you all night and the phone just keeps ringing."

Celeste didn't look too happy at the intrusion and made no attempt to ask Bernie inside. "I'm fine. I just need some down time and some alone time to think."

"Dorito sleeve."

"What? Celeste looked annoyed.

"Dorito sleeve. You've got Dorito sleeve. I thought you were so intent on sticking with this new diet."

"What are you talking about?"

"Look at your sleeve, Celeste. You've been eating Doritos and the cuff of your sweatshirt is all orange. Dorito sleeve."

Celeste sighed hard enough for Bernie to feel her breath. "Look, Bernie, I am not in the mood for company or criticism. I just want to be left alone to vegetate in front of the TV. What I do or don't eat is not your business at this time. I'm so freaking glad you can stick to a diet and not stain your sleeves. Goodnight." Celeste shut the door.

They'd never had a cross word or confrontation and Bernie's cheeks heated, her eyes started to water and she trembled. She made her way back to the car feeling stupid, confrontational and foolish at having verbally attacked her friend about something that really wasn't her business. Who was she to criticize after the recent secret indiscretions? Not that Celeste knew any of them,

but they still existed and Bernie felt ashamed of herself. She returned to her car, soaking wet and left for home.

The uncontrollable crying was still going on when Tony came through the door. "What's wrong?"

She explained what she had done and Celeste's reaction. "I don't know what I did or why she's acting this way."

"Is it possible that she's had to defend you for something with someone else?"

"She doesn't know how to handle confrontation and that might be it, but what was the issue about and who?"

"Sounds like you're going to have to corner her and find out what's going on. I thought this was just a small matter, but it sounds much larger. You don't need to get depressed and upset over it. This is the type of thing that can spiral you out of control, too. Your friendship means so much, but it's not worth beating yourself up over right now. Let's just try to find out if someone confronted her and she ran away. Celeste seems like the type of person to run away from conflict instead of face it head on.

"Honey, I wouldn't go back to her house until she is ready to talk. She may have something personal going on, too. You never know."

"Yeah, but how am I going to find out unless I can talk to her. She doesn't want to talk right now. It was unfair about the Doritos, too. God knows I like my wine and she has every right to eat what she wants. It's just that she really is losing weight and it shows in her face. She

really has pretty features and she's looking so much better right now. I just have to find a way to get her attention to get to the bottom of this. It's killing me. Any suggestions?"

"Yes, try writing an email or a letter. Tell her how frustrated you are by not knowing what happened between the two of you. She may read it and reach out to you."

"What if she doesn't read it?"

"Mail it with her goat cheese. If you mail it tomorrow, she'll get it Saturday. Mike should be home with her and he'll be curious to know what's in the package."

"Ok, I'll do it."

THIRTY EIGHT

Friday Bernie went to the farm to talk to Carl and tell him what was going on and to garner a little extra goat cheese for Celeste. Carl was surveying the hay fields, "It's a little too damp yet to cut. The forecast says it's to be warm and dry for the next five days. I think we need to start cutting in two days. I'm calling your brothers and getting them out here. We can't do this alone."

"Celeste wanted to do hay with you this year. I don't think she can throw a bale to the top of the pile, but she may be able to walk behind the wagon and lift them that far. Why don't you give her a call? We can invite her and Mike to grill out with the rest of us after we put it in the barn."

"She's a sweet little thing, and I don't want her to think I'm taking advantage of her right now."

"But, she asked if she could do hay with you."

"Really? Ok, I'll give her a call and see what she says."

No one knew the outcome of the conversation between Carl and Celeste, but she and Mike did show up to do hay. Mike just wanted to be with Celeste and see the goats and Tony decided it would be a good idea to meet

Mike. Cut and turned hay was baled, loaded and put in the barn in record time.

Celeste stayed away from Bernie most of the time, but Mike and Tony seemed to be in a competition to get the stacks higher and higher without tottering off the trailer. With so many people helping, the work was easy and didn't seem like such a sweat burden this time.

Bernie walked behind the wagon and picked up bales on the opposite side from Celeste. ***I need to treat Celeste like an onion and peel back a layer at a time until I find out what happened*****, thought Bernie. She looked over at Celeste's grimacing face and realized that the woman was physically pushing herself hard to keep up.**

"Celeste, take a break and get some water or Gatorade. You're face is bright red and you can collapse out here in this heat"

"I'm fine. I just don't do that much lifting. This will strengthen my arms."

"No, really, take it from someone who knows, take a break." Bernie yelled toward Dad that everyone needed a rest. They stopped and poured water from the jugs and chugged down Gatorade while sitting on the wagon. Celeste was out of breath. Mike, used to construction work, was laughing at Tony whose face was red, too.

"What's the matter, paper jockey, too much heat and stress for you?" Mike chided Tony.

"Not exactly what I had planned for my Saturday, but useful for the girls and Dad. I guess I'm a little out of

shape. You can continue stacking and I'll trade driving the tractor."

"Not gonna happen, son," said Carl.

"Yeah, I never told you that Dad never lets anyone drive his tractors," Bernie said. "Although, at this point I think Celeste should be allowed to rest and drive the tractor."

"Celeste, have you ever driven a tractor before?" Carl asked her.

"No, and it's big and scary looking. I think I just continue on with the job I'm doing."

"Actually, Celeste, you could stand up here and I can show you how to drive a tractor," Carl said with concern in his voice for the obviously overheated girl.

"You'd let me do that?"

"Sure, that's how all the kids learned to drive a tractor, they watched from up here first. It'll give you a break, too. We are almost done with this wagon and will be dropping it and picking up the next one soon, anyway."

Celeste's continence changed immediately and she climbed up the step to stand next to Carl. Tony changed places with her and he and Bernie walked on either side of the wagon and threw bales to Mike, who became a stacking powerhouse. Relief showed up in the form of Josh and Matt just in time to switch wagons. Carl left them to start stacking the empty wagon from the field while he gave the first crew a ride to the barn to unload.

The day was getting warmer and everyone was getting hungry.

When the hay was stacked and salted to prevent spontaneous combustion, Mom appeared in the barn with lemonade and beers. Everyone pulled up a bale and enjoyed a rest for 30 minutes. "I've got the grill going and some nice sides ready when everyone wants to eat," she said.

"I don't know if I can eat right now," Celeste moaned.

"This is called heat exhaustion and I bet you're slightly nauseous, too, aren't you?" Carl asked her.

"Yeah, I do feel a little queasy."

"Just down some of that lemonade until you feel better and cool off. Your appetite will return shortly.

Bernie looked at Tony as soon as Dad said the word 'appetite.'" He moved his eyes from side to side to indicate that she should not say anything and that it was Ok. He winked at her and she smiled back.

The group rested and talked for a while then made their way toward the house. Mom and set up folding chairs and tables and had ice filled glasses at the ready. The grill was full of chicken thighs and vegetables and there was a cooler of cold beers and wine coolers.

Bernie wasn't sure how to approach Celeste and let her have her distance. She and Mike walked off toward the barns so she could show him the herd and the kids. Tony took advantage of their absence to approach Bernie and Carl. "How do we bring up this rift and get to the

bottom of it. This is the first time Celeste has been out for a while and I know she's exhausted, but this is the opportunity Bernie's been waiting for."

Carl sucked on his pipe and said, "I don't know, it seems Bernie embarrassed and insulted her and that has to be dealt with first off. Maybe I can get them to do some job in the barn and have them work together. I hate to see that little girl have to do anything else physical today, but it would be an excuse for me to get them together. Let me think a bit here."

After dinner Carl suggested that the girls come to the milk parlor with him because he wanted to show them how to replace parts on the mechanical milkers. He quietly left as they worked together.

"Celeste, I've wronged you in some way, and I don't know what I did to create a chasm between us. I adore you and I'm so sorry for invading your space the other night. What caused us to separate in the first place?"

"You've been taking advantage of me," Celeste said without looking up or meeting Bernie's eyes.

"How so? I thought you loved the goats and you always seemed so happy on Thursdays to be here. My Dad has the greatest admiration for your skills, too. I don't understand."

"Charlene said I'm nothing more than your lackey and that only reason you associate with me and no one else, is because no one else would be stupid enough to come out here and work for free."

At the mention of Charlene, Bernie's neck hairs tingled. "Charlene? You bought into her vituperative nature? How could you believe anything she says? You used to not trust her."

"She's a very nice person and has her life together."

"Together how?"

Celeste stopped inserting rubber pieces and put her hands on her ample hips and faced Bernie. "You don't know anything about her. She's been very kind to me and treated me like a friend." Her voice was accusatory.

"How have I not been kind and not treated you as a friend? Do you think I would abandon you if you didn't milk on Thursdays? You knew going into this that I milked to help my Mom and Dad and to offset Noir's board here. You were the one who volunteered to help. I never asked you. But you insisted on learning because you fell in love with goats and the job." Bernie tried to keep the frustration out of her voice, but she could hear her pitch rising. She stopped talking for a minute and took a deep breath.

Celeste hands still on her hips was staring down at Bernie sitting on a stool. "I know," she sounded a little embarrassed. "I love this job. I also love teaching and I've made a friend who thinks you are taking advantage of me. She believes you to be the most antisocial person at school, too."

Bernie's mind was racing to think of incidents where she might be considered antisocial. She stared at Celeste with nothing to say. The only person she was really

antisocial with was McGinty, and there were reasons for that.

Although, Celeste might be half right because Bernie really didn't feel she had much of a connection to the other teachers. She still thought of herself as a business person and a little above the other teachers. The only people she had any mental connection with were Gene Morgan and Celeste. Oh, and Cathy when they were showing.

"Celeste, do you remember you telling me last winter how you didn't trust Charlene? What changed?"

"Charlene reached out to me and invited me to go shopping one evening. We enjoyed our time at the mall. I got to know her a little and she started to confide in me. No one confides in me."

"I do."

"Yes and no. You didn't tell me about your medications or your relationship with Cathy Jones the counselor."

"Because I was scared and confused about the medications and the diagnosis. Cathy was sprung on me by the barn where Noir was in training. You're more than welcome to come to come to shows with us, but I think you'll be bored to tears after a watching a few rides. It just never occurred to me that you might be interested in that."

"You locked me out of that part of your life."

"I truly did not. I might have been assumptive, but I did not intend to lock you out. Cathy's involvement with

my horse was a big conundrum for me. I was confused about how to proceed with it. She's a nice gal and she rides Noir well. Noir is a very difficult horse to deal with. It's not like we're socializing all the time or talk on the phone about anything other than lessons and the upcoming shows. I did not mean to make you feel that way.

"How did you find out about Cathy, anyway? I mean it wasn't a secret, but I didn't go advertising it."

"Charlene told me."

"How the hell does Charlene know? The only person I know who knows is my husband!"

"Charlene seems to know a lot about you."

"Did you know that Gene made me talk to Cathy and I was embarrassed? Did you know that I didn't know the rider they were going to recommend over at Thousand Pines was Cathy Jones until the day she was supposed to ride? How could Charlene know things about me that no one else knows? Is she following me around? Does she have a private detective on me? What's her fascination, anyway?"

"I don't know, I didn't ask her."

"Well, at this point I feel my privacy has been violated and that I'm being unfairly scrutinized by someone I don't trust. Why's she so damn interested in my life? Doesn't she have one of her own?

"Here, I wanted to apologize to you for whatever it was that I did to cause you to be upset with me and I feel like someone ought to be apologizing to me right now."

It was getting close to milking time and Carl walked into the milk parlor. "Girls, I'm about to start chores here, any volunteers for help? After hay and that big lunch, I may need a little assistance."

It was clear to him that Bernie and Celeste were in a standoff. Whatever they were talking about was not about to be resolved in the next few minutes.

"Sure, Carl, let me ask Mike if he's interested in watching. I've been trying to get him out here to see this for over a year now. If you let me milk you can get some rest earlier, too."

"Bernie?"

"Sure, Dad. Just give me a minute to tell Tony. He may just want to go home."

Tony did want to go and he asked if Celeste would give Bernie a ride on her way home. Celeste agreed. This indicated to Tony that there was a resolution in the works and going home might be the wisest idea. He beat feet off the farm after saying thanks and goodbye to Bernie's brothers and Mom.

"Bernie, Tony asked if Mike and I could give you a ride home because he wants to leave. I guess this bores him."

Bernie looked hopeful and said. "Thanks. Too many people in the milk parlor would only confuse things. I appreciate the offer. Did he leave already?"

The three of them finished the job in record time. It was still light out and they went to survey the hay stacks with pride. "So, Celeste, how do you feel about your first experience putting up hay?" Carl asked her.

"I feel a sense of accomplishment like when we finish milking and cleaning up. Like something got completed."

"Enough so, that you'll be back for the second cutting?" he laughed.

"The jury's still out on that one. I'll let you know. I didn't know you could ache so much. I'll definitely be taking some pain reliever tonight. I'm starting to stiffen up already."

Carl sucked on his unlit pipe and thanked the girls and left them standing in the hay shed.

Bernie decided to go for broke. "Celeste, you're about my only friend and I miss you so much. I'll be very honest with you, I don't trust Charlene and feel she has an agenda of some kind. Maybe it's simply to divide us, I don't know. We both agreed we didn't trust her and now you're chumming around with her. That upsets me a little. I can't choose your friends for you, but I am not climbing into bed with Charlene. I don't care what she's selling.

"I'm asking you to be my friend again. It wasn't fair of me to pick on you about the diet and for that I apologize. I was just frustrated that you weren't taking my calls or talking to me at school, or even graduation.

"I thought it was hilarious with the seniors and the marbles and Gene. I thought you'd appreciate that one, but you snubbed me that day and sat with Charlene.

"All this time I thought you'd been confronted by someone about me and didn't know how to deal with it. You're not very good at dealing with confrontation and I worried that you might be making yourself sick over having to defend one of my stupid antics."

"Oh my God, the marbles. Charlene didn't think it was funny and I couldn't stop giggling. Every time he handed a senior a diploma they handed him a marble and he kept putting them in his pocket. I thought I was going to bust a gut about the time the 30th one was handed over. His pockets were full and he was running out of places to put them. Can you imagine what his pockets weighed after the 100th student? I'm surprised his pants stayed on with all that weight! I was missing your reaction, too."

They laughed together at the memory of the harmless senior prank and the atmosphere relaxed a little.

"Why didn't Charlene think it was funny?"

"I don't know. She doesn't have your sense of humor, I guess."

"Celeste, I don't believe she has a sense of humor at all. Now wait, before you say anything, I'll tell you I don't know her well, but I think she's the one responsible for a lot of the problems I have with other teachers. After I get to know them, the problems go away. It's as if they believe I'm the big bad wolf and then they get to know

me a little and their suddenly on my side. Not that I'm creating sides, just saying that they become comfortable around me and include me in conversations."

"I don't know, Bernie, I just don't know. It was nice to be included in a shopping trip, even though I didn't buy anything. It was something different. I can't say I didn't miss my nannies, though. I miss you, too. We laugh all the time in the barn.

Celeste continued, "Charlene is a targeted shopper. She has an eagle eye and shops like a predator. I've never seen anything like it before. It's not that she knows what she wants and goes and gets it, it's more like she knows what she wants when she sees it. It was a strange experience, but interesting. I honestly can't say I do trust her, but she's been awfully kind to me."

"Yeah, interesting that it's always on a Thursday, too."

"I never looked at it that way. I just know that I was mad at you and felt left out of your life. I don't want to ride a horse, but it would have been nice to know what you were doing and be included in some of it."

"Again, my apologies. It just never occurred to me that you'd be interested in watching a lesson or seeing a show. I told you about my goal, but didn't include you because you seem afraid of my horse. Speaking of which, I need to check water. She drinks a lot more than goats and I don't think Dad checked it. Do you want to go out with me?"

"Sure. I wonder where Mike is right now."

"Probably with Mom and Dad and my brothers."

Thursday Celeste showed up to milk, but the air was ripe with unexpressed feelings. They finished at their regular time and Celeste was the one who suggested the pump house. Bernie felt a little more confident in their relationship when Celeste brought her own bottle of Jack out of her tote.

The answering machine at home had a message on it from Cathy when Bernie returned. She decided to call her back after her shower. "Hi, what's up?"

"I was just wondering if you were planning on the July show."

"Wow, is the show bill out already?"

"No, I just know when it is and wondered if you were bringing Noir back to Thousand Pines."

"Cathy, I'll be very frank with you, I cannot afford to take her back there and board her. If you want to ride Noir, I can invite you out here, but I just can't take her back there for a two week stint. You've seen the arena and we built jumps, is there any way you can drive over to practice? I can always be on hand to spot you."

"I was afraid you were going to say that. It's a long drive, but I don't have a horse, so could I come out Tuesday?"

"Sure, I'll have ridden her already and she'll be warmed up for you about three o'clock. How's that sound?"

Monday Bernie rode Noir around the large circle and impetuously decided to flirt with danger. She saw Jack

at the head of the clearing and they rode off together down his paths as though it were prearranged. He didn't mention the stolen kiss and seemed to slightly distance himself from her. She wondered if the two of them had come to their senses, but her own senses were telling her differently. She wanted to repeat and explore the depth of the carnal passion she felt. It lingered on her and he didn't miss it. He stopped, dismounted and tied Red to a tree. She dismounted and anticipated what was to come.

He talked for a little bit about moss on the north side of trees. She wondered if she was supposed to make the first move and did. They clung to one another like teenagers in a first exploratory venture. He kissed her neck and she crumpled. He was too smart to leave marks, but the sear of his lips was left on her libido and her back was pressed against a tree. The kisses grew longer and deeper and he finally pulled away.

"Where's this going?"

"Where do you want it to go?"

"Oh, men are pigs, you should know that." He pressed himself against her and she could feel his physical need. She wasn't quite sure she wanted to go any further than this and moved sideways.

"Look, we're both married and this is not right, but I'm very attracted to you and can't seem to keep my hands off you."

"Yes, we are married to others, but this is not hurting anyone. It's fun."

"I'm not sure I'm looking for fun. I love the affection, though."

He covered her mouth again and no more words were spoken for a good length of time.

"Let's come up for air. I feel like a kid out here with you," she said.

"Like?" I'm madly attracted and think about you often."

"I'm sure your wife thinks about you often, as well."

"She's busy with the kids and has a job at the barn. She doesn't care what I do as long as I provide for the kids. She basically ignores me lately."

"Jack, we can't keep this up. If we do, it's going to end badly and others will get hurt. I don't want to take the chance of getting caught, either. My husband is a very forgiving guy, but he's got a temper deep down and I don't want to run into it. We need to discuss this more."

Jack discussed it with another flurry of kisses to her neck. He'd figured out the key to making her melt. "Just shut up, Bernie, and enjoy the beautiful day."

"No, I think I'm heading back now. I already feel guilty and this is not making any sense in a logical way." She fled as fast as she could. Noir was mounted in lightning speed and she flew away down the path and didn't slow down until she hit the clearing with the arena. Running away was her only recourse. Noir was put up and she drove extra fast on the way home. At home she flooded the bathtub with water and bubbles and nearly jumped in. The guilt, the feeling of being soiled and

the thought of what she may have done was inundating her mind. She'd always been so cautious with men and this situation made no sense to her. She became angry at herself for having let it happen. ***Good grief, the way we were going at it could have resulting in not stopping and going even further.*** **She shuddered at the thought of cheating on Tony.**

She wrapped herself in a light robe and went to the kitchen in search of wine. The bath didn't last long because it was unsatisfying and her hair hung in wet strands and dripped down the back of her neck. ***This is not how I want to live my life. "What just happened out there?*** **Her emotions were scarred and raw, she tried to wipe the scene from her vision.**

I've got to avoid that area from now on. I need a trailer to drive Noir to Thousand Pines to practice and take lessons. **She remembered that she forgot to tell Jack that Cathy would be using the arena tomorrow and she panicked. What if Jack showed up at the trail head tomorrow when they were practicing? How was she supposed to deny the attraction between the two of them and hide the relationship? Her mind was racing and she forgot to start dinner for Tony. She aimlessly wandered around looking for things to do when she remembered Tony's expected arrival and dinner. She grabbed some hotdogs and started the grill.** ***Hot dogs, oh boy, he's going to wonder what I've been up to.*** **She quickly prepared some vegetables to grill with them and brought out a cast iron pan for potatoes. This was a cobbled together dinner by a panicked woman, and it looked like it. She hoped she didn't look too flustered or upset.**

I can't even discuss this with anyone, she reminded herself. *Oh, if I just had someone to talk to right now. I have no one to confide in and if my father gets wind of this, my life is over. I don't want him to know, let alone disappoint him.* She felt dirty again and decided that the bathrobe wasn't the best appearance she could make when Tony arrived home.

She began to wonder what Jack thought and where his thoughts were. Her esteem of him was lessened when she started to think about his lovely children and his wife. *Does he do this a lot? Why me? Where does he think this is going? Does he think he's going to get some and then leave? Does he think this is going to get more involved and leave his wife? Does he think at all?*

As much fun and camaraderie was had at the last show, Bernie felt she needed to find another barn for lessons and wondered if Cathy was game for a change of plans. Cathy did express an interest in Dressage, but she had other plans and Bernie doubted that she could change her mind. It'd be a very uncomfortable situation if she changed barns in the middle of the show season and let Cathy standing alone without a horse to show and no explanation. *Oh, what a mess I've created here, by just kissing someone.*

How do I tell Jack to leave me alone without remembering what it's like to kiss him? She picked up the phone and called his cell.

"Jack, we have to stop this. It's out of control and I'm not playing this game any longer."

"Oh, I thought you were calling to schedule another rendezvous."

"No, I'm calling to ask you to leave me alone. I can't do this any longer. It is very flattering to think you're attracted to me, but I can't be in this position. What were you even thinking in the first place? Is this something you do on a regular basis with the women from the barn?"

"Oh, that's not fair. I'm a good person and this is the first time I've been attracted to anyone. You're enticing, Lady. You hide your emotions, but they show, anyway."

"I'm not hiding anything here. I just want you to go away."

"OK, I'll go away."

"Thank you and now, goodbye." She hung up the phone and called the doctor's office.

"I think I'm in a manic upswing and have done something inappropriate and need to talk about it. Can I get an appointment on Wednesday afternoon?" If this was what the result of an upswing was, she was going to curb it as fast as she could.

****

Cathy showed up on time and Bernie said that Noir was off. "She looks a little sore to me and she seems lame." Cathy, not to be deterred, wanted to see Noir lunged. Bernie had no other option without looking like a liar than to let Cathy lunge her.

"She looks fine to me, Bernie."

"She just looked a little off this afternoon and I thought we'd give her a break."

"Did you ride her this afternoon? Was she bobbing her head?"

Cathy obviously could tell the signs of lameness and knew that Noir wasn't lame, sore or tired.

"I didn't ride her this afternoon; I thought we could just ride her around the bridle paths and give her a break."

"She loves to work, Bernie and since we only have one horse between the two of us, that's not realistic."

"Oh, but you've never seem my bridle paths. I could let you just hack her out and you could meet me back here in an hour."

"Are you sure?"

"Yes, she needs to rest her mind. We can't keep hopping on her and working her each time she's ridden. You go and I'll help my dad in the barn. You can't get lost if you stick to the larger path and circle round." Bernie wasn't thinking that the larger path led around to the arena and the trail head. "Go ahead, saddle her up and take a nice leisurely ride."

After Cathy left on Noir Bernie realized that Jack might be at the trail head. Her hands started fluttering like her thoughts. She jumped on the four wheeler and headed out to the woods. She caught up with Cathy about halfway down the big path. "Hey, I thought I'd show

you how the trail winds in and out so you had a better ride. Noir gets bored just going on a big circle, she loves to explore the seldom used paths."

Cathy looked at her strangely. "Bernie, is there some other reason we're not supposed to practice today? What are you not telling me?"

"Nothing. I just thought that Noir needed a break. I rode her yesterday for about two hours and I didn't want to cancel your ride, but felt sorry for her."

"But, you ride her all the time on trail, don't you? I thought this was good for her head."

"It is. Don't you think she feels sore to you?" Bernie grasped at anything.

"She feels perfectly lovely and relaxed to me."

"Ok, let me show you some other paths and we can do this again another day. I wish we had two horses here, so we could ride together. It would make it more enjoyable."

"Well the noise of that machine isn't very pleasant. Can I get lost in there? Are the paths marked?"

"Not really. I made them and I know them, but if you keep the sun on your right, it should take you back to the main path and back to the barns. I'll leave you to your ride." She left hoping that Jack wasn't waiting at the trail head and hoping she'd deterred Cathy from going in that direction.

Cathy and Noir returned and they seemed relaxed. "That was fun. You've made some interesting bridle paths over the years and Noir is very comfortable. This is really my first trail ride alone and I'm grateful to you for suggesting it," Cathy said as she unsaddled the horse.

"Yeah, maybe it was the best thing." Bernie was relieved that Cathy and Noir didn't run into Jack. Noir would have cried out and that would have been a telltale sign to Cathy that something was up. Not that she hadn't already been suspicious.

"What made you think she was lame?"

"Oh, I just saw her standing around today and not grazing, so I thought she was sore or lame. She usually grazes with the goats and they stay in a close herd. Just a hunch," Bernie lied.

"Well, she did just fine. I think it was a good idea so she doesn't always associate me with work. I know she loves to jump, but it's work and I push her sometimes late in the afternoons at shows. I've been really thinking about how I could afford my own horse. I can't afford to board at Thousand Pines because I feel their fees are outrageous, but they do take good care of the horses. They also have Jack, and he seems like he really pays attention to the horses and riders.

"Would your father consider boarding another horse here with Noir?"

"Oh, God, no. You don't know what I have to do just to have him accept her here. Unless you're willing to drive

from Jackson once a week and milk goats and clean up the milking parlor, he wouldn't be interested. Right now I have a friend who milks with me on Thursdays and it's all we can do to keep up some days. She doesn't get paid, either, other than some cheese once in a while."

The thought of Cathy in the milk house was beyond Bernie's sense of humor. She was so consumed with the thought of Cathy leaving that she didn't find this funny. "You know, I never asked, but I bet Thousand Pines has rough board or pasture board for some of those horses out there. You might ask Sue. First, you need to find a horse. Do you have the resources to care for one? I know that's a nosy question, but it has to be asked."

"I really don't know what upkeep on a horse entails. I know they need hoof trims and shoes and I don't have my own bridle or brushes or anything. But what else is involved?"

They chatted for a while about horse upkeep and unexpected bills. Cathy seemed genuinely discouraged by the end of the conversation. "I guess I don't have those resources or opportunities. I'd really like a horse of my own, but I have children to think of. It would take a lot of time, too. Their father is getting more involved with his girlfriend and I seem to have the kids for longer periods of time now. I guess I'll just have to keep sharing Noir until something happens."

The thought of continuing to share Noir was starting to irritate Bernie. There was no reason that they couldn't do so, just her guilt about Jack and her indiscretion. Cathy was astute and had already noticed the attraction between them. It didn't seem obvious to Bernie, but

Cathy had already mentioned it twice. What would happen during the July show, she wondered.

The doctor's appointment the next day was an exercise in futility. "I don't know if I'm in an upswing or not. This is what happened and I have no idea why. Nor, was I thinking clearly when it started to escalate." She expounded on the events and when they happened.

"You told me you won all your classes at this last show. Were you elated?"

"Hell yes, I was elated. I told you the horse cannot lose because she's so great."

"This is the event that may have pushed you a little too far. You were happy, elated and didn't use good judgment. Lack of judgment is one of the signs of mania. I'm glad you came in. I'm thinking ancillary counseling on a weekly basis to help you change behavior patterns."

"What patterns? This is the first time in my life something like this has happened. I've never done anything like this and don't plan to again."

"Bernie, you didn't use sound judgment before and you didn't think anything was wrong. That was manic behavior and it got you into a lot of trouble. You almost lost your job over those incidents. This could lose you your marriage if it continues. You said you practically ran away after the tryst in the woods. I'm surprised it didn't go further from what you've told me about the attraction between the two of you."

"I'm not going into weekly counseling. I just want to know if this was considered a manic episode and how to control it."

"A lot of reactions to things are learned behavior."

"This is not *learned* behavior, it's the first time for something like this. I've always mistrusted men and their intentions. I just want to know how to recognize the signs of an upswing and stop them."

They argued back and forth for most of the hour without any reconciliation. He was insisting on counseling and she arguing against it. There were not going to be hour long drives to Ann Arbor once a week and she didn't want to have to start over again with an additional person. She felt as though she were putting her life out there for the world to criticize at will.

There was talk about upping the medication again and she refused. Bernie felt the medications she was on were enough to keep her level headed and in control. This was a mistake making the appointment and wanting to talk to someone about Jack. Sitting there she made a decision. She'd eschew all contact with Jack and find another avenue for her urges. She didn't need this doctor and she didn't need medications. What she needed was willpower and discipline. Who was he to tell her to up the meds again and to talk to some other stranger about this behavior? She would fight this on her own without his help or anyone else's. And, she told him this.

"I predicted something like this was going to happen at our last appointment. I knew it was just a matter

of time; especially if you won at that horse show. You cannot fight this battle alone, no one can."

"I can and I will. I'll stay on the dose of meds I am currently taking and be more self-aware. I'm not keen on seeing you because of your smugness, either."

He raised his eyebrows and chuckled at her. "This is my job, Bernie, this is what I do all day, this is what I went to school for. I know mania and depression and I know bipolar disorder. I've seen and heard it all. I've yet to meet someone who fought this battle alone and unaided. You, however, are an adult and you can choose to run, or ruin, your life the way you see fit. I can only offer what help I can give and pray for the best results. It takes a lot of counseling, medication and changes, and it takes a willing person to alter this behavior. I'm not saying you may not be strong enough to do this unaided, I'm saying that with help, you can control this. I'm offering the help."

"I'll continue my monthly appointments and keep you apprised of changes, but I'm not driving here once a week and then again once a month to see a person who will sit in judgment of me. Bottom line."

"The psychologists are not judgmental. They just counsel. You won't even consider this for a short timeframe?"

"Not in the cards. I'm holding the cards."

He sighed and stared at her for a moment, then wrote a name and number on a prescription pad and handed it to her. "OK, here's the name of the counselor if you change your mind. She is very good, very understanding

and a good listener. I'll tell her to make room for you should you change your mind and call. I wish you luck."

Nearly bedding Jack Reems made her extra cautious around people and highly sensitive to her reactions to happenings and events. She still had to deal with Jack to transport her horse to the July show and she felt foolish acting as though nothing had happened between them. Squaring up was not easy to do, but she made the call to Sue Riker and requested that her horse be picked up two days before the show so Cathy and she could practice with additional help. She was at the farm when his rig pulled in and she had Noir standing near the driveway waiting. Her attitude toward him was strictly business; nearly cold. He seemed to mope a little and acted hurt. She did not allow him time alone with her in the barn or in the driveway because her father conveniently appeared as the horse was stepping into the trailer. *Bless you, Dad.*

Thousand Pines was buzzing with activity that evening and she and Cathy got right to work. Bernie purposely did not follow the trailer to the facility because she didn't want to give Jack the impression that she needed him. He was conspicuously absent when she got there.

"Cathy, I did a little too much drinking and partying last time we showed and I wondered if you'd be offended if we stayed in a different hotel closer to the show this time."

"Oh, but we had so much fun at the last show."

"I think I had too much fun. I suffered for it later. What do you think?"

"Bernie, we don't have to stay up and party all night, we can get to bed early. I just loved being with the whole group and we bonded so well. Let's stay at the same place as the rest of them."

"OK, but we may not get in because I haven't yet made our reservation," Bernie said.

"Oh, I wish you'd told me, I could have done it online this week."

"I'll attempt it tonight. Let's just hit the sack early this time and not stay up all night." Bernie knew she wasn't going to win this argument and didn't put up much of a fuss. Besides, it had just occurred to her that Jack would probably be staying on the grounds that night and not be at the hotel. She meant to avoid him at all costs.

Just as she suspected, Jack was assigned to night duty at the show grounds and Sue was at the hotel. Cathy and Bernie finished braiding in good time and stopped at the hotel bar with the others. Cathy nudged her, "I promise this won't be a late night. I just have few chances to spend with others and this is always a treat for me."

"That's Ok, Cathy, I'm feeling pretty rested tonight. We can spend some time with the others and enjoy ourselves. I'm feeling pretty confident about tomorrow, too. Can I buy you a drink?"

THIRTY NINE

"Hi, Babe."

Bernie swung around quickly at the sound of Tony's voice. He was wearing shorts, sneaks and a T-shirt with his sunglasses hung on the collar making him look like a high profile celebrity.

"You surprised me. When did you get here?"

"I decided that Kalamazoo wasn't that far away and thought I'd get some photos of you and Noir for us. I keep promising to watch you show and wanted to surprise you."

"Thank you. I hope we do well. We'll be in the ring together in about 20 minutes. Did you have any problem finding us?"

"Nope, the logos are all over the trailers and they were easy to spot."

"Hi, Jack. How ya doing?" Jack was assisting a junior rider with a leg up for her class.

"Hello, Tony, I'm doin great. Should be a good show. You just get here?"

"No, I've been looking for the barns and you guys for a few minutes. I parked somewhere out there," he waved his hand to the side. "I wanted to support my lovely wife's last show before the season ends."

"Last show? We have two more coming up. She didn't tell you?"

"No, she never mentioned it." He turned and looked at Bernie who was fastening the keepers on Noir's bridle and keeping busy wiping the slobber off the bit in Noir's mouth.

"You never mentioned any more shows."

"Well, we budgeted for three and Cathy budgeted for three, so this is the last show. If I'm lucky and Cathy's lucky, we will both have a shot at high point even if we don't go to any more shows this year."

"I see. What can I do to help?"

"Not a thing. We're all lunged and warmed up and ready to go. It's just a matter of mounting up again, putting on my coat and heading to the ring. My camera is in my tack trunk right over there."

"I've got another surprise for you."

"What's that?"

"Your folks are here too. I got up and went to the barn early this morning and helped your dad milk. Well, I actually cleaned up like you and Celeste taught me and we got out of there in time to make it here."

"Where are they?"

"They're at the concession stand trying to decide if they want cow's milk in their coffee." Tony laughed. "I'm serious."

"Oh, I know you're serious. That's a big debate when they go out. Can you get them and bring them to ring two? I've got to get down to the gate before I miss my class."

Carl came right up to Noir and stoked her forehead at the gate. "I've never been to a horse show before and I have to tell you that it looks exciting. You look pretty damn good yourself, Kid."

"Thanks Dad. Wish me luck."

Bernie's mother fussed over the formal attire and how lovely Bernie looked on Noir. It was typical mother behavior and she seemed very nervous for Bernie. She'd never really watched Bernie ride before because she was always busy doing something at that time of day, so her ministrations were a little irksome. Bernie could feel herself getting nervous by osmosis and a little irritated at her mother.

"Mom, I have to get myself calm and in the right frame of mind here, so do you mind going and standing near Tony and Dad?"

"Oh, am I making you nervous? I'm sorry. I didn't even know I was doing it."

Bernie's mind was spinning. She was grateful for Tony's presence and him helping Dad in the barn so he could

bring them. She was glad he was here to keep Jack in line, but she was nervous about showing in front of them. She'd made major presentations, spoke in front of crowds, showed to first place in front of people she didn't know, but the planting of her parents and Tony on the same grounds with Jack kept flooding her mind.

Sue came over and said, "You look edgy."

"I am edgy. My husband just showed up with my parents and I think they're making me nervous. How can you get a case of the jitters in your 30's?"

Sue laughed. "You'll do fine. Just give Noir her head and let her carry you until you focus again. I'll be right here ringside to encourage you. You're eligible for high point."

"Thanks a lot, Sue. I really needed to be reminded of that right now."

Bernie knew she had to perform and she had to keep Noir from getting jiggy. She needed to calm down and gain her focus to do this. For some reason the crowd at the rail seemed larger than usual, the competitors looked more competitive and the sun was starting to bake her in the wool coat. She could feel her hands sweating under the gloves. "Well, if my gloves get wet, I'll have a better grip on the reins," she consoled herself.

She took one last glance at the little party standing at the rail with her parents. Cathy and Jack were with them. "Let the tranquilizer you took take effect and get this job done," she thought. "Let the meds do what they ought to be doing and don't let us wobble."

When the gate opened, she was ready; Noir was ready. "Let our show begin. They want to see me win, let's win." She patted Noir's neck and hit the gate.

The class seemed to last forever. The sun was merciless and she could feel the sweat dripping down the back of her shirt and the seat of her breeches. She just let Noir do her thing and she watched the two judges and kept her hands and seat as still as possible. "Invisible aids, invisible aids," she kept telling herself. Her focus was on. They won the class.

For the first time at a show, she was breathless and soaked to the skin. The discomfort was unbearable. The group converged on her as she exited. There was a happy babble among them and she basked in it for a few seconds until she noticed Jack's arm around Cathy. ***What? Is that friendly or overly friendly?***

Sue took her ribbon from her sweaty gloves and congratulated her. Sue's face was jubilant. "One more class and then you can get those wet clothes off and rest. I'll let you spend time with your family and I'll take care of Cathy. By now, you trust her with Noir, so no big deal."

"Thanks, Sue, but I'll be there for Cathy like she's always there for me. Besides, they have a chance a high point as well in their division. I wouldn't let her down now."

The second class was nearly a shoe in because it was judged on the horse's movement and gaits and Noir certainly had those. The second blue ribbon was handed up to her by the ring steward when Bernie remembered Jack's arm around Cathy. She thanked the woman and

looked toward the group. Cathy and Jack were nowhere near the rail and Bernie began to wonder.

"You look distracted, Hon, Tony said as she slid off the horse and loosened her girth.

"I do?"

Bernie fairly dragged Noir to the barn to see if Cathy and Jack were there. The group straggled behind her thinking she had something important to do.

When she got to the barn and unsaddled the horse she immediately went to the wash rack and hosed the sweat off her. The sun was quickly tiring horses today. She scraped off the water and put Noir in her stall. Still no Cathy appeared. Cathy didn't have to be saddled up and in the ring till after lunch, so she may have gone off somewhere. *Somewhere with Jack?* She was single and Bernie got the impression that she thought Jack attractive. *Hmm.*

"You did great, Bernie. I'm so proud of you. Sue introduced herself and told us you had a chance at a high point award. She sounded disappointed that you weren't planning to show in August and September. Do you want to?" Tony asked.

Bernie was chugging down an electrolyte drink and took a second to address Tony's question. "I really don't know. When school starts I am more involved than earlier years. I should start to accompany you to the games and support your efforts at advertising this year. I can't answer that question right now. Have you seen Jack, by the way?"

"No, I haven't. He didn't watch your second class. We really should discuss this. You had a goal and you are about to attain it. If no one else on this circuit does as well as you, you could be high point winner this year. Just think, your first year showing hunters and a high point."

"They're all flat classes. I'm not allowed to jump yet at shows. I still wobble out there and the instructor told me she'd tell me when I was ready. I don't think I want to do any over fences classes this year, anyway. I'm not too excited because I have a great horse that knows her stuff in my area of showing. Let's find some lunch. I could eat a cow right now. I'm also soaking wet with sweat and need to keep hydrated so I don't get disoriented."

She got very close to him and whispered, "You're not supposed to sweat a lot on these medications because it runs the meds out faster. That last thing I need right now is a meltdown."

Conspiratorially he whispered back, "Gotcha. Let's get you fed and sit down with your folks for a little while."

Tony bought lunch for everyone. He got a bottle of Gatorade for Bernie and stayed close to her. She had already taken off her show shirt and choker and changed into a t-shirt. It was pretty obvious who had already shown and who had not. A t-shirt was the apparel of choice after long sleeves, chokers and gloves. "Mom and Dad, if you need to be back at the farm early, take my car and I'll ride back with Bernie. That way you'll be on schedule and everything will be ready when Noir is delivered without disrupting the regular schedule."

They took Tony up on his offer and left after lunch. Tony strolled the grounds and through other barns with Bernie until it was time to assist Cathy. They entered the barn to find Jack helping Cathy saddle Noir.

Bernie knew that Cathy didn't need help saddling, and Jack had never offered assistance before. Cathy couldn't quite meet Bernie's eyes and Bernie knew that she had been dropped like a hot stone by Jack. *Fine, suits me and keeps me out of trouble.* But it bit her. As far as she was concerned, she was standing here with one of the most handsome men in the country, and yet slightly jealous about whatever had transpired between Jack and Cathy. Her face colored slightly.

Jack would not meet her eyes, either. She had to laugh a little about her mother's warning when she was a teenager about "fast men." She knew what the true meaning was now. Jack had wasted no time in replacing her and she wondered who else had been prey for him. She felt a little stupid. *Just dumb luck,* she told herself. *I was lucky and inspired to run away. See, I don't need counseling, he does. I wonder if his wife knows about his dalliances.*

Tony, oblivious to her thoughts had his arm causally draped over her shoulder and watched as Noir was readied for her next class.

"Cathy, said Bernie, Noir was really sweated up good from the flat classes. Take it easy on her. It's sweltering out there.

"Did she drink water, Jack?"

"Yes, and we put electrolytes in the feed this morning. She should be well hydrated and ready to jump." He still didn't look toward her, but stayed on the other side of the horse looking as though he were talking to the ground.

Bernie had a relatively evil thought about blowing Cathy's confidence, but didn't want to hurt Noir's chances for another shot at high point. She had a great horse and that's all she cared about. Besides, Cathy was single and could do what she wanted. Maybe she watched Jack so closely before because she desired him. Who knew? Who cared at this point? She reached her face up to Tony and gave him a kiss. *Stick that in your pipe and smoke it, Bub.* She fully knew she was playing a high school game, but she wanted to do something to make her indifference known.

She knew that both Jack and Cathy were observing her and neither knew what the other was thinking. Cathy was probably embarrassed and Jack did not want confrontations with either of them. He certainly didn't want Bernie to know what she already knew. Bernie's new concern was whether or not Cathy could keep it together through her classes after whatever had transpired earlier.

"We'll see you ringside after you warm up, Cathy," Bernie said to the air.

It was obvious to Bernie that Cathy was a little discombobulated and was having a difficult time concentrating on her warm up. Noir ticked a rail on a practice jump and Bernie started to grow concerned. She needed her fabulous horse to win and the mare

needed Cathy's concentration. Bernie walked into the warm up ring and approached Cathy. "You are up for high point, you need to concentrate and keep it together today. Use that focus you use on those kids at school, Cath.

"I lost my focus earlier because of Tony and my parents. Who would think at my age that my parent's presence could make me nervous?" She forced a laugh for Cathy's benefit.

"Just think how much you deserve a cold beer and that Noir has to earn it for you today. That should give you motivation."

Frazzled Cathy said, "She's a little lazy right now. I heard her tick that rail back there. Should I push her a little? She's probably as hot as the rest of us and wants to just quit. No one told me these clothes were going to be this awful to wear in the summer. I'm already soaking wet and I can't imagine that she wants to canter around and jump right now."

"She's in great shape. Push her just a little. Do you want to use a crop for a few minutes?"

"No, I'll just put my leg on her stronger before a fence. I can hang in there with her for two classes. I know I can."

"Ok, we'll hose you off with her after you're done!" Bernie said, thinking that Cathy probably needed to be hosed down after her run with Jack. Where did they hide? she wondered. Was it in the dressing room of his trailer? Men are pigs, he was right. He seemed to be proving his own words. Why did he decide today was

the day? Why not wait until Cathy had a lesson at the barn where they could find a place with privacy? Why did he do this at the show? Her thoughts were drifting to their last meeting in the woods. *Oh, I can't believe I got suckered into this. Here I have the world's most understanding, handsome and loving husband and I was taken by a piece of trash like that.*

"What?" She answered Cathy. "I didn't hear what you said."

"Nothing, I just feel like a wet dishrag and I'm wondering if she feels the same way."

"Don't worry about it, she's been ridden harder and longer in hotter weather. I have ridden her through hotter summers, all day for long distances. She can handle this. She's just giving you one of her famous opinions. You'll do fine as long as you don't take anything from her. That's why I let you ride her in the first place. Hey, it could be worse, and you could be riding a school horse right now. At least she's still got spirit enough to tell you what she doesn't want to do."

Bernie surveyed the warm up ring and noticed other horses looking sluggish and tired. Noir, on the other hand, still had fire in her eyes and looked alert. Bernie felt their chances were good.

Cathy had two clear rounds and won both classes. Bernie took the reins from her as she exited the ring and walked Noir to the barns. She had the kindness to buy Cathy a Gatorade between classes and handed the half empty bottle to her.

"You'd think I'd have to pee after drinking a quart of this stuff, but I think I sweated it all out," Cathy said as she used her sleeve to wipe her forehead. Her helmet was dangling off her fingers and Bernie noticed that the cuffs of her blouse were wet.

When they got to the barn Bernie took Noir back to the wash rack and hosed her off for the second time. Cathy left and came back with a t-shirt in place of her show blouse. I'm sorry, I just wanted to get that wet shirt off. I should be hosing her down because you did it earlier. God, I don't think I've ever been this hot in my life. Now I know what you guys were talking about concerning dehydration. You can really get unfocused in a hurry out there." Her face was florid and it made the streaks in her hair look even more fake.

Bernie had decided earlier not to mention anything to Cathy. She suddenly perceived Cathy as lonely and needy for company. How could she even approach the subject without betraying herself? She couldn't, and she wasn't about to bring it up. She did decide, though, to help Cathy meet some nice man who would respect her for the person she was. Where she would find such a person was a little bit of a confused mystery right now. *Later*, she thought. At this moment she was concerned that she cool down the horse and get her to the shade of the stall and a water bucket.

Tony approached them and stood a respectful distance from the splashing water. "You girls need to discuss the next two shows. I know summer school is starting soon and that doesn't leave much time for practice and work,

but if you both have a chance at high point, you should go for it."

"Cathy and I will discuss it next week." She tried to get Tony to shut up because he didn't know Cathy's financial situation or about the kids and not getting all of her child support checks.

He didn't let up. "Really, if you are that close, why not nail it down?"

"Tony, we'll discuss it next week. Right now we have a hot horse that needs a drink and some rest." She frowned at him and his face registered some recognition to let it be.

Noir was sluggish getting off Jack's trailer at the farm. She and Tony lifted the tack trunk out of the truck and set it down in the driveway with intentions to move it later.

Jack said, "I'd give her a few days off, Bernie. She really worked hard today and Cathy had to push her over jumps. The heat was really bad and you've got to remember that she's a black horse. She probably heats up more than any other color."

"I'll do that. Thanks for your help today, Jack. I'll see you around." Bernie looked him directly in the eyes and he registered her knowledge immediately. His ears got red.

"Well, I've got horses to get to Jackson, see ya." He hopped in the truck and left.

Bernie and Tony hauled the tack trunk to the barn near Noir's stall. She was already sighing and eating her hay.

They would withhold all grain tonight in the event of a colic situation. Tony embraced Bernie and planted a big, wide kiss on her lips. “I’m so proud of you. You took a difficult horse and made her a champ.”

“She’s always had the potential to be a champion, Tony. I am just firm with her. Even when I didn’t ride her and couldn’t drag myself out here, she was a potential champ.” She returned his kiss with as much passion as she could muster in the heat.

“I bet you want to get out of those clothes and take a shower, huh?”

“Yeah, you read my mind.”

“How’s about I take you to dinner in celebration tonight?”

She mimicked him back, “How’s about you take me to dinner in celebration?”

At home she could barely peel off the damp breeches and two pair of nylon socks. She lay back on the bed and just enjoyed the air conditioning for a few minutes. Tony yelled up the stairs. “How long before we can leave?”

“Depends on where you’re taking me. I don’t feel like getting really dressed for anything big time, but I don’t want a pizza or a hamburger, either.”

He walked into the bedroom and laughed at her prone position. “Too bad we don’t have takeout Chinese here. I’d just offer to drive and pick it up.”

"I'm bushed. Don't expect me to run with you tomorrow morning."

"I can see that. I imagine the heat wasted you today."

"It more wasted Cathy. Did you notice that Cathy and Jack seem to be attracted to each other?"

He walked to the bathroom and stripped off his clothes for a shower. She stayed cooling off on the bed under the ceiling fan. When he was done, she showered, put on shorts and they left.

FORTY

(I know she smokes on Thursdays. She thinks I can't tell because she showers and brushes her teeth, but the smell is still there and I can taste it when I kiss her. I haven't mentioned it to her because she needs a little secret; with such a transparent life that she now feels everyone is examining. I don't like it, but it's only on Thursdays that I notice it, so how much harm can she be doing?

The last two years have been tenuous both in my practice and with my wife. I'm never sure what is about to happen next and I sometimes think I'm married to a miscreant kid. She's impetuous and her next act is always a surprise to me. It's like living in some sort of tragic comedy. My mother thinks she's the greatest thing to come into my life and I worry because Bernie is never accountable. She seems to slide through these incidents without any responsibility.

Bernie was never like this in our early years and it's only increased in frequency. I've studied the finer points and she exhibits many of the telltale signs of bipolar disorder, but avoids some of them, as well. She doesn't exactly have grandiose ideas and she hasn't shown me any signs of sexual misbehavior. I don't think either of these are in her makeup. But I always wait for the other shoe to drop.

I love the fact that she is disciplined in so many ways. Our house is always immaculate; laundry is not just done, but folded and returned. I don't want for anything in the food department and can't tell you what a great cook she is. She's imaginative and steady at home.

The shopping incident did rile me a lot, but I have to blame the disorder because there was no logic to it. I know she sacrifices a lot of things for us and herself, but the shopping trip was over the top. It happened on a day she saw her doctor, too, and I wonder if he had anything to do with it. Did he encourage her to go out and spend to feel good, or was this something she had preplanned? I'm about to consider counseling for myself at this point. I just don't know what's next on her agenda. Does she have an agenda I wonder?

She loves to teach and has gotten over, from what I can tell, the horrors of teaching the children of the very people she went to school with. They seem to respect her position and the kids are apparently letting their parents know how exciting her classes are. I know her to be strict and there is one little girl in an advanced class that she worries about because the girl is slender and underdeveloped the way Bernie said she was as a teen. I know she is well protected because I've heard that authoritative voice myself and I cringe to know that teens in her classes have heard it when she doesn't like something.

The Nash kid incident was one I understand, but she handled it wrong. The school said they couldn't do anything about it because it was a civil matter and didn't involve them. That's were Bernie turns into a raging

bull. I know that the situation would never have come to light if she didn't do what she did, but she was wrong and nearly lost her job over it. She believes she has no friends, but my understanding is that many people sided with her actions that day because they had all thought of doing the same thing. If it were me, I'd have gone to the authorities and let them investigate it. Not Bernie. No, she has to rush right in and take matters into her own hands. Literally.

Living with someone with bipolar disorder is disorderly, at best. I never know what kind of mood she will be in and last year's depression was scary. She barely got out of bed, didn't care about her appearance and had no interest in anything. She loves to cook and we ate a lot of lackluster meals. I'm not complaining about the meals, just the lack of interest in anything, including sex. Her horse was also neglected from what her father stated. Her parents and I were worried that she'd have to be institutionalized to get over her depression. I'm not sure what brought her out of it, but I got tired of taking meals to her bedside because she would come home and put on a bathrobe and go to bed. I'm not creative in the kitchen and am no cooking genius. She barely ate during that episode and she started dropping weight. Now that I've done some research I marvel at her ability to teach during that time.

Making her take her medication was a chore, too. She felt it wasn't doing her any good and she would often refuse to take the two prescribed pills. I had to force them on her each morning. I started to doubt their efficacy and considered calling her doctor. If it wasn't for Thursdays and milking goats, I don't think she would

have survived that bout of depression. I'm convinced that the routine of Thursdays kept her moving and motivated a little to accept the low period and start to recover from it. She didn't just snap out of it, she just gradually became herself again. The experts tell you not to tell someone with the disorder to "snap out of it." I really don't understand it because I'm not bipolar and my depressions are just disappointments in my life. They don't last long because I'm a doer. Bernie is also a doer, but she can overdo things to the extreme.

The shopping sprees they warn you about are very evident by the way she hoards food in the freezer and the pantry. She buys several of everything and we have it on hand forever. Thank God she's creative in the kitchen and uses most of it, but our spice cabinet looks like a store shelf. I don't know what Star Anise is used for or juniper berries, but we've got them. Many of the things we've got are in large containers, too. How much curry powder can one use for two people?

When she was single she had a high stress job, but supportive people around her. I think she flounders now because the support is gone and the stress kicks off either a depressive mood or an upswing in her personality. She's talked to me about what the doctor says and I do a lot of research on the Internet to back up what I'm told. I know that her libido is either very high or very low. When she's in a manic phase the libido is high and it excites me. I can deal with that part! It's the moping, slumping Bernie that I can't deal with because I don't know what to do for her. I offer to take her out and she's just not interested. She obediently goes to my parent's for dinners, but you can tell by her quiet demeanor that

she is not up to par. She's actually fallen asleep at their house a few times and I just tell everyone that she's exhausted. I don't tell them that she's in a depressive phase. I don't discuss her disorder with my parents. They still see her as the lively person she can be and that's the way we'll keep it.

Her parents, on the other hand, are very concerned. Apparently this all started to manifest itself in her teens and they just thought she was difficult, hormonal and the youngest child. I don't think it was any of those. I believe she was under constant stress from school and her parent's wishes for good grades. She does have a strong will and her decision to go to college out of state was a real coup for her. Apparently they couldn't say much because of the academic scholarship offered. I don't see them stand down much, either, so it must have been very tense in that household for a while. The whole family is stubborn in decisions and I see where her will comes from. Things are done a certain way and there is no allowance for change.

Bernie doesn't like change very much and it sends her spiraling down. She grew up with rigid personalities and she has one herself. Getting her to start jogging with me was a major effort. She hates to run and I drag her out each morning except Sundays and we increase our time each week. She's gotten in much better shape and is keeping the weight at a decent level. I know she feels ugly again because of the weight gain, but this is the only thing I know to do to help her manage it.

Speaking of ugly. My wife is a stunning woman with black hair and deep blue eyes. She has stature and

curves in all the right places. She just has more curves since her diagnosis. She looks fabulous in my opinion, but she feels logy and fat and lets me know it. I know this affects her self confidence, but there is nothing I can do other than keep encouraging her to run with me and stop drinking.

Alcohol is a depressant and it's a way for her to self medicate when she's manic. The problem is that she just doesn't do it in a manic phase, but all the time. I don't really know how much she drinks, but her father put the kibosh on the liquor at the farm. He even stopped drinking in front of her at family meals. I haven't. I feel she needs to be around people who do drink and have good discipline. This always starts an argument because she so loves her wine and Scotch. I have two glasses of wine each evening and then stop. She can't stop and I'm afraid that alcoholism is next on her plate. There are many reports about manic depressives becoming alcoholics.

I don't know if she drinks to cope or it's just a habit she acquired. It certainly looks like a habit when you see the wine boxes in the recycling area of our garage. She thinks I don't know about the box of wine in her trunk, either. I have the cars cleaned by some of my young clients and they vacuum the trunk. I guess she figures they ignore it, but they tell me about it. It's pretty evident by the garage, anyway.

We've discussed children before and we both seem to want them. I'm just concerned about the hereditary nature of the illness and her alcohol consumption. Can we cope with another manic depressive in the home?

What if she can't take her medication while she's pregnant or nursing? What kind of hell awaits us in that situation? I have been researching a lot lately and have read articles about others who have gone off their meds while pregnant and nursing, but they seem to be in counseling. The doctor told her that much of her behavior was "learned." She learned to react a certain way to certain stressors and stimuli and act out. The question is whether or not counseling will help her unlearn some of her behavior. Can behavior be unlearned? I question this all the time, but it's not a discussion because of her belief about not needing counseling.

She refuses to investigate counseling and support groups, so the children issue is at a standoff right now. I'm not getting any younger, either and she will have to make a decision pretty soon. I am approaching my forties and will be set in ways that do not include continuous vigilance over children. At this point, I don't know how to approach the subject again with her. She is stubborn and sees a stigma attached to both her doctor and the counseling she so desperately needs. I'm not a counselor; I'm married to her and have to live with the consequences she brings on herself.

As far as I know, there is only one person who knows a little about her disorder and that is her friend Celeste. They are an unlikely pair, but Celeste compliments Bernie's gregarious personality. I say gregarious, but you should see her with strangers. She's like a coil about to unwind.

I often do not want to go to restaurants and stores with her because of her sharp tongue and cruel remarks.

I know she's made a few sales clerks nearly cry. She doesn't trust new people and it takes a long time for her to warm up to them and find them harmless. She is always on the lookout for the next barb thrown her way. I know this came from the school experiences from Cold Lake and I can't erase those. Oh, how I wish I could. This place doesn't like strangers and insecure ones at that. What people don't know is that she is mushy and vulnerable and puts on a tiger posture to counteract what she feels might be a threat to her. It comes across as all diva and rude. I see through it, but I can't stop her from doing it. It's ingrained already. She's right, the residents of Cold Lake proved how ugly they were when she was an adolescent. And Bernie can be ugly to people; the only thing ugly about her is her attitude and personality toward them.

I can't believe this part of her personality hasn't shown up in her lessons at the barn in Jackson. I know it's part of the reason other teachers don't trust her. They eventually come around when she lets her guard down or considers them nonthreatening. Her friendship with Celeste is such because Celeste is a walking warm fuzzy. I don't know anyone who doesn't like Celeste and I don't know anyone who would want to hurt her. She, too, is a vulnerable person who will cry if you say "boo" to her. Bernie has a soft spot for Celeste and would not purposely do anything to hurt her.

Their little rift was a mistrust issue. I don't know the Charlene Bernie talks about, but I can tell you I don't trust her motives. I haven't yet met her, but she seems to me to be a divide and conquer type of person. Maybe she has some mental issues of her own. I don't know.

I do know that Bernie hates to drive her beautiful car around town. She loves that car and loves to drive it, but feels like it imposes some image on her that she doesn't want. We just can't let her drive the big old Bronco around because she's already proved how physically dangerous she can be when she's in a manic phase. Not that she couldn't be dangerous in the BMW, but she's less apt to have killer thoughts in it, in my opinion.

One good thing about school for her is that students make her laugh. Laughter is a great healer and she laughs with and about them a lot. She even seems to like the rowdy and disrespectful ones and they obviously know this and treat her well. She's a pretty funny lady when you get to know her and her comments either make you laugh or squirm a little because of their truthful nature. She's just Bernie. I love her. I don't know what to do to assist her in finding more of herself. I'd like to change her behavior, but then I'm sure she'd like to change some of mine. That's marriage. I can only hope that she understands the need for counseling and trusts someone enough to consider it. I pray for someone who will just listen and not condemn her or her previous actions. She doesn't need to be admonished any more than I already do with her. She needs a sympathetic, trained ear with a good handle on bipolar disorder.)

FORTY ONE

"Hi, whatcha doin?"

"Talkin to you!"

"No, really what are you doing right now? Am I interrupting anything?"

"Not at all, I'm sewing."

"Well, you said you'd like to watch me ride. Tony has agreed that we can take Noir back to Thousand Pines for two weeks before the next show and I thought you'd like to accompany me and watch my lesson and then watch Cathy's. I'm back in the flat class because I'm up for high point for the year and Tony has suddenly come up with the money for two weeks more boarding. Noir is being transported today; right now, as a matter of fact."

Celeste's voice got an octave higher. "Oh, that'd be wonderful. I haven't met Cathy yet, either. Do I have to dress a certain way?"

"No, silly, you don't have to wear riding clothes. Your Capri's should be good and cool for you in this heat. I'll pick you up in the morning about 9:30. My lesson is at 10:30 and it takes about half an hour to get there. I'll even treat you to lunch in Jackson afterward."

"Oh, I'm so excited. What can I bring?"

"Nothing other than your water bottle. I have two folding chairs in my trunk and we can use them at the outdoor ring for Cathy's jumping lesson. You might want to bring a hat or something."

Celeste was awed by the big barns and indoor arenas, the viewing room, the horses, the teenaged riders, the good behavior of the children and everything in general. She was polite to Cathy, but a little reserved. She was probably intimidated by the fact that another person was jumping rails with what Celeste considered a big horse. Bernie didn't invite Cathy to lunch and she and Celeste left after Noir was put back in her stall.

At lunch Celeste asked if she could go to the next show and Bernie wanted to know if she was willing to drive to Lansing early in the morning on a Saturday because she and Cathy would be splitting a hotel room again on the prior Friday. Celeste seemed a little hurt that she didn't get to share the hotel room with Bernie and Bernie had to explain the expense thing to her and the arrangement that they had made earlier in the year. Celeste seemed to pout a little.

Bernie mentioned this to Tony at dinner that evening. They were eating on the deck and Tony suggested that she and Cathy allow Celeste to stay with them and order a cot for her at the hotel.

"I love Celeste, but she'll only be in the way on Friday. Cathy and I have a tandem thing going with show prep and all."

"It's just a suggestion. But I think she should be included because that upset her."

"I'll talk to Cathy and see what she says," Bernie said without much conviction or enthusiasm.

That night Bernie called Cathy and presented the idea to her. She explained this was a close friend and that Celeste was feeling left out lately and that's why she was at their lessons. Cathy seemed amenable to the idea and it was decided to invite Celeste. She seemed unfazed and Bernie got the distinct feeling that Cathy felt the more the merrier.

Bernie called Celeste and told her about the potential arrangement and Celeste breathed a sigh of what was, evidently, relief.

Bernie resigned herself to the situation and called the hotel to order a cot for their room.

Celeste and Bernie arrived at the show grounds about 15 minutes before Cathy the day before the show and Celeste immediately got in the way in her efforts to be helpful. She felt she had to do something and it slowed them down getting tacked up for practice. Bernie started to get irritated and Celeste, at one point, looked at Bernie and asked, "Did you take your pills today?"

Nothing set Bernie off faster than Tony asking the same question when he was irritated with her behavior and Bernie exploded. "Yes, damn it, I took my pills today," she said with fire in her eyes. Celeste was taken aback because Bernie had never spoken to her in that manner and she was unprepared to be verbally attacked.

Cathy watched this and asked, "What pills?"

"Nothing."

"No, really, what pills?"

Flustered and off guard, Bernie shot a look at Celeste that could have started a fire. She stammered a little and said, "My doctor has prescribed a tranquilizer for me prior to shows."

"Oh great, our horses get drug tested after a show, but the riders don't," Cathy laughed.

The laugh was enough to break the tension and the incident was shoved to the back of Bernie's mind for a few minutes; not forgotten, though. Bernie was irked at Celeste and had never thought to tell her that people don't know about her disorder and she wasn't interested in making it public knowledge. They had discussed it together so much that Celeste just wasn't thinking. Celeste had reacted out of hurt.

Celeste just stood there as they washed and braided Noir, put her sheet and slinky on and put her back in her stall. During this activity other riders were doing similar activities and joshing around with one another. The cohesive group was back in action and everyone was excited about tomorrow. It was obvious to Celeste that she was the fifth wheel and out of place; the outsider who felt useless. Her stature seemed to shrink a little more from the action and people who seemed to be a clique with an active purpose.

Jack was at the hotel again so Sue must have been on the grounds for the night. The group as usual gathered in the bar after dinner. He was introduced to Celeste and shook her hand, "So, are you going to be taking lessons at Thousand Pines and be showing with us?"

"Me? I'm afraid of horses! What a funny question."

"Most riders are afraid of horses when they first start, that shouldn't stop you."

"I don't think you have a horse big enough for me," Celeste was obviously embarrassed and looked at the floor."

"Nonsense, Sue has horses for all ages and body types for learning on."

"Really, people my size ride horses?"

Jack was not aware that he was making Celeste uncomfortable. "Of course, you just have to want to."

Celeste perked up, "Really? No shit?"

Bernie and Cathy watched this exchange and saw Celeste start to brighten up after the blowup in the barn.

"Part of the fun of showing is the party we have the night before the show. We are about to start dancing and drinking. Didn't Bernie and Cathy tell you?"

"Ah, no,"

Celeste looked out of place again and Cathy interrupted with, "We try to get everyone involved the night before

so we have a winning attitude the next day." Cathy was attempting to sooth Celeste's obvious feelings of inadequacy. Bernie was still fried at Celeste's earlier question and made no effort to overcome Celeste's discomfort.

The regular show group was in full swing party mood and they drank, toasted and danced. The highpoint awards for each division were discussed and many people came to Bernie and Cathy and hugged them with wishes of luck. Celeste watched and listened and felt like the new kid at school. They all knew one another, had been working together for a while and were at complete ease with each other. Celeste felt even more out of place. Bernie understood very well, but didn't care to ease Celeste's discomfort. She felt mean.

Jack hugged Cathy, wishing her the best luck and ride tomorrow, but didn't hug Bernie. Bernie was stewing about Celeste and was rather distracted and barely noticed that Jack was pursuing Cathy again on the dance floor.

The three of them went to their room about 9:30 and Cathy decided to shower. Bernie turned on Celeste, "What were you thinking?" she hissed at her. I haven't told anyone but my parents and Tony and you about this. I could have died of embarrassment this afternoon!"

Celeste sitting on the cot was fiddling with the TV remote and put her head in her hands and said, "Bernie, I'm so sorry. I just saw how closely you two work together and thought you had confided in your friends as well."

"Cathy is not my friend. She borrows my horse to ride and show. She's the freaking county counselor at school for the kids, too. I had to talk to her after Morgan took me to task. I didn't choose her for Noir, the barn owner did. That's how we met. It was a hard decision to have to make and I don't want her to know anything that she could use to judge me," Bernie whispered. She did not want Cathy to hear them and she was listening to the sounds in the bathroom to know when Cathy was done. This conversation had to be kept on the QT.

The shower stopped and Bernie rapidly grabbed the remote control from Celeste's lap and turned the volume up on the local news channel. Celeste made a supplication posture and whispered back, "I'm so sorry, Bernie. I would never betray you or tell secrets. I love you so much and don't want to be at the receiving end of your bad side. Not that I've ever seen you to have a bad side, but I just want to apologize again. I'll stay out of your way tomorrow. It's obvious that you have a group of friends that just love you and Noir and hold you in high esteem."

"Look, forget it. Let's just get some sleep. Cathy and I usually shower in the morning to wake up and feel refreshed. I think she sacrificed her wake up for you. Just be polite and be ready when we have to leave. We eat breakfast at the show now, so you'll be on your own tomorrow morning. We need to focus and concentrate on Noir. Noir can be naughty and we both understand that."

The bathroom door opened and Cathy came out with a towel around her head. "I hate sleeping in wet hair

because it makes it wild in the morning. If you guys need the bathroom use it now because I'm going to blow dry my hair."

"We're good," Celeste said.

Bernie stifled a giggle about Celeste's hair and the frizz.

****

The August humidity was up and the sun was blazing in the cloudless sky when they arrived at the show grounds. It was going to be another uncomfortable show day.

Bernie woke up distracted and felt as though people could read her thoughts and knew about her disorder. Her transparency and vulnerability caused her actions to be jerky with Noir. Noir immediately picked up on her mood and started acting like a diva. She had to be lunged longer that morning and Bernie, not realizing that she was the cause of the horse's misbehavior, worried about tiring the mare before her five classes. Cathy was still doing one flat class in the morning.

Celeste, true to her word stayed out of the way and hauled a chair ringside and sat there nursing a cup of coffee and a donut. Cathy helped Bernie tack up Noir and gave her a leg up before she went to the practice ring. Noir started little rears immediately.

Bernie had taken a dressage whip with her and gave her little taps to get her under control. This was baby behavior and Noir had figured out that if she was at a show, she'd have to work and couldn't be disciplined. The whip would be handed to Cathy before the in gate.

Bernie needed to let Noir know that she was serious and needed to move out with flowing strides and pay attention. She was the only person for flat classes carrying a whip. Other riders stared at her.

Bernie's first class was a bust and she took a second place ribbon. Sue, who was ringside, looked confused and walked to Bernie's side. "What happened out there?"

"She's opinionated today."

"I can see that. Why?"

"I don't know."

"You and Cathy know this horse inside and out, what's going on, Bernie? We need the wins for highpoint. You can't blow the equitation class. If she keeps trying to speed up and slow down, you will lose the class. You've got to focus and also get her attention."

"I'll do my best."

Bernie and Noir placed second again and Bernie's brain started to broil. Noir didn't lose classes. The second winner is the first loser and she felt every bit of that saying. Sue approached her again.

"Bernie, are you off today? Noir is not being controlled and I would have placed that class the same way. You're still in the running, from our calculations for high point, but you'll have to do the September show to clinch it."

"I need to talk to the technical delegate."

"No, you do not," Sue said forcibly.

"Yes, we were good and I think the judge was unfair and prejudiced."

"Bernie, the judge was fair, we don't need an issue with the judges and technical delegates. You didn't do your best in that class and Noir wasn't listening."

"Noir knows her business in the ring. I know what I have to do. Did I do anything that was obvious to you? I don't think so."

"Yes, Noir slowed down and you made an obvious bump with your legs to move her out. It was clear to everyone. I'm surprised you got a second. Do me a favor and get her over to Cathy for a tack change and leave the show officials alone. I mean it. We don't need trouble with the ribbons and placings."

"Fine." It was the type of answer a teenager would give an adult and Bernie wasn't feeling too adult right now. She was feeling confrontational and looking for an outlook for her unhappiness. She spun Noir around and headed toward the barns. Cathy met her there and read her facial clues.

"I'll get her untacked and put your gear in the trunk. I'll have Jack hold her while I tack up and you can get some lunch. We're cutting it close. You don't need to be ringside. You look hot and tired and you probably need some lunch," Cathy said with caution. She had noticed the explosion of anger yesterday and didn't want a fractious horse in the ring because Bernie was upset over something. Whatever it was, she didn't have a clue. It involved Bernie's friend and pills. That's all she could determine.

Noir was not an angel for Cathy and she had to carry a whip into the schooling arena. It wasn't allowed in the flat classes, but she could, however, carry a small bat into the ring and use it in the jumping classes. Her rounds just had to be clear for jumping, but she was worried about her first flat class and no whip. Noir tested every fiber in Cathy's body and found her to be firm and consistent; she won her flat class and later in the afternoon won both over fences classes. The jumping classes were after lunch and Cathy clinched her high point for the year with Noir. She was ecstatic and hugged and spun Bernie around. It didn't matter if she showed again. She had done it with Noir.

Bernie was seething. "I lost, I lost, I lost. I have the greatest horse at the show and I lost. Cathy won. What happened, did I warm the horse up for her or is she a better rider than me?"

Bernie tried to show support and elation, but her heart wasn't in it for Cathy. She had been distracted and didn't know it through her anger at Celeste. She and Celeste rode home to Cold Lake. Celeste suspected that her gaff had caused Bernie to shut off her brain and was relatively quiet on the ride back. She got in her little green Explorer and drove off after saying hello to Tony at the farm.

Tony wanted details and Bernie was not forthcoming. He suspected a loss would spiral her downward again. Noir was delivered via Jack and Bernie and Tony went through the motions of putting her out with the herd and replacing the tack trunk. Tony kept a steady sidelong glance on his wife. He has suspected for a long time what would do this and it was happening before his eyes. His antenna was keenly tuned this time.

Sunday morning was spent lounging around the house with the restless Bernie. She and Celeste did not speak on the phone and Tony suspected something had happened between the two. He made an excuse to drive to the grocery store and called Celeste from his cell phone en route. Celeste met him at the store and they had the opportunity to earnestly talk about Bernie's rapid downturn and sudden change of mood.

"Tony, is she in any way dangerous?"

"No, only to herself if she gets really depressed. She fights depression with anger and she is mighty angry right now. She didn't even bring in her saddle pads from the car yesterday and I retrieved them this morning because I know she cleans them immediately to keep the show pads clean. The heat in the trunk sets the stains and she soaks them as soon as she gets home.

"Right now, we need to intercede and I need to see if I can't contact her doctor and tell him about this recent event. Do you have any idea what set her off?"

"Yeah, I mentioned her pills in front of that other rider."

"What do you mean?"

"She got very irritable with me and I asked her if she had taken her pills that morning. It was an innocent enough question, but she lost it. I really thought she was going to smack me."

"Oh Lord, that's about the one thing that always sets her off. I didn't realize for the longest time that every time someone asks her that she feels as though she has no control over her life and that her personality is controlled by others and drugs. It took me a long time to learn that it's like slapping her in the face and saying, 'Honey, you're being bipolar and you're pills will calm you down.'"

Celeste's eyes got wide and she looked at Tony in alarm. "I had no idea, it was just the logical question at the time. She was really testy. I guess I can understand how she'd feel, or I would feel if someone asked me that question. As though I had no control over my world and it was being decided by someone or something else."

"Well, you're a lot more astute than I. It took me almost two years to learn not to snap that question at her when she's agitated. Good for you, but also bad for you right now. She will not forgive easily and holds grudges for a long time. She's held a grudge against Cold Lake for almost two decades now. Do you know a little of her school history here?"

"Some. We don't talk about it a lot, but every once in a while a student from one of her former classmates surfaces and she withdraws a little. I can't imagine what parent teacher conferences are like for her. It must be hell."

"From what I've deduced, she is well liked by the students and they admire her because of her sense of humor and intellectual permissiveness. Is this true?"

"Oh, yes, very much so."

"Hey, Celeste, I made an excuse to come here for something and I don't want to be gone too long. It looks suspicious. I've got to run. I'll just grab some snacks and tell her I wanted something to munch on tonight. I'll keep in touch with you when I can. I have an idea about her doctor and a therapist. She is adamantly against therapy, but I think it will help a great deal. I just don't know how to persuade her to rethink the suggestion her doctor gave her. I hope she doesn't go off the deep end and do something weird again. I'll see you later. Thanks for talking to me."

Retail therapy was out of the question so Bernie began to cook. It was hot outside, but the process of chopping, stirring and baking took the edge off her foul mood. *I lost. How could I lose? My horse is the best. I lost.* The thought buzzed in her head and looped again and again.

Tony came through the mud room laden with bags of chips, dips, crackers and cheeses. "Well, it looks like we're not going to my parent's for dinner tonight."

"We can go if you want. I just wanted to get a jump on dinners for the freezer and September. I don't think beef stew and chili is the best summer food."

"Maybe we can get over there early and take a swim. How's that sound?"

"I'm too fat for a bathing suit and public viewing."

"That's not true and you know it. I don't know where your bad self image came from, but you look lovely in a bathing suit. It will do us good to just lounge around the pool for a while and have a cocktail. I bought a lot

more junk food than I needed because I was hungry, we can take some of it over to Mom and Dad's."

"OK, fine, if that's what you want to do. I just have to get this stuff cooled, into containers and the freezer first." Bernie was in no mood to lie on a float in the pool. She wanted to go to the barn and ride Noir to see what kind of mood she was in today. Sunday was usually Noir's day off, but Bernie was still fidgety and jumpy about yesterday.

"Bernie, we need to talk about your excited behavior," Tony whispered as he stopped and sat at the kitchen table.

"What excited behavior?"

"You are extra flighty today and I sense it has something to do with yesterday or the weekend's show. We need to sit and just talk. Can you spend some time with me in the pool and just talk?"

"I don't have anything to say. I lost yesterday. I have the best horse and I lost both my classes."

"You did not lose, you placed second in those classes."

"Second place is the first loser. I lost."

Tony ran his hands through his thick hair and said, "You and I see things differently. It's possible to have an off day with an animal that thinks for itself. You just had one of those."

She didn't reply as she busied herself in the kitchen wiping down surfaces. When she was done she went

upstairs to their room and packed a few clothes. She put on a one piece suit and a cover up. She met Tony downstairs as he was repacking a bag full of goodies.

"Why don't you change and I'll go through the stuff and see what we might want here and what will work over there?" Bernie repacked the bag and wondered how thoughtless Tony could be by buying all the junk food when she was seriously watching every ounce of body weight. Packing the bag she began to steam a little more.

Mr. Romanelli met them in the driveway. He had been hosing down the surface around the pool and was wearing swim trunks and a polo shirt. "Hey, we thought you'd two would be too tired to come out today. How'd the show go, Bernie?"

"I lost," she said despondently.

"She did not lose, she took two second places," Tony said and put his arm around her shoulders.

"This is good news, then," Mr. Romanelli smiled. "So, the pool is nice and comfortable, are you going to get some sun?"

"Yes, Dad, we thought we'd impose on you and have a couple of drinks and talk before the rest of the Sunday crowd gets here."

"By all means, enjoy." Mr. Romanelli sauntered off toward the house. He reappeared several minutes after Bernie and Tony had placed their belongings on chairs and gotten in the pool. He hoisted two insulated

tumblers. “I thought you’d like a nice summer drink, Mom made frozen Margaritas.”

They clambered onto floats and paddled to the edge to retrieve the drinks and put them in the built in cup holders. Tony splashed water in her direction.

“Hey, I’m not in the mood to play. I just want to float around and think.”

“What do you want to think about, Bernie?”

“Nothing really.”

“You haven’t been much fun lately and you never want to play. We are starting to drift apart.”

“Who says?”

“Me.”

“What, I’m not fun any longer?”

“Not really. You used to be playful and lighthearted. Now I suspect you have anhedonia. That’s what they call the phase of not being interested in anything that used to give you pleasure or joy.”

“I don’t feel very playful and lighthearted. I didn’t win. I wish you’d stop beaming about yesterday. I did so much better before. I don’t know what happened.”

“Do you have a clue? Anything at all?”

“No, other than Celeste really pissed me off on Friday.”

“What happened Friday?”

"Nothing you'd understand."

"Try me."

Bernie reached for her glass and took a long pull on the frosty drink. "Mmm, your Mom sure makes a good 'rita,'" she avoided Tony's penetrating eyes.

"Bernie, we have to talk. I'm losing you right in front of me. You're dissipating. Your personality is evaporating."

"OK, Celeste was in the way and causing us to have to take out braids and rebraid mane because she wanted to help. She started getting on my nerves and I let her know it. I wasn't unkind, I was just irritated with her. She looked me right in the eye and asked me if I took my pills that morning. She really fired me up. I hate that damn question. It's no one's business whether or not I take a prescription. She needs to watch her mouth."

Tony, not immediately saying anything splashed some water onto his chest and then folded his arms over it. He thoughtfully glanced at her and said, "So you got pissed off." It wasn't a question.

"Yes. She almost busted me in front of Cathy. I don't need the school counselor knowing about my prescriptions or what they're for."

"You feel it's a stigma, don't you?" he asked softly.

"It is a stigma! She's nuts, crazy, insane, men tal ly ill." She pronounced each syllable. "There's something wrong with her, stay away from her. She's unstable and dangerous. She's whacked out completely. . ." She sighed.

"So, you don't want anyone to know that you feel different. You've felt different your entire life and this only makes it worse."

She nodded. "Yeah, watch out for the crazy bitch."

"Do you feel that way when you ride Noir? Does she make you feel out of place?"

"No, why would you ask me that?"

"Because you're perfectly normal unless you're upset and on a mission or tirade. You're beautiful, sympathetic, loving and a great wife to me. That's all I've ever wanted from you. Oh, and your sense of fun and sense of humor."

"What? You think I lost my sense of humor?"

"Yes, I think you lost your sense of humor. Last semester you weren't as entertained by the kids in your classes with the exception of graduation. You've changed since you've been treated for bipolar disorder. It's killing me. I feel as though I'm losing the love of my life and the intimacy that marriage provides, both physically and intellectually. It's not the pills you've been prescribed, it's the attitude you've adopted since you started them. Your stigma is your own. You need to own this, Babe. You need to embrace your peculiarity. I've done some research and you probably don't know this because you eschew so much of the information that the National Institute of Mental Health provides. You, with your disorder, are considered in the higher percentile of intelligence. It's a bizarre fact, but a fact, nonetheless. There are a lot of bipolar celebrities and geniuses." He kept comments and questions open ended.

"Tony, I have like one friend. Others I don't trust and if they found that I, if I did, have bipolar disorder they would run in the other direction faster than I can drink this," She tipped the glass back and drained it.

The alcohol was loosening her tongue and Tony went for broke, "Let me get two more of these and I'll be right back. Do you want some sunscreen?"

"Nope, I want to get rid of my farmer's tan. Thanks." She relaxed back on the float.

It seemed like an instant and he was back handing her a full tumbler. He eased his way back into the pool and up on the float. Tony grabbed at her hand and they held hands for a few minutes before he resumed his questioning. "Surely I'm not the only person you talk to about this?"

She let go of his hand and paddled a little further from him. "Yes."

"You don't talk to your doctor?"

"Some."

"Do you tell him how you feel when you get angry? Do you tell him about going off on tangents? Do you tell him what goes through your mind when something you don't like happens? These are things I need to know because right now we are at odds with one another and I don't feel as close to you as in the beginning of our relationship."

"I tell him what he needs to know."

"What does that mean, Bernie?"

"I told him I think I'm bipolar, manic depressive, losing my mind."

"That's a huge admission from you since you seem to be adverse to the diagnosis. That's my opinion, but it's still something I observe. I'm not saying you weren't bipolar when we met, you probably were, but the stress level was lower and you had backup with Timmy and coworkers. You just didn't exhibit any signs like you do now. I am losing my wife, whom I love to death. Where did she go?"

"I'm right here," she said between sips of her drink.

"No, you're not."

"So, Doctor Romanelli, what do you propose I do?"

"I'd like us to seek counseling?"

"Like marriage counseling? I'm not good with that."

"No, I mean counseling for you to accept that you're bipolar and that it's affecting everything in our lives. I'll go with you. I'll help you pick out someone. Just do this with me. I love you so much, but I can't live this way much longer."

"Tony, I don't need a counselor. I have accepted that I'm bipolar and will work it out myself."

"Yourself? At what cost?"

"What do you mean?"

"Bipolar, two sides. We're splitting apart and I wanted to grow a family with you, share rocking chairs on the deck; watch your hair go gray. Right now I'm the one who's going gray from tension."

"What are you talking about? You make it sound as though I cause all the tension."

"I can't have you going off again because of *learned behavior.* You have learned to react a certain way to specific stimuli. Those catalysts are causing tension and the walking on egg shells effect in our relationship and at your job. I can't sweet talk another person into not pressing charges against you. You don't know what happened with the Nash kid and his grandfather. I kept that all from you. He was a kindly old man, but he was angry that you interfered with their lives. He was willing to go to jail for a Camaro."

"What? This is all news to me."

"Yes, he loves his grandson, faults and deviancy; all of it. He was perfectly willing to give the kid a car for love. I didn't tell you because it got really ugly at the end. The kid dropped out of school, the sister has a badge attached to her because of her brother and the old man has lost a companion. He already lost his daughter to drink. I couldn't tell you what happened in my office because you were on to your next *adventure.*

"I can't talk to you any longer and I don't trust to talk to you. I hate to say that after this weekend, but you've gone nearly ballistic about not winning first place with Noir. You have no idea what a grandiose thought that is. You feel you can't lose because of a 1,000 pound horse

between your legs. It hasn't arrived in your brain yet that the horse is tuned in to your thoughts and feelings and attitudes. Anyone with a horse knows that they adopt their emotions from their riders. You were angry at Celeste for a legitimate question and your horse was attuned to this. You blew your own classes."

"You're so full of shit, Tony Romanelli."

"No, I'm not. You need to seek help outside of drugs."

"Oh so well-read doctor, what do you suggest I do?"

"I'll go with you, but you need a little extra help to undo what is called 'learned behavior.'"

"And you've learned to treat me a certain way since this diagnosis. You look at me sideways and I think you want to hide the knives in the house. That's learned behavior as well."

Tony rolled his eyes. "OK, maybe I have watched you more closely. Maybe I don't know when the other shoe is going to drop. I can't live like that. I want us to be us again, not someone who has to put out fires on a continuous basis because of behavior that I have no idea about what's going to set it off and then have to deal with it. I'm being as honest here as I can possibly be."

"Do your parents know?"

"No, absolutely not. They worship you."

"Funny."

"I'm dead serious. Please, let's consider outside counseling to add to what is obviously working with the prescriptions. An adjunct, if you will."

"My doctor made a recommendation for a counselor, but I'm not sure."

"I promise, I'll go with you. If we don't agree or like the counselor, we'll find another. Please, Bernie, save our relationship, let's go back to who we were."

"You really feel strongly about this and our marriage? Is it really affected?"

"Yes, Bernie. And it affecting our relationships with others. My office staff, school, and all your potential friends. Let's do this and see if it eases a little tension and pain."

"OK, I'll try, but I'm not happy about this. What if they want to know about our sex life?"

"So be it. It's all confidential and what are they going to do about it?" He laughed at her and fell off the float and tipped her into the pool. He didn't mention that since the start of the prescriptions her interest in sex had lessened and about disappeared. He did know, however, that this was a side effect of the drugs he researched.

"Hey, kids, put your tops on, we have company," Guy yelled at them. "Let the Sunday begin."

FORTY TWO

Sasha Patel was obviously Indian and very fashionably dressed. Red skirt, black camisole; the red stiletto heels were over the top. She wasn't a tall woman, but looked tall in the heels. Very pretty with chocolate eyes and lots of eye shadow to match; arched brows and highlights at the brow and inner corners. Bernie abhorred her immediately. Tony was stoic.

During the interview Patel propped her shoe on her toe and kept bouncing it up and down during the session. Bernie disliked her and her rhetoric. She was more concerned about her abilities than with Bernie's perceived problems.

"I'm a licensed psychiatrist too, and can be very creative with drugs," she smirked. "But I specialize in counseling."

Bernie cut the interview short and nearly dragged Tony out of her office. They made the co-pay and left. In the car she raged at Tony, "Do you see what I have to put up with? That woman is insufferable and I'm not going back."

"I agree with you. You need to find someone else, but where?"

"I agreed to do this and there has to be someone who will listen and understand and help me. I agree with you, too. I need to talk to someone, but that's not the right person. What the hell did she mean when she said she could be very creative with drugs? I'm not an experiment for her. She'd have me locked in a psych ward in a second if she knew my history. I don't trust her as far as I could pitch those red shoes."

"Yeah, they were a bit much, huh?"

"This is not going to be easy. I may have to change doctors to find a good counselor. If that's who my doctor recommends, I am seriously considering his sanity. I wonder if he has even ever met her or if he knows her. How can they work together?"

Bernie met her regular monthly appointment and gave the doctor hell about the counselor. She reviewed for him her thoughts and observations and he seemed surprised about the counselor's comments. He recommended another counselor and set up the appointment for her. She went alone this time.

The waiting room and office were small and dark. The receptionist was a bright and cheery person about 23. "Dr. Patel will be with you in a few minutes, in the meantime we need you to fill out these forms"

Bernie thought to herself, "What is the deal with all the doctors named Patel? I wonder if he's related to the crazy lady." Her attitude changed and she started scowling with narrowed eyes when the short man with dark features came to the waiting room and said, "Ms. Romanelli, if you'll follow me."

He didn't bother to introduce himself and Bernie was a little confused. "Are you the counselor?"

"Yes, I'm doctor Patel." He had a slight accent.

She narrowed her eyes more. There was a prejudice forming about Indian doctors and she wasn't too pleased about finding another one. What did his culture know about hers? She sat on the edge of the chair and frowned at him.

It was nearly 45 minutes before she relaxed with him enough to fully sit in the chair and cross her legs. She'd been ready to flounce out of his office until she realized that this was a very different animal from the first counselor. They parted with smiles and handshakes. An appointment for the next week was set by the smiling receptionist.

"How'd the counseling session go today," Tony asked as he poured himself a glass of wine that evening.

"You won't believe this, but Dr. *Patel* is also Indian! He is soft spoken, humble and I don't feel threatened by him in the least. It took me a while to warm up to him, but I really think he will listen and help a little. This is hard for me to admit, you know."

"Sounds like you found someone to listen and who knows what might need to be done. If he gives you mental exercises and self control ones, listen to him and do them."

"What kind of self control exercises?"

"That's a counseling technique I learned about online and it's supposed to work really well. Just do what he says and I'm sure we'll be on a better, easier path."

After the third session Bernie trusted the counselor completely and felt at ease with him enough to cry and laugh. She reiterated the incidents at school and with McGinty, her horse and the disappointment at not winning. She also told him that there was another show coming up in September that she had to win to garner the high point award for her division. He seemed supportive and encouraging. Never once did he ask her what she'd feel if she didn't win, he just acted as though she had things in place to win. He gave her confidence and allayed her fears. When she left his offices, she felt buoyed and had confidence in her step. She felt as though she were accepted by someone for a change.

The onion loomed again and Bernie found herself driving to school with the big portfolio of enlarged documents. Celeste, too, was there and doing something similar with her room. They discussed the smell of the school and the behavior of its occupants. "It still reminds me of an onion," Bernie laughed.

"It is an onion. You peeled it a little, but we need to cook this sucker and fry it."

"And, what do you think we need to do with it after that?"

"Eat it and inoculate ourselves!"

"What, so we're impervious to it and don't give a damn?"

"Something like that, but I have a suspicion that we'll both always care."

"Celeste, I think it's always going to grow a new layer."

"We'll deal with it."

"Want to go to lunch?"

"Sure, how about the café. We might run into your husband and his father."

"Deal. They can buy us lunch," she giggled.

Celeste tilted her head and gave Bernie a strange look. "You just giggled. I've never heard you do that before."

"I'm in counseling, Celeste and finally am starting to feel free of encumbrances and as though I'm not carrying the weight of the world on my shoulders. I'm actually looking forward to meeting the new students and their parents this year. This is a big year for me because I have so many students whose parents I went to school with. I'm no longer afraid."

"Oooh, tell me about counseling."

"No, it's a conversation for the pump house."

"I think the timing for this question is all wrong, but there is no better timing. Can I go to your next show with you? I promise not to get in the way and I'll be encouraging. I won't mention drugs to Cathy. She seems really nice and I bet the two of you could be good friends if you let her in."

"Yeah, I've been thinking about that and no one bothered to explain anything to you at the last show. You never had a chance to know what you were watching other than the jumping part. I wasn't fair to you and I was angry. For that I'm sorry."

"I blew it for you, or almost did; and for that I'm sorry, too."

"Let's not discuss this now, let's discuss it during milking on Thursday. Right now let's go get a free lunch!"

****

In the middle of cooking dinner Wednesday the phone rang. It was Dad.

"Hey, Kid, you might want to drive out here and look at your horse. She appears lame to me."

"What do you mean?" Bernie asked distractedly.

"She's holding one foot off the ground. I don't really know anything about horses other than what you've explained about them eating their own rations, but this doesn't look right to me."

"I'll be right there." Bernie shut off the oven and stove, grabbed her light jacket and ran to the garage.

Noir was, indeed, holding up one front foot, but eating her hay without concern. "We'd better call the vet", Bernie said to her father.

"It's after hours and it's going to cost you."

"I don't know what's wrong, there is no heat in her leg and it seems as though she's just sore on that foot. I cleaned out her hooves and there doesn't appear to be anything stuck in there that she stepped on. I need a vet. She is up for high point in four weeks and I can't have her off right now."

The vet arrived around supper time and the three of them went to her stall. Bernie haltered the mare and brought her out for inspection. The vet had Bernie walk her in a circle and stopped her and picked up the foot.

"Might be an abscess. Hand me those hoof testers, Bernie."

Sure enough, the mare pulled her foot back when he hit the sore spot. "Yup, looks like an abscess."

He tested the spot again and then started paring down the bottom with a hoof knife. "I'm going to have to pull this shoe because I can't get in deep enough to reach the abscess and open the spot."

Bernie was on auto pilot and wasn't thinking about the future ramifications or the work an abscessed hoof was going to take. Luckily the abscess was close to the sole and the vet managed to hit it and dig deeply enough to release the pressure.

"You're going to have to soak this hoof twice a day for twenty minutes in hot water and Epson salts. As hot as she can stand." He instructed her in the soaking and daily wrapping procedures and left. He handed the invoice to Carl, who stuffed it in his pocket.

"Dad, I've never done this before and I need a rubber tub because I think if we stick her foot in a regular bucket, she could pull it out and get it caught on the handle. Do you have a tub I can clean and use?

"I'm going to have to take a trip to the store and get diapers, duct tape and Epsom salts. I don't have anything like that here. I'm just going to stick her back in her stall for a little while.

"It just occurred to me that I'm going to have to come out here each morning and soak her foot before school, too. So much for running with Tony."

The task proved to be a little too much work in the morning before school and Carl took pity on Bernie and offered, after watching the process, to do the morning soakings. To keep the open wound clean, it was wrapped in a waterproof diaper and adhered to her leg with a duct tape platform so the mare could be turned out.

On Thursday evening Celeste watched the process and asked, "What if she doesn't heal all the way before your next show?"

The very same thought had been bubbling in Bernie's mind for a few days. Noir was still off and sore, indicating that the abscess was still draining and being drawn out by the Epsom salt's soak. Bernie gritted her teeth and didn't answer Celeste.

Her thoughts, however, were not so much compassion for the mare, but more about that big prize within reach. Bernie battened down the emotional hatches and started calculating how many days until the next show

and how long before a shoe could be put back on and the horse pressed into service again.

Tony and Celeste both noticed that Bernie's demeanor seemed a little jittery and nervous. Tony called Celeste and asked her to watch for rapid speech patterns and irritability; classic signs of an upswing.

By the end of the week, Noir was still limping and the abscess didn't seem to be going away. She called the vet, who came back out. He tested her again and determined that there might be a second abscess somewhere within the hoof. The soaking had to continue and there was only three weeks before the September show. Bernie's personality took on a very dark persona. Cathy had already clinched her highpoint award for the region and Bernie needed one to two more wins to earn hers. This became an all consuming thought and she was not kind around others.

Her doctor's appointment didn't go well and he decided to put her on a new anti-anxiety drug. He handed her the prescription and told her to stop taking the former one.

She filled the prescription and immediately upon getting in the car, she swallowed one pill, which was to be taken three times a day. Pill scheduling interfered with her classes and became a minor annoyance.

The new prescription made her a little lightheaded, but she ignored the side effect because she had classes to teach. On the second day she was driving to the barn to soak Noir's hoof when she felt overwhelmingly sleepy. She nodded off and swerved into a tree on the county road that served her parent's farm. The front end of

the BMW was crumpled and she went ballistic. Her first call was to the doctor, whom she screamed at for wrecking her car. He listened to her and suggested she get someone to drive her to Ann Arbor to the hospital and check herself in for observation.

He failed to tell her that the place for observation was the psychiatric ward. Tony helped her pack for a week's stay and drove her to Ann Arbor. When they got there the admittance people went through her bag and took away her nail polish, cuticle scissors, mirror, perfume bottles and anything that could be used for a possible suicide attempt.

Bernie had a meltdown in the hospital when this was done and she learned that she was on the psych floor. Her doctor met her and explained that it was going to be easier to monitor new medication if she was in a controlled environment. "I have a horse to care for and show in a few weeks. I need to practice and get ready for the show."

The doctor's words were slow and measured, "Bernie, your body reacted strongly to the new drug and we can't have you driving or riding with this type of reaction. Consider it a vacation."

"Who's going to teach my classes?"

Tony interjected at this point, "They will bring in a sub and she can follow your syllabus. Right now I agree. You need observation to adjust to the new drug."

"Why can't I just stay on the old one? It was working fine, until he changed it and wrecked my beautiful car."

"I'm not concerned about your car; I'm worried about you and what could happen if you don't adjust to the new drug."

Bernie was escorted to a locked ward and given a room of her own. The floor was well lit, brightly painted and full of people. Her room had its own bathroom. She left her bag on her bed and left the room to find out what she was supposed to be doing there. Women of all ages seemed to be lounging in chairs and sofas; some were in their rooms. It was close to dinner service and many people were exiting their rooms. A nurse introduced herself and said she would need to sit down with Bernie after dinner and ask her a few questions. Bernie was also told that since she was new on the floor, an orderly would be sitting outside her door at lights out. Why? Bernie wasn't sure. She did not like that she was being monitored and observed.

The nurse further explained what time breakfast was served and that Bernie would be expected to participate in group therapy, crafts and spend some one-on-one time with a psychiatrist at some point. The entire day was scheduled like a school and left very little personal time. It seemed as though there was a little time to read before dinner. Bernie had packed a novel and intended to wake as early as possible for some bathroom and reading time. She hoped she'd have some privacy.

Dinner was wheeled in and people began to stake out chairs and tables after visiting the food cart. Fried chicken, French fries, lukewarm coffee, a carton of milk and corn were dinner. "I thought this was a hospital, why all the fried food? Didn't they serve healthy salads

and low fat foods?" Bernie mused. But, she was hungry and ate anyway.

When the dinner trolley was wheeled out and the doors locked behind it, the nurse came into Bernie's room looking for her. She had a clipboard and sat in the one and only chair while Bernie perched on the bed. She asked, "On a scale of one to ten, how do you feel emotionally at this moment?"

"Confused. I was told I was here to be monitored for a drug reaction and I seem to be locked up in the crazy ward."

"This is not a 'crazy' ward. We have people here with emotional issues that need to be overcome. What do you mean when you say 'monitored for a drug reaction?"

"Just what I said. I was told that my reaction to a new drug for bipolar disorder was severe and I needed to acclimate to the high dosage. Why am I on a locked ward?"

"Your doctor obviously felt this was the best way to *observe* you."

"Then why do I have to go through group therapy and talk to an unknown doctor?"

"I don't know, you'll have to ask your doctor when he visits. My job is to make you as comfortable as possible and get you up to speed on our daily schedule. There is a coffee pot in the mini kitchen, there are juices in the refrigerator and snacks are provided during the day. In the morning you have to present yourself for a

temperature and blood pressure reading. We suggest you do this before you have coffee. It can skew our results.

"There are magazines, puzzles, games and cards here. We encourage you to make friends and find something you like to do. We also have a group crafting workshop each day. It's a lot of fun."

"I'm not exactly into crafts."

"It's a requirement. You'll enjoy it."

"I doubt it."

"Also, meds are distributed as required. Your chart says three times a day. A nurse will come to your room and give you your medications and wait until you take them. Do you understand this?"

"Yes." Bernie was starting to feel a little cramped and demeaned. "What about my nail polish, etc? That was all taken away from me at admission."

"After a few days we will determine, based on behavior, if those things can be used. They will be kept in the nursing station and checked out by you, then returned."

"Can I have visitors? Can I leave?"

"You are a voluntary check in and can leave at any time. However, your doctor does not recommend it and you may not return. We have you scheduled for two weeks here and you may have visitors. Your cell phone is in the nurse's station and it can be checked out upon good behavior; it must be checked back in.

Or, you may use the outgoing line. Only incoming calls will come to the nurse's station and be monitored. This is not punishment, but a way to access your moods and restrict the number of times you use a phone. You are here to get well."

"I'm not sick." Bernie's ire was ignited. Without excusing herself or apologizing to the nurse, she stood up and walked to the bathroom and shut the door. When she returned the nurse was gone. She walked down the hall and scoped out the ward.

There was a smoking room with about five women in there in a cloud of gray haze. Several people sat across from one another at small tables doing jigsaw puzzles in a room with a television. One girl was furiously marking a coloring book with crayons, another was setting up a Scrabble board and looking around for a partner and several women were in their rooms, either talking to other residents or laying alone on their beds.

An orderly approached Bernie and asked if she wanted to do a jigsaw puzzle with him. Something in Bernie's brain warned her to be nice to him and accept his offer. They moved to the TV room and sorted through several boxes. Bernie was drawn to one of an elaborate fairy character in flight. "I'm Dustin, what's your name?"

"Bernie. What do you do here?"

"Whatever they need me to do. I will be the person outside your door tonight and I thought you might want to get to know me. Tomorrow I'll also be in crafts with you because I assist with supplies."

"Oh. Why do I need someone outside my door all night?"

"It's just something we do for a few nights so no one wanders around and everyone gets a good night's sleep. Sleep is very important to the minds and moods of our patients."

Bernie didn't say anything as she looked for corners for the puzzle. Dustin followed her lead and didn't say any more.

At 8:30 the ward doors opened and someone wheeled in a trolley with ice cream and fruit on it. Dustin urged Bernie to get some ice cream. "We only have ice cream once a week, but fruit every night. Enjoy it."

At 10:00 and lights out Bernie retired to her room. Dustin pulled a chair to the side of her door and opened a book that looked like a text book. Bernie went into the bathroom and put on a T-shirt and sweat pants, then climbed into the hospital style bed. She couldn't fall asleep and got back up in search of her novel. She read for a while and drifted off. Her door stayed open all night.

At six she woke, slipped into the bathroom and showered. She dressed in a camisole and running pants, put on sneakers and reported to the nurse's station for temperature and blood pressure readings. Only one other woman was waiting. The nurses seemed to ignore them and Bernie stood up and asked if she could please have her temperature taken so she could get a cup of coffee. The other woman laughed. Bernie turned around with a puzzled look.

"You'll just have to wait until they're good and ready."

"Why?"

Because they don't start until seven. I'm here for the same reason. Some days they do it early for me and others they just wait. I'm Becky."

"Bernie."

A younger nurse approached them, asked their names, checked their wrist bands and retrieved their charts. She took their temperatures, checked their blood pressure and said, "You can get your coffee now." Bernie was grateful. Both she and Becky headed toward the small kitchen and prepared themselves cups of coffee.

Breakfast was trollied in at 7:30. Dry scrambled eggs, two pieces of bacon, cold buttered toast, a carton of milk and the lukewarm plastic cup of coffee. At 8:30 everyone was supposed to be dressed and heading to various activities. Bernie had to ask where she was supposed to be, and was directed to a small room with a circle of chairs. She picked one.

"That's my chair," a woman in sloppy looking sweats said to Bernie.

"Oh, sorry, I'm new."

"Yeah, I can see that, you find another chair." The statement was challenging.

Bernie stood up and looked around the circle. It seemed as though there was going to be only one chair open as other women came in and sat down. The chair Bernie

chose was next to a man with a clipboard and pen. He had everyone identify themselves and asked if anyone wanted to speak first.

Never having been in group therapy, Bernie didn't know what to expect. She just listened to others talk and kept quiet. The man asked Bernie if she had anything to say.

"No, I'm just observing. I really don't know what I'm doing here and I don't have anything to say."

"Everyone has to speak in each session. Please tell us what you are doing here," he asked her.

"I had a bad reaction to a drug prescribed by my doctor and he put me here to acclimate to the new drug." Bernie watched while he wrote "denial" on his clipboard. "I just saw you write 'denial' on your papers. I'm not in denial, that's what I'm here for."

"It's a river in Egypt," said an older, frazzled looking woman. The group laughed and Bernie felt her cheeks heat.

The man said, "Denial is the first step in recognizing your illness."

"I'm not ill. I had a bad drug reaction and needed to be someplace where it could be monitored and I could get used to it." The group laughed in unison again. Bernie felt her temper flair and asked, "What are you all here for?"

The answers came rapidly from the circle, "Paranoid delusions," "Schizophrenia," "Bipolar disorder," "I'm crazy." "Suicidal." Bernie looked at the person who

had said 'Bipolar' and studied her face for a minute. She looked perfectly at home and comfortable in the group and completely normal. She didn't know what to say and looked around at the group. Each of the women present were not well groomed, looked like they had just crawled out of bed and no one had bothered to put on makeup. Bernie, by comparison was freshly showered, had applied mascara and lipstick and matched her outfit. She seemed to have no identification with the group.

She looked at the man, whom she figured was a psychologist and realized that he wore khakis, a blue button down shirt and tie and street shoes. He looked incongruous with these women. Didn't they care what they looked like? Was this their illnesses speaking? She decided that she would haunt the nurse's station that evening and ask for her nail polish. She did not want to identify with these people and she was going to go out of her way to look like she was not part of this group.

The group was dismissed and Bernie went to her room to search through her bag for perfume. "It's imperative that I look as normal as possible and do normal things."

Arts and Crafts started after lunch and they assembled and were going to build birdhouses. Bernie was bored, but everyone else seemed excited to be building birdhouses. The chattered like children in school about what colors and designs they planned to paint them.

At 6:30 Tony called Bernie on the nurse's line. "How you doing in there?"

"I'm bored and miserable. I should be helping milk goats and riding my mare."

"Look, Babe, you need to be there to dig to the bottom of this hole. I support you all the way."

"What support? You knew I was going to a locked ward and seemed to encourage the doctor's suggestion. If I had known this wasn't a hospital stay and I'd be making birdhouses and going to group therapy, I would have refused to be here. I'm not sure I have enough words at this point to convey my disdain for you."

"Disdain? Bernie, you cracked up your car because of the prescriptions. You need to be there. I had nothing to do with this. I'm coming tomorrow to visit you after work. I should leave early enough to be there before dinner."

"I'm not sure I want to see you right now. Did you tell Celeste where I was?"

"Yes, she's going to try to visit you as well."

"Tony, do me a favor and don't come. I've only been here one day and already I feel like I was entrapped in some sort of scheme you cooked up. You've been campaigning for me to get outside help, but I didn't realize this was what you were referring to. The people in here are not living normal lives and they seem delighted to be here. I'm not," she hung up and walked away from the nurse's station.

After dinner she dug into her novel. There was a soft knock on the door frame and the evening nurse

responsible for doling out medications walked in. She handed Bernie a small paper cup with pills and a plastic one with water.

Bernie took the paper cup and looked inside. "What's this?"

"Your medications, you're supposed to take them on time."

"I can tell you right now that I don't recognize that large capsule and it's not my medication. I'm not taking something I don't recognize and won't be switching meds without talking to my doctor first."

The nurse left looking a little confused. She returned about 30 minutes later with familiar looking pills. There had obviously been an error when the medications were set up. Bernie became very suspicious and knew she had to watch every move they made. She didn't need to be taking drugs that were not hers. Good God, someone had said that they were schizophrenic, what if those were the drugs mistakenly given to her earlier? She'd already had a bad drug reaction, what could have happened if she didn't question the nurse and took someone else's medications? She'd be in here for the rest of her life.

The next morning she showered, applied makeup and went to the nurse's desk early again. Becky was there and they asked the nurses for temperatures and blood pressure so they could get their coffee fix. Bernie had chosen a pair of jeans, a pullover sweater and flat shoes. It seemed as though everyone else was dressed in sweatpants and oversized sweatshirts and hospital

slippers. Bernie asked Becky why she was here while they fixed their coffee.

Becky was a petite blonde about 25. "I was held hostage by my new husband and then watched him shoot himself."

Bernie didn't know what to say and couldn't imagine what had happened to put Becky in the hospital.

Becky continued, "I'm getting out of here in a week. The doctors feel I'm able to cope again. I've been here three months."

"Three months?" Bernie was shocked. They walked with their coffee cups to one of the day rooms and sat next to one another on a sofa.

"Yes, three months. My parents helped me get here and I've learned coping skills and finally realized that what happened was not my fault. For the first month I did nothing be sit and smoke. I didn't even talk to anyone else. I stopped eating and lost a lot of weight and didn't participate in group therapy or even talk to the doctors who visited me. They kept me pretty stoned for the first month. I finally started to realize what I was missing in life again and embraced the program. I let my parents come to visit and I even went out for a few weekends. The doctors told me that I was in a post traumatic shock and it would take time for the horror to wear off. I never attended my husband's funeral; I didn't want to."

"Were the police involved when this happened?"

"Yes, our apartment building was surrounded by police and firemen. He had threatened to kill me."

"What did you do for him to threaten you like that?"

"Nothing. But in the beginning, I felt it was entirely my fault. He just cracked up and it caused me to crawl into a hole. I wasn't sure I could crawl out on my own, but they helped me here."

"Good God, how do you feel now?"

"Like life is worth living again. I was unreachable and despondent for almost two months. My doctor was cool and gave me a lot to read about the shock factor and how it affects your life and how you view yourself. I'm looking forward to getting back to a normal life. I just hope I can be a flight attendant again and this little soiree doesn't end up a permanent stain on my record. I'm not going back to our old apartment. I'm moving in with my parents again and they cleaned the apartment out. I never want to go back there."

In group therapy that day Bernie decided to ask a question. It was based on what she had read and understood from her doctor and therapist. "Yesterday you said I was in denial. Is denial a learned behavior?"

The psychologist leaned back in his chair and looked at Bernie, then addressed the group, "Well, ladies, what do you think the answer to Bernie's question is?"

The answers were all a variation of the same thing. "Yes, one learns to deny a fact long enough so it becomes the truth to that person." The obviously complicated question

set off a series of stories from the group members and the psychologist had a difficult time breaking the session. Several women put their arms around Bernie as they left the room. Somehow her question had broken the ice and started interactions between group members.

The gal who had blurted out that she was bipolar spent a lot of time sitting in a chair outside her room with a thin hospital blanket on her lap. She was always seen talking to another woman, but didn't join any of the game players or groups. Bernie introduced herself and the woman asked who her doctor was. Bernie told her and they realized they shared a doctor. "You can't trust him."

"Why not?"

"He makes his money by putting people in here and holding them captive. What are you in for?"

"I had a bad drug reaction and smashed up my car."

"Oh, that's what you think. Did you come in voluntarily or did he interfere in your life and commit you?"

"I came in voluntarily. Why would that matter?"

"He's slick and wants people to think they made their own decision. I've been here six months and I want out now. He just keeps telling me I'm not ready. He also tells me that I'm a wise ass and that isn't helping me cope with my problem."

"You said in group that you were bipolar. I'm bipolar, but had a drug reaction. I haven't had any other problems other than weight gain from the drugs he's put me on."

"Oh yeah? Just wait till he starts testing new drugs on you," she laughed.

"It was a new drug to me."

"You've got to be careful. He's pill crazy and will try all kinds of drug cocktails. It was recommended that I go home a few months ago by one of the resident shrinks here and he wouldn't hear of it. He's got them all convinced they need to move me to Mayo in Minnesota. Like you could die of being bipolar."

Bernie paused to consider what she just heard. "I've been pretty adamant about not increasing dosages and trying new drugs. I just had a big disappointment that set me off a little and he suggested we try a new drug."

"That was your first mistake. I used to have a good job and I thought I trusted him until I landed in here. Welcome to the nut house. You were smart to not trust him in the beginning. They're all drug happy and we are their guinea pigs. Only difference is we are captive here. You be careful what you say and who you say it to. Trust me.

"If you want to gain a lot of weight, just keep trusting them. Look at me, I didn't have this stomach when I first got here. I used to work out in a gym, be a hundred and fifteen pounds and now I'm a hundred and seventy. I'm higher than a kite most days and if you don't take your pills, you get written up as being belligerent. That doesn't go over well here."

"I was almost given someone else's drugs yesterday night."

"Oh yeah? Doesn't surprise me at all. They don't pay attention to what they're doing back there most of the time. They really don't like babysitting us. The orderlies are cool, though. Just don't trust anyone here. Be very careful what you say to other patients, too."

Bernie walked back to her room confused and thinking about the conversation. She climbed into bed and opened her book. A knock on her door made her look up. Tony stood in the doorway with a vase of flowers in his hand. "Hi."

"Hi. I asked you not to come unless you're willing to spring me from this place."

"Yeah, seems a little excessive. They took the vase from me and gave me a plastic one. I guess you're not allowed to have glass in here." He seemed a little sheepish.

"That includes my perfume bottles and nail polish. Pisses me off."

"Well, you need to be under observation to acclimate to this new drug."

"Ha. You should have been around about thirty minutes ago for a conversation I had with another patient. She has the same doctor and she gave me an earful. She seems very distrustful of him and said he was pill happy. She's a bit of a wise mouth, but she made an awful lot of sense to me. If we weren't both in here I have a feeling I'd be one of her friends. Didn't seem like there was anything really wrong with her."

"Honey, she's here for a good reason."

"Maybe, maybe not." I don't know, Tony, she seems perfectly normal to me. She feels manipulated by the doctor and told me to tow the line here or I'd never get out."

"You're only supposed to be here two weeks."

"I think that's what she initially thought too."

"You're acting paranoid."

"You would too, if you were administered the wrong pills last night."

"What?"

"I'm not kidding. I refused to take a capsule I've never seen before. It was large and purple. I don't take anything purple and all my prescriptions are pills, not capsules."

She explained the look on the nurse's face and the subsequent actions. He studied her face during the story and his brow creased.

"You're cognizant, that's good."

"I'm not sure if they increase dosages that I'll stay that way. The new prescription he put me on made me fall asleep. There was no warning. One minute I was driving and the next I was kissing an airbag.

"Speaking of which, how do I look to you, is the bruising going down a little in your opinion?"

"Yes, it's barely noticeable. You didn't tell anyone I beat you did you?" he laughed.

"Oh, you should hear some of the stories of people in here. One girl was held hostage by her husband and then he committed suicide in front of her.

"They have us making birdhouses in art therapy. Any particular color you want?" her voice was caustic.

"No, I'm more worried about what you told me about the mixed up prescriptions. Have you felt sleepy or dizzy since you've been here?"

"Not that I've noticed, but I'm on high alert right now and becoming very distrustful of my doctor from some of the things I've heard. Some of these girls have been in here several months.

"Also, the food they serve is all fried and not on our regular diet. I've eaten fried fish, fried chicken, mashed potatoes, and only one salad in two days. I'm concerned that the sedentary nature of this place will pack on pounds. Others have complained about it, too."

"I doubt that two weeks is going to make much of a difference."

"How's Noir? Did you talk to my folks?"

"Noir is no longer limping and your dad said that she had another blowout. I don't know much more than that."

"Oh, maybe I can make the show after all and we can get a high point award."

"Look, Bernie, the horse is what set you off in the first place and you should be more concerned with getting better than getting an award. Have you seen your doctor yet?"

"No, he hasn't been here. I'm in group therapy and it seems like a useless endeavor to me. Just busy work. I understand that I'll be talking to some other doctors and I can't wait to see what they have to say. Did you bring me anything else to read?"

"Yes, and I found that they have a small library here, but it's on another floor. Maybe they bring books in. Here's what I brought you," he pulled a paperback out of his coat pocket.

Bernie stood up and faced Tony as he sat on the bed. She stood over him. "I want to talk to Dad and the vet and then Sue at Thousand Pines. If I can get out of here on time, I can make the next show. You haven't talked to Cathy, have you?"

"No, I haven't talked to anyone other than your parents and Celeste. I just called the school and told them that you had to have minor surgery and would be out for a few weeks. They didn't ask me and I didn't tell them.

About your horse, we need to talk." He stood as well, faced her and took her hands in his. "Bernie, what happens if you have a bad ride and don't win high point? Is that going to send you into another tailspin? Are you going to go into a depression again and mope around the house and take it out on everyone in sight?

"Are you going to contemplate suicide? Do you need constant supervision? Did it occur to you that's why you're here, for supervision?"

"I'm in here because I had a bad drug reaction and they need to stabilize them. I'm not going to have a bad ride on Noir and I'm going to go after my goal. It's the first time I've ever had a chance like this. I want out of here right now so I can get my horse shod and over to Thousand Pines and ready for the upcoming show. I can't believe *you*, of all people, have bought into this horseshit about supervision. That lowers your esteem in my estimation quite a bit. You're the one who's behind this, aren't you?" Her voice was getting louder and shrill. She walked to the door and shut it. She didn't need the nursing staff reporting an argument to the doctors. "Tony, leave now before I go nuts on your head. I am very angry about all this. I'm angry at the doctor for screwing with the drugs, I'm angry about being in here and wasting my time and I'm angry about not being able to ride my horse and pursue my dream. I know you have no idea what I've done to be so close to obtaining something I really want. If you leave now, I might forgive you."

Tony never got a chance to say anything because the door was opened by a nurse. "This door has to stay open at all times until the doctor clears it with us."

Tony looked contrite. "Sorry, we were having a private conversation."

Bernie glared at the nurse, who raised her eyebrows. The nurse shrugged, "Rules." She walked down the hall.

Tony left as the dinner trolley was wheeled in. Bernie didn't say any more to him and had already walked out of the room.

Celeste called before lights out and Bernie was reluctant to take the call. "Hello?"

"Hi, Kitten. Are they treating you right in there?"

"If being a prisoner is right, then I guess things are peachy."

"Uh oh, that doesn't sound good. I was going to drive over and visit you, but you don't sound like you want company."

"Tony was here and he is clearly pasting this *visit* squarely on me. I'm a little upset with him. Actually, no, I'm pissed at him. I have the distinct impression that he had a hand in all this."

"Bernie," Celeste said softly, "You cracked up your car."

"Yes, I certainly did, but I feel like this was all preordained and Tony had a hand in me being put in here. It's unbelievable here. You should come to visit and get a gander."

"Can I come tomorrow?"

"Sure. We have group therapy at 9:30 and then arts and crafts, I'm not shittin you, at 2." Anytime between or after that is cool. I'll be waiting. Bring a box of Kleenex because I may need them by tomorrow."

"Are we allowed to bring in drinks and food?"

"You know, I just don't know. Try it and let's see how much trouble I can get into. Right now I could just spit nickels I'm so pissed. I feel like instigating something."

"Now, don't go doing something that will keep you in there longer, Bernie. I wanted to go to the next horse show. If you get out when they said, we'll be going to the next show together."

"Now, that's the kind of attitude I wanted to hear. Thanks. I do love you, Celeste." Bernie gently placed the phone back in the cradle.

She then flagged down a nurse and explained how her nail polish was taken away at check in and that she wanted to do her nails. "We have your stuff right here in a locker and all we need to do is see who wants to help you."

"Help me?"

"I mean any orderly who wants to sit with you while you do your nails."

"Oh, OK. Do you mean that my stuff has been up here the whole time and I could get access to my perfume?"

"Sure, all you've got to do is ask."

Dustin sat across from her in the day room as she pared her cuticles applied a base coat and put two coats of color on her nails. They talked about his college classes and her students. She applied a top coat and fanned her hands to dry. "I can't put a puzzle together with you, but I bet we can play a game of Scrabble without me wrecking my nails. You game?"

"Sure." He got up, found and started setting up the board.

"Hey, can I get in?"

They both turned to see an older woman about 49 heading in their direction. Dustin said, "Sure Debbie. This is Bernie. Bernie, watch her, she's a deadly player."

"OK, sounds like fun. Nice to meet you, Debbie."

Debbie was, indeed, a competent player and they finished the game with Debbie winning. It was fun and relaxing for Bernie and she forgot she was on a locked ward. The fruit trolley rolled in and everyone chose something. Bernie chose an apple to eat while she was reading in bed. Dustin returned her nail polishes to the nurse's station and again planted himself in the chair outside her door.

At 6:30 the next morning while Bernie was applying mascara someone knocked on her bathroom door. She opened it and a nurse was standing outside. "There is a doctor who needs to meet with you now."

"Now? Can you tell him I'm showering and can't until I'm done?"

"Sure."

A minute later the nurse came back. "He said unless you come out right now he is leaving someone at your door at night."

"What kind of crap is this? I am getting dressed. What doesn't he understand about getting dressed?"

"I don't know, he's not very nice. I told him you were hurrying, but his insisted."

"Well, tell him I feel safe with someone outside my door and he'll just have to come back when I'm dressed. This is ridiculous." The nurse smiled and left.

Bernie finished dressing and got coffee with Becky. She told her about the doctor's unreasonable demand so early in the morning. Becky listened and reiterated what the bipolar girl had said. "You need to be very nice to the doctors here."

"He wasn't even my own doctor."

"Doesn't matter, you have to give them what they want, when they want it."

"Don't you find 6:30 a little excessive? Nobody needs to be anywhere until 7:30 for breakfast."

"They do it for some reason, but I don't know the reason."

"Probably to catch you off guard."

Bernie forgot about the incident by the time group therapy started and only remembered it when she saw nurses talking behind the big counter top and then looking at her. She wondered if she had made a huge blunder.

Celeste arrived after crafts. She must have left right from school. She carried in a tote bag of Vitamin water, chocolates, cookies and goat cheese and crackers. "I got frisked before I could get in here!"

"Yeah, I know. They took away anything in glass from my bags. I bet you have nothing to spread the cheese with, huh?"

"Right. Any ideas?"

"Sure, let's go to the kitchen area and see what's in the drawers that we might be able to use. We can have a picnic in my room. You know you're spoiling my dinner, don't you?"

"Everyone at school wants to know what kind of surgery you're having. I told them it was a fanny lift."

"You did not."

"Nah, I told them it was female and they all stopped asking."

"Did you milk on Thursday?"

"Yes and your Dad isn't half as much fun to be with. He's bad on gossip and I miss my drink afterwards."

"You know, I haven't once thought about a glass of wine until you mentioned it."

"There was no way I could smuggle in wine. The chocolates will have to do. I'm leaving this stuff with you so you can share."

"I think I'll give it to the nursing staff and orderlies. They'll appreciate it.

"Did you see Noir? How's she look?"

"Um, like a horse? I don't know how to answer that question because I only saw the soaking part. Your dad has done a good job with her and she is walking on all four legs. Does she need to jump for the next show?"

"Oh, man, I never thought of Cathy riding her and jumping her. I don't know. I'd have to talk to the vet first. Maybe I can get cell phone privileges tomorrow and call and ask him. Wow, what a mess.

"I'm here, I should be practicing at Thousand Pines, Noir should be sound and I'm stuck and clueless. I'm not being a very responsible person in here because they have us on a schedule like school children. Every second of every day is planned for you and you have to adhere to their schedule." She told Celeste about the 6:30 doctor visit that morning.

"This place is an onion, too?" Celeste asked.

"Yup, but I don't have a clue how to peel it or even if want to. I just want out. So far I haven't had any adverse drug reactions, haven't fallen asleep anywhere and I feel a little above them all. That includes the rude doctor's visit."

"You should blog about it all."

"Are you crazy? They'd crucify me. As a matter of fact, I find it odd that no one has a laptop in here or computer privileges. Tony found out that there is a library here, but on another floor. They sure don't encourage using it. I guess people are supposed to be centered on themselves and whatever their problem is."

After a lengthy conversation Celeste left all the goodies to be delivered to the nurse's station and departed. Bernie felt an odd sense of desertion and began to feel controlled. She gathered up the remains of the picnic and walked to the nurse's desk.

"I have a peace offering or bribery depending on how you view it," she said with brightness in her voice.

The ohs and ahs over the delectables was enough for Bernie to know that she was not in trouble from this morning, but somehow admired for sticking up for herself.

FORTY THREE

Bernie's doctor made an appearance the next morning after group. "So, how are you faring in here?"

"I'm myself and no one else. What I'd like to know from you is why I'm here. I think your *suggestion* to be here is bullshit and I could have done this by staying home for a week. I don't need someone sleeping outside my door each night and I'm perfectly capable of taking care of myself. Right now I'm losing valuable training and practice time on my horse and wasting my time playing games and putting together birdhouses. And, don't try to tell me you don't know about this crap."

"I understand you refused to see a doctor yesterday morning."

"Oh, is that how it was presented to you? Let me set the record straight. I was using the toilet, it was 6:30 in the morning and the jerk refused to let me take my time and demanded and then administered punishment. His opinion of punishment is to have someone sit outside me door each evening. Frankly, I like Dustin sitting outside my door each night. This is the best sleep I've gotten in years."

His open mouth and raised eyebrows might have been slight gestures, but they were not missed by Bernie. She

dug in further, "Where the hell have you been since I've been in here? Our insurance pays you an inordinate sum of money to take care of me and all I've done is camp activities. Is this supposed to be a curing effect or a soothing space of time wasting?"

"I have other patients to attend to."

"How many of them are incarcerated on a mental ward?

"Several."

"Oh, so this is convenient for you to observe your patients in a controlled environment?"

She was clearly exasperating him because he sighed and took a measured breath. "No, you need to be here so we can decide the best course of treatment. The therapy I've prescribed is apparently not working and we may also need to increase your medication or change it. This is the best environment for that."

"How is *this* the best environment? There are no stimuli here to set off a behavior anomaly. It's not the real world with its day to day pressures and interaction with similarly affected people isn't conducive to setting off a bipolar phase. It's all sterile and controlled. Tell me, exactly, how this works."

"I've never looked at the hospital environment quite like you do. I see a program that works because patients can be monitored when we change treatments."

He wasn't allowed to finish because Bernie cut right in, "Whoa, Pal. We are not changing treatments. The medication I was on was working just fine. I told you

about a small glitch and you radically changed my medication which caused me to pass out. You're damn lucky I was on a country road and not a super highway. I could have taken out a lot of people because of your rash decision. Furthermore, I did a little research here and found out that one doesn't just up someone's meds in one giant leap, not to mention we have no way of knowing how my body would react to a new one. I find you to be irresponsible and to blame for what happened to me, my car and my plans."

"You are not the doctor here and you need to understand that this is not an exact science."

"Science?" She laughed and then covered her mouth. "Science isn't where you go and blow something up for shits and grins, it's something done on a controlled scale in increments. Which is what, if you're telling me the truth, you should be doing instead of trying to prove something to your ego by keeping me at the new and high dose you prescribed for me. My dosages were not backed down and increased slowly. They are the same as you radically changed them to.

"Also, you should be aware that I was mistakenly given the wrong medication one evening. A big purple capsule was given to me and I refused to take it. Did they bother to tell you about that when they told you I refused to see the shrink they assigned? No, I'm sure they didn't tell you about their own screw up. It's a good thing I was awake and not drugged out of my mind or I could have taken someone else's meds. I have a stinking suspicion you are completely clueless about what really happens in here. Why don't you tell me about the people you've

put on this ward to observe for a few weeks and they're still here months later!" Bernie's eyes burned fire and she wasn't going to be his little Petrie dish.

"You should be concerned about your own problems and not someone else's."

"What? You want me to sit here and not talk to anyone. I'm talking to as many people as I can while I'm here. I sincerely believe that this could have been done at home under normal *pressures* and not an artificial environment. I've also grown a very healthy distrust of you and am going to be asking for a new doctor while I'm here."

"That's your prerogative, Bernie. I talked to your husband and he says only one incident set you off. It had to do with your horse. This looks to me to be a repeating pattern."

"My husband, for your information, believes I should be drugged, have no opinions of my own and be compliant. The very things he fell in love with are now a nuisance to him. I'll deal with him on my own, but you, Sir, have to go. I don't want to end up at the Mayo clinic trying to convince people of my sanity because I've become your experiment. I told you about the doctor you sent me to and you sent me to another. As I recall, he is also a psychiatrist and I think I'll call him and see if he can't visit me while I'm here and we can find a course of medications and treatments that will serve me throughout my life. You're fired."

They'd been sitting on opposite ends of a sofa and Bernie stood up and walked away. She turned back, "Your

account of today's conversation might be pretty funny to read. I'd like my records turned over to Dr. Patel. I'm sure at some point he'll let me read them or convey to me what your reaction to being dismissed is."

She didn't look back and walked to her room and into the bathroom to peer at herself in the mirror. She noticed that her face was a little flushed and red, but she felt she looked fairly normal. Dismissing the education and experience of a doctor seemed a little excessive and over reactive, but she knew for her own good that it had to be done. Her next task was to get her hands on her cell phone and call Dr. Patel and then Tony. The cell phone had to be procured before her doctor talked to the nurses.

"Hi, I've been cleared to use my cell phone to call my therapist and my husband. Will it take long to get it?"

It was close to lunch and the nurse was a little distracted. Bernie hated to manipulate, but she was desperate. The nurse was the same one who had given her the nail polish and she didn't question anything. She left the desk and returned with Bernie's cell phone and leather case. Bernie wasted no time in leaving a message for Tony to call her at the hospital desk and then dialed Dr. Patel's number. The receptionist put her right through.

"Dr. Patel, this is Bernie Romanelli and I'm in the psych ward. I don't know if you work with this particular hospital, but I'd like to schedule our next session in here. I'm not due to leave for another week and a half and I've just fired my regular doctor. I'd like you to take over for him." She gave him the details as quickly as she could. She was afraid the nursing staff would

take her phone away and she needed to see Dr. Patel as quickly as possible before her regular doctor poisoned everything surrounding her. He said that he did work with the hospital and would be on his way over in a little while. He sounded genuinely concerned.

Bernie took another chance and left a message on Celeste's cell and quickly left some intriguing details about firing her doctor for Celeste. That would ensure Celeste calling as well.

When Bernie left her room she did not see her doctor and no nurses approached her as she picked up a lunch tray from the trolley. "Hmm. The most important decision I have to make today is what color to paint a birdhouse," She smiled.

In the craft room the wisecracking woman formally introduced herself. "I never told you my name and you never told me yours. I'm Janice. I stopped participating a long time ago, but you did something today to our doctor that made him a little flighty. What was it?"

"I canned his ass."

"What? Are you saying you fired him?"

"Ten four, Buddy."

"Wow. I never thought of that. He sure was distracted by something when he came to talk to me. He wants to transfer me to Mayo right away. That's what he told me, anyway."

"How sane do you think you are?"

"No nuttier than the next person. Wasn't it Silvia Plath whose ward mate asked if mental illness was contagious?"

"I don't know, I never read any of her stuff that I recall, and if I did, I certainly did not retain any of it. That's pretty funny."

Bernie was on fire with an idea about painting her birdhouse and she was picking out brushes and colors. She glanced sideways at Janice, "So if I come to visit tonight, will you tell me what landed you in here and then kept you here all this time? I don't plan on being here more than the originally scheduled allotment. I'm not letting someone push me around, either. He made a huge error and I paid for it. He prescribed a new drug at a high dose three times a day and I conked out and wrecked my pretty car. He refuses to admit this."

"Sure. I'm supposed to be incurable, so what have I got to lose? I just can't believe you had the balls to tell him to take a hike. He's a doctor and they need reverence and worship, you know."

Bernie tossed her head and howled. People looked up from their tables and then looked away. Janice said, "You know, I may need a birdhouse in Minnesota. Hey, Dustin, can I do one of these, too?"

Instead of painting the birdhouse a solid color, Bernie painted the sides in little bricks with windows that held tiny plants and were hung with curtains. She put a welcome matt under the perch at the entrance. "I'll think about this place every time I see this."

Others noticed and changed their ideas a little. "Sheep," Janice said. All of them sheep. Not one original thought in their heads. They need to be led because they cannot think for themselves. I bet that's what upset him today, you thought for yourself. You told him what you thought, didn't you?"

"We'll talk about it tonight. I saw some hot cocoa packages in the kitchen and I'll make us two cups and bring them down to your room tonight. I may have to watch myself because I lied and told them I had my cell phone privileges back. I wouldn't hang out with me right now if you want to be treated well today. I'm serious. I'm on the unwritten shit list."

Dr. Patel was waiting when crafts were over. Bernie smiled wide at the sight of him and he smiled back. His eyes seemed to be twinkling and Bernie led him to her room. She shut the door as he started to speak. "I highly doubt I'll be getting any more referrals from him thanks to you. I just read his remarks and your chart. Why don't you start at the beginning?"

The story took an hour and she added as many details as she remembered. Life was moving a good clip right now and she didn't want to leave out anything he may consider important. Together they decided which drugs and how much of them would be used for the duration of her stay. They parted like old friends and she initiated a hug with him. He seemed a little embarrassed at first, but Bernie meant it and he didn't push her away. He mentioned that he had a little bit of paperwork to do in her regard and left the ward with a promise to be back.

During dinner, Dustin approached her, "I don't have to guard the drawbridge tonight. You've been cleared for takeoff."

Bernie laughed and told him that he'd better find a good puzzle for them to put together tonight so she could hear more college stories and he left her to finish the bland cube steak with the gelatinous gravy. She had forgotten about Janice and the cup of cocoa. If she had to access her mood right then, it would be light, controlled, but light. She watched her step with the nursing staff, but was herself.

Celeste called early and Bernie tried to get her story out without crowing on the phone at the nurse's station. She had found out that they were allowed to make outgoing calls on their cell phones, but not allowed incoming calls. Celeste was being purposefully obtuse and Bernie was getting a little impatient with her as she tried to explain her day. Bernie took a cooling breath and told Celeste that if she visited she would fill her in on the details. Tony called as soon as Bernie walked away from the nurse's station.

"Hey," she said

"Hey to you. What's happening on your planet?"

"It's started revolving again. I fired my doctor today," she whispered into the phone.

"You what?"

"That's right, I told him to take a hike and met with Dr. Patel instead. He's taking over my *case.*

"You're the person who told me to 'own' this, so I'm owning it. I'm taking charge of my own treatment and life. No one is going to walk over me, drug me silly and take away my dreams. That goes for our marriage as well. I have a few things I'd like to discuss with you, but the phone is not the place. Besides, I'm standing here at the nurse's station and I can be overheard. When are you visiting again so we can talk?"

"Um, wow. You just floored me and I need some time to think about this. Is tomorrow too soon?"

"Nope, works for me. Also, I'm going to get hold of Cathy Jones and see if any of this is going to affect my job or go on permanent record. I have a lot of explaining to do to her and I think the best place would be the barn. Why don't you spring me outta here this weekend?"

"Are you allowed to leave?"

"I don't see why Dr. Patel would put any restrictions on me since I'm here of my own volition. You could call and ask."

"You sound very sure of yourself right now. Are you on an upswing again?"

"Nope, just taking control of my life. I've let someone else do it for me and it wasn't a pleasant experience. We'll talk about it in the car and at home. I'd also like to sit down with my parents and explain a few things."

"Okay," he said the word very slowly as though not quite believing her.

"Tony, you've got to trust me and know that I have an entire life to live and want to live it. I just don't want anyone messing with it. The doctor had his own agenda and it didn't jive with mine. I can't talk any longer because I promised to talk to someone else and I just remembered. I have to get out of a jigsaw puzzle appointment and then go down the hall and talk to a new friend. Gotta ring off, Babe."

Tony seemed baffled by the change in her demeanor. He was silent a moment and then said, "Alright, I'll call you tomorrow and also find out if you can leave for a day or two."

"Good. I am also running out of clothes. We only put enough in my bag for a week and I need to run some laundry and pack some other things. I'll tell you a theory on the way home. I love you, talk you to tomorrow." She hung up and went in search of Dustin.

Janice's story was one of depression, but she just didn't tell it like a depressed person. She had been with their doctor for five years and said she didn't feel as though they had progressed. She felt he made fun of her and didn't take her seriously. She admitted that she was unable to get out of bed for a long time and lost her job over the depression, but at the same time the antidepressants he prescribed didn't do much for her low mood. Bernie listened well, but kept noticing Janice's sense of humor was entertaining and self depreciating.

"Do you really believe you can't beat this?"

"Yeah, he tells me that I need more treatment at a better place. Hence the Mayo Clinic."

"What would they do there that they can't do here?"

"Beats me. But, I'm so beaten down that it really doesn't matter anymore."

"Really, truly, do you believe that? Remember in group we talked about hearing something so often that you start to believe it? Are you sure you just haven't been talked into this?"

"Listen, Kiddo, I gave up participating in anything other than group therapy because they insist on it. Mostly I sit here in the hall and watch the head bangers and the people who just want a government check each month so they act nutty. That's my entertainment all day."

"Don't you read?"

"Read what? I don't like books that much and I miss my old job. I was an accountant in a big office. I feel like a piece of unredeemable shit."

"Janice, do you have any outside interests or hobbies?"

"Like what? How many freaking birdhouses can you make before you want to stick your finger down your throat?"

"Is that all they have you do is build birdhouses?"

"Just about."

"Have you made any friends in here?"

"Yup, they all get cured and go home. I just stay and watch the parade of freaks."

Tony called early Friday morning and told her to be ready to leave by 5 PM. He said he'd bring a dress and heels and they could go to dinner in Ann Arbor before returning home. After group Bernie showered again, spent extra time on her makeup and redid her nails. She needed to be ready to just change into a dress and leave. She packed her suitcase for cleaning and repacking at home.

Tony's arrival on the floor created a stir among the patients and the staff. His good looks and suit drew admiring glances from everyone. While Bernie changed clothes, he chatted up the nurses and orderlies. Bernie emerged from her room dressed and caused her own sensation. The patients and staff were unaccustomed to seeing anyone dressed for dinner and seemed to sink down into their sofas and chairs. Bernie immediately noted the change in postures. She certainly had a few things to talk to Tony about, and one of them was her theory about the way people dressed on the ward.

They left arm in arm with Tony carrying her suitcase and makeup bag in his other hand. He had made reservations at a steak house and this was much appreciated by Bernie who had been struggling with the hospital selection, but not complaining.

Upon being seated, Bernie ordered a glass of Pinot Noir and took appreciative sips. Tony didn't initially say much, but stared at her as though he expected her to morph into someone else. Bernie laughed at him and said, "No, I'm not cured and it's going to be a lifelong job to work with this, but I'm gaining perspective this week."

The lovely couple stayed for hours talking and finally left for home. Being at home made Bernie a little irritable because she missed it and still thought the hospital was a rather dumb idea. The idea of sleeping in her own bed with her husband seemed almost novel after a week.

The next morning she made breakfast for both of them and called Cathy. She asked Cathy if she could meet her at Thousand Pines because she had something she needed to discuss with her. Cathy agreed and Bernie borrowed Tony's car and left for Jackson. Tony was concerned about her driving alone and has asked her if he should accompany her. "I need to do this myself and you need to wrangle an evening at your parent's tonight so we can talk to them as well."

Bernie wore jeans and a sweater and felt a little out of place in a barn full of breeches. Cathy met her in the parking area and Bernie suggested they drive into Jackson and get coffee. After receiving their orders they found a nice quiet table and Bernie said, "Cathy, there is something I need your help with.

"A few shows ago I brought my friend Celeste and I snapped at her for getting in the way and she asked me if I had taken my pills that morning."

Cathy grinned at Bernie over her coffee cup and said, "Oh, I remember it well and my first thought was that you were bipolar. You exhibit a lot of the classic signs with rapid speech and irritability. Are you?"

Bernie's jaw dropped, "Yes. You knew?"

"It's my job."

"Oh, well I don't know what to say then. I need to know if this is going to affect my job if anyone finds out."

"Hell no! There are teachers who make no bones about letting you know they are on antidepressants. Being a teacher in this day and age is no easy job and what might have been a lifelong dream turns into a nightmare with the kids, parents and the school system, itself."

"I don't know you well enough to ask what I'm planning on, but I hope you keep an open mind."

Cathy nodded over her cup. "Shoot away. I consider you my friend and was wondering how long it would take before you realized that. Hit me."

"Well, you're leaving me speechless here. You're one step ahead of me and I wonder if we have anything to talk about at all," Bernie laughed.

Cathy smiled back and said, "You don't make friends easily and I can tell that you seldom trust people, especially new ones. You're not going to lose your job over a chemical imbalance. Consider it like a thyroid problem that you need medication for."

"Again, I'm speechless here."

Bernie proceeded to tell Cathy the tale of the doctors and the car accident and the hospital. She outlined the mistrust of the doctors and the therapist and firing her first doctor. She told her about having to return to the hospital tomorrow and her reservations about it being the best environment for testing medications.

"You know, I agree with that part, but you had no skilled personnel to help you at that junction. I doubt Tony is equipped to deal with the mood swings or medicine side effects, either, so you probably made the right decision at the wrong hands. I know Dr. Patel, by the way. He's very good and all his patients seem to like him very much. He seems very empathetic. Did you know that he counsels several of your students at school?"

"No kidding? I have a few concerns about all these meds though and he's going to have to do some research for me about the rest of my life's plans."

"What would those be?"

"Cathy, I'm confiding in you before I tell my husband. I'm not getting any younger and I want a family with Tony. I don't know if I can take meds and be pregnant. How do I go about a plan like that one?"

"Bernie, bipolar women have children all the time. I can't say they are all being treated, but I know that they have perfect little families and are good mothers. I bet that's crossed your mind as well; whether or not you'd be a good mother."

"Yes, it has and it bothers me a great deal. I care for my husband and animals all the time, but would a baby send me over the edge? That's a big concern. I'd like to be drug free during pregnancies and have no resources to learn what to do. I know that so much of my behavior is *learned*, but I don't know how much of it is and how it can be unlearned."

"You're on the right track right now. I can do some research for you and so can Dr. Patel. You say you like and trust him, then let him guide you through the process."

"I'm not too sure Tony will want to follow through on this, I know he very much wants children, but his wife is nuts."

"How well do you know his wife?"

They both laughed.

The conversation turned serious again and they finished their second cups of coffee and returned to Thousand Pines to pick up Cathy's car. Cathy hugged Bernie before she left. "I promise to start right in on the research and get back to you. Let's discuss the next show before you leave.

"Also, do you want me to visit you this week?"

"You're kidding me, right?"

"Hell no, I'll drive over and keep you company. Need any good books to read? They don't have a lot to do over there and I know you love to read."

"Celeste is coming Monday and if you have time and can get free of the kids, you could just ride over with her. That would be a huge surprise for the other residents. I seem to be the only one there with visitors. Also, it's gotten around that I fired my doctor and found another right away."

"The kids are in a day care until 6 because I usually don't finish my day until then, so if we leave right after school, I

can do it on Monday. Sound good to you? I've never been to this ward before and it would be a real education for me. Just call me nosey," She crinkled her eyes.

"OK, it's a date. Let's get Noir over here and you're in charge of taking my lessons, keeping her legged up and I'll just have to wing it at the next show. I should be okay and have things under control by then. Celeste has asked to come again, so if you don't mind, we can share a room again. I'm getting excited just thinking about it. Cathy, I really want that high point award and being in the hospital just threw a wrench in the works."

"Listen, we'll get you through this and you'll seal the high point. We still have another show to get through after this one. I'll make the hotel reservations, pay the entry fees and schedule Noir to be transported. You just take care of what you need to and I'll see you at the show. Oh, and on Monday, too."

Dinner at the Romanelli's was a little tense that evening. They had a lot to mentally digest and listened carefully to the things Bernie said. Bernie's parents had been invited because of time constraints. Both her parents barely spoke a word, but seemed proud to be her parents. Bernie felt confident in her decisions and the way in which she presented the facts to them. Tony held her hand through most of dinner.

"Hey, wife."

"Yeah, husband?"

"I think you dodged a bullet with grace tonight. I'm proud of you and now my parents have a little inkling of

what you've been going through for the past three years here. I think the way you presented your thoughts was lucid and well thought out. I'm very proud to be your husband. And, I love you."

'So, you're onboard with this new way of thinking and tackling the problem?"

"Yeah, I am." The sparkle in his eyes was hard to miss.

"So what do you think about the theory that most of the residents don't care for themselves and dress as though they're hopeless in that place?"

"Well, I wouldn't exactly tell you to wear a suit and heels, but I think you're on to something. I also believe you did the right thing by firing your doctor. A radical move, for sure. And a touch impetuous, but well decided. How long did it take you to realize this and cut bait and run?"

"Honestly, Tony, it was a spur of the moment thing. The more I thought about it the angrier I became at him. There is some sort of conspiracy going on in the medical minds of this country and they think they can drug you into submission. Me? I'm not into feeling like a zombie and unable to remember what I did one day to the next. It was an *on the spot thing* as it was unfolding, it felt like the right thing. I'm just lucky to have had a doctor in my back pocket to call instead of having to go through a series of them until I found one I could deal with. Dr. Patel seemed slightly amused by the whole process. Although, he says he'll probably never get another referral from what's his face." She chuckled at the conversation with Dr. Patel and felt like she had won some battle.

"We can work together and fix this. You're going to be involved and be kind without being critical and help me think through some of those impetuous thoughts I have. I need to slow down a little when I'm manic and think into the future about the domino effect of actions. I'm expecting help with that from you and Celeste and Cathy and our families.

"Did I tell you about Cathy already having guessed at my disorder and helping me do some research?"

"What kind of research?"

"Let's agree to have this conversation, or that part of it, in about two weeks. I have a surprise life's goal and I need to think about it some before I go off into the wild blue with something not well researched and though out. How's that sound?"

"Like a secret."

"OK, agreed, it's a secret and I'll tell you when I'm ready!"

Tony shook his head and laughed, "Don't tell me you're going to change careers again."

"Nope, maybe. That's all I'm saying for now. Agreed?"

"I'm going to have to trust you on this one, then?"

"Yes Sir. It's something good and something we want. I just have to get to the right place to make it happen. Again, that's all I'm saying for now. Let's go up and raid my closet and help me get some laundry done so I don't

come home to a mess at the end of the week before a show." She dragged her suitcase downstairs to the laundry room.

Tony followed her and put his arms around her while she was sorting and loading the washer. He nuzzled her hair and spun her around for a long and deep kiss. She responded in kind.

Back upstairs she started digging things out of the closet and drawers. "I need some contemporary clothes that look good, not too out of place and have a good rotation of bright colors. I refuse to wear gray sweats and baggy pants. Help me decide here. Also, I want a dress to leave in on Friday. If he will let me, I'd like to leave Thursday so I have one night in my own bed and can drive to the show on Friday afternoon. I'm still out of school, so I should be on the grounds before anyone else, other than the horses.

"I also owe Cathy the entry fees and half a hotel room and I don't want to forget that. Are you interested in driving up for the show?"

"Nope, I'm letting you handle this yourself. Besides, football games have started and I don't want to miss any. We both have jobs to do and we can reunite at home and be together afterward. I'm glad we set aside money for this." His face showed all the confidence it used to when they were single.

Bernie felt loved.

The next morning they took a run together, ate a leisurely breakfast in the nook and read the papers before getting dressed to go see Noir. Carl met them at the car and hugged Bernie. "I'm proud of you, Kid. What you did

last night took moxie and a lot of courage. It couldn't have been easy to tell someone for the first time about all this."

"Thanks, Dad. I'm just committed, no pun intended, to running as much of my own life as I can. Thank you so much for putting all the effort into Noir and getting her sound again. Tony told me you had the farrier out and she got four new shoes. What do I owe you for them?"

"Nothing, it's a get well present from me and Mom." He grinned at Tony over her head.

Noir was in her stall and Bernie haltered her and lunged her outside to see how the horse moved and if there was any soreness that might interfere with her classes or jumping with Cathy. Noir was showing off and full of herself and Bernie couldn't help but grin with pride at the beauty of her gaits and Noir's opinionated head tossing the first few revolutions. "She's as little wound up. I thought she was turned out with the girls the whole time."

Carl sucked on his pipe and said, "I had the vet out to look at her and he felt that two days of stall rest would help increase her recovery. I just knew you wouldn't miss this show. Thousand Pines is sending a trailer over tomorrow for her and she will only have one week there before she gets hauled to the show. Mom and I don't plan to go and figure you need a girl's weekend; Noir included."

Bernie hugged him, "I can always count on you in a pinch, Dad. Thanks so much for what you've done for the both of us. I'll bring home that high point for everyone involved."

FORTY FOUR

"When was the last time you put together a puzzle? We seem to have a great many here, both cardboard and human, Bernie said to Cathy and Celeste. Both women looked at her askance.

"I'm serious. We can play in the dayroom and you can observe people all you want," she whispered to them.

They were sitting on her bed and cleaning up the wrappings of the snacks they brought. Both were still dressed from school and looked very professional. Patients had gawked at them when they were escorted in, each carrying a wicker basket of goodies.

"Cathy and I talked about bipolar disorder on the way over and I understand a little more now than I did before. You are not responsible for everything you do, but you can control it with the right drug combination. She said it was like rewiring your brain so you could get used to *normal* behavior. Am I wrong?" Celeste asked Bernie.

"Well, I guess. You need to ask yourself what the definition of normal is. I think it's just a setting on the dryer!

"I really don't know what the triggers are that make me manic and I have to learn to step back from my thoughts and think them through. A little like counting to ten when you're angry." Bernie said as they left her room and headed down the hall.

In the dayroom they selected a puzzle and the three of them started turning pieces over. Bernie could tell by the look on Cathy's face that she was really enjoying herself. Celeste, always happy, was more focused on the puzzle than the patients. They were the two who spent the most amount of time working on the pieces while Cathy observed other patients.

"This is good for you, isn't it?" Bernie asked Cathy.

"Yeah, I have to say this is a treat. Leave it to you to supply the excitement for an evening. We have to get going pretty soon because I have to pick up the kids. Thanks for letting me come along."

Janice sought out Bernie after the girls left and Bernie was still in her room collecting the goodies to take to the nurse's station. "Janice, do you like goat cheese and crackers?"

The girl hungrily eyed the goodies and was obviously flattered to be asked. Bernie shared with her and took the opportunity to ask a few questions. She found that Janice had only one visitor, her mother, since she'd been on the ward. Bernie also found that the girl's mother had since passed away and Janice was not allowed by the doctor to go home for her own mother's funeral.

"That's absurd. Who decided that?"

"He did. He felt I would have a relapse. Instead it spiraled me into a depression that I couldn't shake."

"You need to find another doctor before he ruins the rest of your life. You're only in your twenties and if you end up at Mayo like you told me, I suspect you'll be there forever. You also need to find some outside activities in your life for passion."

"I don't have any passions any longer. I'm too drugged to feel anything. I didn't feel much and was very numb when my mother passed. She died of a heart attack and I wasn't even allowed to see her and say goodbye. I kind of died myself that week."

"Oh, I'm so very sorry," Bernie didn't know what else to say and knew nothing of Janice's problems to counsel her about finding some doctor who would be more compassionate. This information, did however, make Bernie's resolve even stronger.

In her room, Bernie thought a little about how she could help Janice, who seemed to be a perfectly decent and reasonable person. Yes, she may be diagnosed correctly, but it seemed to Bernie that her treatment was being mishandled. *How do I help people like her? How do they find those types of doctors, anyway? What got her placed in here in the beginning?* This all confused her and she was distracted because she had her own agenda of being released a day early so she could show.

This thinking process produced guilt about Noir. Bernie realized that she did not treat or feel like Noir was a loving companion and dependent. It finally occurred to her that she had treated Noir like a possession and

a machine when the first abscess presented itself. All she could think of was winning, not the pain the horse was in or even how she had left her in the hands of her father. Her father, she realized had more compassion for the animal than she did at that point. She felt ashamed by her greed. Being alone in this environment gave her pause to reflect. She fell asleep without reading any of her current book.

Dr. Patel arrived after breakfast around group time. She was excused to spend time with him. "You don't seem to have any noticeable side effects from the new drug and it seems to be leveling out for you. How do you feel?"

"Reflective."

"Reflective?"

"Yes, this is a sterile environment without any pressures and I have time to think. I can't tell you if the new prescription is working or not, but I don't feel anything untold. I really can't answer the question you are really asking."

He nodded and looked at her expectantly.

"The question you are really asking is if this drug is working and I feel good enough to go home and resume my regular life."

"Yes."

"I want to be honest with you, but I can't assess my own personality and feelings right now. Help me here. Do you think I can go home and compete and take the chance of not winning that big prize I'm chasing? Do you think I can go back and face a classroom of unruly teens and live through it? Do you think with counseling I can go off drugs long enough to carry a baby to term?"

"Wow." He smiled at her. "This is a lot of thinking and questioning. I can't answer those questions, only you can."

"Yeah, that's what I was afraid you'd say. I don't want to spend any more time in here than I have to, but at the same time, I'm starting to question myself about a lot of things. Who am I, really?"

Staff at the nurse's station looked up when he laughed. "Ah, the age old question. You became a philosopher in here and have stepped up to the plate of acceptance.

"I don't see any more denial and I feel that you're ready to leave. You expressed a desire to leave Thursday to prepare for another horse show and sleep in your own bed. My gut tells me you can do that.

"However, I do want to warn you that drugs tap out at various times and you may need to be keenly aware of your moods and feelings and tell me when you falter. This, I need you to understand, may happen at any time. Right now you seem to be on a good course and from our short time together I think they are working. How long, how many years they work will be up to you to determine and seek help. We'll work together on this and keep our weekly appointments. I know you don't want to drive to Ann Arbor for this and I have a suggestion. I also counsel for the school system where

you teach. We can set up every two weeks and monitor you if you will meet me in Jackson."

"Yes, I've heard that you treat some of the very same people I teach. I also understand that they like you. I see you as a reasonable person who is not drug crazed or experimental. I can do that. It may be a little embarrassing to me in the beginning if I run into anyone I know, but I can do that."

"Then let's sign you out on Thursday morning so you can go home, be with your husband, prepare and resume normal duties and activities again.

"I also want to wish you luck and concentration on your show this weekend." He grinned at her and she laughed.

"Thank you for caring. I'm glad I made the choice I did and I have to apologize for my first meeting with you. I had a bad and threatening session with someone and just assumed you'd be the same way. I also want to thank you for taking me on as a patient."

He nodded.

"Can you counsel me through starting and raising a family? Will you do some research for me? I'm not getting younger and Tony and I really wanted to have a family. I just don't want to be on any potentially harmful drugs during a pregnancy; at the same time, I don't want to endanger anyone or myself during that time."

Dr. Patel raised his eyebrows and asked, "Do you want to do this immediately, like in the next month or so?"

"Good God, no. I just want this to happen naturally for me and Tony. We discussed it prior to marriage and I'd like to tell him when it's safe to start. I haven't said anything to him lately because of all the hoopla surrounding me. I just need some good advice and someone to hold my hand through it."

"Then we will work on it. I'd like to meet your husband at some point and get his views and opinions on this. I don't know enough about the current drugs you are on to make an educated statement about pregnancy with them. We are also fairly new to one another and we will have to work through this together. You husband may have to see me a few times to cope if you go off medications completely through the process. Is this fair?"

"Entirely. Thank you. Do you need to be here Thursday or can I just walk out the door?"

"No. I'll have to write up discharge papers for you today and you are free to leave at any time on Thursday. I don't want you to just run out the door because there is always the possibility that you have to return for one reason or another and we need the hospital to be on your side. Do you agree and understand?"

"I guess so. I don't want to come back, but I see that this fine hotel could be a landing place again without the prescriptions and any future antics. Yes, I understand. Thank you for being honest."

****

"Let me call you back from a landline," Tony said. "I'm home already and digging through the fridge for something to eat. I can hear you better off the cell phone."

She stayed at the nurse's station and waited for him to call. "Hey!"

"Yeah, how'd it go today?"

"I don't know what your schedule is on Thursday, but I'm sprung and can leave."

"Oh, that's great. What time do you want me to pick you up?"

"I'd like to tell you I want to leave as early as possible, but that's not feasible for you and I also want to attend group therapy. I know it's an hour drive, but maybe you could get some work done early and then leave."

"Works for me. I can't wait to get you home. Can I ask you a huge favor then?"

"Ah, I guess so. What?"

"Will you make me dinner?"

FORTY FIVE

There were six for dinner. The house was lit up like Christmas and the aroma of fish and paella filled it. They had stopped in Ann Arbor before coming home and picked up the ingredients, including the saffron. Bernie had a glass of wine while doing the majority of the cooking, but eschewed wine at dinner in the presence of parents.

Nothing was said about the hospital and everyone left early, giving Bernie time to pack her show clothes and drop her bag in her car. Tony had it driven to the body shop immediately after the accident and it was ready within the week. "Just don't wash it or have it waxed, was what I was told because the paint needs to cure," Tony had told her.

Celeste drove directly from school to Bernie's house and they left for Kalamazoo. Cathy met them at the barn where Noir was just being unloaded from Jack's trailer. She settled in easily and the girls looked over the show grounds and left for their hotel after a quick job of braiding. There was an unbroken bond of secrecy and friendship between them and they checked in and went right to their room.

"Let's not eat at the hotel tonight, but find something outside that's interesting, Cathy suggested. "We certainly have the time and we can come back and have a drink with the group later."

Bernie felt a little strange, but freed from the confines of the hospital. She also watched her friends for signs of distrust. They decided on Sushi and Bernie drove downtown, and no one said anything about accidents or medications. She was grateful they trusted her.

Upon their return and a few Saki's each, they sought out the bar. All three were a little tipsy and tired from the hot wine. The regular show people were there and having a grand time dancing and drinking. Cathy initiated their early departure.

In the room Celeste headed for the shower in consideration for their morning routines. Cathy took that opportunity to talk to Bernie. "I've been doing some quick research about pregnancy and the drugs you are taking. Have you talked to your doctor about this yet?"

"No, I just left prison on Thursday and I don't see him for a week. What did you learn?"

"It's a gamble. There are so many women who just can't go off their meds to counterbalance the hormones, and there are others who do and suffer for it. It all depends on you and the type of therapy you've got."

Bernie admitted she had done a quick look on the Internet and found a site where women wrote about their experiences both ways "So it sounds as though

it's up to the doctor and me. I need to get used to this new drug and keep stress to a minimum from what I understand. I'm willing to stop all drugs and alcohol, but I don't know if I won't have an episode somewhere in the middle."

Cathy said, "There is some controversy. It's not been studied enough, but some women go off and start again in the second trimester and then step the drugs down in the third so that babies aren't affected. That might be something to look into."

"Right now I hear Celeste shutting the water down and I don't want to discuss this in front of her because I haven't mentioned it and she has no children. I don't want to make her want something that may not be possible in her life."

"OK, got it."

Celeste exited the bathroom with wet hair and a bottle of anti frizz product. "Don't either of you laugh at me, but my hair has a mind of its own and I have to apply this while it's wet, and then comb it through."

Bernie smiled, "Celeste, I've known you for years and know when you don't use it or don't have time. We put makeup on each morning and you don't make fun of us. Apply away. I have to admit that I have a bottle of that stuff in Noir's grooming kit to control her tail!"

"No shit?"

"No shit," and Bernie laughed with her.

****

The show was comfortable and familiar and the weather was mild. No one melted or became dehydrated. Bernie, unpracticed, but mentally intact, won her classes. Cathy won all three of hers and they packed up to return to Cold Lake and Jackson. The hug that Cathy gave Bernie was genuine and filled with unspoken words. Celeste and Bernie drove to the farm to unload Noir.

"Do you think you are still a contender for the high point award you want?"

Bernie pursed her lips as she watched Noir pulling out mouthfuls of hay in her home stall. "I don't really know because I had a meltdown last time and didn't talk to Sue this time. I'll call her tomorrow on her cell. She only has four people participating in the dressage portion of the show and will be more able to talk to me. I so very much hope so, though.

"As much as I love showing, I'm getting a little tired. I had a major life upset recently and have a new path to research and follow. I need to spend time with Tony and discuss something very serious in our marriage."

"Anything I should know about or could help with?"

"Celeste, the time isn't right to tell you and I haven't yet had a chance to sit down and talk to Tony about it. I'll tell you when the time is right. You've got to trust me enough to wait. OK?"

"Sure, Bernie. I think you've been through a small part of hell lately and I don't want to push you into talking about things you aren't ready for."

"It's not that, it's more that I need to make a major decision with my husband and he's clueless yet."

"Oh. OK."

They knocked on the back door and said hello to her parents before leaving the farm.

Tony was waiting for her with a salad, steak and purchased side dishes. "Hey, it's the only thing I know to do and I figured you'd be too tired to want to cook. Also, I didn't think it appropriate to impose on our parents tonight and I didn't want to go out. I bet you're exhausted and just want to rest. You kinda think you've been pushing yourself a little since you left the hospital, ran home, made a fabulous dinner for everyone and flashed off to a show in three days. You need a break."

Standing with the saddle pads draped over her arm, Bernie smiled slightly and let out a long sigh of exhaustion and relief. "I'll just take these downstairs and soak them and I'll be up to eat in a minute. Are you using the grill?"

He walked to where she stood and enfolded her. She collapsed into his arms and started weeping tears she had been holding back for two weeks.

****

School seemed out of sync the first week back. Milking on Thursday was the closest to "normal" that Bernie felt. Celeste's presence was welcomed, but Bernie felt hammered into a behavioral box without an outlet for creative expression. Everything seemed to be turning

and revolving in the same way as it had before her accident. "Hmm, I'm a little bored by the same routines and life. Everyone wants to go back to the way things were before, but I'm still stuck at school and with goats. I need some creative outlet. Even showing my horse is boring me."

Tony and Bernie had spent a lot of hours discussing the possibility of having a family and the ramifications of bipolar disorder affecting children. They both started research in earnest and reported back to one another. Dr. Patel, too, discussed this with Bernie. He urged her to continue her medications if the couple decided to stop birth control. "Right now the antidepressant you're taking should not cause any problems, however, not a lot of research has been done on some of the newer ones. I would eventually take you off the anti-anxiety drug because it has shown itself to be slightly addictive and could cause problems with a newborn. You aren't planning on doing this immediately, are you?"

"No, Tony and I are discussing it and doing research on the various drugs, their efficacy and their effects on subsequent children. I'm still on the pill and we will let you know as I progress. I'm not under any undue stress at this time and I don't know how I'll react yet. The learned behavior thing is a small problem and that's why I'm keeping my appointments. I'm also grateful to not have to drive to Ann Arbor each week."

FORTY SIX

Problems did start when parent teacher conferences began that semester. One of Bernie's nemeses from high school was also a PTA member with clout. She kept insisting that her son was Advanced Placement material even though he didn't keep up with the work and participate in class. The kid was a thug and a football star. He had a lot of the qualities Todd seemed to rub off on his boys. Slouching, legs in the desk rows, disruptive to the point of pulling the other students off the subject matter and disrespectful to Bernie.

After what was to be a civilized conversation with the woman, Bernie could feel her heart beating faster and the old feeling of unworthiness beginning. She attempted to talk quietly to the sneering parent, who obviously hadn't matured past high school. Bernie could feel her temper flaring and informed the woman that she was influencing her son to misbehave because she had no respect for current authority.

"You're just a teacher, what kind of authority do you want?"

Bernie paused to control her voice and replied, "I'm a teacher now, I wasn't before and I know that if you want

a good career for your son, he's going to have to learn to respect people and his elders."

"He's going to be a big football star, he can do what he wants."

"In order for him to be a *football* star he's going to have to be accepted to a good school. If he doesn't get his act together soon, no colleges will consider him because of failing grades. I suggest he be put back into the regular classes to give him a chance to succeed."

"You can pass him in the Advanced Placement class of yours."

"No, and I'm empathic, there is no skating in my classes. My students work too hard for me to let someone just get by without a little respect and studying. I don't know why you cannot understand this." Bernie was getting increasingly angry because her students were diligent and participated, showing her they read the work and thought a lot about it. She so wanted to just dismiss the woman and ask her why she bothered to show up for the meeting.

She was saved from saying something regrettable by a knock on the door as the next parent arrived. She stood up, "That is my recommendation and I suggest you discuss it with your son." The woman left in a huff when Bernie walked to the door and greeted the next parent. She concentrated on dispelling the old feelings and anger. The attitude of the woman didn't seem as though it was going to go away and she wondered why she wasn't able to convey her point. It rubbed her that

the woman had said she was just a teacher. She was starting to miss her old job.

At dinner that evening she bled her heart out to Tony concerning the attitude of former classmates.

"This is the type of deep seated stress that can set you off. Are you sure you can handle it?"

"We'll have to wait and see. I don't know who has who for a parent. I left this place with no intentions of returning, so I don't know who married who or who stayed here and had children. Tonight was tough because I really wanted to punch her. I already want to punch her kid."

"Bernie!"

"Really, I'm just blowing off steam here to you."

"Do you know any other teachers who may know the kids and their parents?"

"The only teacher still around is Audrey, and I'm certainly not going to sit down with her and relive my past and ask questions. She's pretty tight lipped about the kids she teaches, anyway."

"You just hit the nail on the head. Don't relive your past. Your past defined you at one time and it causes undue stress in your current life. Working with and meeting the very people who made your past life miserable is only going to set off another stress inducer and either depress you or make you manic. Right now you're even keeled and doing well. It helped with the horse winning, but you can't base your happiness on a horse's performance."

"I'm not basing my happiness on a horse, Tony. I'm just going after a goal. I have two friends now who support me and gently nudge me when my mood changes. One is well schooled in the disorder and the other just wants to be with me. I think I entertain both of them!"

"Parent teacher conferences are going to be hell and you have to get through them. You don't know the parents of the students you're teaching, but you have to not be shocked and have to control your emotions through this week. Is there anything I can do to make this exercise easier on you?"

"Nothing I can think of. Just be supportive and if I spout off, just listen. So far I've only wanted to punch one person because she said I was only a teacher. I used to have a great job in business and I feel like I dropped my goals and lessened my chances of success. What is success in teaching? You try to adjust attitudes, you deal with kids going through hormonal changes, you see teachers affecting moods and relationships in the kids, you deal with the politics and you live there all day long without any outside stimulation. It doesn't help that the syllabus stays the same year after year and you lose your spontaneity in the classroom. I need a creative outlet that isn't goats and horses."

"Well, I don't know what to tell you or suggest anything to you. You love to read and you love to research using the computer; is that getting boring, too?"

"I don't know any other things to do. The garden is gone for the season, there is only one horse show left and I'm not milking on Thursday because of conferences. I don't paint, I'm certainly not going to be making birdhouses or do carpentry. But, you're right, I need a new hobby to throw myself into to distract me. Dr. Patel said there is a group that meets in Jackson once a week for bipolar disorder. I didn't ask him if it was like group therapy or they actually did some project together. I will."

****

Thursday was cold and wet. She sat at her desk and waited for the first parent to arrive. She dreaded recognizing someone she went to high school with. The first person was, indeed, someone from high school and she seemed delighted to recognize Bernie. It was one of the higher achievers from Bernie's senior year.

"Oh, I always wondered what happened to you. So nice to see you. I hear great things from Karen about your classes."

"Well thank you. Karen is a great student with a sense of humor and well liked by her classmates. She's targeted at recognizing flaws in the characters she studies and is not afraid to speak up like so many are."

In reality Karen was overweight and made fun of and left out of school activities. Bernie often thought of her like she did Celeste. Karen had skin issues as well and wasn't beauty queen material. She was not popular outside of Bernie's class and Bernie often felt sorry for her. These were the students she couldn't help, but would succeed after high school, where less judgment would happen. Bernie knew that Karen would find herself in college and join with a group of like-minded people. Karen was a high academic achiever who was in the honor society

and all advanced placement classes just like her mother had been.

Bernie really wanted to address the issue of Karen's acclimation in school, but wasn't able to because of the topic brought up by her mother.

"I always knew you were bright and intelligent and picked on. You really shined your senior year and there was a group of us who wanted to get to know you better, but you didn't let anyone in. We all did things together and often wanted to invite you to join us, but felt uncomfortable because you were so bottled up."

Bernie held her breath. This was not the topic she wanted to discuss and it was painful to relive those years. "I needed to see you because Karen's creative writing has become a little dark. Are you aware of this?"

The mother shifted uncomfortably in her seat. "Yes, my husband and I are very aware of her writing and painting. She loves art class as much as she loves your class, but she seems depressed. That's why I thought of the things you endured as a big target in our high school days. We never thought of it until Karen's personality began to change. She is withdrawn, spends most of her time in her room and has stopped going to school functions. She really wanted to be in the school play last year and we encouraged her to believe in herself and do it. She refused.

"Right now she is on a diet, but it's slow to come off and her complexion is a big confidence killer. We have her seeing a dermatologist, but we're not making much headway. She has no sparkle any longer. I don't know

what you can do about this, but after what I watched you go through, I thought you'd be able to shed some light on Karen."

"I protect a lot of my kids in class, but can't do much after they leave the room. Have you tried counseling? There are several good ones out there and they might be able to help her regain some confidence. But, and I warn you, if she is sinking down into a big depression, you need to intervene now or she will be scarred for life."

"You were, weren't you?"

The direct question unbalanced Bernie's professional demeanor and she felt exposed. She stumbled with an answer. How was it possible for someone else to have any idea the kind of psychological damage that had been done to her? Were people really aware of their actions back then? Did they know how ugly and cruel they were; or was this just an observer who suddenly had a child in a similar situation?

Bernie stood up and clasped her hands together. She sat back down, placed her hands on the desk and started with, "At least you are seeing this in Karen and not blaming her for her lack of socializing. My parents didn't see my predicament and refused to believe what I told them. You're taking the first step here today." They sat and talked for the full hour and Bernie opened up a little about her past and what it did to her psyche. When the mother departed Bernie felt spent and exhausted. Luckily the next two parents were given easy and quick glowing reports.

Her return home sent her straight to the wine box. She started a fire and sat in the living room twirling her glass until Tony walked in at seven. She relayed the afternoon to him.

"I'd have thought that would have been cathartic for you."

"Not."

"Why?"

"It's making me relive those years. I ignore a lot of that stuff at school because I don't know what to do about it; just like I didn't back then. I'm confused. I know that other people have problems and that Karma is a bitch, but I don't want to be involved. I want to run away again, not dig in and solve their problems."

"Honey, these are the very same issues you dealt with in high school. Don't you have some ideas of how to solve them?"

"No." Her voice was loud and empathic. She looked around at the lovely home, stood up and said, "I don't feel like cooking dinner, let's get out of here. End of conversation until I can chew on this a while. I don't know if I want to get intimately involved with the people who tortured me when I was a teenager. I know about their angst. I know their pain, but I also know their parents and what they did. The sins of the parents and all that."

Tony had the maturity and foresight not to say anything, but he was thinking. "Let's just stay in town and go to the inn tonight."

Her appointment with Dr. Patel was after school on Friday in Ann Arbor. She drove in silence without the radio or CD's. Her mind was whirling and nervous.

She didn't have to wait long as a patient left and she went right in to the quiet office. The blinds were always drawn and there was always a sense of peace because nothing was bright and glaring. She opened the dialog with an account of the two disturbing conversations with the parents and some of her feelings about them. Dr. Patel was relatively quiet and listened while leaning forward in his chair across from her.

"Are there bullying programs at your school?"

"No. Unless they discuss that in health class, I have no knowledge of them."

"Maybe you could start one or buy a speaker for the school."

"I wouldn't know where to start. There are budgets I'm not privy to and I don't know if I want to get involved to that degree."

"Your husband is half right about catharsis. He doesn't have those memories to draw upon so he can't feel your pain, but I agree with the healing power of what opened before you. Did this person actively participate in the bullying when you were in school?"

"Not that I remember, but everyone was my enemy back then. I do remember her at lunch time. She always brought a bagged lunch and I don't feel as though her family could afford the cafeteria lunches. She was not extremely trendy in the dressing department, but she was in the honor society and had the support of others in her classes. She had friends and they stuck together. I, on the other hand, was afloat without an anchor."

"Did you see her participating in school activities?"

"How would I know? I didn't participate in any school activities myself. I do remember she had an older brother who seemed popular to me, but that's because he was so cheerful all the time. In reality, I don't know."

"How can you reach out to this woman and make a new friend?"

"What?" She narrowed her eyes and stared at him.

"From what you just reiterated, she sounds as though she is as lost as you were and feels you have a handle on her child's situation. She is reaching out to you to help her and your student. You already know the particulars, but you aren't connecting the dots yet. She is appealing to you to help her because she feels you already know what can happen if this goes much farther for her *baby*."

"I don't want to reach out. I'm aware that other people have illnesses, personal problems and families to care for. Even deaths that cause great pain, but I'm not the problem solver here."

"Ah, but I think you are. You're just unwilling to put on the new robes of advocate."

"Advocate? What? Do I look like a revolutionary? I don't care about them. I don't even want to live in Cold Lake; I'm there because of my husband and my family. I want to put as much distance between them and my life as possible. Just because I teach in their school system does not make me responsible for having to solve their problems."

"Who better educated on the subject of bullying and its ramifications than you, I ask?"

"I have no interest. That may sound selfish to you, but I'm not interested in telling my story and having people find out, in addition, about my disorder."

"Why does it even have to come up?"

Upon returning home, Bernie did some Internet research about school bullying and read a lot of stories about suicide and kids. The stories were told from the parent's point of view and absolutely heartbreaking. Who in her classes was being bullied and how could she find out more about the students who swung in and out of her door? She still had doubts about advocacy, but decided to bounce it off Celeste and Cathy.

She initiated a three way call with Cathy and Celeste and they gave her an earful. "I didn't realize this was even still happening in our school."

"Oh, Bernie, I hear about it all the time, especially from the students who just can't cope and have no home support," Cathy said.

Celeste said, "I thought it was the younger kids just reaching puberty and hormone swings. I wonder how many of them have underlying issues like yours and feel helpless."

Cathy interjected,"Most of them feel helpless. That's why I refer them to counseling if their parents can afford it. The state funds a little here and there, but I never hear from these kids again because there is a stigma attached to talking to the school counselor and they avoid me after initial contact."

"Cathy, is it possible that some of them are bipolar as well? Bernie asked.

"Because of their age and the amount of sadness surrounding teens, it's almost impossible to tell. They don't exhibit some of the symptoms of an older person, and it's difficult to discern if new hormones are the cause. They just seem out of control or weepy. I've been concerned about some of them in the past, but, as I said, I don't see these kids again or often. I cover so many schools that I can't keep them all straight."

Bernie outlined what the doctor had suggested and asked their opinions. "Cathy, you have the resources to research some of the national programs and possibly get one to our school. Would you be willing to do that?"

"Bernie, Celeste and I will investigate this and get it done. I think right now you have more important things

to do. I have a website for you to look at that may hold the promise of some understanding about being bipolar. I'll email you the link. I think you should work on other things. Besides, if you get too involved in this, you might be distracted and reminded of the past. You've got to start dispelling the past and let someone else handle this while you research your new goals."

"What new goals?" Celeste asked.

"Celeste, why don't you come over for dinner tonight with Tony and me and I can sit down and tell you about something I'm wanting to do."

"What's for dinner?"

"OK, you never ask that question. Does it matter?"

"No, I was just being cute."

"Well, let's go through my pantry and freezer and see what we can come up with. We can sit later and talk. Tony would enjoy seeing you because we always eat alone. Besides, I owe you a dinner."

"Sounds good to me. Mike is out of town again and I was not looking forward to cooking for one tonight."

"Deal. Cathy, thanks, I'll talk to you later."

Celeste arrived as Bernie was unloading the dishwasher. They went downstairs to the big freezer, chose the beef stew Bernie had made months earlier and set about making savory muffins to compliment it.

"Celeste, I married for love and children were part of the thought process. This was before I was diagnosed and I'm concerned right now about passing this disease to a child, upsetting my home and making more stress for Tony. We've sat many hours and talked about it and have agreed to try, but I must be in complete control of myself and my surroundings without catalytic stressors. I'm still not certain about what sets me off swinging either way. I'm also on a new medication and we don't have a history of tracking time to see how I'll react to certain incidents on it.

"Dr. Patel is researching medications and pregnancy. Right now it's been determined that I stay on the meds and go off the pill. I didn't mention this to you earlier because you always wanted a house full of children with Mike and I didn't want to tease or hurt your feelings."

"Oh, Bernie, this is your life, not mine. Mike and I haven't completely ruled out children, but my weight and his problem may prevent us from being successful. I'm not jealous, if that's a concern for you. I'm actually happy that you're checking it out. What effects will the drugs have on a baby?"

Bernie strung out a breath and didn't say anything for a minute. "All the bloggers say that they have healthy children. Some stayed on meds, some alternated and some only used them when needed. It's been suggested to go off the drugs prior to conception and start again during the second trimester, and then wean yourself off them prior to birth. Another school of thought is to stay on them and go off the second trimester, start again then

go off as you get close to birth day. There is no concrete advice out there.

"Postpartum depression is always a concern. The stress, from what I've read, is tremendous. Right now the doctor and I are researching and discussing it. Tony seems delighted that I'm open to starting a family, and doesn't seem to think any of this is a problem.

"He's thinking this is going to be a walk in the park, but I'm very concerned about deformed and addicted babies. We need to explore this further."

"You should do your research and go for it."

"Ah, but the consequences are huge from what I've read. There are also the optimists out there who feel they have healthy children and they're happy about them. Many of them went off drugs completely and went through the ups and downs of the rollercoaster ride during pregnancy. There is also the issue of breast feeding. I don't think I'd do it after the first few weeks because of the drugs I'd be back on. It's all confusing and a huge decision for us to make."

"Well here's hoping you find an even keel and a solution. I'll get to be an aunt!" She raised her glass.

FORTY SEVEN

The site that Cathy emailed was for the National Alliance on Mental Illness (NAMI) and Bernie joined and started reading the comments. She also found a Face Book page dedicated to bipolar disorder and that proved to be more useful because many spoke of pregnancies. Bernie didn't identify with some of the laments and comments. They seemed to be really out there and relating to them was somewhat surreal. Everyone, however, complained about the same things she did concerning meds. They made everyone fat, sluggish, killed sex drive, made them forgetful and slightly off kilter.

Face Book monikers like "nuttiebabie," "pingpongballs," "hollowgurl," "moody," "stigmas" and "polar bear" were revealing and a little comical. It defined the illness and their states of mind. They put their pathos and lives out there for everyone to see. They didn't seem ashamed, but a few parents asked why their adult children couldn't "snap out of it." She considered herself lucky that no one had uttered that phrase in her presence.

She was a part of a larger group and learned that there were many people with the disorder and struggling with it. Some of their struggles she understood and some of them just whined a lot. Many of them admitted to being "cutters" where they cut their arms and legs to disfigure

themselves. Each of them admitted they were diagnosed and on various chemical cocktails. Some related that their doctors switched meds mid stream and drastically. She began to see through their eyes; and saw a lot of depression in the whole of things.

One person wondered what pregnancy hormones would do to her and Bernie started to think about this. Many of the mothers writing related that their pregnancies were either hell or easy. Bernie couldn't use this group for only a decision she and Tony could make. She shut down the computer and went to the farm to ride.

Noir had her number as soon as she saw the halter and evaded her for nearly an hour. With the days becoming shorter, there wouldn't be much time to ride, but Bernie knew that if she didn't win this game, the mare would learn not to be caught. She doggedly pursued her and finally contact was made. Instead of a ride, Bernie decided to just groom her and teach her that all catches weren't work. She put her in her stall with her hay and feed and helped Dad round up the nannies. Milk production dropped off in fall, so Bernie left her father to do the short job of milking and left for home again.

During dinner she told Tony about the sites that Cathy had forwarded and the comments made concerning pregnancy and medications. He indicated that he was worried the stress of this plan might spin her into a downward passage.

"Yes, it is stressful and it's heartbreaking to read those posts. But this is the acid test about my meds and therapy working in combination to get through this. Do you feel the same way?"

"I don't know. We'll just have to wait and watch for trigger points and stress levels. I'd like to read some of them myself."

"I'll forward you the links, but you don't have a Face Book page and you can't access that one. There is one blog, however, that is just related to pregnancies and medications. I'll warn you right now, there is a lot of marital discord portrayed in there and I don't want you to get discouraged."

****

The last show of the season was due and Noir moved back to Thousand Pines for two weeks. Since she was being ridden five days a week and sometimes by two people, she was in fantastic shape. Neither Cathy nor Bernie worried about her abilities in the ring. Bernie hadn't grasped the entire concept of jumping and still wasn't confident, so no over rails classes were entered. Cathy, on the other hand, had advanced and dropped her flat class and entered one class of higher jumps. Noir proved herself a good jumper and needed no prodding.

The coming show was in Battle Creek and it was Bernie's chance to seal the high point award for the year. She had wrapped her mind around the prospect of losing. Cathy snapped her out of it by telling her to envision good rides and think of past successes. Bernie became optimistic.

The girls gathered at the farm and drove over together on Friday afternoon. It was the first time they had driven to the show together and Celeste was picking up on their show nerves and was extra jumpy on the hour's drive.

"Celeste, you've got to stay calm for us because we need to be calm to keep the horse from picking up on our excitement and getting hyper," Cathy explained to Celeste.

"Dr. Patel suggested I take an additional anti-anxiety pill about an hour before I show. I'm not blowing this," Bernie blurted.

"You should have invited him to the show to watch," Cathy said. "He would have a better understanding of your life."

"Oh, yeah, that's just what I need, my psychiatrist at a horse show," Bernie laughed.

After the grooming and braiding process, they settled the mare and left for the hotel. Dinner was eaten early and they found themselves in the hotel lounge with the others. Jack was there. Bernie watched Cathy dance with him and noticed that they seemed to be doing more speaking than dancing. *What the hell was I thinking with him?* She mused to herself, W*as I so out of control?*

Celeste sat sipping her drink and watched Bernie. "Whatcha thinking?"

"Nothing much, just watching the crowd."

"You seem to be deep in thought."

"Really, I'm not. I'm just thinking back to earlier shows."

Celeste, never one to pry, just said, "OK."

As hoped, wished and predicted, Bernie sealed her high point award in her division. She believed that she would be elated and proud, but she felt a little empty. Cathy and Celeste were beaming for her, but she just couldn't seem to show her enthusiasm and was a little confused by her feelings.

They drove back to Cold Lake and Tony, in anticipation of her win, met them at the farm with champagne, chocolates and a fully prepared pasta dish from his mother's. He sensed Bernie's mood.

"What's wrong, Honey? You just achieved your goal for the year."

"I just realized that I did it and have no further goals. It's such a weird feeling."

While Cathy and Celeste helped Mom prepare a salad and garlic cheese bread, Tony dragged Bernie outdoors. "You have a goal. You have more than one goal right now. It's getting through this and beginning to start a family. You also wanted to go back to dressage with your horse. I guess I'm a little confused."

"Tony, I got what I wanted and through all this craziness, I just feel like everything else is a long-term process and I don't have an immediate need to complete anything." She leaned into his embrace and buried her head in his chest.

He held her tightly for a few moments then realized that she was shivering in the October weather. "Let's get through dinner and not dampen anyone's mood. Cathy also won a highpoint and your mare is a star. Celeste

is back into the fold and we owe it to them to put on a happy face right now." They re-entered the house.

Back home he helped her take the saddle pads down for soaking. "Do we need to talk about this or are you OK?"

"I'm alright, I have an appointment this week and it will be discussed. Right now I'm a little scared about the future and the possibility of going off the deep end again without medication. I need to be totally stabilized before I go off the pill. I don't want to endanger our relationship again or a baby. The doctor should have some answers this week. At least he promised to."

"Right now you need to understand that many people are proud of you and your progress. If you want, I can go to that appointment with you and be another set of ears."

"I hate to have you leave the office and drive all the way over there for an hour's appointment."

"Let's just say that it's time for me to become more involved because this is about more than one person.

"I have to tell you, though, this disorder is very self-centered."

"What do you mean?"

"It's a strange disease that focuses you on yourself. I've never encountered anything like this before. Your actions affect others, but you focus inward to deal with them. Do you constantly feel as though you're second guessing yourself?"

"No. And, I've never looked at it that way. I don't second guess myself, I just react to certain stimuli with anger or learned behavior.

"Actually, Tony, I've never thought of it as being self-centered, but now that you mention it, it really does make you wonder too much about yourself. Unusual comment."

"Seems to me that right now you're in a mixed state. You're not manic and you're not depressed. But you're disappointed for some reason and restless."

"Yup, a mixed state. Very good description."

"That's what the doctors call it, a mixed state. It's neither up nor down, but mixed together. That's why you feel a little empty, but antsy."

"Huh? Does it last long from what you've read?"

"Couldn't tell ya, Babe. Couldn't tell ya. Only you will know. And you will be the only person to know if your meds are working properly. I can't help you with this. You must be the one to tune into yourself."

"You've been unusually supportive. Most of the stories I've heard portray husbands and partners who want people to be superhuman and start and finish feats that seem unattainable."

FORTY EIGHT

Bernie awoke in a puddle of blood. Copious amounts of it. She sprang out of bed and a crimson trail followed her to the bathroom. "Oh my God. TONY!"

"Oh my God," she heard from the bedroom. His face registered the same emotions as hers. "Oh Bernie, my love, I'm so sorry."

She wasn't just crying, she was keening. The pregnancy had them both overjoyed and cautious at the same time. They hadn't told anyone because it was early. She has skipped a cycle two weeks earlier and she had peed on several pregnancy stick tests to confirm. The first doctor's appointment was already made and this was not in the cards.

The blood trail to the bathroom looked like an animal had been slaughtered and the sheets were ruined. Bernie was ruined. She got off the toilet and Tony pushed her back down onto it. His face registered shock as well as horror. The grief immersed both of them and Tony was very worried about Bernie's state of mind.

The last six months had been easy and glorious for them. Their marriage had more depth and they were inseparable. Knowledge of the baby made them both glow and the excitement was contagious, even if others

didn't know what was so wonderful. Her doctor and Cathy had both agreed that the antidepressant Bernie was taking seemed to pose no side effects to a fetus and she stayed on it, albeit at a half dose. Therapy and talking to someone on a weekly basis did, indeed, help.

She had gone off the anti-anxiety drug as instructed, but a prescription was handy in the bathroom drawer if she felt she was out of control and going into an upswing because of stress. Hormones from the pregnancy had carried her to the complacency of pregnancy for the last three weeks.

The bleeding stopped as quickly as it had happened. Tony stayed home to watch Bernie and be with her through the disappointment and grief. The OB/GYN was called and he said that since the miscarriage had happened so early there would probably be no need to visit. He urged her to stay on the prenatal vitamins and give it a month for a good healing before attempting again. This included sexual activity for two weeks.

What had started as a delirious two weeks became weeks of depression on both their parts. Tony knew that running or exercise would be beneficial for Bernie's state of mind and they kept running in the mornings. Bernie continued to the farm each day and rode Noir. The spring shows would be coming up soon and she was both depressed and excited at entering a new realm with her horse. Her lessons were now on a Warmblood gelding on Wednesday evenings with the Dressage group. Cathy joined the group and lent a sympathetic ear about the miscarriage. Celeste was devastated and

worried. She didn't want to nurse a dragging and low Bernie through school and Thursday evenings.

To not add people's emotions into their state of mind, Bernie and Tony never mentioned the pregnancy to their parents. Bernie's mother, however, seemed to pick up on something and asked Bernie if something had shifted in her treatment. Bernie brushed aside the concern and kept quiet. She did tell Tony about her mom's premonition and they decided that if she were to get pregnant again, they would share the information early.

Spring came upon them fast and kids were born without incident. Celeste and Bernie continued their Thursday milkings. Bernie was restless and still reeling from the horror of losing a baby. Celeste was her usual cheerful self and didn't seem to notice Bernie's sluggishness.

****

From many standpoints, Bernie had led a privileged life with few devastating events. Other than the bullying at school, she had supportive parents, a loving husband and now good friends to share with. Never really having girlfriends before, she was delighted at the subjects that came up and were discussed between them. Their continuing support helped her through the first few weeks, but the downside started again after the pregnancy hormones waned from her system.

Not only were the hormones leaving, but depression was setting in on a larger scale than at any previous time. The bedroom became a constant reminder of that day and she slept less. Lack of sleep contributed to her extra

irritability and set Tony on edge. He was acutely aware of the consequences of too little sleep on her moods and their swings. He asked if she could get a prescription for some sleep aids that would not be addictive or harmful. These, too, became part of the chemical cocktail in her system; but they helped keep things at an even keel.

Dr. Patel played a larger part in her life and he suggested that she go back on a full dose of her antidepressant. Bernie lapsed back into old habits and wine became part of her daily routine. Tony ignored this to a degree because he felt she needed normalcy again. It wasn't as much of a depressive mood as disappointment. Glances between them were searching. Each looking to the other for answers to which there were none.

Tony made a concentrated effort to include her in the scholastic spring sports programs and she found accompanying him was rather fun. She'd never been a team sport watcher, so he had to explain a lot of moves and maneuvers to her. This kept them occupied and close.

Her husband, she found, was a very popular person and much loved in the community. Strangers were introduced and she found them to be engaging and excellent company during their soirees together. Tony seemed to know everyone and everyone knew him. His sponsorship banners were prominently displayed and Bernie began to feel part of her own school system and closer to Tony's immersion in the community. She learned of other people's lives and began to recognize folks and care about them.

Noir, having been ridden all winter and in the same patterns with both Cathy and Bernie in her own arena became very irritable. She started tossing her head and fighting the bit. Both women were riding schooling horses at Thousand Pines on Wednesday evenings and then practicing what they were learning at the farm. Noir's behavior became perplexing to them because they had no prior experience with horses. They had no idea they had caused the rank attitude by schooling her over and over again in the same patterns. This gave Bernie something else to focus on.

"We need to call someone. This isn't the same horse we rode all last year," Cathy lamented.

"Who can we call?"

"Well, didn't Jack retool her for you last spring?"

"Yes, but he's not a dressage rider."

"Let me call him and ask him what he thinks and I'll split the training with you for whatever he recommends."

Cathy's suggestion wasn't expected and Bernie hesitated a second too long. Cathy immediately picked up on this. "You knew the whole time that he was attracted to you, didn't you?"

"Uh, I guess so. But, I'm married and so is he. If I were single I might have gone out with him a few times."

"Even with him being married?"

Slowly Bernie met Cathy's eyes, "Yeah, I think so. He's an attractive person. I think he has the ability to charm women very easily. He was certainly charmed by you!"

"Ah, yeah, about that, I was flattered to be noticed by any man, even a married one with two kids. I have a confession to make. I did play a little with him at the shows. Nothing came of it and I started feeling guilty about his family. If someone did that to me, I'd be furious. I met his wife and she's drop dead gorgeous and a lovely person. I felt so bad that I just started ignoring him and his advances.

Cathy continued, "It'd be lovely to have someone to go out with once in a while and have a love interest outside of my children. But I'm just going to have to bide my time and hope that I meet someone soon. I'm basically a very lonely person right now and our friendship has eased some of that discomfort in the past few months. That, and the bullying programs we're instituting at the schools. Those have kept my mind occupied and me very busy."

They were watching Noir graze with the goats and Bernie said nothing at first as they stood silently side by side at the edge of the pasture. Bernie reached for both of Cathy's hands and held them as she faced her, "OK, let's call Jack and Sue together and see what they say. In the meantime, I'll pray for you to meet a wonderful person. I know how lucky I am with Tony and I wish for the same thing for you." Cathy's embrace was welcomed.

****

If Jack was surprised by the call from Cathy he didn't seem to show it. He started laughing, instead. Sue, on the three way call, also chuckled. "You've bored the horse, Cathy, and she needs some excitement. In your earnest haste to compete this spring, you've made the horse arena sour and she's developed an aversion to being in the ring. She's also a lone horse without an outlet for excess energy. My best suggestion is to get her back here and get her focused on something other than the same schooling she's been doing with the two of you," Sue summed up.

"I'll talk to Bernie and we'll see what we can do. I never thought of that because we are riding the same tests for the upcoming shows and not mixing it up for her. She hasn't even been trail ridden because we've both been riding her for long periods of time in the arena. I bet she'd benefit from a few trail rides as well."

Cathy phoned Bernie after dinner. "They laughed at us because we did it to her ourselves."

"What? I don't understand."

Cathy outlined the conversation with Sue and Jack. "We are back to trail riding and finding a way to get her back to Thousand Pines. At least we can both ride her and split a lesson. That's the good news. The bad news is we have to have Jack or me start jumping her again to mix it up a bit to ease the boredom."

"Hmm, this is both good news and bad news. We will have to show her on two days at the shows and that means longer weekends, two day shows and a lot more money shelled out between us.

"I really hate to ask this, but can you contribute to this?"

"Well, here comes the good news. My ex has caught up on his child support and I have a little to contribute. I can even help with the board bill at Thousand Pines! I never thought he'd do it and I was very surprised. I put it in savings. He even set up college funds for the kids."

"Oh, Cathy, you never said anything. That's great."

"OK, you give me the date and I'll have her picked up at your Dad's farm and back she goes. Will you need to discuss this with your husband?"

"Oh, I sure will. I have a lot of explaining to do, too," Bernie started laughing.

Tony, not have heard Bernie really laugh for a long time, came up the stairs to the kitchen where she was on the phone. "What's so funny?"

Bernie didn't even bother to cover the phone and said, "I have something to tell you."

She said into the handset, "Cathy, I guess I'm telling him sooner than later. I'll talk to you tomorrow."

"Well, Tony, dear, I've got good news and bad news. Which do you want first?"

FORTY NINE

As much as Bernie did not want to be part of the bullying programs at school, she was fully entrenched and responsible through her classes. The staff training urged teachers to suggest reading material on the subject and teach empathy. The health teacher had his hands full and English and physical education teachers were heavily involved. Bernie scoured the Internet for books that would be relevant, but useful for her curriculum. After having classics read in the classroom she now had to find something relevant for the various age groups she worked with. Not a lot of literature was forthcoming in the problem solving department. Much literature held bullies of all kinds and shapes, but relevancy was a different matter.

The school assemblies tried to involve the community and parents by teaching new skills for behavioral change. Most parents were working during school hours and evening meetings were scheduled. Bernie found herself among the parents of those who were bullied and not the parents of the bullies.

Consequently, the schools had to initiate appropriate punishment for transgressions turned in by teachers and students. This program nearly back fired when jealous or angry students started turning one another in. Mayhem ensued and was a regular topic at staff meetings. McGinty, in particular, was against the program and was very vocal. During one of his tirades Audrey Kresge stiffened, turned her entire body in her chair and accused McGinty of being the "biggest chauvinistic teacher" in the room and "part of the problem."

McGinty, never having heard much from Audrey and having been in the same system for decades with her was flabbergasted and started yelling. The voices raised in earnest when other teachers ganged up against him and sided with Audrey. Morgan said this, itself, was a form of bullying. That shut up everyone in the room, giving pause for much thought.

The hollow feeling of losing the baby started to fade a little as Bernie gained focus and perspective on doing hunter and dressage classes in the first upcoming spring show.

Tony, ever vigilant about the budget, judiciously suggested to both women one afternoon that the lower levels of dressage allowed the rider to show in hunt seat clothing. They both objected vehemently and drove to Ann Arbor to the tack shop to buy white full seat breeches. Stock ties were discussed, but the full seat breeches were so expensive that they both decided on purchasing extra chokers and promised to be scrupulously clean at the first show so they could both wear their one and only blouses the next day.

Cathy and Bernie wore their full seat breeches for the first time to their class and both were surprised at the odd feeling of someone continually grabbing their

buttocks. Bernie had many pair of full seat breeches from her previous life, but didn't recall the sensation. They laughed about it after class and decided that a good washing may prevent them from discomfort during the upcoming show.

Noir, with Jack's nearly daily jumping and training, settled back down and was interested in her work again. Both women split a lesson on her each Wednesday and felt they were back on track, albeit both were nervous about attempting something new in the ring. Neither could afford two lessons a week and they decided to wing the hunter and jumping classes on their own because they were only doing them for Noir's sanity. Sue seemed to be on board with this plan and didn't press them. The dressage faction at Thousand Pines had grown and the instructor now taught twice a week.

Bernie really wasn't tracking her menstrual cycles and realized the day before they drove to the show that she hadn't started yet. She assumed the show nerves were interfering with her cycle and never gave it a second thought. The night before the show the odd thought struck again while the three women were in the lounge after dinner. Celeste had become their regular sidekick and the three of them were enjoying their cocktails.

"I will probably get my period tomorrow during my first class."

"Oh, crap, are you due?" Cathy groaned.

"Yeah, I really didn't pay any attention because I was off cycle and didn't know when I was due to start again.

I sure hope it doesn't start on Sunday in the dressage ring while I'm wearing white breeches."

Celeste, hearing this, looked at Bernie with an open mouth. "Oh! Do you think you could be preggers again? Do you think you should ride? What would happen if you fell? Is it safe to be on a horse at a delicate time like this?" Her anxiety was palpable and both women looked at her and cracked up.

"What's so funny?"

"Most doctors will tell you not to change anything in your lifestyle in early pregnancy because a baby is so well protected. My Ob/Gyn urged me to continue riding because it was a form of exercise and relatively safe."

Cathy, trying to stop the anxious conversation and soothe Celeste said, "I rode with my second pregnancy and it was all good. Let's just say a small prayer that Bernie is pregnant and it holds this time."

Bernie's brow creased because the thought of being pregnant again hadn't occurred to her and she felt a gripping in her heart. Terror set in and she pushed her glass away. "OK, I can't think like this right now. I have to put this out of my mind because we have two tough days ahead of us. I'll probably start this weekend. It's so soon after the miscarriage and I'm still a little raw around the edges."

Cathy put her arm around Bernie's shoulders, grabbed Celeste's hand and said, "Let's call it a night and get some rest. I'm a little jittery about Sunday and I need to concentrate on the brat child being back in the ring

tomorrow and jumping fences with her. We haven't had a lot of practice since we've been concentrating on something else."

****

The routine was easy on Saturday and confusing on Sunday. Saturday had yielded four wins for them and they handily changed saddles for the different classes. Saturday evening they pulled the hunter braids and made button braids for the dressage ring. Not having done this before, it took them a little longer. Celeste came to their rescue because of her sewing ability. She competently took the blunt pointed needle and stood on her toes on a mounting block, reached up and sewed in the knotted balls. It almost looked professional.

More confusion was created between classes because Cathy and Bernie were competing against one another and did not have time for a tack change. They had agreed to use Bernie's saddle, which Cathy was relatively unfamiliar with.

Bernie and Noir wobbled up the centerline and looked like drunken sailors before their halt. "Cathy, she just refuses to ride a really straight line. You don't see it on the rail in hunter classes, but the judge will. Do your best. I think I'd use more closed legs on her to keep her straight."

"Whew, I'm not sure about this, Bernie. You guys did pretty well after the salute, so I don't know if it counts. I know nothing about the judging of dressage tests. I just hope I can remember my test and not go off course."

"You'll do fine. Just trust her. I wish you luck," she said as she patted Noir's neck. "Just remember what it should feel like."

Cathy's mouth was set in a firm line and Bernie reminded her to smile. "Look, we both have one most test to do, consider this one practice."

It took nearly an hour for score sheets to be posted and ribbons given out. They put Noir away after their second tests and went for coffee at the concession stand. Celeste, ever relentless over Bernie's health, whispered, "Did you get your period today?"

"Celeste! Honestly, I had forgotten about it because of the show. Don't remind Cathy. We need to get our tests and judge's comments and talk about this later. I'm nervous enough as it is and I'm back on full medication and I'm still worried about the effects it might have on a developing fetus. Let's just go to the scoring stall and wait." Bernie drilled her eyes at her friend.

"OK, I'm sorry. I just worry, too. I want so much for things to start going right in your life and I just say what's on my mind."

Cup in hand, Cathy walked up, "What's up?"

"Oh, nothing, I'm just coming down from a bad case of the nerves. This is the first time I've competed in dressage for a very long time. Noir did much better, I think, on the second test. You did wonderfully on the first."

"Oh, by the way, did you get your period this morning?"

"Not you, too!"

"What, did Celeste already ask you?"

"Yeah."

"Bernie, relax, you're going to make a great mother and God will grant you children. Just go with the flow, so to speak."

When they reached the scoring stall, Sue was waiting for them with papers and ribbons in hand. "You two really did well for your first show, a sour horse and what looked like a bad case of show nerves." She waved matching ribbons and score sheets in the air.

"Really?" Cathy was excited.

"Two thirds and two fourths out of a lineup of 12 riders and six ribbons," Sue said as she handed them the sheets and ribbons.

"Oh, we get to hold them?" Bernie asked with sarcasm.

"You know, I think I'll keep these and put them on the other side of the office wall," she replied as she reached for the ribbons. Sue winked at Cathy and Cathy threw Bernie a withering look.

"Not bad for a hunter in a dressage show. I see the judge asked for more impulsion at the walk and trot. You'll both have to work on that. So I will have to start taking lessons with the two of you to learn more. Congratulations.

"I took the liberty of going into your tack box and borrowing your camera, Bernie, so you'd have some photos. Hope you don't mind."

"I'd completely forgotten to grab the camera, thanks, Sue."

No celebratory dinner was held that evening. The girls drove back to the farm behind Jack's truck and unloaded the horse and the gear. They were pooped and tomorrow was a school day. Hugs were gathered and Bernie got in her car and drove home. Tony met her at the garage door and helped her bring in the saddle pads.

"So?"

"What? You, too?"

"What?"

"No, I did not get my period this weekend."

"OH! I was asking about the show. You didn't text or call, so I just assumed it went badly. You were due?"

"I swear to God that Cathy and Celeste were badgering me about it."

He reached out and gently held her. They stood this way for a few minutes and he stood back and looked at her. "You're afraid." It was a simple statement full of double meaning.

"Yes. I'm afraid of deformed children, I'm afraid of addicted children, I'm afraid of children at all right now. Can we really do this? What happens if I get really

depressed after a live birth and can't cope? There are so many questions and there are no answers."

"How long before we can know?"

"Well, there are some early home pregnancy tests out there. I just don't want a repeat of last time. I actually feel pregnant. I'll be mighty disappointed, to tell you the truth, if I get my period."

****

The week ground by slowly and they waited. Neither said any more about it, but it was front and center in their minds. Tony, not wanting to jinx the situation or upset Bernie visited his parent's home after work on the twelfth day. He asked his mother if he could cut a few tulips from her abundant beds to take to Bernie.

"Is this a special occasion?"

"Maybe, Mom. Bernie's flower beds are sparse and I know you have year's worth of multiplying tulips. I wanted to bring her flowers, but grocery store ones didn't cut it."

"Is there something I should know?" his mother asked, cocking one eyebrow and studying him with a very direct look.

"She just needs a little gift right now and a homemade one is better than a store bought one."

"Anthony Romanelli! Mothers have second senses. You should know that by now."

"I do, and maybe that's why I stopped here. You should be praying right now for good outcomes. And, that's all I'm going to say."

Mrs. Romanelli surveyed her son's face and then said, "OK, let's us go out and cut some flowers and find some greens and a vase. If it's that important you should do it right."

"Thanks for not asking too many questions right now. It's not her health issue, I'll tell you that much."

"I think I already know. I wish you luck, son. You're my first born and you need a first born of your own."

Tony stepped through the door precariously balancing a vase and his briefcase. Bernie was in the kitchen looking provocative in a tank top, shorts and a pair of sandals. She was cutting vegetables and smiling. He took this to be a good sign.

"I come bearing gifts, my queen."

"Oh, those are lovely. Where did you get them?"

"Mom's," he said simply without further explanation.

"I stopped at the drugstore on the way home and made a few purchases. Now everyone in town is going to suspect. What if it doesn't hold?"

"We're pregnant?" He sought her embrace with a little too much pressure.

Bernie sighed and hugged him back, "Yes, from what the stick test says, we're pregnant again."

"What do we do now?" he asked with excitement.

"Um, wait, I guess. No wine for me for dinner." She smiled. "I can drink juice or milk. I don't even want any alcohol if this is true."

"Neither do I."

"Really?"

"Really. If you can't drink, then I'm supporting you all the way and not drinking either. I really think we'll get lucky this time. We need to sit and talk about the last experience, though. I don't want you sliding into a depression if we lose this one. When can you see the doctor?" He was leaning against the counter top and studying her face. It seemed to glow and he said a silent prayer.

"I've already called and have an appointment on Thursday afternoon. That means that Dad will have to milk with or without Celeste."

"I want to shout from the rooftops, Babe. I want to tell everyone, but we have to wait, don't we, for the doctor's conformation?"

"Don't know if we should, but those new tests are considered very accurate. I think Cathy and Celeste knew at the show. Do I look different to you?"

"You were smiling when I came in. Yes, I think you do look different. I know we're both scared, but I have a good feeling about this one. You checked out as very physically healthy and we'll deal with any mood swings as they happen. I'll be there all the way for you,

I promise. We'll deal with what comes along and you'll be fine. You will make a great mother and we'll inch through this."

****

The doctor's waiting room was full of pregnant bellies and toddlers. Bernie felt as though she were in another world, maybe a different planet. Having been childless to such a late age and having been very career oriented in the beginning, she felt out of place. One mother had a briefcase on the floor and was reading some sort of report. Bernie studied her with intent.

The outside door opened and Tony strolled in. "I just wanted to be here with you. I thought you could use a little support."

"You drove all the way from Cold Lake for this?"

"Yup. It's important. Maybe we can figure out what happened before. Besides, I need to know as much as you for us to get through this with success."

"Have I told you recently that I love you?"

"You tell me every day in the little things you do."

They held hands, "Thank you. I feel out of place. It feels surreal."

The doctor pronounced Bernie healthy and pregnant at about five weeks. They discussed the antidepressant and anti-anxiety drug she was taking. He suggested, like Dr. Patel, that she not take the anti-anxiety med unless it was severely needed and told her to cut her other to

half dose. He also said that he'd dealt with the bipolar situation and drugs before and assured them that they had a very good chance of a healthy baby. Calculations were done and a January baby was estimated.

"Oh, nuts, I hate to have a child whose birthday is so close to holidays. They always get cheated on birthdays."

The doctor laughed and said, "Well, let's hope for a safe and sound pregnancy and you can make it up to the child over the years."

"Do we have any idea why my body rejected the first pregnancy?"

"No one can ever answer that question. I highly doubt that it had anything to do with the drugs you are taking. I'm providing you with a sheet of the most commonly asked questions and I suggest a few books in there for you to read. They will give you a good idea of what is happening in your body and Tony will enjoy reading them with you. I wish you the best of luck. Let's see you back here in four weeks."

When they reached the parking lot and were going to separate cars, she stopped Tony. "Should we tell our parents?"

"I think my Mom already suspects and your mother is no dummy. She'll know right away. I think it will be a bigger surprise to our fathers. Let's invite them over for dinner on Sunday. We have time to prepare and talk about telling them about the last time. Mothers have special direct lines to God, so we'll be protecting our own."

"You're so funny. I'm going to the farm to ride Noir. Doc says it's good exercise and he also gave us a thumbs up for continuing to run. Now you are really going to see me get fat!" She kissed him goodbye and drove toward Cold Lake.

Both sets of parents seemed to be delighted to enjoy dinner at their house and plans were set in motion. Bernie called both Cathy and Celeste and told them the news they already suspected. Celeste had to be warned and stopped by both of them to not immediately go out and start shopping for baby related things.

"Oh my Gawd, I'm gonna be an aunt. I can't wait to shop."

"Celeste, I think that Charlene ruined you on your shopping trips and you'll be spending more than you can afford. Right now I just need moral support to get through this. I don't want to lose this one and I can't deal with the horror of it all again."

"Bernie, you'll be fine. Just wait and see," Cathy supported.

"We're telling our parents on Sunday. I am making an old fashioned dinner, meatloaf, mashed potatoes, green beans, etc. And a pie. We didn't tell them before and I'm glad we didn't. Now, we need their support and prayers."

Both women talked at once. "I'll be praying for you." "Prayers sent your way."

"Do you want a boy or girl?" Celeste excitedly asked.

“Celeste, I just want one big, healthy baby who is not addicted or deformed or affected by the drugs. I’ll be going off them during the second trimester and we decide by my behavior whether or not I’ll need them in the third. I’m still frightened by what I’ve read from doctors and heartened by what I’ve read from bipolar mothers.”

Freshly showered from milking on Thursday, Bernie started dinner. She was absorbed in thought and didn’t hear Tony’s car enter the garage. He banged through the door into the mudroom and barreled into the kitchen. “Hey, I figured out who Charlene is.

“We had an old client of Dad’s walk in today to make some changes in his will. It was Charlene’s father. I didn’t recognize him right away.”

“You know Charlene’s father?”

“Oh, yeah, and it’s a long story. I never told you that I asked a girl to the prom when I was a senior. She was a junior and had a little sister named Charlie. Charlie is Charlene!

“You’d have thought I asked her sister to marry me. Her parents were ecstatic and invited mine over for dinner prior to the event. They went all out and went shopping for a very expensive dress and accessories. They even bought Charlie, Charlene, a new dress that looked like a gown.

“I knew that little Charlie had a crush on me, but I was a kid and didn’t think too much of it. I teased her a lot when she was about fourteen. Her sister was my age,

but a junior and thought we were going steady. She even asked to wear my class ring."

Bernie sat in one of the kitchen chairs with an astounded look on her face. "So you took Charlene's sister to the prom?"

"Oh yes and it was a nightmare. Her parents hosted an early morning breakfast for half the school. I'm telling you they thought we were an item and were going to get married. You know, a lawyer's son and all."

"What was her name?"

"Kendra. She died an early death in a car accident. She never went to college and got in with a bad element. I had the distinct feeling that her family blamed me for not marrying her before I left for college. They were a very blue collar family and her father worked at the abrasives plant as some kind of supervisor. The family was large like ours and there were five kids. Charlie was the youngest. I think they wanted to better their children through marriage and Kendra was pretty, but not asked out a lot. You never saw her at the local hangouts. To tell you the truth, I asked her because I felt sorry for her.

"I went to her funeral between college and law school. They acted like I shouldn't be there at the time. I never saw anyone in the family again until today. And, I'd venture to say that Charlene still has a crush on me. That's why she acts the way she does toward you. You were the interloper.

"Frankly, I never saw her again and was off to bigger and better things. I still don't know what she looks like to this day."

"I can give you a short description. She's the math teacher and is always dressed to the nines. She drives a little convertible and Celeste says she's a predatory shopper. As far as I know, she's not married, but it'd be impossible to tell because she wears rings on all her fingers. She has a lot of free time on her hands and, as I've told you, she's shown up at the farm during milkings. We can tell she doesn't like animals very much and she seems lonely and in search of something unknown.

"Maybe she thought she'd have a shot at marrying you as she got older."

"Whew, it was one weird scenario today. The old man looks haggard. His will was done many years ago and he wanted to take Kendra and his wife out of it and change the division of property. I also learned that Charlie's mother had died of cancer a few years back. I didn't know about that. Charlie, I found, still lives with her father and the old man is willing the house to her. The others are off into the wild blue with their own lives. Now you know why she has so much disposable income for shopping trips and clothes."

"Wow, that's a story I would never had imagined. I bet she's going to have a conniption fit when I start showing a baby bump. Tony, do me a favor and don't have any interaction with her. I told Celeste a while ago that she was stalking me because she seemed to know so much about my life. How she does it is still a mystery to me."

"What color is this little convertible?"

"Red."

"Well, I've seen it. Do you remember when we did a heavy duty cleaning on the garage and you went to recycling?

"That day a little red car was driving very slowly by the house. I had moved everything out to the driveway and when I was walking out of the garage again, it sped up and flew away. She is stalking. I bet it's me and not you. You just got in the way of her better life."

"Honestly, did she think you were coming back for her? How could she believe that without any contact with you after you moved to Chicago?

"I've already told you about her relative silence during staff meetings and her knowledge of my daily life. She tried to poison Celeste about me, but Celeste is loyal to a fault and she stopped hanging out with Charlene. You don't think she could cause any trouble, do you?"

"I doubt it, but I'd be extra careful what you say to other teachers. I know Cathy said she knows many who make no secrets about taking antidepressants, but it seems to me that Charlene would find a way to use that against you; from all you've said about her. Just be careful.

"I'll do a little digging and see what I can find out. I will ask around town and see if I can learn anything. In the meantime, don't announce your pregnancy right away. You've already told the girls, but I'd caution them to be judicious about what they mention and to whom."

After dinner, Bernie called Cathy and Celeste and told them the story Tony had relayed to her. "Celeste, be very careful. She may be trying to get to me through you. I don't want to ruin any fledgling friendships for you, but I've got to watch my back. Right now I don't need any trauma or drama in my life so I can get through this pregnancy without complications. I'm considering myself a high risk because of the drugs. I just want you to be careful. I wouldn't be rude to her, but at the same time, I wouldn't go out of my way to engage her. You even said she doesn't have much of a sense of humor."

Cathy piped in, "Yeah, Celeste, you can be a little naïve and this gal could cause some serious problems for Bernie. You so much want to shop for baby things and that would tip her off early that Bernie is pregnant. She doesn't need to know about the miscarriage. I already don't like her and I don't even know her.

"However, on the other hand, Bernie is right. She's your friend and you can do what you want."

Celeste didn't say much and the subject was changed. Bernie told them about the morning sickness and the loss of appetite. Cathy laughed and told her it wouldn't last long if she was lucky.

Then Celeste dropped a bombshell on the two of them. "I missed a period."

There was pandemonium on the phone.

Bernie offered the unused pregnancy tests and Celeste said she'd be right over to get them. Cathy screamed in delight.

"I thought you said you couldn't get pregnant," Cathy crowed.

"That's what I thought. Mike is going to freak right out. After ten years of marriage, I suddenly skip a period. Oh, Bernie, we can raise our kids together."

"Don't get too excited until you find out. There is no disappointment like false hope and it will really depress you. How many days?" Bernie asked.

"Thirteen."

"Get over here right now."

"I wanted to tell both of you at the same time. Maybe it's thinking about it being hopeless and giving up that did it. Mike will have to either find a job closer to home or stop traveling. I couldn't do this by myself. I so want to shop for things."

"Just go to Bernie's and let me know. Don't get your hopes up yet."

Celeste arrived a few minutes later as it was starting to get dark. "Hey," she said as she came through the open garage door. Her face was bright red and her cheeks looked like they were burning.

Bernie ushered her to the downstairs bathroom, handed her a white pharmacy paper bag and closed the door. She really wanted to stand outside, but returned to the kitchen. It was ten minutes before Celeste entered the kitchen. She was breathing hard and Bernie became concerned.

"Are you OK? You look weird."

"I feel weird. It's positive. I did it twice with two different brands."

Tony chose that moment to come upstairs for a drink. He scrutinized two faces and went to the refrigerator for juice. "What is up with you two?"

Celeste was sitting with a shocked look and Bernie quietly said, "Celeste just did a pregnancy test here and it was positive."

Tony, being on the expectant father's high spirited list was overjoyed for her. Then he softly said, "Great, two throwing up women and mood swings. Who's going to milk on Thursdays?"

FIFTY

Bernie's second trimester was not easy. She cried at the drop of a hat, was irritable and starting to feel physically uncomfortable. The puking had stopped, but running with Tony in the mornings was a little nauseating in the heat. Tony accommodated her by walking instead. They just went further distances and were later to get dressed for work.

The ultrasound technician had asked if they wanted to know the sex of the baby and both of them vehemently said, "NO!"

It was quite obvious that Bernie was pregnant and there was a lot of talk around school and town before graduation exercises. Celeste, on the other hand wasn't so visible because of her weight. Mike was joyful and extra attentive to Celeste. He had applied for a non traveling job and won it. He was now working as a supervisor from the company offices in Jackson. Things seemed to be on track for both women.

Bernie and Cathy competed again in May and June and did well. Noir was everybody's star. Celeste grew accustomed to being so near the horse and was more comfortable around them. She went to each show. In support of the two pregnant women Cathy did not drink

any alcohol and lost a few pounds in the process. All was good.

Good until Charlene learned of the pregnancies that summer. She had seen Bernie, Cathy and Celeste at the mall in Jackson shopping for baby things and made the correct assumption. She accosted them at the food court.

"So, it's true, you're both pregnant." The words and attitude were clearly jealousy.

"Oh, Hi, Char. We didn't tell anyone. How'd you find out? Bernie asked.

"It's pretty obvious with maternity shop and Baby's R Us bags for both of you."

Cathy ushered her kids to the table and was introduced to Charlene. She, in turn, introduced them to her. Both children politely offered their hands to shake and Charlene ignored them. Her eyes were burning at Bernie. Cathy moved a little closer to Charlene, "My children just put their hands out to shake and you dismissed them. That doesn't teach respect for adults."

Charlene's eyes widened and she focused on Cathy, stammered and walked away.

"Oh my God, Cathy, why did you do that?"

"I couldn't help myself. She's clearly a nasty person and jealous of both of you."

Celeste, looking very hurt began to cry. "She's just got an ugly personality, I guess. I thought she was a friend."

****

School started again in late August. She had worked hard to continue an exercise program and get a good night's sleep so that it didn't affect and cause manic highs. Everyone concerned had warned her to do her best to sleep. Sleep deprivation was a leading cause of manic highs and she didn't want to start hyper manic activities. Chamomile tea, other herbal teas and hot milk were administered by Tony. This was a group effort and it was working. Pregnancy hormones kept a lot of odd behaviors in check.

She was high just knowing she was getting through this without too many glitches. Horseback riding had become a thing of the past because it was uncomfortable and difficult for her to mount. A deal was struck with Thousand Pines and Noir went there to live and be half leased by Cathy. Noir was used the rest of the time as a school mount. People who knew her reputation as a winner clamored to ride the mare.

Celeste's pregnancy, which all thought to be high risk, went along without complications. Celeste had begun a walking program and continued to spend Thursday evenings at the farm with Bernie. The two of them stayed mobile and active. During the late spring, Cathy had joined them a few Thursdays to learn to milk, but the drive was too long for her to get home to her children. Cathy considered buying property in Cold Lake, but would need to market and sell her home and relocate the children. She felt it best to stay put after she leased Noir.

As much as Tony wanted to shop, he did not. Knowing that excessive shopping and mindless spending was a

bipolar reaction, he restrained himself and only went with Bernie to pick out nursery furniture. He did, however, begin to baby proof the house with great anticipation.

Many changes were made and each one was a potential trigger point for Bernie. Change is never readily accepted by most and Bernie was no different. For the sake of the baby and the families Tony kept change to a minimum, walked on eggshells and tiptoed around some conversations. Bernie's mind, though, was singly focused on a healthy pregnancy and Dr. Patel played a major role. She did not want to go back on the antidepressant until after birth. Dr. P, as she affectionately referred to him, was especially concerned, but acquiesced on one condition: that she see him twice a week so he could monitor her continence and any mood swings.

Knowing her temperament and now aware that it was bipolar induced, Bernie's mother kept advice to a minimum. Tony's mom, never have seen or heard one of Bernie's tantrums or tirades was not so judicious. Tony had to intervene a few times before discussions became heated. Mrs. Romanelli just did not understand why Bernie could not breast feed after a four week period.

"Mom, Bernie will need to go back on medications to prevent mood swings and depression. Just think about what would happen if post partum depression sets in for her. It would be disastrous and potentially harmful for the baby. They need to bond and this disorder sometimes prevents people from being able to do that. I've been doing a lot of reading and it's just better that we get through this the best way possible. We'll be in much better shape to plan a second after we get through our first.

"Also, Bernie is resisting taking any drugs during the third trimester and this is dangerous because she could let loose at any time. I'm telling you, she is a wonderful person, but the disorder can send her into a temper fit or an untoward action. You've just never seen it because she has great control since she's now aware of repercussions.

"I so much want to shop for our baby, but I know that shopping sprees are a manifestation of the disease and I might spin her out of control." Tony explained. "Frankly, I don't think I'd have the presence of mind to rein her in," he laughed. "I'm not sure I have as much self control as she has right now."

"Does this drug therapy mean the baby is going to be bottle fed most of the time?"

"She will breast feed for the first month, but after that she needs to go back on full medication. We don't want to endanger the baby in any way. You need to understand that a chemical imbalance needs to be rebalanced with *chemicals*. The good news is that you get to feed the baby on a regular basis."

"Is she aware of the lack of sleep a new baby brings?"

Tony blew out a long breath, "Yes, and that's something we are very worried about. Lack of sleep and proper sleep is something that can send her into a manic mode. It's very important that I be there so she can rest. We'll be on shifts and have to rely on you and her mother to help at times so she can sleep. Sleep is critical to keeping her mind and moods stable."

"This is more complicated than I imagined."

"That's why I tell you not to give her advice or argue with her. I know you've raised five kids with finesse, but she has different issues we have to address. Right now I'd like to see her on something to take the edge off the nervous energy and the impending doom she is expecting. She still feels she could lose the baby and is very edgy."

"Well my doctor used to dole out little green pills for pregnant mommies. Why can't they give her a tranquilizer?"

"Mother! That's a drug. Do you want her drinking, too?"

"Oh, I never thought of it that way. But nothing happened to you kids."

****

Before the holidays in October Bernie and Tony grocery shopped together at the local store. They had spent an entire day toodling around town at the various shops like the hardware store, visiting Noir in Jackson and then decided to restock the shelves at home. They found themselves at the grocery with two carts full. Bernie had actively started making a lot of dinners and freezing them in anticipation of the arrival in January. Ingredients for even more dinners were in the carts and they bought several bottles of sparkling grape juice for fun. Although it was sweet, it was fun to put in a wine glass and have on the dinner table.

Bernie's belly was larger than expected and she was already waddling. She pushed one cart and Tony pushed the other. He stopped occasionally in different parts of the store to ask if they needed something from a

particular shelf. Bernie laughed to herself because her husband was not a good shopper and really had no clue what was needed for meals.

When they arrived at the checkout a cheery voice said, "Hi Mr. and Mrs. Romanelli!" Bernie looked up, but did not recognize the middle aged cashier.

"Hi," was Bernie's buoyant reply. "We're stocking up for the holidays."

"You look like you're stocking up for a soon to be arriving family."

"Ah, Sherry, we have three months to go yet. Bernie is making and freezing meals so we are not caught off guard and can spend more time being a family than cooking," Tony said as he glowed.

"That's a wise move. I wish I had the foresight to do that when I was pregnant. You look so much closer than three months, Mrs. Romanelli."

Bernie laughed, "I am having a whopper, not twins. Romanelli's have big personalities," she said as she started placing items on the belt. "Please call me Bernie."

Tony beamed at her because this was the first trip to the local grocery where Bernie wasn't on edge and nervous about running into people and co-mingling with them. She'd come a long way in behavioral patterns and people found her to be a kind and engaging person. Her demeanor today was friendly and inviting. If there was an onion to be peeled, it was certainly Bernie's personality layers.

"Have you picked out names yet?" the cashier asked.

"We are considering some," Tony replied, "but we haven't decided."

Sherry reached around the register and picked up a small pocket book next to the candy bars and gum. "We still sell these." She showed them a tiny book of baby names and meanings.

Tony took the book from her and looked up his name. "It says 'Anthony means worthy of praise.' Let's look up yours."

He thumbed through the little book, "Bernie, your full name means victorious; Bernice. You are, you really are. You beat all the odds so far and I'm so very proud of you. Be forewarned about a public display of affection!"

END

Bonnie Palis is a freelance writer specializing in personality profiles. She and her husband live on a horse breeding farm in Kentucky. This is her first novel.

Face Book: "Uglier"
www.bonniepalis.com

Resources:

More than 10 million Americans alone have bipolar disorder. Because of its irregular patterns, bipolar disorder is often hard to diagnose and can be combined with any number of other mental and physical illnesses, making it difficult to treat.

National Alliance on Mental Illness
3803 N. Fairfax Dr. - Suite 100
Arlington, VA 22203
Help Line: (800) 950-NAMI
http://www.nami.org/template.cfm?section=About_NAMI

National Institute of Mental Health
6001 Executive Boulevard
Bethesda, MD 20892
http://www.nimh.nih.gov/index.shtml

Helpguide.org
http://www.helpguide.org/mental/
bipolar_disorder_self_help.htm

Depression and Bipolar Support Alliance
http://www.dbsalliance.org/site/
PageServer?pagename=home

Everyday Health

http://www.everydayhealth.com/bipolar-disorder/bipolar-disorder-tips.aspx

Printed in the United States
By Bookmasters